CW01066570

Born in Grangetown, near Middlesbrough, in 1954, Colin Farrington was brought up within sight of blast-furnaces and flare-stacks, but now lives in rural North Yorkshire with Sarah, his partner of twenty-five years.

Off and on he attended Eston Grammar School. Introduced to foreign parts by the Army, he subsequently travelled extensively and was able to put his love of learning languages to good use.

Colin's first novel **In the Shadow of the Kestrel** was published as a Vanguard imprint in 2012. He is currently working on a third novel set in Sierra Leone.

FIVE MASTS IN THE BAY

By the same author

In the Shadow of the Kestrel
Vanguard Press (2012)
ISBN: 978 1 84386 836 1

Colin Farrington

FIVE MASTS IN THE BAY

Vanguard Press

VANGUARD PAPERBACK

© Copyright 2013
Colin Farrington

The right of Colin Farrington to be identified as author of
this work has been asserted by him in accordance with the
Copyright, Designs and Patents Act 1988.

A CIP catalogue record for this title is
available from the British Library.

ISBN 978 1 84386 813 2

*Vanguard Press is an imprint of
Pegasus Elliot MacKenzie Publishers Ltd.*
www.pegasuspublishers.com

First Published in 2013

**Vanguard Press
Sheraton House Castle Park
Cambridge England**

Printed & Bound in Great Britain

This book is dedicated to my brothers Stephen and Paul, and to my sons, Andrew and Robert.

Acknowledgement

Thanks to Robin Lidster of Scarborough for having compiled the book of photographs which provided the inspiration for this novel.

Chapter One

My Family and the Sea

The mechanical digger driver renowned throughout the hamlet for clearing the stream that flows down from the moor, told me that he once caught two eels in its shallow water. A year later, when we had got to know each other well enough for me not to be aggravated by a manner which, with greater familiarity, had become more abrasive, he extended my knowledge by informing me that eels similar to those he had caught migrate to the Sargasso Sea. I learned that they spawn in its clear, deep, blue water. If, among the keys to life's mystery, the notion of incarnation is real, then I believe it unlikely that I was ever an eel. Nor was it probable that I was ever a fish, or a crab, or a turtle. I can also say, with certainty I might add, that I was never a shark.

Such is my disdain for salt water that in the human sphere also certain groups are better off without me. For indeed, the seafarers of the world, be they trawlers trying to grub up a living from the diminishing bounty the sea has to offer, or passengers enjoying the sybaritic life in the restaurants and on the sun-decks of the floating hotels that are ocean liners, be they South Sea islanders paddling long canoes with warrior vigour, or the crews aboard the war ships of the American Sixth Fleet tasked to patrol one or other of the world's trouble spots, they are probably not even remotely aware that their chances of being despatched to revel, feast and cavort in the mythical cornucopia that is Fiddler's Green were reduced considerably by my decision at an early age not to go to sea.

My decision to become a soldier rather than a sailor was largely influenced by two events decades apart, the most recent being the near disaster for which my father, a graduate of Britannia Royal Naval College, Dartmouth, was deemed partly responsible, even though he was absent from his ship at the time. Several decades earlier, and this time in the context of the Merchant Marine, it was the ship under my grandfather's command which, for all the wrong reasons, hit the news. The ship he grounded and wrecked in a bay close to where the eels were caught was the United States registered schooner *Cape Canaveral*. This earlier nautical mishap was how half my forty-six chromosomes came to be American in origin rather than the total number being wholly British, although I suspect that the Yankee bits have simply returned to these shores following an earlier migration. My provenance prior to the twentieth century still lies buried.

My name is John Gilchrist. My father was Captain Gordon Gilchrist, RN, a fact which will no doubt provide a trigger for many people to remember the unfortunate incident involving *Her Majesty's Ship York*, and how she nearly sank whilst on a goodwill visit to Australia and New Zealand in 1966. The vessel presently bearing the name of the erstwhile capital city is not the same destroyer which became impaled on a piece of jagged rock in that part of the Coral Sea lapping the shores of the Chesterfield Islands. It has always struck me as being ironic that the town in Derbyshire renowned, certainly throughout the land if not throughout the world, for its church with a crooked spire should, apparently, have provided the nomenclature for a group of islands thousands of miles away, though the irony only comes into sharp relief when one is aware that the archipelago in question is under French jurisdiction, and that it was a piece of French rock, a piece perhaps smaller in scale but similar in shape to Chesterfield's twisted spire, which pierced the hull of my father's ship. In point of fact the islands were named after a ship which founded there in a previous century, though it's highly likely that that earlier ill-fated vessel was named after the Derbyshire town.

With a view to organising a barbecue, my dad was conducting an aerial survey of the islands in the ship's Lynx helicopter when the incident happened, and, as he told me months later, made a beeline back to the destroyer as soon as he received the unwelcome news over the radio. I was twelve years old and had probably just awakened to the sound of birdsong or, at that hour of the morning – the hour when boys and girls mount their bicycles burdened by sacks filled with newspapers and the milkman is halfway through his round – the now steady drone of traffic passing on the nearby main road leading down the hill into town when my father was quelling his angst and wondering if his ship would still be afloat and the chopper be able to land. People with only a passing interest in the 'beautiful game' that is Association Football will appreciate that 1966 was the year when England won the World Cup, and as it was on the day of the home team's victory over Portugal in the semi-final that HMS York got spiked, for a long time after I suspected that the officers in charge of the ship in my father's absence had been distracted in their duty to the point of negligence by listening to the radio commentary of the match, conjecturing also that they had become increasingly euphoric as they listened to the description of how the net bulged with the formidable power of Bobby Charlton's goal. Only when I realised and took into account the time difference between Eskmouth and the Chesterfield Islands, bearing in mind that the collision occurred at five past five in the afternoon local time, did I come to the conclusion that people wiser and more knowledgeable than I, namely adults, would have arrived at sooner; that conclusion being that the recreational pursuit of watching football had not been the cause of the accident. A cause, or causes, there had to have been. Needless to say, following the ignominious repatriation of the damaged ship at a cost to the British taxpayer of umpteen millions of pounds, a Board of Trade Enquiry and Courts Martial were convened. The officers to have been found most negligent, and therefore most culpable, were dismissed from the ship. My father considered himself to have been fortunate in receiving a severe reprimand. It was deemed that he had not ensured that the correct procedures were followed, that, in naval parlance, he had not run a tight ship. In the belief that his career in the senior service had been seriously blighted by the incident, and imagining himself to be the butt of many a joke and derisory comment from ratings and fellow officers alike, he lasted another six months before he resigned his commission to become a life assurance salesman for one of the leading Canadian companies then operating in the United Kingdom. There were obvious advantages and disadvantages to this change in our family's circumstances. The most obvious advantage was that instead of his being away at sea for months at a time my father was able to sleep in his own bed at home. I have always assumed that this more or less permanent sleeping arrangement which came into being once dad became a civilian was welcome to both my parents. The most obvious disadvantage to the new status quo was that the family income suffered. This was because dad was paid commission on what he sold, and sometimes his sales figures were below par. The regular and substantial income which we as a family had been used to for years seemed the product of a golden, bygone age, an age that was unlikely to return. Consequently my mother found herself having to supplement my father's income by working two days in five at Eskmouth Grammar School. She taught French to pupils aged eleven and twelve. I think so now, and I thought at the time that it was a good thing that I didn't have to inform my mother about the whereabouts of the pen of my Aunt in class. This was because I was in third-form when mother assumed her new role in life in return for some much-needed monthly pay.

For myself, I readily admit to having felt considerable disappointment in what I perceived to have been my father's drop in status. Regardless of our being able to continue to live in a nice house and wear nice clothes, the fact that my father was no longer a daring sea captain in the tradition of Sir Francis Drake or Admiral Lord Nelson, but a suited individual who earned a precarious living in the then little-known world, or so it was to me, of financial services, irked me more than a little. Dad's new job in "civvies" just didn't have the kudos I admired. Moreover, in the weeks and months after the near sinking, I had to put up with an incredible amount of stick on the school field at break times. These days it would be called bullying. It goes without saying that a third-former's knowledge of the world at large is limited, and that feeling as I did about my father's changed occupation and perceived drop in status, I had no idea as to just how fortunate we were as a family.

The tale of woe relating to the holing of *HMS York*, though the incident was considered important enough to be featured on national television news, is, however, as I have already intimated, not the main thrust of our tale. I would emphasise that the sorry episode I have just described should first and foremost be considered a warning, and then as a stepping-stone back in time to the strange dichotomy that was the consequence of my grandfather's arrival, first off our shores in his schooner, and then on shore in the eponymously named fishing village which from the south overlooks the great curve of the North Sea framed by cliffs that is Rankin Bay. This dichotomy involved creative forces which were barely fathomable for being barely visible working in tandem with the formidable power of Nature when she is most rampant, most destructive. It is the gist of our tale, tossing together in the maelstrom of life people from different shores whose chances of meeting were about as likely as my meeting the President of the country from which my grandfather hailed.

Chapter Two

Immingham Bound

"Thanks," said Captain Andrew Gilchrist as he reached with both hands to grasp a mug of steaming hot cocoa being handed to him by Walker, the donkeyman.

Prior to his being offered the refreshment the man who was my grandfather had been leaning against the foremast of the five-mast schooner of which he was the skipper, feeling more than a little pleased with himself as he watched the ship's prow gently rise and fall in the moonlight as the *Canaveral* ploughed through an unusually calm sea. The prevailing weather conditions, and the effect they had upon the inky water, mirrored the Captain's frame of mind. All were free of turbulence. Thus far Captain Gilchrist had good reason to be pleased with the voyage. After purchasing a twelve per cent stake in the ship back in Boston, Massachusetts, their home port, this was his first mastery. He had sailed with a crew of five, three-and-a-half thousand miles across the Atlantic Ocean without mishap. Indeed, having run before a moderate westerly for most of the voyage, by carrying full sail he had been able to maintain an average speed of ten knots, which for a ship of this type and size was commendable. They had reached the Port of Bristol in thirteen days, and had successfully unloaded a third of their cargo of timber, and most of their tobacco. After a night ashore, during which time Henley, one of the five able seamen on board, had managed to extricate himself from a fracas over a woman outside the public house they – he and the mysterious woman – had just vacated. According to Henley's version of events three 'limeys' had picked on him without reason. Despite his being half-cut at the time, subsequently he maintained that the punishment he had meted out with his fists was much more severe than that which he had suffered. From the impression he had gained of Henley's character over the preceding fortnight, Captain Gilchrist – or Gill as he was affectionately known to his men – was at first somewhat sceptical of the man from Maine's account of events, but in the face of additional testimony from three other members of the *Cape Canaveral's* crew, all of whom had turned up in the nick of time to assist their shipmate, he had no choice but to consider Henley an innocent victim who had acted violently only in self-defence. That had been two days ago, and presently the *Canaveral* was shadowing the Lincolnshire coast as she made her way north to Immingham, where the plan was to unload the remainder of her cargo of timber and have the auxiliary engine serviced. The necessity of having to undertake the latter irked the Captain. He had resorted to using the oil-burning engine only twice before on the entire voyage, the first occasion being upon entering the Bristol Channel, the second upon leaving. The engine had functioned perfectly – driving the two bronze propellers – on sailing up the channel, but not so well the second time. It hadn't faltered completely, but it had been obvious to all on board that it hadn't been running as smoothly, and therefore as efficiently, as it should; and this despite the fact that the ship and its engine, having been built ad assembled in Vancouver at the beginning of the year, were almost new. Presently, for the third time, the screws were turning.

"Allow me to offer you my congratulations on completing your first successful voyage as skipper, skipper," said the donkeyman.

The sailor who had uttered these words was a compatriot of my grandfather in the sense that he too had been born and brought up in New Hampshire, just as my antecedent had been. The donkeyman was a citizen of Manchester if he was a citizen of anywhere, and for the edification of people on the Monarchist side of the pond, Canada notwithstanding, I can tell you that Manchester is the next major centre of population when heading south from Concord, the New Hampshire state capital, on the Merrimack River. In turn Concord is the nearest large town to the village of Penacook, the settlement where my grandfather was born and spent most of his formative years. Despite the obvious differences in rank and status between the two men, the cultural inheritance they shared, and the pride and loyalty they felt for the Granite State – the first to have gained independence – had created a bond which was special for being unspoken.

Whenever Walker handed the Captain anything, be it a mug of cocoa or a spanner, the latter's eyes couldn't help but focus on the back of the donkeyman's hands. They were unusually hirsute, a fact which was noticeable even in the moonlight. Moreover, it wasn't just Walker's hands which were hairy in the extreme, for he sported a full set which was magnificent in its luxuriance. The beard, at its extremity, he kept neatly trimmed. The lower edge resembled part of a disc which, despite the obvious flexibility of hair, seemed to be a thing which had been forged with geometric precision. Conversely, however, and most obviously noticeable whenever he shook his head from side to side in silent negation, the thick mass of hair seemed to be an entity with a life of its own, an entity which may have had a symbiotic relationship with its host, or one which was just as likely to have been parasitic. Within its considerable mass there were many shades of grey, and in the regions either side of Walker's resolute head just in front of each ear, the growth was almost silver. Walker's deeply set eyes were brown, sad, and ponderous. In combination with his furrowed brow and a nose which, though not so noticeably flattened as to convince the beholder that the object of curiosity belonged to a boxer, the snout in question being unable to hide the fact that it had received a few well-aimed blows in its time, the impression Walker's demeanour invariably created was that of an old man of the sea. After having turned fifty last July fourth, an old seadog is precisely what he felt he was.

"We aren't home and dry yet," commented the Captain as he wrapped his bare hands around the mug for warmth: this being the middle of October, in the North Sea off the English coast the air was chill and Autumnal. Being a man of smaller stature physically than the donkeyman, Captain Gilchrist had to look up in order to address his words to Walker's face. "You must have made this trip a hundred times before," the Captain said before turning the focus of his vision towards the ship's prow as he took a slurp of the hot, frothy liquid: finding it too sweet, he nonetheless gave no sign of dissatisfaction.

"I reckon twice that," Walker replied, "But strange as it may seem, this will be my first time into Immingham. Mainly I've greased the engine and worked the lines on ships bound for Liverpool. I reckon I know that city like the back of my hand; well, at least its seedier parts."

Captain Gilchrist gave a barely perceptible nod of the head and smiled knowingly; and though he thought it for the best that he should not be apprised of each and every sordid detail of what individual crew members got up to ashore, he had a pretty good idea nonetheless. He was well aware of the basic needs of sailors when released from duty after having been cooped up for weeks on end at sea. He had indulged, and some might say over-indulged, in the Bacchanalian revels which forty-eight hours ashore allowed on a number of occasions himself; but that was in the dim and distant past, and in this instance the past was another ship sailing from a port to which he could never return. All he asked of his crew was that they stayed clear of entanglements and escapades involving the forces of law and order, and they reported back for duty sober at the stipulated time. Other than abiding by these two ordnances he was happy to let his crew behave as they saw fit in their free time. After all, his forefathers hadn't fought to free themselves of British tyranny to become slaves to a plethora of unnecessary rules and regulations subsequently. It was undoubtedly true that he had been concerned about the ruckus in which Henley had become embroiled, but that was because the seaman in question could easily have ended up in jail. The inconvenience and additional paperwork that would have caused would have been tedious in the extreme. No; nobody could say of Captain Gilbert that he was a hard taskmaster; yet, by virtue of certain innate qualities, he was able to command loyalty and respect.

Much of that loyalty and respect was generated by a subtle combination of manner and appearance. Standing at five feet eleven inches, a good five inches nearer to the deck than the man whose main role in life was to attend to the needs of the engine – the donkeyman no less – in terms of his height the Captain was hardly domineering.

Like Walker, he too sported a full set, but his was of an inferior kind, for the skipper's facial hair, being all of two weeks in the making, was nowhere near as luxuriant as that which adorned the face of the man who was now standing beside him, shoulder to shoulder as it were. Going without a shave for a fortnight was about all the skipper could put up with, for once a certain length and softness had been attained he began to feel uncomfortable, not quite clean, and in respect of polite society, hardly presentable. Presently on board ship the latter point was not an important consideration, but now that the *Canaveral* was within hours of reaching her final destination, the Captain had more than once thought that the time had come, once again, for him to become clean-shaven. Feeling suddenly cold he fastened the topmost button of his jacket. He regretted having come on deck hatless, and unconsciously he freed one hand from holding the mug to brush his wavy fair hair using only his fingers and thumb. It was as if he needed to confirm that he had indeed left the item of apparel in his cabin, an item no less important for projecting status as for providing protection against the elements. At that moment a ripple of cold air chilled the right side of Gilchrist's face.

"There's a breeze getting up," commented Walker: evidently he too had felt the slight gust, the first sign.

Like a pair of wild animals sniffing the air for signs of danger, these mariners' senses became instantly sharper, for not only had they felt the first indications of a change in pressure on their faces, but they had seen, and even above the noise of the engine, heard, the unmistakeable sounds and vibrations in the rigging. The questions to which Gilchrist had to provide answers occupied his mind as he turned to observe three sets of lights, each set about a quarter of a mile away from its neighbour, on the horizon. He assumed they were trawlers fishing for cod or haddock. The questions were obvious: was that first gust the harbinger of stormy weather? At their present speed of eight knots how long would it be before they entered the Humber, where, if a storm had blown up by that time, conditions would be far less turbulent than they would be in open water? Finally, the skipper had to determine whether the anticipated increase in wind speed was going to be of benefit or a hindrance, and that would depend on from which direction it blew. He estimated that, taking into account the passage up the river, they were as yet a couple of hours from berthing, but he didn't have much confidence in the accuracy of this estimation. If he could be certain that the expected wind was going to blow from astern, this would be the moment to summon the crew from their quarters in the forecastle by getting Walker to shout, in time-honoured fashion, "all hands on deck", whereupon their immediate task would be to hoist the sails. Presently the *Cape Canaveral* was showing 'bare poles' as she chugged north under the power of her suspect engine.

"Do you think she's going to blow hard?" asked Gilchrist of Walker.

This willingness on the part of the Captain to seek out another's opinion was not an unusual occurrence in respect of any member of the crew who happened to be standing close-by. He was not under any illusion about the fact that he was solely responsible for the decisions he made, but that didn't deter the Captain from striving to involve his crew, particularly the more senior members, in the decision-making process.

"I can't be absolutely certain, but I would put my shirt on it blowing from the north-east afore midnight," replied Walker, nodding his head in the direction of the deepening gloom off the starboard quarter. "How far do you reckon we are from the Humber?"

Turning about with the intention of returning to his cabin situated aft the Captain said, "That's what I'm about to check. We'll keep things as they are for the time being, but be sure to let me know immediately of any significant changes."

"Sure thing Gil," responded Walker with probing familiarity.

The Captain, though aware that half his face would be in shadow, checked his progress towards the stern to give Walker a look which could not be mistaken. Stern describes the look aptly. The Captain had no objection to being addressed as "skipper", and he didn't worry one jot about what the crew called him behind his back, but he drew the line at being called "Gil" to his face.

"I mean aye, aye skipper," said Walker, surprisingly sheepishly for a man of his years and experience.

"I know we come from the same neck of the woods, but don't overstep the mark, particularly when we're on duty," warned the Captain, peremptorily.

Once the attempted mutiny had been thwarted and discipline restored, Captain Gilchrist put his sea legs in motion, and, having turned his back on the errant subordinate, proceeded aft, unconsciously adopting the lurching gait peculiar to all seafarers as the individual concerned attempts to obviate the unbalancing effect of the ship's roll. It almost goes without saying that the rougher the sea the greater the roll, and the greater the roll the more apparently eccentric the gait. The Captain was well-practised at anticipating the rise and fall of the deck beneath his feet, as were the rest of the crew. This was because on a ship which was two hundred and thirty-five feet from bow to stern, and forty-six feet in the beam, the number of nautical miles walked on a voyage of this duration was considerable.

"Oh and Walker!" hailed the skipper, turning once more to face forward as he paused by the second of the schooner's five masts, "Tell Landowska to check with Humber Radio if they have anything for us."

In the as yet clear night air the Captain's voice carried without his having to make a stentorian effort.

26

"Aye skipper," Walker replied.

The skipper resumed his perambulation towards the stern. After pausing to check the halyards on the jigger (the fourth mast from the bow), he poked his head inside the pilot-house located aft of the mainmast. The sailor at the wheel, and the only other man on deck at that precise moment, was none other than the doughty Henley, the man from Maine for whom, of all his crew, Captain Gilchrist had the least empathy. When considered sympathetically and in the best of lights there was much about Henley which repelled, but in the eerie light cast by the pilot-house lamp, the visage which turned to face the Captain appeared hauntingly grotesque, so much so that at that instant the image he projected, the impression he created, was that of a man showing incipient signs of insanity. He achieved this simply by looking, his eyes staring fixedly at his interlocutor, whoever that may be. This gaze of unwavering intensity was emphasised further by the fact that Henley's eyes were of disproportionate size to the rest of his face, which was gaunt and weather-beaten. It hardly seems worth mentioning seeing that two-thirds of the *Canaveral's* crew presently sported full sets in one form or another, but Henley too could boast of a full set which was thick and just a shade lighter than the hair on his head, which was black. Adding to his intimidating appearance was the bushiness of his eyebrows, which met above the bridge of a sharply pointed, slightly upturned nose. The appearance of latent madness was enhanced by the subject's choice of headwear. His hat resembled an inverted dustpan surmounted by a dome: the whole appeared to be two hats in one. Insofar as Henley's prowess as a fighter was concerned, being of wiry frame and small stature, he hardly looked the part. That said, we all know that appearances can be deceptive, and in respect of the helmsman that was true in more ways than one. He might have looked half-mad but he undoubtedly wasn't. If anything, he was possessed of a shrewd, calculating mind which sought to turn every eventuality to his own advantage. Similarly, though most of his antagonists in a bout of fisticuffs not governed by Marquess of Queensbury rules were likely to be bigger and stronger, he had proved that he had been able to scrap with the tenacity of a terrier, for, after being knocked down by a series of telling punches, he had the remarkable ability to get up repeatedly in order to continue the fray.

"If a wind gets up nor-nor-east, as I'm expecting it to, keep her head into it; but whatever you do don't lose sight of land," ordered the Captain firmly.

Ordinarily, for the very reason that he disliked Henley innately, when on duty Captain Gilchrist made a point of asking after him, as if concern for the sailor's welfare was all that mattered at the moment the question was posed. Alternatively he would try to find some common ground over which they could share a joke or hold a brief discussion. In short, when it came to dealings with Henley, grandfather thought it necessary to make an extra special effort. On this occasion, however, the skipper's orders were more peremptory than usual, and once his instructions had been acknowledged with the usual, "Aye, skipper," he closed the pilot-house door and descended to his cabin via the hatch located between the mainmast and the transom.

Chapter Three
Old Boys Reminiscing

The village of Rankin Bay, almost one year on from the date when the guns fell silent on the Western Front to end the war that would end all wars, was a very different place from what it is today. The plethora of shops, some selling books, some selling fancy goods, and a bevy of restaurants and pubs catering to the needs of middle-income tourists, give a clear indication of how much the formerly dingy little fishing village has changed. In October 1919, when fishing was the mainstay of the people that lived in the tightly packed rows of cottages which tumbled (once or twice literally) down the hillside towards the sea, presented to the world a much more humble demeanour than it does today. Back then, the wives of fishermen hung out their washing on lines strung out across the communal drying ground in front of a row of terraced cottages officially named, 'Esplanade'. The row was known locally as 'Sentry Box Row' because of the line of earth closets in the cottage gardens. Back then the road leading down Rankin Bay bank was just as steep as it is today, but unlike the modern thoroughfare, it was more likely to resound with the metallic ring of horses' hooves striking the cobblestones, for the most commonly used method of carrying goods up and down the bank was to harness the strength of three or four such animals to a cart. Back then, the Rankin Bay lifeboat crew could be seen manhandling and launching, either in response to a real emergency or as a practice run, the *Henrietta Maria*, a boat which in twenty-five years of service had been launched forty-two times, and thereby saved sixty lives. In this context the skill and endeavour of the crew manning the Board of Trade Rocket apparatus could be observed as they too practised their procedures for saving the lives of people aboard ships stranded close to shore. Back then, as the Captain of the *Cape Canaveral* studied the charts spread across the oak table situated in his spacious, but hardly sumptuous, cabin, two Rankin Bay characters were puffing away at the last remnant of tobacco each had stuffed into his pipe an hour before. These two old-timers were none other than Jamie Cullen, the illiterate town crier whose job it was to tour the streets of Rankin Bay town, and, with the assistance of a bell salvaged from the *Visitor*, a ship which was wrecked in the bay about forty years previously, inform the residents of forthcoming events and recent disasters. At seventy-nine years of age, 'Cull the bellman' as he was known, was five years younger than the man sitting on the bench beside him. The older man was former sailor and local fisherman, John Gretton. John supplemented his pension by delivering somewhere in the region of seventy litres of paraffin to residents each week, all of which he carried in cans slung from a yoke balanced across his shoulders. Even if he didn't have need of the extra income which the demandingly physical work provided, John would have been loath to stop for the simple reason that he believed, and it was probably true, that the strenuous activity kept him in good health and, for his age, remarkably fit. The wooden bench in question was positioned against the whitewashed wall of the Rankin Bay Hotel, directly beneath the lounge bar window. This was the two men's usual perch of an evening, whenever the weather allowed. Indeed, so accustomed had they become to being able to sit on their favourite seat whenever they chose, they had come to think of the bench as their own. Of course, notwithstanding the fact that both men were sound in mind and body, being the venerable ages that they were respectively, they could have done little to oust a usurper or two, but the strange fact was that this particular bench, with its panoramic view across the bay from which, or to which, the village either derived or gave its name, was rarely occupied, as if it were indeed this pair's private property. The tide was out, but would soon be on the turn to make slow but steady progress towards the eccentric arc of cliffs which gave the shape to Rankin Bay as far as Seal Point and Point Pleasant about three miles away as the crow flies. (It may seem more appropriate in this instance to state as the seagull flies, but having watched herring-gulls wheel and dive on numerous occasions, the larger-winged bird would undoubtedly make the distance twice as long). Point Pleasant and Seal Point are the top and bottom of the same promontory jutting out into the North Sea to form the southernmost part of the bay's periphery, and as such the difference in height between them is six hundred feet. Moreover, both points are aptly named, and for reasons which require no further elucidation, though it's not every day that seals can be seen basking on the rocks, and the pleasantness of the view from the top of the cliff may at times be obscured by sea mist or low cloud. On the night in question the focus of the men's vision was on the distant lights shining from the hotel perched atop Point Pleasant, and from the houses, few in number, straddling the road which leads inland ultimately to link up with the main road between Eskmouth and the spa town of Ravensborough. At the turn of the century, when Britain was fighting the Boers in South Africa, plans had been drawn up to develop the land around Point Pleasant so as to establish a community which would thrive and grow, but apart from the laying of foundations for a small fraction of the intended overall number of houses, nothing was built, and the plans came to nought, even in respect of the foundations already laid. In the opinion of the old salts puffing on their pipes in the clear night air, the failure of the project was to be expected, for Point Pleasant was a bleak place to be on an inclement day, and there were more than enough of them in a year on this coast.

"I hear the parish council intend putting up the rent for the drying ground," said Jamie, without taking the pipe from his mouth.

"That'll upset a few folks," John Gretton responded, staring fixedly ahead of him at the far promontory. "How much is it now, and how much is it likely to increase by?" he asked.

"Mrs Draycot told me that she pays one shilling per annum, and that from the first of January she'll have to pay two shillings: that's an increase of…"

"One hundred per cent," John Gretton jumped in, eager to demonstrate his arithmetical skills.

The mention of Mrs Draycot was sufficient to dispel all further talk about the proposed increases to the rent for the drying ground.

"She's a handsome woman that Sally Draycot; and not only that, but she's got a good head on her shoulders as well, in the brains department I mean," commented old John, and after a pause, during which time he pondered the wisdom of what he was about to say, and indeed, whether he should give voice to his thoughts in this context at all, he nonetheless continued, "For the life of me I can't understand why she took up with that husband of hers. She's far too good for him I reckon."

"You're just saying that because you're jealous and wanted to marry her yourself," said Jamie in jest.

Cull the bellman was renowned for his ribald sense of humour, and being dressed in his customary apparel of waistcoat, jacket and trousers, items of clothing which a decade ago belonged to three separate suits, he cut a comic, Chaplinesque figure. The jacket, which was patched at the elbows, but with little regard for symmetry, was too short in the sleeve, and the trousers, which were secured around his waist by twine, were too long in the leg. The quirkiness of his appearance he enhanced further by the wearing of a top hat, though this was only when he was engaged on official duties. At such times he would make his way from The Dock, the place where old John and he were presently sitting and where he invariably began his round of vocal pronouncements, along New Street to his second proscenium, as it were, at Bridge End, doffing his hat and bowing slightly to the people he met along the way, particularly the ladies.

In response to the accusation that he could possibly be jealous of Sally's husband, John's initial retort was to say, "Get away with yourself man," which was a phrase he often uttered when in conversation with his comical chum.

Jamie, realising that the last shred of tobacco in his pipe had turned to ash, stood and took a stride towards the fence which had been put in place to deter people from falling into the stream below. The drop was about twelve feet into a concrete gully. The water running through the gully, and which a short distance inland flowed as a beck through the centre of the village, was fresh for having recently fallen as rain in the surrounding hills. In all probability the pointed slats that formed the fence had saved a significant number of people from hurting themselves, particularly those inebriated souls exiting through the portal of the Rankin Bay Hotel on a Friday or Saturday night, and not really knowing which way to turn. After turning his pipe upside down, Jamie tapped the bowl now empty of tobacco against one of the fence slats, his purpose being to encourage the burnt contents to fall into the stream which led out to sea. In the bar behind and above their heads a man with a strong baritone voice had begun to sing the verse of a popular sea shanty, and with gusto an indeterminate number of male voices could be heard as they joined in the simple chorus: "Heave away... haul away... we're bound for California." Old John tapped his heel in time with the rhythm of the song. Jamie reached into his pocket for the tool which, as a prodigious pipe smoker, he would have been lost without, namely his penknife, and with a gnarled but steady hand proceeded to prise out the debris which had refused to respond to gravity and a gentle tap.

"I suppose you've got your eye on Jenny Fewster," commented old John wryly.

He was referring to Sally's younger sister, who at twenty-two years of age and single, was reputed to be the prettiest girl in the village. The problem for any would-be suitor, however, was that he would first have to impress and gain the approval of Henry Fewster, Sally's and Jenny's father, and as Henry was coxswain of the Rankin Bay lifeboat, that was going to be no easy task for any man. It should be made clear that, notwithstanding their seemingly licentious comments regarding the younger women, one of whom was married, in reality there was no wicked intent in the minds of the old fogeys, and if push were to come to shove, they would have protected Fewster's daughters with their lives. In short they would behave more like kindly uncles or grandfathers than dirty old men. Their suggestive comments constituted no more than a joke between themselves. This assessment of Jamie's and John's respective characters was the opinion prevalent throughout the Rankin Bay community, for though they were hardly the leading lights of village life, it was generally thought that Rankin Bay would be a poorer place when the two old salts finally keeled over. Being both widowers, it was also generally thought that the pair were good for each other in the same way that a man and his wife are good for each other in their twilight years, and that is by providing a sounding-board for each other, by indulging in a little verbal cut and thrust – without, of course, overstepping the mark – to keep each other emotionally strong, mentally sharp. Of considerable significance was the fact that both men were on the friendliest of terms with Fewster.

"I would hazard a guess that this is Henry and his boys coming in now," said Jamie Cullen, who from his standpoint was able to see more of the bay to the north, the direction from which the single light shown by the fishing cobble was approaching the shore, though as yet the boat was about half a mile from The Dock.

Before the war there had been two families living in Rankin Bay and earning their livelihood, in the main, from the bounty the sea has to offer. Usually within sight of each other the Comptons and the Fewsters used to fish for cod and haddock during the winter months, and get tremendously excited about catching lobster in fleets of pots during the summer. The fishermen of both families had enjoyed the rivalry, and would often stay out longer than was wise with the aim of bringing home a bigger catch than the opposition. The competition may have been friendly most of the time, but there had been occasions when the comments drifting across the water towards the Fewster's boat from the Compton's cobble, and vice versa, had given the impression that a state of war was in the offing. The patriarch in charge of each boat would see to it that the rivalry didn't ever get out of hand, and whenever a really serious need required there to be a friend indeed assistance would be offered, and needless to say, when appropriate, it would also be reciprocated. With the outbreak of hostilities, however, and I mean in France and Belgium rather than the dock of Rankin Bay, had come change, though not in the way that you would probably imagine; for the Comptons had not volunteered for active service and fallen victim to the slaughter, but had simply moved to the opposite end of the country, to continue in the industry which they knew and loved off the Cornish coast. Thus it came about that the only serious fishing carried out in the often choppy waters of Rankin Bay was done by the Fewsters, the occasional exception being when a cobble from Eskmouth made the relatively short journey south, or when a boat out of Ravensborough made the longer journey north.

"They're in early," commented Jamie Cullman, before adding, "Henry has either caught all the fish he can handle, or he's expecting the weather to change for the worse."

At this point John Gretton rose to his feet, and after encouraging his old, stiff joints into action, hobbled over to where his friend was standing, the better to be able to see what was happening out to sea. It was difficult to make out exactly what was going on in the darkness enveloping the scars between The Dock, wherein the two men with time on their hands were now standing, and Gunny Point. This rocky outcrop which formed the northern extremity of Rankin Bay was not nearly as impressive as its opposite number to the south – Seal Point and Point Pleasant – for it wasn't as high and didn't jut into the sea as far.

"I think they must have had a good night's fishing," said old John: "I've never known Henry Fewster come home empty handed afore: he'd still be at it when the rest of us had run for shelter and had begun to batten down the hatches."

"Well it looks to me as if they're intending to bring her into The Dock," said Jamie referring to the coble *Red Lobster* as he observed a figure making his way over the scaur, a figure recognisable as a human being by virtue of the lantern that he carried. The movement of the lantern was occasionally erratic, which was hardly surprising considering the nature of the ground, ground which in a few hours time would be the bottom of the sea. "If you ask me that's Jack the lad coming to get Dobbin to haul the boat up on the trailer," said Cull, standing now with his shoulders hunched against a gust of wind which, having sprung up suddenly and seemingly from nowhere, had a chilling effect on the two men's geriatric bones.

Dobbin was the Fewster's piebald horse which they kept tethered on the open ground beyond Bridge End adjacent to King's Beck. Standing sixteen hands high, the gelding was a big specimen of horse flesh. They had bought the animal for its strength from a group of gypsies that had spent several days camped by the side of the winding lane that links Rankin Bay and Kingscliffe, a village straddling the main road a couple of miles inland. Effectively semi-retired, Dobbin spent most of his days grazing serenely; but whenever horsepower was likely to be the answer, his plodding strength invariably proved invaluable.

Cull's right hand was affectionately fondling the pipe he had returned to his jacket pocket: his left hand played with a couple of tanners (sixpences), all the money he had on his person, and possibly all the money he had in the world until he was next able to draw his pension, which fortunately for him would be on the morrow. To all intents and purposes Cull's analysis was spot on, for if the weather was expected to stay fine Henry would have tied the *Red Lobster* to the buoy marking the entrance to the main channel between the scaurs, but whenever a storm was brewing the wiser option was to haul the cobble into The Dock. The fact that the coxswain had brought his boat in sooner than observers in the know might have expected was a clear indication that Henry Fewster, a man renowned in Ravensborough and Eskmouth, as well as in Rankin, for being able to read the runes when it came to forecasting the weather – a skill not to be underestimated when the North Sea is your place of work – was expecting a storm.

"Shall we ask if he wants a hand?" muttered old John, feeling the icy blasts penetrate the thick wool of his pullover, or 'gansey' as the item of apparel was referred to locally.

Old John's gansey, which had been the creation of his deceased wife Edna and was at least two decades old, had, in keeping with tradition, been knitted in the pattern in which all Rankin Bay ganseys were knitted. Similarly, the wives of Eskmouth and Ravensborough fishermen knitted ganseys using a pattern unique to their respective town cum port, thereby making it possible to identify from where a man had come simply by looking at his pullover. This was of sombre practical use whenever a boat was lost at sea, a tragedy which was likely to lead to bodies being washed ashore, possibly far from home. In this way a man who could no longer speak for himself was able to inform his finders as to the whereabouts of his loved ones.

"Is that you Jack? Do you need a hand bringing the boat up?" questioned Cull the bellman when the figure approaching was about a dozen yards from the slipway.

"Aye, it's me," was the clear reply.

Jack Fewster stood six feet six inches tall, was twenty-two years of age and was the coxswain's nephew. He instantly recognised the voice which had hailed him as belonging to Jamie Cullman, and guessing that the shadowy figure standing behind Jamie's right shoulder was John Gretton, he had no hesitation in declining the offer of assistance. He didn't want to be responsible for either of the old codgers slipping on a rock covered with slimy seaweed.

"You can set them up in the bar for Henry, Cotty, and me," prompted Jack as he splashed, just a couple of yards from the slipway's relatively smooth concrete surface, through a pool left behind by the previous high tide. "I'll pay you for them as soon as we've taken our catch to market."

"Tell him to get away with himself," muttered old John in a volume audible only to the person closest to him.

"John here says you're to go and get away with yourself," echoed Jamie loudly, to the slight embarrassment of his friend.

"Good idea," Jack replied, and, after first dropping a coin into the gaping mouth of a cast-iron representation of a large cod which served, and still serves, as a collection box for contributions used to benefit the family of some poor soul lost at sea, he set off along New Road towards Bridge End. In the sloping field nearby was where Dobbin was tethered. Before he was able to disappear from his would-be helpers' view completely, however, Jack was hailed once more by the more vociferous of the two reprobates. Questioned as to whether Henry and he were expecting foul weather by morning, the giant of a man paused to look over his shoulder before replying succinctly, "Aye!"

Chapter Four

Storm Force

Captain Gilchrist had been in his cabin for a full ten minutes before he felt the first indications of a sea change. He was standing, staring down at the chart spread out on the table before him when the ship rolled first to starboard, and then to port, with an abruptness which almost unbalanced him. In the event he was able to remain vertical by taking a lateral check pace to the right whilst at the same time reaching forward to steady himself by grabbing hold of the edge of the table. Measuring six feet by four, the largest item of furniture in the cabin was fortunately immovable, having been bolted into place. The five serviceable though hardly matching chairs were a different matter, but because they were used only on those rare occasions when the Captain entertained or held a conference, they were, bar one, lashed securely together in the corner of the cabin diagonally opposite to where my grandfather was accustomed to lay his head. The chair which had been left untied had overturned with a clatter and had slid across the cabin floor until, in obeisance to Newton's first law of motion, its progress to starboard was arrested by the unpredictable movement of the ship acting in response to the action of the wind and the moon upon the water, and it was propelled back from whence it came to crash against the immovable object that was the leg of the table. Despite the noise generated by the apparent severity of the impact no serious damage was sustained by either item of furniture. A longer lasting consequence of the sudden upheaval, however, might have resulted from three of the four items atop the table falling to the floor, these being a rule, a protractor and the Captain's ink pot. Serendipity was maintained by virtue of the fact that this pot was empty, and that the small treasured possession which he had bought in the general store in Penacook did not break. Captain Gilchrist was in the midst of restoring order to his accommodation when there was a knock on the door. Recognising the distinctive pattern the knuckle in question made as it rapped loudly, the Captain knew before the door opened who his caller was.

"Come in Walker," the Captain commanded.

The door opened outwards to reveal Walker holding in his left hand a piece of paper. The donkeyman had to stoop to enter through the portal, but once inside, no doubt mindful of the dressing-down for the over familiarity which he had demonstrated earlier, he regained his full height and gave a clenched-fist salute to his right temple before handing the communication to the skipper.

"Sparks has just received this from Humber Radio," informed Walker: "it seems that we're about to run into some bad weather."

"I think we're already in it," interjected the Captain, wary of the pendulum motion of the lantern swaying alarmingly close to Walker's head. "How's the engine holding up?" he enquired as he took the paper on which he assumed were written details of the imminent fall in barometric pressure, and nothing else.

The radio message may have been smeared with engine oil, but at least all the words and numbers were legible.

"I think she'll get us to Eskmouth," informed Walker with an expression which revealed a transient sense of superiority for being the bearer of crucially important intelligence.

"We're not going to Eskmouth, are we?" asked the Captain with a perplexed look on his face.

"It would seem that we are," Walker replied. "It's the only practical course of action open to us seeing as how the docks along the Humber are idle.

Not for the first time Captain Gilchrist had the sense that to all intents and purposes Walker was in charge of the ship, or at least aspiring to be, and that he – the real skipper – was the willing factotum.

"The stevedores, or whatever they're called here, have walked out. They must have known we were coming skipper," said Walker, concluding his report with a philosophical shrug of the shoulders.

The Captain's first impulse was to accuse Walker of playing a joke on him, but he managed to stifle the expression of such a thought, a thought which would have only demeaned himself had it been voiced. Instead he said nothing prior to scrutinising every word before his eyes. In the meantime Walker reached up to steady the dangling lamp's violent oscillations, but realising, and soon, that his actions were going to be of no avail, he took it upon himself to unhook the cabin's one and only functioning means of illumination on his own initiative. He carried the lamp round behind the Captain to the back of the cabin, where he secured it in position in such a way that oscillations were negligible. This antiquated but reliable means of providing luminosity had replaced the electric lighting normally available throughout the ship, but which, since leaving the Severn estuary, and for a reason which as yet remained a mystery, had failed to operate aft of the radio shack.

It was another gremlin, or possibly an act of sabotage by Henley, which the Captain had hoped to sort out in Immingham. Meanwhile he read the message for the second time, just to make sure that he had grasped its meaning completely. At the top of the piece of lined paper smudged with engine oil was the date and time of transmission. The date was October 18th: the time indicated was 1900 hours. There followed the call-sign of the sender and the name of the receiver: GKZ to *Cape Canaveral*. The text of the message read as follows: "Warning of northerly gale in North Sea developing by 2200 hours; increasing in severity to force 10 or 11 by dawn; wind veering to North East later. Station GKZ also advises that docks at Immingham and Kingston upon Hull are non-operational because of strike by dockers. Arrangements have been made for you to unload cargo of timber at Eskmouth. Do you have anything for me?"

To this last question the man maintaining the radio watch, which is not quite the same thing as being an expert radio operator, had replied: "*Cape Canaveral* nil for now."

The man in question, who, though everyone on board referred to him as 'Sparks', was actually named Landowska, a name which gave a clear indication of his Polish pedigree, although Nikodem considered himself to be as American as apple-pie by virtue of the fact that he had been born and brought up in Connecticut. The Constitution State – Westbury to be precise – was the place to which his parents, their three children in tow, had emigrated from Lodz before the turn of the century. Presently Sparks was in the radio room aft of the forecastle where the remainder of the crew were checking that their gear was totally secure.

The Captain, still in his cabin, once again adopted the stance which would provide him with the greatest support as he leaned forward to peruse the chart. In this exigency he was joined by

Walker who, somewhat assertively, effectively mimicked the skipper's posture whilst standing at a right angle to him. Captain Gilchrist carefully measured the inches from the Humber estuary along the coast to Eskmouth, and estimated the distance they would now have to travel to be in the region of ninety nautical miles. Assuming that they would be able to make less headway as the wind increased in strength from the north, he came to the conclusion that it would be touch and go whether they would escape the worst of the weather. He expressed as much out loud to Walker as both men stared down at the chart from different angles, different perspectives, and all the while they felt the motion of the ship becoming more extreme by the minute.

"I think I would like to confirm this message," said Captain Gilchrist, his lack of experience in command revealing itself in the now taut lines of his face, in the repetitive actions of his hands as he tapped the rule against his left palm.

It was not the deteriorating weather conditions which were predominantly disconcerting to the Captain, though they didn't help matters. It was every sailor's lot to be able to take the rough with the smooth, the calm with the turbulent, and anybody that couldn't put up with the discomfort and likely nausea of sailing a ship in rough weather would no doubt be better suited to an occupation with a firmer base, namely dry land. No; it was this business of having to change his plans at the last minute and so near to the end of the outward leg of their voyage which caused him to frown. Through no fault of his the *Cape Canaveral* would more than likely have to bear the brunt of a severe storm when she would otherwise have been tied up safely alongside a jetty. It might just have been his good fortune, but never in all his years at sea had the skipper been aboard a ship which had been diverted to an alternative port because the men that operated the land-based cranes were on strike. In his mind's eye he could see a line of skeletal structures standing idly along the quayside, the dark silhouettes of their jibs pointing at various angles aimlessly towards the night sky. In short he felt as if he had been let down, that he had been placed in a difficult position.

"Don't worry skipper," said Walker, perceptive to his Captain's somewhat anxious demeanour, "I've sailed through typhoons in tubs much less sturdy than this. The *Cape Canaveral* will be able to handle anything the elements throw at her: you mark my words."

The donkeyman's tone and choice of words were meant to be reassuring, and in the sense that the Captain's immediate response was to gird his mental faculties so that he was able to take action they were. He had been about to express his concerns to the older and more experienced sailor, but after having heard the old salt's words of encouragement he said merely, "Let's go topside and see what havoc the weather gods are wreaking, as if we didn't know."

"Sure thing skipper," Walker assented.

The Captain gathered the various small items which he had picked up from the floor and rather absent-mindedly placed back on the table, and deposited them in a drawer in the same said item of furniture. That done he made his way with a renewed sense of purpose towards the cabin door, where he paused to unhook a sou'wester for himself and a less pristine but no less serviceable coat for Walker, the latter having delivered the radio message wearing togs which the skipper considered poor protection against the elements. Upon handing over the windproof jacket Captain Gilchrist quite naturally noticed the hirsute hand reaching towards him, and he wondered if Walker's thicker natural skin covering made him less susceptible to the effects of a bitterly cold wind-chill factor. It was a passing thought, one which was quickly subsumed by a more weighty concern, specifically whether the engine would continue to function satisfactorily. The two men donned their sou'westers. Walker was undoubtedly a tough nut to crack in any situation, but after reminding himself of the adage which states that any fool can be uncomfortable, and thinking himself more than a little foolish for having delivered a warning of imminent bad weather as inadequately dressed as he was in sweater and trousers, he gratefully accepted the Captain's offer. It was at this juncture, just as Captain Gilchrist opened the cabin door to leave for the radio room, that Walker gave some indication that he was possibly telepathic.

"If it's all right with you, I'll give Henley a hand with the wheel… he's probably exhausted by now."

The Captain had been thinking the exact same thought barely a moment before Walker had voiced his suggestion. It was approaching the end of the second dogwatch, and given the present roughness of the sea, he knew how much concentration and physical effort were required to keep the ship on course. From what he could gather Henley wasn't making a bad job of it, and being approximately only two miles from shore it was crucial that he didn't. After a quick glance at the clock which was nailed to the cabin wall to the left of the door, the Captain merely nodded his acquiescence prior to exiting the cabin and leading the way up the flight of steps to emerge, eventually, onto the pitching deck.

The word 'eventually' implies delay, and the delay in this instance came about because just as the Captain was about to open the hatch a huge wave broke along the starboard side of the ship to send a minor deluge of spray and water over the deck and, unfortunately for my grandfather, into his upturned face. This was one ablution he could have done without. His reaction, which was immediate for being instinctive, was to close the hatch, which he had opened almost fully, and then wipe the salt-water from his eyes, which he attempted to do with the sleeve of his sou'wester. This was hardly efficacious because his sleeve had not escaped the drenching. Walker, who had taken a step back on the lower deck so as to escape the inundation, and consequently had barely got his boots wet, laughed at his leader's misfortune. It was a good-natured laugh.

"Bad timing skipper," he said, stating the obvious.

Captain Gilchrist shook his head in order to clear the remnants of the North Sea that were trickling down his face. Then, after making a gesture with his hand in the direction of the person who was laughing, a gesture which he realised at once would not be discerned in near darkness, he pushed open the hatch and emerged on deck. The Captain first steadied himself before turning to hold out his hand for Walker, following hard on his heels, to grasp. The donkeyman took the proffered hand just as another voluminous wave broke over the ship's side. His back turned towards the most recent cascade, this time it was my grandfather's turn to laugh as he beheld the crewman's discomfort, Walker's face having been thoroughly wetted. Despite the severity of the weather and the unwelcome news that gave the Captain no alternative but to chug ninety miles farther north, his stalwart and he were in good spirits. In moments such as these it was as if the life of adventure they had come to sea to find was truly theirs, and, like boys playing at being pirates in the river, they were revelling in the experience. The playful mood was necessarily transient, for there was information to be confirmed, a course to be checked.

The first destination on deck for Walker and the Captain was the wheelhouse, in the light of which Henley could be seen from behind manfully struggling with the wheel. Not only did Captain Gilchrist think it necessary to check up on the morale of his least favourite crewman, but he also wanted to cast his eye over the equipment housed in the binnacle located directly in front of the wheel, the most important item therein being the magnetic compass. Originated by the survivors of more than one wrecked ship, tales had assailed the Captain's ears of how the only possible explanation for their having ended up on the rocks was that the ship's compass had been faulty. Of course, if the compass on the *Cape Canaveral* were faulty, the only way the discovery would be made would be if she were to meet with a fate similar to that which had befallen those many other wrecked ships, either that, or by sighting the coast of Holland. The truth was that there was no way of knowing for the present whether their one and only compass was faulty or not; but, reasoned Captain Gilchrist, there was considerable reassurance to be gained by ensuring that for this part of the voyage the schooner's bows were in line with the direction indicated by the arrow.

The distance between the opening through which the two men had emerged on deck and the wheelhouse was only a few yards, but in those strides it was impossible not to get a feel for how capriciously changeable Mother Nature can be in this part of the world. It seemed an aeon ago that Walker had handed his Captain the mug of cocoa in conditions which were relatively calm, when in reality the time that had elapsed was no more than an hour. Now the men had to lean forward to make progress against the wind sweeping along the deck from bow to stern, the whine in the rigging rising to a crescendo with each gust. Despite the difficulty, the Captain sought to make note of the bigger picture by looking to left and right, port and starboard, and was somewhat disconcerted to observe that, in the driving rain, beyond the confines of the ship hardly anything was visible. He was surprised to find that there were no lights showing in the direction where land should be. He surmised that this could be because they were sailing past an uninhabited stretch of coast. An equally plausible alternative which came to mind, but which was hastily dismissed by the Captain, was that they were farther from Lincoln County than he had estimated. The search along the starboard side from aft to forward so far as the view remained unrestricted proved equally unrewarding, for the signs of human activity which the skipper had taken to be trawlers were no longer in sight. No doubt they had made for their home port whilst he had been down below studying his charts. It was a wise move if they had. No; with her bows rising and falling with determined thrust as her diesel engine supplied the power, to the perspective of those on deck the *Cape Canaveral* appeared to be a lone entity in a vast and presently inhospitable sea, the nearer surging waves of which were just discernible at the dim extremities of the light emanating from the wheelhouse. Walker, moving with a simpler and, therefore, more clearly defined sense of purpose than the Captain, reached the door of the wheelhouse first, and, upon gaining entry, grasped hold of the left-hand side of the wheel to assist the struggling Henley in getting the ship back on course. By the time the skipper had squeezed in everything was shipshape. They were heading a few degrees west of north.

Chapter Five

The Milkmaid

Jenny Fewster had been awakened by an unmistakeable sound coming from the adjoining bedroom of the two-bedroom cottage in which she lived with her parents on Chapel Street. The street was so named because there was a Methodist chapel at the end nearest the sea, where Chapel Street gives way to King Street, which in turn leads steeply down past the Endeavour Inn towards The Dock and the Rankin Bay Hotel. The building that was the Methodist chapel stands to this day, but now serves during the day as a cafe, and on certain evenings as a venue for concerts and for showing films. The sound heard by Jenny was that of a person using a chamber pot to have a pee, and judging by the creaking of the bed prior to the prolonged tinkling as yet more waste liquid was added to the pool already formed in the ceramic container, that person could only be Jenny's father, Henry. Being of much slighter build than the burly fisherman and lifeboat coxswain, Jenny's mother, Enid, would have created, in getting out of bed, about as much noise as her husband's shadow in comparison. The night's sonority was compounded by the weather raging outside the cramped but cosy cottage. At frequent intervals the wind gusted percussively along the street which wasn't really a street, but merely a paved walkway wide enough for no more than two people to wend their way side by side. The pedestrian thoroughfare separated the contiguous cottages from their respective gardens, and, more significantly, from their respective lavatories. At that time the denizens of Rankin Bay may have been looking forward to the beginning of the third decade of the twentieth century with renewed hope following the recent four years of carnage and slaughter in Europe, and for many that hope might have included the installation of an inside toilet, a feature which was presently lacking in the Fewster household. Rather than fumble with matches to light the candle perched in its brass holder on the bedside table, instead Jenny picked up the adjacent clock, and walked barefoot in her nightdress with it to the sash window, where, after drawing back the curtain a little, by the light of a usefully positioned gas streetlamp she was able to discern the time. It was ten past four, twenty minutes before she normally woke six days out of seven to dress and get ready for a morning stint milking a herd of thirty Friesian cows at Millbeck Farm, a mixed farm of fifty acres the centre of which – the farmhouse and buildings – was situated about a mile from home. Not surprisingly Jenny enjoyed her job working as a milkmaid more during the summer months, when she found the task of getting up of a morning relatively easy, than in winter, when the bone-chilling early starts could be an ordeal. Judging by the wind, how it was apparently trying to uproot the trees which had grown tall on the narrow banks channelling the beck running thirty or so feet below the wall rising from the cliff which marked the boundary to the Fewster's tiny garden, the onset of winter was imminent, the halcyon days of summer a pleasant but distant memory.

Jenny climbed back into bed and snuggled down beneath the covers for warmth, reprimanding herself as she made a mental note not to leave the bedclothes thrown back in future, at least on those occasions when she intended to regain their comfort after an absence of minutes. In the event her bed could and should have been warmer than it was. Once the noises from the adjacent room had become less obvious, and no longer formed part of a narrative, Jenny lay in bed listening to the effects of the drop in barometric pressure. On quiescent days she was able to hear the gentle gurgling of King's Beck as the stream of fresh water flowed over pebble islands on its journey to the sea. Here and there it also washed over a securely wedged broken branch. This particular melodic sound, normally so pleasing for being so evocative, was no longer audible for having been drowned out by the turbulence of trees and the crashing of waves against the cliffs a hundred yards away. Intermittently Jenny heard the high-pitched and seemingly plaintive cry of a gull descrying the fact, as she imagined, that it was about to be blown from its perch.

This young woman – Jenny had just turned twenty-two – had no intention of going back to sleep. No; there wasn't enough time for that delightful prospect seeing as how she would have to get up at four-thirty. By her estimation she now had a further fifteen minutes to savour her comfort, and being mindful of this she began to plan her day. She would have liked to have spent the sybaritic time that was left to her imagining riding Aerial – one of two working Fell ponies kept on the farm – along the beach, but unfortunately thoughts about work came to the fore. In this regard she wondered whether she would have to bring the cows in from the field for milking, rather than what she was accustomed to doing in less inclement weather, which was to carry a stool and a bucket to them. She concluded that she would have to do the milking indoors. Her first thought prompted a second, and she wondered whether she should make her way to Millbeck Farm by her normal route, which was to leave Rankin Bay via Albion Street, and, after ascending Flagstaff Steps, follow the narrow path between the farm fields and the edge of the cliff. The only practical alternative was for her to take the one and only road suitable for vehicles out of the village, and undertake a journey which was thrice the length of her normal route, and which, not surprisingly, took three times as long. There was a chance that she would be offered a lift on a passing cart, but it wasn't an eventuality she could count on, and the chances of her getting a lift in a car or van going her way at that time of morning were too remote to consider. The realisation dawned on her that if she was to go by the longer, safer route, ideally she should have got out of bed a quarter of an hour ago. There was still just about enough time for her to take the safer option and, provided she put her skates on as they say in this part of the world, arrive at the farm by five-thirty, her normal start time. Cocooned, however, as she was in the ambient heat provided by the bedclothes drawn up to her chin, Jenny had set her mind on savouring the extra few minutes in bed. Her reasoning proceeded along the lines that the weather always seems much worse than it really is when you're on the inside looking out: it was then that, rather portentously, as if to add emphasis to this thought, a squall of rain pelted the window. No sooner had she made up her mind to go to work by her normal route and stay in bed a little longer, when her reverie was disturbed by a gentle knock on the door. Jenny knew at once who had knocked, but remained silent rather than bid her father enter. She would have only called out if he had chosen an inopportune moment, and the command then would have been for her father to wait until she had made herself decent. Smiling with expectation, Jenny watched as the person whose identity she had yet to confirm tentatively opened the door wider. Sure enough, within a few moments, his face illuminated luridly by the lamp he was carrying and which he held out in front of him at about head height, appeared Henry Fewster.

"Are you awake yet Jenny?" Henry questioned softly, his hushed tones demonstrating his consideration for the neighbours, who in one direction happened to be his eldest daughter and her husband, rather than any paternal concern for his youngest daughter's beauty sleep, and that was simply because if she wasn't already awake he would have soon made sure that she was.

"I woke up a quarter of an hour ago," said Jenny in a mildly reproving tone; "Awakened by a call of nature."

"It's funny you should say that," said Henry with a chuckle. "It was about then that I had call to use the piss pot: the result of my having a couple of jars in the Endeavour with the boys. Anyway, I'm glad that it wasn't my nocturnal tinkling that woke you. If the truth be known I'm quite self-conscious about using the pot at times: I'm not concerned in the slightest about what your mother thinks, but I do feel a little embarrassed for your sake, and for the sake of the neighbours. Any noise seems twice as loud at night and travels twice as far."

Jenny was content to let her father think that she had woken in response to her own needs rather than in response to his.

"I'm well and truly awake now father, if that's what you came to make sure of," said Jenny.

The solidly imposing yet at the same time, in this instance at least, ghostly presence of Henry Fewster was neither a terrifying nor unwelcome sight to Jenny, for she knew that her father had come to ensure that she did not oversleep. His early morning call was not a daily occurrence, although the act was sufficiently regular to make the omission a surprise. Bearing in mind her father's occupation, and not forgetting his dangerous vocation, at this time of year Henry was usually pushing the boat out well before dawn.

"Look Jenny," said Henry in earnest, "I really do think you ought to take the road to work this morning, rather than risk the cliff top path. It's blowing a gale out there and you're likely to be blown right off and break your neck or something. Old Bob Higginbottom won't mind you being a few minutes late in weather like this, and if he does mind tell him it was my concern for your safety that made you late."

Henry Fewster, in mentioning Bob Higginbottom, was referring to the proprietor of Millbeck Farm, Jenny's boss.

"Don't be such a fusspot father. I've been out many a time in worse weather than this, and I don't need to tell you that I know that path like the back of my hand; and besides I can always steady myself against the worst the wind can do by keeping hold of the fence: I'll be perfectly all right."

Perhaps she had learned the technique from her father, for no sooner had she said that she would be perfectly all right when she qualified this preliminary statement with a second which in effect was a contradiction of the first, specifically that if she were to be blown off the cliff, then more than likely she would escape serious injury. She had uttered this addendum on the basis that the cliffs to the south of the village in the main were not sheer like those to the north, and depending of course on the precise location of the prospective unfortunate incident, there was a good chance that the person who had lost his or her footing would not plummet to the rocks below, their descent having been arrested by a gorse bush growing outwards rather than upwards, or by a hand which was an integral part of the falling body reaching out to grasp a clump of grass, or a stone.

Henry was not convinced. The very idea of his pride and joy, the apple of his eye, of his youngest daughter injuring herself even slightly was anathema to him, and in seeking to ensure that such an eventuality did not occur, he tried a different tack.

"What if I come with you as far as the gate where you turn inland to go up to the farm: that way you'll get to work on time and I'll not have to worry about you," suggested Henry.

Henry Fewster's reputation for being as tough a character as they come was widespread. In point of fact there wasn't a man in the county with a greater reputation for mental and physical toughness, but when it came to dealing with his daughters, he was likely to become doe-eyed and as gentle as old Dobbin. Indeed, it was probably a wise move on Henry's part that the only persons to whom he showed this softer side of his nature were his daughters, and his wife on her birthday and whenever she fell ill. To the crews of his cobble and the *Henrietta Maria,* his demeanour was sometimes inscrutable, often severe, but never soft. His severity manifested itself as a scowl delineated most emphatically by a narrowing of the eyes – which made him look fierce – and a pronounced, asymmetrical curving upwards of the mouth from the corners of the lips either side. His mouth's usual stern aspect, set approximately halfway between the bottom of his beard and the top of his balding head, was reminiscent of a wave racing towards the shore. His barrel chest notwithstanding, everything else about Henry Fewster was relatively normal, but this didn't hinder people from thinking that this was a man who was not to be tangled with, and not surprisingly nobody did tangle with him. In contrast to the men that obeyed their skipper's commands, Jenny saw her father as a gentle giant whom she knew she could twist round her little finger, and this she often did, though rarely with a dishonourable motive in mind. More often than not she would use her feminine wiles, and that peculiar sense of privilege and power she felt at being her father's daughter, mainly to keep his over protectiveness, as she perceived his paternal attitude towards her to be, at arm's length: she felt a need to assert her independence.

"There's really no need for you to come with me father," said Jenny, before adding in a tone which was imitative of her mother when she and her youngest child were approximately eighteen years younger, "Now go back to bed this minute, or you'll wake up half the street with your fussing."

To give emphasis to her verbal instruction Jenny pointed to the wall on the other side of which Mrs Fewster lay sleeping oblivious to the conversation taking place only feet away. Reluctant to impose his will on his headstrong daughter, and realising that he had run out of persuasive ammunition, Henry, after placing the lamp on the dressing table for the young lady to dress by, muttered a few parting words. The complete sense of this valediction, being barely audible, was lost on Jenny, for, before her dad had closed the door behind him, she had been able to discern only one word, and that word was, "…women."

Soon after Henry's departure Jenny leapt out of bed and began to dress in the clothes which she had laid out on a chair the night before, items of apparel chosen more for the warmth and comfort they provided than for their appearance. For this early riser not to get everything ready beforehand, an eventuality which was now rare, would, come the next morning, invariably lead to her experiencing a sense of panic as barely awake she would have to rummage about for one thing or another. Her outer garments consisted of the plainest skirt imaginable, one which she didn't mind getting dirty as she attended to the cows. Resembling a bell in which her legs – a secret to the world at large – by a stretch of the imagination could be perceived as clangers, the hem of the workaday garment swayed a mere two or three inches above the ground, which meant that this milkmaid's feet were barely visible. Above the waist Jenny had put on a woollen blouse the plainness of which was in perfect harmony with her skirt, though the contrast in colour between the two garments was stark. For maximum warmth, and motivated also by an innate sense of propriety, she had buttoned the blouse right up to her collarless neck. She intended, if there happened to be such a garment lying around, to borrow one of her dad's old pullovers, and perhaps one of his hats; though not his favourite of course.

Before she had finished her breakfast consisting of a slice of bread spread with honey derived, in the first instance, from heather growing on the nearby moor, Jenny blew out the lamp which she had carried downstairs, and then proceeded to exit the cottage by passing through the two doors at the front, there being no way in or out at the rear other than through the diminutive bathroom window.

Dressed in her composite attire, Jenny's first recourse on stepping into Chapel Street was to hold on to her charmingly eccentric hat with her free hand. In her right hand she still held a half-eaten piece of bread and honey. Once the initial gust of wind that had greeted her emergence into the open air had abated, Jenny began to wonder what her father had been so concerned about, for although the tops of the trees were being blown and shaken wildly, the bluster in the vicinity of her own front door had diminished. Confident that for the time being her hat would stay securely on her head, Jenny let go at the same time as she turned to close the door behind her. Now if it isn't, it should be common knowledge that many tasks which appear to be straightforward at first in reality soon reveal their idiosyncrasies, their niggling complications, and in this context closing the door of Camberwell

Cottage was not the mindless task one would imagine, particularly at ten to five in the morning. Between the exit on to the street and the parlour there was an inner door, and when both doors were closed they created a porch which resembled an airlock, and in which it was possible for one person to stand comfortably and two people to be squashed together in danger of standing on each other's toes. The complication which required specific knowledge in this instance was that in order to be able to close the front door with sufficient force for it to lock, the person leaving had to ensure that the inner door, which opened inwards, was open wide so as to relieve the pressure of air in the porch. In the business of coming and going this undoubted complication was a relatively new development, having first arisen about two years previously. Prior to the problem's sudden inception it had been possible to close the inner and lock the outer door without difficulty. For a time Henry had been baffled, but once he had found a procedure that worked, he had been happy to instruct the other members of his family on what to do, and had argued convincingly that it wasn't necessary to make any material changes to either the lock or the door. In this regard, for Jenny the new *modus operandi* had contradicted the previous two decades' instructions, making them not only irrelevant, but if acted upon, counter-productive. This morning, as if by instinct, she had reverted to the old ways of doing things. The inevitable outcome was failure and frustration, and in reaching for the inner door to reopen it, unintentionally she dropped the remainder of her breakfast. The honey-smeared bread landed face down on the porch carpet. By way of admonishment she muttered to herself, cursing her clumsiness. Then she stooped to retrieve the remnant of food, and, having decided that the morsel was no longer fit for human consumption, attempted to throw it into the flight path of a fortunate gull, the bird in question seeming to prove the aphorism, almost literally, that the early bird catches the worm. Not surprisingly Jenny, like the vast majority of her gender, was not particularly good at throwing, and the flight path of the bird and the trajectory of the bread diverged with each passing moment until the gull, having caught sight of the offering despite the poor light, changed course suddenly to swoop out of sight below the garden wall. Whether the agile creature had been able to catch the tasty morsel before the latter had landed on the bank of the stream or actually in the water Jenny had no idea, but she had no doubt that the large yellow-beaked bird would find its meal.

She set off towards the chapel, and beyond that imposing edifice, King Street, consciously aware of how strong the wind was in places without as yet being put under any great duress. That situation changed dramatically when she turned into the thoroughfare that was royally named. At this point on her journey she caught sight of the mainly dark expanse of the sea stretching, as revealed by the gap between two buildings, in the shape of a triangle, its apex inverted, from close to shore to touch the less dark sky miles out to sea. Here there was little protection from the full force of the wind blowing from the north, and she was propelled down the steep gradient that is King Street towards The Dock faster than she would have wished. Unlike the cottages in Chapel Street, buildings in this street acted as a wind-tunnel. Nonetheless, as Jenny approached The Endeavour Inn she was still sufficiently in control of her legs to be able to veer a couple of yards to the left. It was not that she had any aversion to the inn per se, but she was understandably concerned about passing beneath the pub sign swaying backwards and forwards and creaking loudly. The last thing Jenny wanted was to be in the wrong place at the wrong time should the sheet of metal depicting Captain Cook's ship be released from its moorings. It had crossed her mind that if that thing were to be sent flying through the air then decapitation of any unfortunate individual who happened to be passing was a distinct possibility. The thought of it made Jenny shudder, though she didn't have time to be fearful for long, for once again she was propelled along from behind, giving her little option but to break into the kind of run which gives a clear indication of the reluctance of the runner. Specifically she wanted to desist from taking short, sharp steps at the earliest opportunity. Once in The Dock, Jenny deviated from the most direct route to work to stand on the slipway and look down into the seething maelstrom that was the sea. Wave after land-encroaching wave leapt over the cobbles like a demonic being which, though for the moments Jenny stood watching it seemed that its sole aim was to engulf the innocent milkmaid, could not break free of its chains. Jenny held on to the railing which protected the iron codfish – the replica which served as a repository for charitable donations – for she was wary of being taken by surprise by the demon wind and launched into the sea-demon's arms. She could remember the time – it was at New Year the year war broke out – when two visitors to Rankin Bay had paid with their lives for showing the churning sea scant respect. It was assumed that the women had been washed off the slipway in the early hours of New Year's Day whilst larking about under the influence of alcohol. Jenny believed that they had been toying with the waves just as young boys that had probably been drinking nothing stronger than fizzy pop often did during daylight hours. She could picture how one of the inebriated women had lost her footing on the slippery cobbles and how she had then ended up in the briny. Jenny continued to imagine the event which had been tragically real in the guise of outstretched hands, one seeking for, the other offering assistance, a grasp that had had dire consequences for both parties. The scene Jenny imagined as she watched the wave which had come farther up the slipway than previous others quickly recede, sent a shiver down her spine. Letting go the railing, she turned away to make for Albion Street and the steps leading to the top of the cliff.

Ordinarily Jenny was accustomed to pause at the top of Flagstaff Steps and take in the view, which, unless the coast was draped in dense mist or fog, was spellbindingly panoramic. Even in the darkness of a barely incipient Autumnal dawn the view could be enchanting, one's eyes from Jenny's viewpoint naturally focusing on the inky blackness of the promontory that is Seal Point and Point Pleasant where it makes its bold thrust into the sea, on that and the few lamps lit to reveal that even in that remote and exposed location there was human habitation. Today, however, Jenny barely paused to take breath and was heedless of the view. Of all the elements it was possible for people living on the Yorkshire coast to encounter, it was the windy days that she disliked most. Assisted, rather too keenly, by the force which was visible by effect rather than in essence, she proceeded along the cliff top path, her head bowed, keeping one eye on the cliff edge whilst occasionally reaching out with her right hand for the support that was to be gained from taking hold of the wooden fence which enclosed the seaward side of Cowfield Hill.

Obviously this was the most dangerous part of Jenny's journey to work, though she could be thankful for the fact that the distance from the top of Flagstaff Steps to the point along the cliff where she had to turn inland was no more than a furlong. The ground underfoot was well-trodden grass interspersed in a couple of places by sunken pockets of mud around which she had to skirt with extra care. It was after Jenny had just negotiated the second of these small landslides that she caught sight of a light out to sea. Intrigued, she stopped dead in her tracks in order to make sense of what she was looking at, realising in an instant that the focus of her attention had to be a vessel, one which seemed to be making painfully slow progress towards Eskmouth. By Jenny's reckoning the boat or ship's present position was approximately mid-way between Seal Point and the horizon. From the cliff the light appeared to be intermittent, coming in and out of view at irregular intervals. Jenny could only surmise that the apparent inconstancy had much to do with the weather. The thought which ran through her mind as she stood watching for those few seconds was, "Rather them than me." A quarter of an hour later she had forgotten all about the sailors that, if they were not in mortal peril were certainly having a rough passage, and in the relative comfort and safety provided by the byre she set to work milking her first cow.

Chapter Six

At the Mercy of the Elements

The light which Jenny had espied out to sea did indeed belong to a vessel ploughing its way steadily northwards through the pounding waves. That ship was none other than the *Cape Canaveral* being driven into the wind by the power provided by her engine. Over an hour into the morning watch, occupying the wheelhouse as the schooner rounded Seal Point were two unlikely and, therefore, remarkable crewmen. Being as different from each other as the proverbial chalk is from the equally proverbial cheese, they could nonetheless claim to have one crucial factor in common, and it was this denominator which had caused them to become good friends. The frail thread which had attracted rather than repelled initially had become wound by sequential experience into a steely ligature, a seemingly unbreakable bond based on mutual trust and respect. Less obvious than the ball of twine which Ariadne rolled out for Theseus to follow in his quest to kill the Minotaur and then make good his escape, by simply asking the right questions this psychic thread could be followed in one instance back to the lush plantations of Texas, and in the other to the great treeless expanse of the Canadian prairie in the province of Alberta. They and their forebears had grown crops, one of cotton, the other wheat, and like the men that had helped to harvest the ready seeds, they too were as dissimilar as the white stuff formed by the skeletal remains of sea creatures and the food made from the fresh curds of milk. The fact was that for the preponderance of their lives on Earth to date, these two predominantly disparate individuals had grown up to become men of the soil, and the land provided for a common language. It was perhaps not insignificant that the places where they as boys had grown to manhood were a long way from either the Atlantic or the Pacific Ocean.

Standing at six feet three inches tall and being of strong, muscular build, Cornelius Cotton could cope with the arduous task of keeping the ship on course in rough weather better than any other member of the crew, the Captain included; but that didn't mean that he wasn't appreciative of his friend's assistance in this present trial of strength and endurance. Upon first being introduced strangers were mildly amused by Cornelius's name, and when asked about its origins he explained that he was in no doubt that its lineage went no farther back than two generations, and was derived from the cash crop growing on the plantations, generally across the subtropical regions of the south, but specifically in his case around the town of English in Red River County, Texas. His grandparents had formed one fifteenth of the original consignment of slaves brought to the settlement established by Oliver English in 1840, although they were actually brought there by a relative of the town's founder in 1852. Following the defeat of the Confederate states in the Civil War, Cornelius' antecedents suddenly found that they were no longer living chattels that could be bought and sold at auction, but were now free to come and go as they pleased. Not surprisingly, however, a great number of the state's two hundred thousand erstwhile slaves found that economic necessity demanded that they continue to toil in the fields as free men and women, so that picking cotton constituted the only work they would ever know as they grubbed a subsistence living as sharecroppers.

For Cornelius, having grown up on the plantations listening to stories of how the white folks that had been their masters had treated his grandparents and his parents when the latter were children, stories of how they treated them sometimes with kindness, but more often with harshness depending upon the slave owner's mood or whim, a world beyond the cotton fields had beckoned, and eventually, after many a year working in those fields, he had made his way via the crowded and far from hospitable streets of New York to begin a new life, a life which he had chosen of his own free will, at sea. It was a life he took to with the same relish that the boll weevil takes to the cotton plant; for aboard ship, admittedly primarily because of the physical strength he had developed in his previous endeavours, he was effectively a big cog in a small wheel. Despite skin colour being the obvious difference between him and his colleagues, on this voyage Cornelius had an easy going, amiable relationship with everyone but Henley. He suspected that the man from Maine, though the latter often expressed the kind of liberal views which would have merited a pat on the back from no lesser person than Abraham Lincoln, was somewhat reluctant to live and work in such close proximity to a black person, a descendent of slaves. Cornelius didn't let this suspicion trouble him, and treated Henley with courteous though phlegmatic coolness whenever he was in his company. On a ship which had a crew of six in total this was more often than he would have wished. Individual differences aside, Able Seaman Cornelius Cotton gained considerable satisfaction from the life he had chosen as exemplified by the singing of shanties as he helped haul on the halyards, and the singing of more tuneful songs (referred to as fore bitters) as soon as he had finished his watch, by many a nocturnal hour spent gazing at the stars, and by the exotic sounds, sights and smells of foreign ports. None of these pleasures was in the offing presently. Instead, notwithstanding the storm, he began to wonder about the lives of the folks asleep in the dwellings indicated by the presence of static gas lamps winding their telltale way from close by the shore up a steep hill. The township in Cornelius Cotton's view, albeit mainly as a darkly filled outline of interconnected roofs, and in his thoughts at this time, was none other than Rankin Bay.

If young Jenny Fewster upon catching sight of the light which denoted the presence of a ship had been blessed, or perhaps cursed, with supernormal sight, she would have observed that the man in control of the helm had neatly cropped black hair, the sideburns of which flared out to form a broader base in front of the ears. He was clean-shaven. More permanent features were a brow which was deeply furrowed, a nose which being broad and somewhat flattened was not unusual for his race, and the broadest smile imaginable. Indeed, so broad was his expression of delight at those aspects of life which gave him pleasure, events which the vast majority of people would probably take for granted, and thereby gain no pleasure from whatsoever, that each row of perfectly formed teeth was revealed in its entirety, right back to the molars which are reputed to denote wisdom. In his musings upon the likely daily existence of the denizens of Rankin Bay, Cornelius Cotton's facial expression indicated wistfulness rather than obvious joy. The fact of the matter was that despite the turbulent conditions, his mind had entered a halcyon state which in the present situation was too serenely contemplative, not only for its own good in the longer term, but also for the good of all on board the *Cape Canaveral*, though on his account the safety of the ship was never really in question. The opposite of 'channel fever', that state of excitement which can grip a crew as the ship approaches the end of a long voyage, in modern parlance it could be said that Cornelius Cotton had taken his eye off the ball, and this slight lapse of concentration was sufficient for him to be caught unawares by the most formidable wave to have crashed against the schooner's hull and washed over her deck thus far. It was only for a matter of seconds that Cornelius lost control as the wheel spun alarmingly in either direction in response to the natural roll and pitch of the ship as she laboured vaguely in a northerly direction.

"For crying out loud!" shouted Sheldon Crossman in an attempt to wake his friend from out of his reverie. Standing to the right of Cornelius he added, "Can't you keep your mind on the job instead of daydreaming about your love-life?"

In the same instant that Crossman voiced his warning, he joined his friend in arresting the previously uncontrolled motion of the wheel, aware that the sudden violence of movement that the ship had just experienced – if it's not stretching the imagination to say that an inanimate construction held together mainly by rivets can experience something – would not have escaped the skipper's attention. Throughout the ship expletives were rife as the majority of the crew sought to vent their feelings for having almost been upended. Of those crew members not presently on deck only Captain Gilchrist refrained from using immoderate language.

"What love life might that be you're referring to?" asked Cornelius once they had regained control, aware that Sheldon and he were, in the same boat in that regard, and that they were both footloose and fancy-free as the saying goes.

Contrary to the notion that sailors have a wife in every port, certainly in Sheldon's and Cornelius's case such a statement could not have been further from the truth, and though both men had experienced the pain and pleasure of deeply felt emotional entanglements back home, these had ended months prior to their having set sail on this present voyage. Perhaps sadly, or perhaps not so sadly from their point of view, neither man had a wife in any port, nor a woman waiting for him over some distant horizon. For the Canadian from the environs of Lethbridge – a town less than fifty miles from the Province's southern border – was a handsome devil by his own account, though it has to be said that the self-expression of this opinion had been echoed by more than one member of the opposite sex; and as for his own gender, who can say? Being relatively small in stature, and in this regard he could have been Henley's double, Sheldon could easily have been mistaken for a youth standing next to his guardian whenever he was in close proximity to his friend Cornelius. The similarity in respective physiques between Henley and himself was the one major likeness they shared, for unlike the American, Crossman looked upon the world with a benign countenance, wherein his small but nonetheless regular features, and in particular his clear, almost translucent pale blue eyes, said to women young and old, whether he encountered them in the streets of his home town, or in the busier thoroughfares of London or Bristol, that Mr Sheldon Crossman could do them no harm. In point of fact he had often pondered over whether that quiet gentleness of manner as depicted in his demeanour was the reason that he had not had as much success with women as he thought was his due. Whatever were his thoughts in the moments after Cornelius and he had regained control of the helm, they were interrupted and banished by a hardly surprising intrusion as the wheelhouse door was flung wide open to reveal the hooded, dripping figure of the skipper. To the men at the wheel, who as one turned to look over their left shoulders, the Captain was obviously in a state of displeasure bordering on anger.

"Is there a problem I should know about?" asked Captain Gilchrist, shouting to be heard above the noise of the wind.

"No sir," replied Crossman truthfully, for in his mind the problem had been resolved.

"No problem sir," replied Cornelius as he turned back to face the bows, though mindful of the fact that the responsibility for keeping the ship's head into the wind was primarily his he added, "If you're referring to that buffeting we experienced a few minutes back... that was my fault. I don't know what I was thinking of at the time, but I have to admit to having had a momentary lapse of concentration and then losing control of the wheel. It won't happen again." There was a slight pause before Cornelius rounded off his little speech with, "Sir."

This explanation, this confession which had begun with Cornelius almost shouting had reduced in volume once the Captain had squeezed into the wheelhouse and slammed shut the door behind him. In a sense the helmsman was pleased with his "momentary lapse of concentration", for he felt a degree of sophistication just by uttering these words. This wasn't the sort of language that he had been accustomed to hear and speak back in Texas.

"You're damned right it won't happen again... not unless the two of you want to go back to picking cotton and milking cows," warned Gilchrist unequivocally.

The fact that there were no such animals on the Crossman family farm revealed that the skipper's knowledge of the respective former lives of his crew was occasionally flawed.

"Here's Donk by the looks of it," informed Cotton as he peered through the barely translucent glass at the figure approaching rather more quickly than he would have done had the wind not been at his back.

Keen to bring the tongue-lashing to an end, mentally Cornelius was grateful to Walker for his sudden appearance, believing that the donkeyman's imminent interruption to the skipper's train of thought would be the distraction that was needed to assuage the latter's anger. The three men who were squeezed into the relative comfort and shelter which the wheelhouse provided collectively focused their attention on the wind-blown figure who, just as he was putting up his thumb to indicate to the three pairs of eyes gawping at him that all was well, was almost blown off his feet by a sudden and particularly strong gust. The trio of safely ensconced observers did not fail to see the comic irony in Walker's near nemesis just as the old sea dog was signalling something like its opposite. Led by the Captain and imitated in quick succession first by Crossman and then by Cotton, they emitted a ripple of sound as each man chuckled. The Captain, evidently unwilling to let Cotton's lapse go without further comment, referred to Walker's near upending in a brief lecture on the necessity of keeping one's mind completely focused in such atrocious conditions.

"There gentlemen," drawled the Captain with didactic seriousness, "You witnessed how the most experienced of our colleagues almost came a cropper for not keeping his mind on what he was doing. He could easily have knocked himself out by banging his head against…"

The object which Walker might have banged his head against was not specified because at that precise moment there was a loud bang. Differentiated from the effects of the storm, a violent judder was felt throughout the ship, though obviously more noticeably the nearer to the bang's epicentre the crew member was. The four men in no doubt that something untoward had just occurred were aft.

"God Almighty!" exclaimed Crossman. "What was that?"

Cotton merely looked at the Captain with face aghast, for in the moments immediately following the disturbance he was the first to realise that the ship, having lost its forward momentum, had become nigh on impossible to handle.

Without wishing to attempt to appropriate powers that he didn't and could never possess, just as he was about to exit the wheelhouse the Captain replied, "In answer to your question Crossman, I can say without fear of contradiction that the noise we've just heard was bad news, very bad news indeed. Do the best you can with the rudder Cornelius," he added prior to departure.

In his eagerness to take stock of the situation and formulate a plan of action accordingly, the Captain initially gave credibility to the maxim 'more haste less speed' by colliding with Walker as the donkeyman was making his way towards the hatch through which he and my grandfather had emerged earlier. Fortunately the collision occurred with insufficient force to cause either party injury. The steps leading down from the hatch led not only to the Captain's cabin, but lower still, down to the engine-room where the four-stroke auxiliary engine was located. Now that the ship was at the mercy of the wind and sea completely, any attempt to make deliberate progress around the ship was not only immensely difficult, but fraught with danger. The *Cape Canaveral* was a big ship, but to those on board at this hour of likely catastrophe, she felt about as steady as an inflatable dinghy. If the hours since the onset of the storm had thus far tested the crew's resilience, in all probability the bad event which the bang betokened would test each man's nerve. Resolute action was called for, and not surprisingly the two men who were about to investigate the incident were not found wanting. Working now as a team, the Captain opened the hatch in order to let the man whose primary responsibility aboard was to tend to the engine go first. Before anybody went anywhere, however, the men recoiled to escape the effects of a cloud of smoke, the sudden appearance of which, on the basis that 'there is no smoke without fire', was seriously ominous. Notwithstanding the cold and wet conditions on deck, prior to turning away, and in addition to the smoke, these two individuals had felt warm air wafting across their faces. It was a strange sensation, but any pleasantness which could be said to be inherent in such an experience was counteracted in this instance by noxious fumes invading their nostrils. They realised in an instant that what they could smell was burning diesel.

"What do you think?" asked the Captain, almost shouting into Walker's ear so as to be heard above the din of the storm, implicitly questioning the older man's expertise prior to the latter making a descent from which, quite conceivably, he may not subsequently emerge.

"Until I've taken a closer look I can't say for certain, but I would put money on a crankshaft explosion. In any event we've lost the use of the engine. If I were you I would…"

Walker didn't bother to finish the sentence for the simple reason that his Captain, as soon as he had ascertained that their one and only engine was totally useless, had already determined what to do, and that was to return to the wheelhouse and order Crossman to go forward and relay the order to the seaman on radio watch – Landowska – to send, and send repeatedly until acknowledged, a mayday signal. Crossman was then to ensure that the entire crew, with the exception of Walker and one obvious other, made ready to abandon ship at a moment's notice. Once the first part of Captain Gilchrist's plan had been delegated, and he had observed Crossman demonstrate the requisite sense of urgency as the Canadian made his way forward, he hastened back to the hatch which he discovered was properly closed. With the intention of following where Walker, by virtue of his greater expertise in things mechanical, had led, the Captain opened the hatch and peered into the inky darkness. There were no signs of flames. His nostrils, however, were immediately invaded, not only by the now familiar pungent smells which he had experienced earlier, but by a new, rather sweet odour, one which he had breathed only once previously, and that was during training. It was carbon tetrachloride, the liquid emitted as a vapour when Walker – for surely there could have been no other operator – had used the fire extinguisher. In the hope of eliciting a brief situation report at the earliest opportunity the Captain called out as he began his descent. There was no reply. Now whether Walker had heard the Captain and was either too preoccupied with his rather pressing task to reply, or whether he had been overwhelmed by the effects of the fire was as yet impossible for the skipper to know. The fact that no flames were as yet visible at least indicated that the fire was not rampant and out of control. Other possibilities as to the reason for the donkeyman's silence presented themselves to the man descending, the most simple of which was that given the generally loud background noise created by the prevailing weather conditions, there was a distinct possibility that Walker had simply failed to hear the perfunctory request for information. These concerns were quickly subsumed, however, when the skipper realised, just as he was about to step onto the deck on which his cabin was located – the deck one above the engine-room – that he had failed to close the hatch above his head, an oversight which was brought to his notice emphatically by another inundation as the ship took a pounding from a wave breaking over her stern. Now Captain Gilchrist would have been the first to admit that he was no expert in dealing with an engine explosion and the likely ensuing fire, but his training had provided him with sufficient savvy to realise that burning oil and water made for a potentially lethal combination. All considerations regarding his disdain for using bad language now forgotten, he swore out loud as he realised that, whatever predicament Walker was now in, he, the ship's master, the man ultimately responsible for the crew's safety, may have exacerbated the situation by effectively enabling water to be poured over troubled oil. It had been the skipper's intention to retrieve the lamp from his cabin, but instead he postponed this course of action as he ascended unencumbered to shut himself in, to envelop himself in darkness which for a time was absolute. The man who was definitely now feeling the burden of responsibility weighing heavily upon his shoulders, a burden that seemed to be getting heavier for being added to by the minute, gingerly felt his way back down the steps, wishing as he lowered one foot after the other that he had chosen to tack under sail rather than having taken the option that he had. Hypothetically speaking, if the engine had not failed, then the skilful seamanship of sailing at an angle to the wind would have lengthened the duration of the voyage considerably simply because the distance which the ship would have covered in maintaining a zigzag course would have been that much greater. Now the circumstances were reversed, and the voyage under sail which did not take place would have seen the *Cape Canaveral* docking in Eskmouth that very afternoon or early evening, a prospect which would have contrasted favourably with the present disaster.

After having collected the oil-lamp from his cabin the Captain descended the second stairway. The descent was relatively easy for being illuminated. He was about to enter the engine-room when he felt the vibration and heard the sickening, grinding noise which informed him, and no doubt the others, that the ship had hit bottom. This sensory information, though far from welcome, at least confirmed to the skipper's dubious satisfaction, that there had been no time to hoist the sails in an attempt to prevent the vessel from grounding. If there was a silver lining to the dense cloud of catastrophe which had hung over the *Cape Canaveral* on her voyage running parallel to the Lincolnshire and Yorkshire coasts, it was that in being stuck fast the movement of the ship was now considerably less erratic.

In the engine-room doorway the sweet smell of carbon tetrachloride was strong, and its lingering vaporous presence made the flame in the lamp flicker tentatively, as if it was on the point of extinction. Instinctively the skipper held the lamp higher, and the flame seemed to strengthen and grow brighter as a consequence. At first, his view impeded by the twisted, mangled mass of metal that only moments ago had been a working engine, Captain Gilchrist failed to see the man who had evidently put out the fire. What he noticed initially was the grimy mix of sea water and engine oil swishing from side to side in keeping with the motion of the ship's stern as it too swayed back and forth through no less than thirty degrees of a circle. The Captain had judged that his ship had grounded near the bows, and that she was stranded between one and two hundred yards from shore.

In places the remains of the engine were still smoking and radiating heat. It seemed that all the engine oil that could have escaped had escaped. In wading ankle-deep through the unwholesome liquid the Captain eventually espied the donkeyman's lower limbs protruding above the surface, his feet pointing uppermost. Captain Gilchrist's first thought upon beholding the apparently lifeless body of his crewman was exactly that – that Walker was dead. He had heard stories about how individuals using the extinguisher in question had suffered consequently, and he wondered if this incident was going to confirm that those stories were true. The Captain strode forward with the same sense of urgency that a wildebeest demonstrates when it is trying to escape from the jaws of a crocodile, or bathers in certain climes when their frolicking in the shallows has been interrupted by the sighting of a predatory shark. He discovered, upon beholding Walker from head to toe, that the donkeyman was lying face up with his head resting on the fire extinguisher which, presumably, he had been using, and which, presumably, had dropped from his hands prior to his having been overcome by the fumes. The irony was not lost on Walker's would-be rescuer that the fire which could have killed them all had been rendered harmless by a chemical which had almost done for the operator, a chemical squirted from the cylinder which was now ensuring that same operator's continued existence. At the point of time's arrow in this heroic sequence of events the good news was that the veteran sailor was still breathing. The empty cylinder was lying in the hollow of Walker's neck, its length at a right angle to the sailor's body. This hard but merciful pillow served to tilt the donkeyman's head back slightly, thereby preventing his mouth and nostrils from becoming submerged in the bilge-water.

The skipper put down the lamp he was carrying, and almost at once he was plunged into darkness as the flame petered out. Without waiting for his eyes to readjust, but working solely from the light of memory, the Captain stooped to grip Walker under the arms, raising the heavy dead-weight with a herculean effort. First he raised the donkeyman to a sitting position, then up on to his right shoulder, thereby adopting a classic fireman's lift. Wading back to the stairs was no easy task, but going up them was twice as difficult. Once he had gained the level of his cabin, the skipper decided that the only sensible course of action was to unburden himself of Walker's weight while he ascended unencumbered in order to open the hatch. This he did. Upon looking around and seeing the others, two of whom were in the wheelhouse and two of whom were standing in close proximity to it, he called to them to come and assist. There now being no reason whatsoever for Cotton to remain at the helm, all four men heeded the summons; though it was only the Texan who followed the skipper down the steps. The consensus was that of all the men on board Cornelius would be best able to manhandle his incapacitated colleague back up into the bracing and hopefully invigorating air. Crossman, Henley and Landowska waited to assist from above.

"What's been happening topside?" asked the skipper as he stooped to haul Walker back over his shoulder, only to be thwarted in this endeavour by the hand of Cotton as the muscular crewman assumed responsibility for transporting the semi-conscious fire-fighter.

"I'll take over now skipper," said Cotton authoritatively; "As for what's been happening, you'll be able to see for yourself as soon as we've got this lump on deck."

To give emphasis to his words, after having adopted a carrying position with his burden not dissimilar to that which had been employed by his Captain, Cotton gave the donkeyman a hefty smack on his posterior, a friendly act of violence to which the victim responded with an encouraging groan. Within two minutes Walker was lying on deck coughing and spluttering as my grandfather applied his trusted resuscitation technique with the aim of expelling the last of the noxious chemical substance from the poisoned lungs, as well as getting pure air into them. Not a man clustered round and staring down at the pathetic figure, who eventually turned on his side to vomit, was in any doubt that Walker was indeed fortunate to have survived.

Chapter Seven

A Call to Oars

When the cannon sounded at a minute after six o' clock in the morning, not all the residents of Rankin Bay and the outlying farms and cottages heard its loud report. Those that did – and at that time of day, bearing in mind that this was a community which subscribed with gusto to what has been referred to as the Protestant work ethic, that number was considerable – knew that people's lives were in danger. They knew because the only other occasions when the cannon was fired was at midday precisely every Sunday, an action carried out to test and ensure that a piece of ordnance which was so important to the saving of lives was in good working order. The signal was effectively a command for two groups of men to assemble in The Dock, the thirteen souls that had volunteered to crew the lifeboat, and a similar number, thereabouts, that had given promise to man the somewhat prosaically named, 'Board of Trade Rocket Apparatus'.

Now in the annals of the sea that surrounds these shores, the heroic efforts of the Royal National Lifeboat Institution are universally recognised to this day, and largely this has to be because a service with a proud tradition continues to be operationally effective. The same cannot be said of the shore-based crews whose role was to fire a rocket-propelled line over the stranded ship in order to attempt a rescue by breeches buoy. Superseded by helicopters, it should not be forgotten that a service which lasted for approximately one hundred and fifty years also gave those formerly in peril reason to be grateful.

When Jenny Fewster heard the cannon being fired by the coastguard from the top of the cliff to the north of Rankin Bay, she was in the byre milking her third cow of the morning. Her response to the bang was physical, and in almost falling off her milking-stool she pulled at Jemima's teats a little too severely for the normally placid Friesian not to make a vocal protest. Aware that her temporary loss of control had caused the cow in her care some discomfort, Jenny duly apologised. Our lovely milkmaid's response wasn't merely reflexive. It wasn't merely her nervous system responding in a way which would be familiar to many were they to be startled suddenly, perhaps by the sound of a shotgun being fired to bring down a rabbit, perhaps by the clichéd report of a car back-firing. Aware of the signal's significance, following her initial judder at being startled, Jenny's physical sensations soon became emotionally based as a feeling not unlike the onset of a new ice age gradually crept over her, for she knew instinctively that the call to duty had everything to do with the vessel showing the light she had espied earlier. With no direct role to play in any attempted rescue, Jenny was, nonetheless, bound to be affected by the danger that her father and brother-in-law were likely to face by putting out to sea in such weather. The *Henrietta Maria* had proved herself to be a reliable craft in that she had not once capsized on her numerous missions in heavy seas; but there was always a first time, and there had been more than one disaster involving lifeboats from other ports along this coast to give Jenny sufficient grounds for concern.

With fishing out of the question for that day, and thinking therefore that he would be able to enjoy a couple more hours in bed, following the conversation with his daughter, Jenny's father had fallen into a deep sleep almost as soon as his head had hit the pillow.

Normally there was a part of his mind which was ever vigilant, ever ready to respond to the cannon's boom, but for no discernible reason on this occasion the signal to man the lifeboat failed to penetrate his dreaming state, and he continued to snore loudly, completely oblivious, at least for a few moments longer than he should have been, to the emergency which was possibly developing from bad to worse between one and two miles from where he lay, and to which it was his duty to respond with the utmost speed. Fortunately for the coxswain of the *Henrietta Maria*, however, Henry Fewster did not sleep alone.

Disturbed by her husband getting back into bed, from the moment that she felt as if the raft of their dreams was about to capsize under his considerable weight, Enid had drifted in and out of sleep. When conscious she had considered the successes and failures of the previous day, or finely tuned her routine for the day yet to come. She was in recapitulation mode when she heard the signal for the respective crews to muster, and though she knew that she really ought to have awakened her husband the very next instant, for at least half a minute she didn't move, but waited as if prepared to let things happen, if not of their own accord, then at least without any incitement on her behalf. At the superficial level of cause and effect custom established by precedent had previously seen Henry leap out of bed with an alacrity and agility which belied his bulk and weight, and this long-established pattern of behaviour undoubtedly had some bearing on Enid, and was possibly, in part, the cause of her procrastination. At a more abstruse level, however, the coxswain's wife found that she was having dark thoughts about the future; and the future in question didn't pertain to when they were likely to be old and grey; nor even to such a remote event as the forthcoming Christmas; but rather to the next few hours and minutes when they would be worlds apart. In these weighty moments Enid gave serious thought to the distinct possibility that when her husband next walked out the cottage door it could be for the last time, and despite her familiarity with the inherent risk involved in his being a fisherman and a lifeboat volunteer, a sadness came upon her which she had not felt before.

This sense of foreboding could not be allowed to continue for long, and so Enid, acting in a manner more in keeping with her birthright, a birthright which had seen generations of women inured by graft and hardship come and go, she shook her snoring husband awake. The shaking being vigorous, Henry awoke with a start, wondering what on earth was happening. Disbelieving that he had slept through a call to action that he had not slept through before, he was angry with himself, and therefore addressed Enid sternly. She spoke just as sharply back to him, and having urged him to get a move on, it took less than a minute for the coxswain to adjust to the reality and urgency of the situation, and dress appropriately to his spending a few hours in an open boat in a storm. Similarly, in cottages throughout the narrow streets and alleys of Rankin Bay men assisted by their wives made ready in a manner which they had practised many times, and which they had done for real just as often.

A number of people whose presence in The Dock was not required also heard the cannon, and among them was Jamie Cullen. Jamie had not gone to bed in his pokey little cottage amid a row of cottages which were collectively known as Bramblewick, but having wrapped himself in a thick Army blanket in order to keep himself warm as he drank a late night cup of cocoa, had fallen asleep fully clothed in front of an unlit fire. Jamie woke to the sound of the cannon feeling, mainly in his left shoulder and the lumbar region of his back, the discomfort generated by several aching bones, but the prospect of his being able to observe a dramatic rescue, and perhaps being able to lend a hand if asked, stirred him into action, and he extricated himself from the blanket tucked into the gaps between the cushion and the arms of the chair in which it was comfortable to sit but not so comfortable to sleep with youthful enthusiasm. In keeping with his basic level of existence this would be one of those days when Jamie omitted to wash. Instead he merely removed the granules of 'sleep' from his eyes with his fingernail. He was feeling peckish, and sated his hunger by eating two of four potatoes which he found in a bowl covered with a plate, and which were leftovers of a meal he had prepared for himself two days previously. Then, after hoisting up his trousers and tightening the twine which served as a belt and which had worked itself loose during the night, he set off from his cottage barely protected from the weather to negotiate the agglomeration of thoroughfares created by Rankin Bay's rows of dwellings. His intention was to call on his friend John Gretton whom he thought could possibly be persuaded to vacate his bed in Sunny Place and come along to witness events as they unfolded rather than necessarily having to learn about them, second-hand so to speak, later; perhaps even at a later date.

Meanwhile, back at Millbeck Farm, Jenny had just finished milking Betty – her fourth cow of the morning – and was getting up from her stool when she saw Bob Higginbottom enter the cowshed. Approaching the extremity of lamplight, his dark silhouette contrasting with the lighter darkness of incipient day outside was unmistakeable, for he was slightly bow-legged, an aspect of his physicality which was most apparent when he walked. The sight of her employer's stocky frame demonstrating what to her eyes was an exceedingly funny gait never failed to make Jenny smile. It was a smile which Bob, as instigator, took to be an outward sign of Jenny's natural amiability. He was wearing a farmer's flat cap which he politely removed from his head as he drew near to the only other person present.

"Good morning Mr Higginbottom," greeted Jenny warmly, her concerns about what may be happening out to sea and in Rankin Bay temporarily subsumed beneath her desire to appear alert and respectful to her boss. "The yield seems a little better this morning, if these four I've done so far are anything to go by."

Before picking up her stool she gave Betty a firm smack on the rump as if this were a proven method of saying thank-you to cows, one which they can easily understand.

"I'm not so sure that it is a good morning Jenny," said Bob, his round, fleshy face no longer in shadow, and appearing unusually sombre in the glow of the lamp that hung from the rafter.

His cheeks were flushed pink and the brow beneath the thin wisps of hair which he normally brushed across his otherwise bald pate, but which were now in disarray after the removal of his cap, were deeply furrowed. His present demeanour depicted a level of anxiety which for him was unusual.

In her youthful innocence Jenny asked simply, "Why? What's the matter?"

"I wouldn't have thought of it myself, but the wife says I've got to let you get off home seeing as how the lifeboat's being launched and it's your dad that's in charge. Didn't you hear the cannon?" he asked, shuffling slightly, as if to shift his weight from one bent leg to the other. "I'll take over from where you've left

84

off," he added, hanging his cap from a handy protuberance before reaching for the half-filled pail resting on the ground by Jenny's right foot.

"Really Mr Higginbottom, I appreciate your concern but I'm much better off here keeping myself busy doing something useful; and besides, father has been out in the lifeboat in weather like this dozens of times. He always comes back," argued the young milkmaid forcibly.

Just as she uttered "in weather like this", as if to give emphasis to her words, the wind gusted through the byre with sufficient vigour to cause a loose piece of sheet metal on the roof to clatter noisily: seemingly supernatural in origin, the commotion made farmer and milkmaid pause as they considered the ineffable. In respect of Jenny's line of reasoning, she was of the opinion that if her boss had been acting on his own initiative in coming to give her the rest of the morning off, her argument would have won the day; but unfortunately for Bob he was in the unenviable and invidious position of being, on this occasion, a mere messenger between two women, and was determined, therefore, not to take "no" for an answer. The salient fact was that the redoubtable Mrs Higginbottom had had some kind of premonition, and her husband knew perfectly well that if he were to return to the house and tell her that Jenny was perfectly happy to continue with the milking, he would only be sent out of the door again with instructions to be more resolute, more adamant. Not wishing to waste the morning performing the ministrations of a go-between, he set about letting Jenny know that she was not the person in charge.

"Now listen here young lady," began the stocky farmer firmly, his greater resolve clearly evident in the slightly increased volume and the deeper tone of his voice, "There's not just you to think of: there's your poor mother down there on her own wondering if and when she'll see Henry again, to say nothing of her son-in-law. The wife says that Enid will want both her daughters to be with her at this time of peril, and so you're to get away home as quick as you can." The farmer, whose family had hailed from Cheshire in the dim and distant past, but who, for having as an individual known no other, was fully inculcated in Yorkshire ways, could hardly believe the evidence of his own ears when he heard himself say, "And don't worry about your wages: they'll be just the same as if you was here for the entire morning as usual."

If the desired effect had been to make the daughter feel guilty for the sake of her mother, there could be no doubting that Bob Higginbottom's words had prodded the former sharply, as sharply in a psychological sense as if, in a physical sense, he had shooed the young woman from his property at the point of a pitchfork. Jenny, her self-centred resolve thus undermined, and having come to the conclusion that there was no point in her pleading with a person who had assumed the role of ventriloquist's dummy, but who wielded an employer's power over her nonetheless, offered no further resistance, and after handing Mr Higginbottom her milkmaid's stool, left the cowshed to make her way home the way she had come.

Just as Jenny was leaving Millbeck Farm, in the village of Rankin Bay two groups of volunteers were parading to ensure that all were present that should be. With regard to the lifeboat crew in particular, there being no time to waste in forming up in ranks, this was hardly undertaken with military precision, but involved Henry Fewster, his neck hidden by the inflated fabric of his life-jacket, making a quick headcount and scanning the faces that had mustered before him in front of the boathouse. For precious seconds that perhaps amounted to a minute, his crew, their rough fisherman's hands dangling limply by their sides, their resolute faces seemingly held in place by the inflated life-saving equipment, awaited the order to launch with the same degree of anticipation that an athlete under starter's orders for a sprint race would demonstrate. No sooner had their Coxswain given the order, than each member of the *Henrietta Maria's* crew set about his well-drilled, allotted task with purposeful speed, with a sense of urgency which never developed into panic.

The task of launching the lifeboat and then rowing out to the schooner, though undoubtedly more hazardous, was a much less complicated business than determining the best course of action to be taken by the crew of the Board of Trade Rocket Apparatus. Their taskmaster was a retired naval officer named Charlie Cook, a lean-faced sexagenarian who, simply by being possessed of the same name as the great explorer, claimed to be a direct descendent of Captain James Cook, RN, though it is known for a fact that the circumnavigator's children produced no heirs. Charlie stood out from the younger volunteers (the youngest two were in their mid forties) in a team identifiable by the white band each man wore diagonally across his upper body – when on duty that is. His distinguishing features were a pure white beard which contrasted with his black moustache. He continued to wear his naval officer's cap.

By this time both rescue crews knew for certain where their quarry had grounded, for the stranded vessel was showing a red light, and had been shooting flares of the same colour at quarterly hour intervals. The ship was stranded on the scaur approximately two hundred and fifty yards from the cliff, far enough out for her to be pummelled by the waves until a couple of hours before the tide was at its lowest. She was listing to starboard, but not to such an extent that those on board became unduly alarmed. Correctly as it turned out, it was generally assumed that the ship's load had shifted, and this was the reason that the *Canaveral's* five masts were no longer vertical. Her position was directly opposite the cliff which separates the gorges of Stoupe Beck and Coldbeck. Presently the tide was midway between high and low, and ebbing. This fact alone added to the dilemma of the land-based rescuers, whereas if the tide had been coming in, the decision to take their cart by road in effect would have been made for them. The choices facing Charlie Cook were whether to wait an hour or two for the tide to have ebbed completely, a scenario which would allow him and his crew to pull and push their cart over the recently exposed sandy stretches of beach and on over the flat-topped rock that forms the scaurs, or, alternatively, set off at once along the road. In essence Charlie's dilemma was not dissimilar to the one which Jenny Fewster had given some thought to over an hour earlier, and although it may seem a perverse idea to head inland to attempt to rescue the crew of a stranded ship, there would undoubtedly be considerable method in such apparent madness. By adopting this method eventually their route would turn south at the village of Thistlethorpe, and then, after about a mile, loop round to meet with the lane leading to the top of the cliff near Stoupe Beck. Charlie knew that with the cart in tow, this journey of between three and four miles would take well over an hour, and he had to weigh this against how long they would have to wait before they would be able to make progress along the beach. By training and character he was a man who was capable, and indeed accustomed, to making reasoned decisions quickly, and on the basis that he and his men would rather be doing something than nothing, and that they could gain up to an hour on waiting for the tide, Charlie ordered the crew of the Board of Trade Rocket Apparatus to turn about from the way they were facing in readiness to set off along New Road towards Bridge End.

"Why not pick up Dobbin on the way and tether him to the cart?" suggested coxswain Fewster in a stentorian voice as soon as he realised the course of action being taken by his terrestrial counterpart. "He'll make your job of getting up the bank that much easier."

"I'll take you up on that Henry," Charlie shouted back appreciatively; "But I hope that old nag of yours doesn't keel over."

The fact that he was being disparaging towards the horse disguised similar concerns he was having regarding the fitness of his men, for Charlie knew that the task he had set them, all of whom, like Dobbin, were past their physical prime, was considerable.

"Don't break a leg in trying to get round to the top of the cliff at Stoupe... we'll probably have everybody off the wreck before you're even half way there," added Henry, consciously creating a competitive edge, a sense of rivalry between the two groups of rescuers.

The foreman of the team manning the Board of Trade Rocket Apparatus said nothing in reply, but instead ordered his men forward. At the same time as the cart wheels bearing the rockets and hundreds of yards of line began to roll, the heavier pair supporting the *Henrietta Maria* rolled past the cast-iron cod that served as a collection-box. They soon picked up momentum on the ramp leading down to the beach and the sea beyond. Amongst the twenty to thirty people that had gathered to watch the launch stood a number – women mainly – with anxious, careworn faces. With their menfolk aboard the boat the reason for their anxiety was obvious. Strangely for him, even Jamie Cullen stood in sombre, respectful silence as the lifeboat crew waded into the dark, seething water. The cries of the gulls wheeling and diving overhead were neither ominous nor distracting. They were just birds going about their business at the beginning of the day. They were foraging for food as usual.

Whilst all this activity was taking place with appropriate haste in The Dock of Rankin Bay, those aboard the *Canaveral* were coming to terms with their predicament. Thanks to the assistance proffered on deck by Cotton and the Captain, Walker had recovered sufficiently to be able to get to his feet and stagger to the port rail, where he proceeded to vomit. The pair of impromptu medical orderlies held on to the donkeyman at either side just in case. It would have been a rum do to have hauled the invalid as a dead weight up from the engine-room only to go and lose him over the side. The others, the radio-operator included, had occupied the wheelhouse in an attempt to keep out of the wind and keep warm. In the cramped space occupied by three bulging bodies movement was difficult, even appearing quite comical whenever one of them attempted to adjust his position, encumbered as each man was by his life-jacket.

"The skipper's going to catch it from the bosses for this fiasco," prophesied Henley, the expression on his face revealing that he was not unduly dismayed at such a prospect.

"That wouldn't cause you to lose any sleep now, would it?" stated Crossman in that mellow accent of his, an accent the timbre and modulation of which seemed to add gravitas to everything he said. "What is it between you and the skipper? Anyone would think that you'd be happy to see him lose his ticket."

"I've got nothing against the skipper personally," retorted Henley, bracing himself as the ship groaned and grumbled upon being struck by a mighty wave in the same instant that she was buffeted by one of those exceptionally strong gusts of wind that occurred now and then, a combination which could easily have caused the upending of the donkeyman had he not been restrained by the two pairs of hands acting as anchors. "What I mean is that my attitude towards him would be different, would be more positive if I thought he was up to the job professionally."

"And the fact is you don't," said Crossman pithily.

"And the truth is I don't," echoed Henley with some distortion. "I'm sure he knows his stuff well enough in theory, but it's a different kettle of fish being in command on a voyage like this. To my mind, such as it is, he obviously lacks experience, and without Walker to hold his hand he wouldn't know which way to turn. That's probably why," continued Henley in a similar vein, "he went to so much trouble to revive Donk and haul him up on deck."

"That's just downright unfair. You can't blame the Captain for the limeys going on strike," said Landowska, a man who by nature was inclined to side with the underdog, and the underdog in this instance he thought was Captain Gilchrist. "And because I'm sure the skipper would be the last person alive to attempt to appropriate powers normally ascribed to God, he can't be blamed for the severity of the storm either; and as for the engine breaking down, well that was just bad luck."

"You're entitled to your opinion," rejoined Henley, "but it's my opinion that Gilchrist is largely responsible for the mess we're in, and I'll tell you for why."

"Please do," interjected Landowska with forced politeness, a technique which he adopted whenever he felt a surge of anger and wished to counteract the effects of getting hot under the collar, so to speak.

"Look, Gilchrist knew perfectly well that the engine was playing up... it hasn't been running properly since we left Bristol, yet he chose to rely on that supposed mechanical marvel that's now a heap of junk rather than tack under sail, and, as events have proven, that was the wrong decision, that was his big mistake. Look," he repeated, though without exclamation, "when all's said and done, it's the job of the Captain to make the right decisions... that's what he's paid for, and that's what he's clearly failed to do big style on this voyage... as a consequence we all have to suffer. You do realise," continued Henley in a more sombre tone, "that we may yet have to pay for this fiasco with our lives."

Evidently, because Henley had omitted to include it in his list of failings, he did not blame the Captain for the lights not working. Perhaps fortunately for the man doing the hatchet job or the expert analysis of Gilchrist's shortcomings, Henley was interrupted by the man in question opening the wheelhouse door. The latter's expression was stern, but there was no indication of anger. Nonetheless, the three men who beheld that face realised that it would probably be a bad career move to try to make light of the situation by cracking a bad joke. Behind and a little to one side of the skipper, his face seemingly drained of blood, stood Walker. Despite his unhealthy pallor, there was clearly enough blood circulating through his veins to enable him to stand on his own two feet, although Cotton, who was bringing up the rear, was ready to provide support should the donkeyman faint. The first man to address the skipper was Henley.

"I'm glad to see that Walker's all right boss. How bad was it down there?" he questioned, but without waiting for a response he set about providing answers to questions which could just as easily have been asked of him, hypothetical questions to which he gave disingenuous answers. "We were just discussing whether it would be feasible to lighten the ship by throwing some of the heavier stuff over the side. For a start, the one thing you don't need when you've run aground is an anchor. We could also..."

The speaker made no suggestion as to how they were going to cut through the anchor chain with the equipment and in the time that was likely to be available. Nonetheless, it was obvious that these plausibly practical thoughts had been running through Henley's sharp mind at some point prior to his expressing his opinion of the Captain, though it didn't seem to matter to the crewman that he had not previously uttered a word on the subject of refloating the ship, to say nothing of their having had a discussion. The individuals who were aware of what had been discussed in the wheelhouse neither confirmed nor denied their shipmate's statement, though whether Captain Gilchrist had even heard Henley's suggestion was not immediately apparent.

"Get out of there you three, and let Donk in out of this wind," ordered the Captain. "Crossman, go and find something for him to sit on. Come on… look lively," he added as the Canadian brushed past him. "What's the situation Landowska? Is help on its way? How long ago did we fire the last distress signal?

The men wearing life-jackets shuffled out of the wheelhouse to leave space for the three who had not yet found time to don theirs. Crossman ventured farther afield than the vicinity of the door in his search for an object which would serve as a chair. He didn't feel the slightest resentment at having been given this task, for he realised just how much they owed to the man from New Hampshire, and the debt had nothing to do with money.

It was obvious from Captain Gilchrist's quick fire questions that equal to his concern for Donk's welfare was his desire to be put in the picture about what was happening and where. The Captain, having guided Walker across the threshold, turned to face the New Yorker. Cotton held the door open.

"They assured me of their best efforts," informed Landowska, referring to the shore-based radio station GKZ."

"I don't suppose you invited the coastguard... I presume it was the coastguard... to be more specific," commented the Captain, irked by the vagueness of Landowska's reply.

In turn the New Yorker of Polish descent, bridling at what he considered to be the skipper's sarcasm, said, "As a matter of fact I did. I was assured that the lifeboat from a place called Rankin Bay would be with us shortly... though it would seem that our would-be rescuers are coming to get us in a rowing boat. The coastguard... I presume it was the coastguard... wouldn't be drawn on how long a time his definition of 'shortly' covered."

"Is that all?" enquired the Captain curtly.

"Give me a chance to finish," responded Landowska, matching his interlocutor's abrupt, impatient manner with equal terseness. "If for any reason the lifeboat can't reach us, they're going to try to get a line aboard. In short they're going to be firing rockets at us from the shore."

To all but Walker and the person meant to hear, the noise of the wind had drowned out most of the conversation between Landowska and the Captain, though the gusting dropped for a time just at the moment when the former was rounding off his report regarding the measures being taken to attempt a rescue. Crossman was not within earshot, but as far as Cotton and Henley were concerned the prospect of coming under sustained rocket attack seemed counter-intuitive and generated a mutually quizzical look. These shared expressions of perplexity disguised their respective need to quell an incipient sense of alarm.

Chapter Eight

False Impressions

In keeping with the diurnal pattern established when the Earth was formed, the sun rose over the sea's horizon. Throughout the morning of the day when my grandfather's life and the lives of the men under his command were in mortal danger, the life-sustaining orb stayed well and truly hidden. From dawn onwards the natural world was no longer draped in black but in varying shades of grey. Even the grass in the fields stretching inland from the edges of the cliffs appeared to have given up their normal hue as they languished rain-sodden beneath the thick blanket of cumulus-nimbus racing over sea and land in a south-westerly direction, clouds which made the exact position of the risen sun difficult to determine.

In order to evade the rocky scaurs which curved around the bay in great arcs to point out to sea in a north-easterly direction at the northern extremity, and a south-easterly direction at the extremity formed by Seal Point, the coxswain of the *Henrietta Maria* ordered his men to row in a direction that if maintained would eventually see the lifeboat and the magnificent but stranded ship lose sight of each other. The schooner showing bare poles was now clearly visible just beyond the raging surf, and to those in the know, it looked as if she had run aground on a rocky outcrop known as Low Balk. Well known to local fishermen as a place to stay clear of, the hazard in question was farther from the shore than the unwary seafarer might have expected. The purpose of rowing away from the *Canaveral* in the first instance was to keep to the channel of deeper water between the scars. For the *Henrietta Maria* to venture out to sea on a heading other than seventy degrees east would see her meet with a fate similar to that which had befallen the American ship, and for a boat crewed by local fishermen such an eventuality would have been ignominious to say the least. The work was gruelling as the open boat breasted and rose to surmount each onrushing breaker. The crew found the task of rowing with any semblance of cohesion difficult in the extreme. A boat which seemed big enough, and sturdy enough, to overcome anything which an angry sea might throw at her when she was being hauled out of the boathouse, appeared small and terrifyingly vulnerable as she struggled to make headway upon the storm-tossed sea, particularly in the eyes of those watching her progress from the shore. After approximately half an hour, Henry, from his commanding position at the helm, turned to look over his shoulder in order to gauge the distance they had rowed, and judging that distance to be far enough for them to be clear of the still submerged rocks, he manipulated the rudder to bring about the required change of course. In the same instant he gave the order to the crew to dip only their port side oars until such time as the *Henrietta's* bows were pointing in a southerly direction. Henry removed his hat and rubbed the salt spray from his eyes with a handkerchief which he had taken from his pocket, an action he performed whenever there was a problem to be solved; for he knew that he would soon have to make a crucial decision.

Brought at breakneck speed by a runner, news which had been delivered to Coxswain Fewster courtesy of Her Majesty's

Coastguard immediately prior to launch (indeed half the men were already up to their respective waists in water prior to hauling themselves aboard), had provided him with an unenviable dilemma. The hastily scribbled message informed that the *SS Moonglow*, a single-funnelled steamship of nearly six hundred tons gross, and inbound to Newcastle-upon-Tyne after sailing from Durban, had reported that she was in difficulty due to engine failure and that she required urgent assistance. The *Moonglow's* reported position was several miles farther south than the schooner, way beyond Seal Point. This meant that the steamship was hidden from view to the crew of the Rankin Bay lifeboat, even when the would-be rescuers had rowed out beyond the scars. The Ravensborough lifeboat had been requested, but the distance involved was considerably greater than the nautical miles the crew from Rankin Bay would have to row, and besides, the Ravensborough boat was already deployed, having been launched to bring safely home a father and his two sons from a sinking locally registered trawler. Ordinarily Coxswain Fewster's course of action would have been straightforward. The *Henrietta Maria* had been launched for the sole purpose of attempting to rescue the crew from the wreck in respect of which the cannon had been fired, and whose predicament was clearly visible: ordinarily it was simply a question of first come, first served. The complication to this time-honoured rule was that the people aboard the *Cape Canaveral* were, without exception, adult males, whereas it had been reported that there were women and children aboard the *SS Moonglow*, notwithstanding the fact that the latter was a freighter carrying a mixed cargo, a cargo which somewhat alarmingly included a number of caged animals bound for a safari park soon to be established in the wilds of Northumberland. The animals included two leopards and twice as many lions. This information

Henry was privy to, and he spent several invaluable moments giving serious thought as to how they would deal with such dangerous beasts, assuming, of course, that there would still be sufficient time available to attend to the fauna after having first ministered to human needs. The seriousness and difficulty of the decision which Henry was soon going to have to make didn't preclude a smile of broad dimension from creeping across his face as he imagined the macabre scenario of the people whom he and his men had saved from drowning being eaten alive by cats. The newspapers would have a field day, and known in every house throughout the land, he would be infamous. In any real sense, however, the prospect of women and children being served up as cat food was too remote an eventuality to be given much consideration, and as Henry turned the rudder so that the *Henrietta Maria's* bows were pointing to the seaward side of the wave-pounded *Cape Canaveral*, and to the seaward side of Seal Point, as succinctly as possible Coxswain Fewster briefed his men on the mission which was to be their first priority.

"We're leaving the schooner till later lads. We're heading for an area due east of Blea Wyke Point. There's a ship in trouble with women and kids aboard," bellowed Henry.

The sheer power of the coxswain's voice ensured that each member of the crew heard every word, and perhaps it was because they were more keenly motivated by the thought of children of an age similar to their own being at risk, or perhaps it was simply the realisation that there was much work to do and so little time in which to do it, that each man seemed to redouble his effort in working the oars. In this exigency, after changing course, they were less hampered by the wind, though they would have been more grateful than they were if the weather had been blowing directly from the north, if the wind had been a tail-wind on their outward journey. Each man jack straining his sinews to propel the *Henrietta Maria* towards her quarry knew that before the morning was over he would be exhausted.

Coxswain Fewster's decision to make for the *SS Moonglow's* last known location was made not only on the basis of what he considered to be a strong emotional and moral imperative, but for a sound practical reason to boot. The steamship was too far away from Rankin Bay for the Board of Trade Rocket Apparatus to reach within a reasonable timescale, but that team could be remarkably successful in being the sole means of assistance in respect of the stricken schooner. In contrast to the smile he had allowed himself in thinking of the unlikely event of a leonine feast, in considering an eventuality which was quite possible, Henry's imposing visage assumed a glum expression as an ignoble thought, one which was not totally out of character, came to mind. By nature highly competitive, Henry was irked at the prospect he envisaged of Charlie Cook being feted not only in Rankin Bay, but in all the lonely farms and neighbourly hamlets between Eskmouth and Ravensborough for being the saviour of the '*Cap*' *Canaveral*'s crew, whilst he and his men were treated, not so much with contempt or disdain – they were generally held in too high a regard for that to happen – but with pity for having failed. Of course, there would be unbounded sympathy for their not having been able to save the women and kids, and no doubt there would be more than one commiserating hand placed on Henry's shoulder, but though not intended, such comments, and such gestures, would serve merely to cut him to the quick and lower his self-esteem. Realising in time that these imaginings were leading him down a dark hole, Henry regained the light of resolve by concluding that the only thing for it was to save the women and children, thereby making for a successful rescue mission all round.

"Come on lads, put your backs into it," he shouted unnecessarily, and he was not surprised to hear not a moan or groan in response.

After half an hour's hard rowing the *Henrietta Maria* had drawn level with the *Cape Canaveral*, but first to the surprise and then to the consternation of the five Americans and one Canadian, the lifeboat appeared to be making no attempt to close a gap of approximately one hundred yards, this being the distance between the two vessels at their closest point. On the contrary, to the men watching, at first from the vicinity of the schooner's wheelhouse, and then from where they stood in line along the starboard rail towards the stern, the boat which they believed had come to save them, after the initial approach, seemed hell-bent upon widening the gap with every stroke. It was as if the lifeboat men had suddenly been made aware that the *Cape Canaveral* was smitten with a deadly contagious or infectious disease. That, however, was not what Captain Gilchrist thought as he braced himself against a sudden upsurge of spray by tightening his grip on the rail. Admittedly somewhat perplexed by the *Henrietta Maria's* manoeuvring – painted in large white letters on a black background, with his naked eye he could just make out her name beneath the starboard gunwale aft of the bow – Captain Gilchrist's mind sought a rational explanation to the course of action being taken by the coxswain, and in this regard he was poorly but wittily assisted by the comments uttered by several of his men.

"Surely they can't all be blind," spoke up Henley.

He was standing adjacent to and to the right of the Captain.

"Perhaps we've already turned into ghosts, and though we can see them, they can't see us," added Cotton, before inviting one of his crewmates to give him a pinch just to make sure that he really was flesh and blood, and not some ethereal spirit destined to walk the decks of a ghostly ship for eternity.

Nobody took Cotton's invitation literally, but as if to prove his friend's material existence all the more emphatically, Crossman gave him a hefty kick up the backside.

After making a monosyllabic exclamation to announce the sudden sensation of pain, Cotton's rather contrary response was to ask, "Hey man, what did you do that for?"

For the fact that no answer was forthcoming, the question was evidently rhetorical. For his part, the skipper gave some credence to the thought that the lifeboat coxswain was undertaking some complicated manoeuvre which involved his having to give the *Cape Canaveral* a wide berth initially, and that soon the rescue boat would turn towards the larger vessel, presently from a point more or less due east. Captain Gilchrist could only hazard a guess as to why such a manoeuvre should be necessary, and several options, each vying for supremacy, sprung to mind as possible practical reasons. A leading contender was based on the assumption by Captain Gilchrist that his counterpart on the smaller craft was probably the most experienced man aboard. If so, it would stand to reason that in knowing these waters like the back of his hand, so to speak, he was probably privy to a vast amount of esoteric knowledge relating to the currents, knowledge which it would have taken decades of working in the bay to accumulate. Alternatively and of no less importance, that knowledge may pertain to the location of submerged rocks the like of which had done for the *Cape Canaveral*. It didn't take many more minutes to pass before those watching from the wind-blown, sea-washed deck of the schooner realised that the lifeboat, which on its present course was steadily increasing the distance between the two vessels, could only possibly be intending to approach the

Canaveral, after having given her a wider berth than Captain Gilchrist had at first envisaged, from the south-east, that is if it was still the coxswain's aim to effect an attempt at a rescue. To the majority of men standing watching, at first with expressions of astonishment, and then with downcast demeanours, such an eventuality seemed unlikely.

In trying to fathom what exactly the lifeboat coxswain was up to Captain Gilchrist was given clues by Coxswain Fewster, the latter pointing his finger in a southerly direction somewhere beyond Seal Point, in the direction from which the *Canaveral* had come. There followed other gesticulations, some of which informed, and some of which confused. Those which my grandfather instantly interpreted correctly involved the bearded giant patting with his hand in a downward direction at about waist height. These hand to crown touches upon the head of an invisible child of say seven or eight years of age signalled paternal or avuncular affection. There followed, Henry having wedged the rudder in position with parts of his body other than his arms, and in a way conducive to keeping the boat on course, a charade in which he imitated the gently swaying motion of a mother cradling her baby in her arms.

"What's the crazy limey trying to tell us?" asked Henley of anyone who cared to answer.

It was perhaps appropriate that the man who was primarily responsible for the sending and receiving of signals in the form of radio waves, but who had, at the Captain's behest, forsaken his radio equipment once the prospect of imminent rescue seemed certain, should voice his interpretation of the coxswain's body language for the benefit of the others. Of a mind not dissimilar to the Captain's, Landowska's interpretation was more or less correct, certainly in the first instance.

"I think he's trying to tell us that we're not actually about to be rescued, and that he's heading south to save some kids," informed Landowska.

Henley, who had been about to voice his opinion of what he thought of English people in general, and of the *Henrietta Maria* and her crew in particular, changed his mind and said instead, "Gee! I hope those guys manage to save those kids."

The next paragraph in the narrative which the lifeboat coxswain was striving to convey had to do with time, and in trying to get the message across that he hoped to be back to deal with the plight of the '*Cap*' *Canaveral*'s crew within a couple of hours, after raising his hands to the level of his right and left temple, he set about clenching and opening his fists to reveal repeatedly a total of ten splayed digits.

The aim of this strange semaphore was to signal to the men aboard the schooner the likely number of ten-minute periods they would have to wait before the *Henrietta Maria's* return. The problem for Henry was that though he was undoubtedly the best fisherman in Rankin Bay, he was by no means a mathematician, and no sooner had he begun the sequence of gestures dividing hours into decimal-based parcels of minutes when it dawned on him that he hadn't worked out how many times he would need to open and close his hands. With his mind thus in a state of some confusion he lost count and decided to give up after having signalled the passing of only thirty minutes. He desisted not only because of the complexity of the maths, but for the more visceral motive that he suddenly realised how foolish he must look, perhaps appearing to the world as personified by the stranded sailors as a clown or a jester rather than as a man of substance. Indeed, at this juncture, Henry almost regretted not having approached to within speaking distance of the schooner to impart vociferously to the

Captain the information he presently was trying to convey by visual means. Naturally he had considered the possibility, but had decided against this course of action for the simple reason that a deviation which would serve little practical purpose, would add at least half an hour on to the time it would take to reach the steamer, and that could be the difference between life and death. When the one and only benefit from speaking with the schooner's skipper would have been to put the latter's mind at rest by providing a sound explanation, the decision Henry had made was absolutely right. Subsequently, and by yet another gallantly courteous hand gesture, Coxswain Fewster strove to condense the message which he had previously tried to communicate using all his fingers and thumbs. The substitution was easy to effect, but, given the circumstances, difficult to interpret. In attempting to signal that it would be at least two hours before his return, Henry simply held up two fingers of his right hand in a style similar to, albeit with the significant modification that his fingernails were facing towards him, that which comprised the gesture favoured by the English archers at Crecy and Agincourt when they wished to communicate a singular message to the French. Two decades after the coxswain's attempt to simplify his semaphore, the exact same configuration of fingers was adopted by Sir Winston Churchill, though over time the meaning changed completely.

Unfortunately for Coxswain Fewster there was no means at his disposal, at least one which was likely to be efficacious, to cancel out the gestures he had already made, and the realisation had not escaped him that the sudden change of signal would probably be the cause of some confusion. In this consideration he was absolutely right.

"What do you think he is trying to tell us now Landowska?" enquired the Captain loudly.

"That he's learning to count on his thumbs and fingers," interjected Henley less vociferously, but not in such subdued tones that his acerbic comment failed to penetrate the Captain's ears.

"Shut up Henley!" barked the Captain before adding, "When I want your opinion on anything I'll ask for it."

"It's my opinion that we're going to have to play second fiddle while he goes to the rescue of a group of women and kids, thirty two of them no less. Is that what you think skipper?"

"You may well be right," replied Captain Gilchrist, "but in any event it looks as if we're going to have to wait to be rescued; as to how long, I have no idea. Was the radio still working okay when you left it?"

"It sure was skipper," replied Landowska.

"Go and try to find out what's going on. The rest of you may as well try to get some warmth back into your bones by squeezing into the wheelhouse. Don't go below decks just in case…"

Captain Gilchrist didn't finish the sentence. He was startled into abrupt silence by a loud report. It came from the direction of the land behind his back, and he turned around, as did the others, just in time to see the rocket fired by Charlie Cook and his team manning the Board of Trade Rocket Apparatus hurtle in the schooner's general direction. The rocket had a line in tow. In the light of this latest development, the Captain called to Landowska, who, having also heard the loud report had stopped in his tracks to witness the spectacle. The skipper instructed him not to proceed further with trying to establish contact with the Coastguard, but instead to return to the vicinity of the wheelhouse on the understanding that it was now quite obvious that no effort was being spared by the Brits in trying to get the five rebels and one colonial off the ship. Following the firing of the first rocket the Captain turned his attention back towards the lifeboat with the intention of signalling to the coxswain, as best he could, that he understood the order of priorities which had led to the now readily apparent division of labour. This he did by giving the thumbs-up sign. Inopportunely Coxswain Fewster was looking in the wrong direction to receive the signal. He was, however, looking in the right direction to be able to spot the steamer in distress. To the *Cape Canaveral's* crew the lifeboat gradually disappeared from sight around the promontory.

Chapter Nine

Gilchrist Breaks a Leg

In the sense that it is no doubt better for a few people to be in mortal danger rather than a great many it may be of interest to know that there were only two children and one woman travelling on the *SS Moonglow*, they being the Captain's wife and her son and daughter. The children had yet to start school. There can be no doubt that the paucity of the number involved, had this figure of three been known to Coxswain Fewster, would not have influenced his decision in any way; as it was he was apprised only of the fact that minors and the fairer sex were desperate for the *Henrietta Maria* to arrive on the scene. Equally the men awaiting rescue aboard the *Cape Canaveral* would not have begrudged being passed by if they had been informed that there weren't thirty-two women and children in trouble somewhere to the south of them, but only three.

The lady in question – the steamship Captain's wife – was a strong character and of the mind that it was a good idea to introduce her children at the earliest practicable age to the more remote and exotic parts of the world, a plan which she was able to put into practice with relative ease given her position. She believed that her children would grow up to be better educated and more rounded people for the experience. In this regard, the fact that she was the daughter of a sea Captain and his wife herself had obviously been a strong influence on her radical opinions and attitudes, and having been taken on several fantastic voyages, including, and without doubt this was the most memorable for being the most exhilarating, a trip up the Amazon to Manaus, with the sole purpose, or so it seemed to the young lady who was to follow in her mother's footsteps, of visiting the new opera house to see and listen to a performance of La Giaconda by Amicare Ponchialli. That was many years ago, and now that that young girl had grown up to be a mother herself she naturally feared for the safety of her children. For as long as the *SS Moonglow* was drifting helplessly in a forbidding sea she questioned the wisdom of her decision to have undertaken the voyage from South Africa, a voyage which would see the family arrive in Britain at the onset of winter. It has to be said that no such doubts or anxieties would have arisen if the ship's engine had functioned properly, but as there had been mechanical failure, and as the diesel turbines were their only means of propulsion, the *SS Moonglow* and all aboard her were in a pretty pickle, so to speak.

If the numbers of women and children in danger were a mystery to the crews of the *Henrietta Maria* and *Cape Canaveral*, then it stands to reason that the biographies of their recent past would also be totally obscure. Indeed, without the writer's or historian's need to conduct painstaking research, it is highly probable that not one of the Yanks ever did discover the identities of the people that caused the *Henrietta Maria* to pass them by, though I know for certain that my grandfather knew of their fate, and had dutifully informed his crew. Surprisingly, a similar level of awareness can be ascribed to the crew of the *Henrietta Maria*, because, as events transpired, they would only become privy to this information following a brief conversation with HM Coastguard, and it was Coxswain Fewster who had in turn informed my grandfather.

Back in the bay, once the lifeboat had completely disappeared from view around Seal Point, the sole focus of attention for the transatlantic sailors was the rocket with the line in tow being hauled back towards the shore from whence it had come. By this time the Captain and his crew had taken up a position on the port side of the ship identical to that which they had just relinquished on the starboard side, for now, regardless of the fact that the rocket crew's first attempt to get a line aboard had obviously failed, they looked towards the land in the hope of imminent rescue. Six pairs of eyes followed the projectile as it was towed through the waves and breaking surf towards the beach, and more than one brain working behind those eyes likened the object being towed to a lifeless fish being reeled in on the end of an angler's line.

"How many times do you think they'll fire that thing before they give up on us skipper?" enquired Cotton without taking his eyes off the rocket, or, whenever it was hidden by surf, where he thought it might be.

Along with the others, he saw the dud torpedo become lodged between a cleft in the scaur only yards from the beach.

"If the Brits operate on a similar basis to our boys back home, they'll have brought at least six rockets with them, so by my reckoning they have the capability to make another five attempts," the Captain advised smilingly as he observed a rocket man approach the obstruction: irked by the nonchalance of the man's approach that hint of a smile soon faded from the Captain's face.

"Judging by the way that guy is moving, you would think that we have all the time in the world," gasped Walker in between breathing in voluminous amounts of sea air and exhaling equal volumes of carbon dioxide, as well as any other noxious substance, in an attempt to clear his system.

Despite his feeling nauseous and having to contend with the devil of a headache Walker was in remarkably good spirits, for he knew that in order to feel pain or discomfort a human being has to be alive.

Once the surf-man had freed the rocket, after signalling with his hand to Charlie and the others atop the cliff that the coast was clear and that they should resume pulling in the line, he followed the spent projectile's progress, first over the exposed scaur, and then on across the sand strewn with seaweed and pebbles large and small to the base of the cliff. At several points along the cliff-face water cascaded in torrents, forming rivulets in the sand on its journey towards the sea, which, paradoxically, seemingly rushed forward to embrace and taint the fresh water whilst presently gradually receding under the moon's magnetic influence; but never so far that it would leave the *Canaveral* completely high and dry. The man on the beach watched the projectile being hauled up the cliff face all the way to the top before he turned to trudge back towards the inlet where the path was located by which he had made his descent. He had, however, only walked half the distance required to reach the path when he stopped in his tracks after having espied two of his Board of Trade comrades as they appeared from around the rocky outcrop which formed part of the cliff and which, on the southernmost side, marked the entrance to the inlet. They were carrying the equipment necessary to set up the breeches buoy were they as a team to be successful in getting a line aboard the stricken schooner. Despite the initial failure their foreman – Charlie Cook – had evidently thought that they would succeed eventually, and had instructed two of his men to begin work on securing the sand anchor. Meanwhile, two or three individuals watching along the *Cape Canaveral's* port side rail were becoming increasingly impatient at the apparent lack of urgency they were witnessing ashore. Their frustration was exacerbated by the cold, which, largely as a consequence of their own lack of activity, began to gnaw at their bones. To compensate, at irregular intervals, and at each man's own volition, a figure would suddenly begin to imitate the actions of a person treading grapes whilst simultaneously performing those of a seal flapping its flippers.

After the stomping and the antics of the performing seals had been in progress for several minutes, Crossman peeled back the cuff of his oilskin jacket in order to tell the time. It was twenty-three minutes past seven, and though it had seemed an age since they had watched the first rocket fall ineffectually short and twenty yards astern, in all probability only a quarter of an hour had elapsed.

"What's taking them so long?" wondered the Canadian aloud, aware that the eyes of the entire group were now focused either on the activity at the foot of the cliff, or events unfolding at the higher level.

"Any minute now they'll down tools and start drinking tea... you watch," said Henley with customary snide.

This time it was Walker's turn to provide enlightenment, his knowledge having been derived not only from his having taken part in a training exercise involving the breeches buoy, but from having been genuinely rescued by that apparatus from a ship which had foundered on Lake Michigan.

"The shot line... that's the line which is tied to the projectile... has to be coiled in the faking box in such a way that when the rocket is fired the line feeds out freely. That takes time. You see those men on the beach," Walker continued didactically, "they're probably digging a cross-shaped trench to bury the sand anchor… and for those of you who don't know what a sand anchor is I'll gladly explain… that is if you're prepared to listen."

"I don't think any of us have anything planned for the next hour or two," responded Henley, thereby implicitly giving Walker the go-ahead for his explanation.

"Listen and learn my hearties," said Walker, lightly parodying a cut-throat pirate. "The sand anchor consists of two wooden planks connected loosely together with an eye bolt, which in turn has a pendant attached. The pendant is used to attach the block and tackle pulling device…"

"Which is called the fall," interjected the skipper, having been eager to make his contribution to the dissemination of knowledge.

"That, as the Captain has just said, is called the fall," Walker echoed before continuing. "Those guys are going to dig down two and a half to three feet, and that should be deep enough to secure the anchor once they fill the trench with sand. That's just the first part of the operation, they then have to…"

At this juncture Walker's impromptu lesson was interrupted by a promising sound; a loud report which was accompanied by a puff of smoke prior to the projectile with the shot line attached arcing its way across the sky. Aboard the schooner all eyes were focused on the rapidly approaching rocket, though soon it was no longer approaching but passing overhead. It flew over the *Canaveral* at approximately the height of the mast spars some distance forward of the foremast. Consequently six heads turned as one to observe the projectile fly over the bowsprit to land in the sea a good thirty yards to the seaward side of the ship. The line it had carried settled precariously roughly halfway along the mast projecting from the bows like a lance or a thrusting sword. It was apparent to everyone aboard that the people firing the rockets had, for this second attempt, altered their point of aim and adjusted the angle of elevation to allow for the climatic conditions. In so doing, however, the rocket crew had almost over-compensated, and now, in the minds of the Captain and the crew gathered aft, it seemed that the line which was so essential was likely to be lost overboard.

The Captain gave orders to Cotton and Crossman to make haste and secure the shot line as quickly as possible. At the same time he motioned to the others to follow as he made his way forward at a measured pace. Given the present location of the line, it was the skipper's intention, once the end tied to the rocket had been retrieved from the briny, to secure it to the foremast, thereby providing sufficient height for the breeches buoy – once it had been installed – to function effectively.

In reality there was little chance that the line, which rose from the sea on the port side to cross the bowsprit before that same length of fluctuating tautness fell away at an equal angle to enter deeper water on the starboard side, would be lost overboard. For such an occurrence the line would have to work its way upwards at an angle of approximately twenty degrees. If the shot line was going to go anywhere, the greater likelihood was that it would work its way down the bowsprit – for the simple reason that movement in this direction would be assisted by gravity – into eagerly awaiting hands.

Sheldon Crossman was the first to arrive at the point farthest forward on the ship where it was possible to stand. The fact that he had been brought up on a farm a long way from the ocean didn't preclude him from demonstrating an uncanny sense of balance in this environment that was never still. He and others attributed this skill to his having learned to ride bareback as a boy, for he had won more than one race when competing against first nation riders. All in all the accomplishment which appeared to be so innate was not to be sniffed at, particularly when the deck heaved with the wild unpredictability of an unbroken stallion.

The Canadian wasted no time in waiting for gravity to work its wonders, but instead, by gripping hold of the shroud which, with the exception of the bobstay, was farthest forward of all the ropes supporting the masts, he clambered on to the bowsprit, positioning himself so that he was sitting on the forward-projecting mast with a leg either side. He placed his hands palm down, and, by using them as a lever, he was able to inch forward towards the line which, in a continuous pattern, alternated between becoming taut in the extreme prior to the tension easing slightly in keeping with the schooner's rise and fall. This would have been a tricky manoeuvre in a sea that was tranquil, but in the prevailing conditions the danger was obvious.

The hazardous nature of the mission presently being undertaken by his friend was not lost on Cotton, who, realising that there was little of a practical nature that he could do to help, at least for the present, from his standpoint at the bows called out to Sheldon to take care. The warning proved to be counter-productive and nearly led to tragedy, for in Crossman's mistaken belief that he was in control, and therefore not in any imminent danger of falling off his perch, for the time it took him to raise his hand to give Cornelius a thumbs-up signal, the Canadian diced with death.

With his back to the man who had uttered the warning, after teetering in response to a sudden squall which drenched him from head to foot, Crossman hurriedly attempted to return his hand to the bowsprit in hope of regaining his balance. The attempt was in vain, for the Canadian toppled alarmingly, and it seemed that the only outcome possible would be that that he would fall into the surf breaking over the rocks tens of feet below. If, indeed, such an event had occurred, there would have been every chance that the brave but somewhat careless seaman would have been knocked out and drowned. Fortunately, tragedy was only averted by a somewhat tardy exhibition of physical agility on the part of the former farm boy. It was a display which caused his shipmates – for by this time the Captain and the others had arrived upon the scene – to be relieved. They were also more than a little impressed, for by interlocking his ankles Crossman had cheated death.

Naturally, after having witnessed his friend dangling precariously by his legs, it was hardly surprising that the greatest anxiety, and subsequently the greatest relief, was felt by Cotton, who, if the worst thing possible had happened, would have borne a considerable burden of guilt for the rest of his life. He was that kind of guy. Evidently Crossman had not wanted anyone – least of all Cornelius – to have to bear such a burden, and had used every fibre of every muscle in his upper body to enable him, by swinging upwards, to grasp hold of the bowsprit with both hands, so that for a time he had been hanging like an animal that had been trapped by a big-game hunter, a living trophy no less. The bowsprit, being wet and therefore slippery, had not been easy to grip, and Crossman, aware that he would not have been able to sustain his present position for long, had wasted no time in embracing the mast with both arms as if his very life had depended upon it, which, of course, it had. Then he had set about performing what had undoubtedly been the most dangerous manoeuvre of the entire episode in reconstituting himself as part of the solution rather than his being one more frightful problem. To achieve this he had had to unlock his ankles and slide one leg over the bowsprit so that he was able to use his leg from the knee down as a lever. After a Herculean effort he had managed to right himself so that he was more or less back where he had started prior to the mishap.

Instigated by Landowska, there was a ripple of applause from watching shipmates, the only people demonstrating their reluctance to take part being Cotton and the Captain. The former did not want to be in any way responsible for a second cock-up, one from which his friend would, more than likely, not emerge unscathed.

For his part Crossman felt a tremendous sense of relief at being able to observe the world from what, to homosapiens, is a normal viewpoint, rather than that observed by a flying-fox at rest. He became dimly aware, above the noise of the waves crashing beneath him, that people were clapping, this unmistakeably human sound emanating from a source presently outside the scope of his peripheral vision, that is to say, from behind his back. At first he failed to appreciate that he could be the cause. When eventually he did make the connection between the successful completion of his acrobatic act and that most basic, and most spontaneous, expression of appreciation, he declined to make a gesture of acknowledgement. Instead, as soon as he had regained his composure by breathing more steadily, and after quelling the effects of the adrenalin which at the time of greatest danger had surged through his body, he focused his mind on completing the mission. Slowly, and latterly surely, he inched his way forward beyond the shot line – at one point in the proceedings he was sitting on the thing – by adopting the *modus operandi* he had thought best at the start. Thinking that it was too risky a venture to attempt to turn around, Crossman's plan, a plan which he had formulated only after his near fall from grace, was to lift the line on to his shoulders in such a way that it would lie across the back of his neck. His fervent hope was that the line hadn't snagged on a rock as yet hidden beneath the surface. Fortunately for Crossman, and for the five Americans looking on with considerable expectation, the plan worked, and the Canadian was able to work

116

his way backwards along the bowsprit without further mishap, bringing in the line as the skipper had ordered.

For a full twenty seconds Sheldon Crossman was treated as a hero, though now the most popular method for his shipmates to show their appreciation was to slap the stout-hearted sailor on the back in a manner redolent of some ancient masculine ritual, a ritual which had evolved to confirm that the individual involved possessed strength enough in his backbone.

"Well done Sheldon," praised the Captain as Walker grabbed hold of the line in order to haul the submerged end in from the starboard side. "You had us worried for a moment or two," the skipper added.

"The little show-off was probably putting on an act for our entertainment," said Cotton grinning broadly. "He probably thought that we all needed a little extra excitement in our lives… as if being shipwrecked on a foreign shore wasn't excitement enough."

"If you think that I would risk life and limb to keep you lot entertained, then you need your head looking at," responded Crossman in a tone which could not disguise the fact that he was feeling rather pleased with himself.

Once the shot line had been hauled aboard and the rocket which had delivered it disposed of, Captain Gilchrist ordered Henley aloft to secure the end that was now free to the spar, at the point where it intersected with the foremast. Normally he would have selected Crossman to carry out such an important task, but being mindful of having already asked much of the Canadian, he allocated the job to the man who was as nimble as a monkey when it came to climbing the rigging. For his part, Henley, perhaps because he sought to emulate Crossman's nail-biting heroics and subsequent triumphant return, stepped forward like a willing volunteer to take the end of the line now minus the rocket from Walker's hand. After tying a bowline at the waist, Henley ascended the rigging with alacrity. Commensurate with the rate of ascent Walker was feeding the line out gradually, ensuring that it trailed loosely – but not too loosely – behind the man from Maine.

Over the next hour Captain Gilchrist and his crew set up the breeches buoy in accordance with the instructions printed on the tally board. If, however, the job had been left solely to Walker, progress would have been very slow indeed. He, it was, who had been the first to attempt to make sense of the instructions which were perfectly clear to the man or woman who had written them. The problem was that the words he initially began to read aloud to his fellows were in French.

"Faites la queue de cet bille…" he commenced, making no attempt whatsoever to inject a little nasal intonation into his customary Yankee drawl.

He began, but realising that by continuing he would only make more of a fool of himself than he had unwittingly accomplished thus far, he stopped, thereby desisting from inflicting further torture, not only on his friends and shipmates, but also on the Gallic tongue.

"Those idiots ashore have somehow got it into their heads that we're French," said Walker. After turning to look towards the stern to check that the flag they were flying was indeed the stars and stripes, and not a red, white and blue tricolour, he added, "Whatever could have given them that idea?"

"You're the idiot," informed Landowska as he stepped forward to take the tally board from out of the donkeyman's hands.

Normally Landowska would have refrained from using such brazen language when addressing the man whom he readily acknowledged was the most experienced sailor aboard, but the

118

events of the past few hours had proved, in some respects, a great leveller. Grinning like the American equivalent of a Cheshire cat, he turned the board over so that the instructions in English were visible. Needless to say Walker was able to read these without difficulty.

If the old salt had taken umbrage at his mild humiliation he hardly showed it. The scowl he made askance in the direction of the man who had revealed to him the error of his ways aptly reflected the donkeyman's transient and superficial sense of ignominy. Hard upon their discovery the instructions in English were, to all intents and purposes, followed to the letter: "Make the tail of the block fast to the mast well up. Cast off shot line. Ensure that the rope in the block runs free and show signal to shore."

Once the main hawser and travelling block, and finally the breeches buoy itself, had been installed so that the contraption appeared to work satisfactorily when pulled back and forth by the men from Charlie Cook's crew who had installed the sand anchor, and who were now acting as surf men, it was time for Captain Gilchrist to designate the order of departure. The easiest decision he had to make was with regard to his own person, for in keeping with maritime tradition there was no doubt in his mind that he would be the last man to leave the stricken vessel. When it came to deciding who should be the first to step into the lifebelt he was grateful to Walker for stepping forward, for being ready and willing to test the apparatus, this amazing contraption made up of ropes, blocks and pulleys which had saved so many lives in the past, and which everyone hoped would be as equally effective in the forthcoming minutes.

Walker's argument for his going first was far from selfish, but was based purely on reason. His reasoning was that as he was probably the heaviest man aboard – for this prize his one and only rival was Cotton, though the answer as to which of the two was really the heavier was, literally, in the balance – if the breeches buoy could bear his weight, then the others had nothing to fear. Captain Gilchrist found the argument convincing, and without more ado, with the exception of Walker, in turn tapped each man on the shoulder at the same time as he uttered the cardinal number stipulating that individual's place in the queue. The order of departure would, therefore, be Walker, Crossman, Henley, Landowska, Cotton, and finally, the Captain.

Everything proceeded as planned until it was the Captain's turn to leave the ship. Prior to stepping into the lifebelt he surveyed the deck of the *Cape Canaveral* from bow to stern. The wind continued to whine through the shrouds and rigging, though now it carried no rain. It rattled the fastenings attached to the bitts. Like a paternal hand it ruffled the skipper's hair, which, now that he was completely bareheaded, was constantly being pulled this way and that. For the fact that the ebbing tide had considerably reduced the depth of water around the schooner, one manifestation of tempestuous power no longer in evidence was the deck being awash with salt water. It was a poignant last look, and as the Captain stepped into the ring he wondered when, if ever, he would see his forlorn and beloved ship refloated.

After signalling to the men in the surf to haul him in, Captain Gilchrist launched himself towards the beach, becoming aware that a sizeable crowd of onlookers had gathered along the shore. Whereas they appeared to be standing in line along the top of the cliff, on the beach they were clustered, here and there, in small family groups. One such group, in which the individuals involved were sitting on, or standing behind, a large rock situated close to the sand anchor, was comprised of his crew. He noted that Walker was waving, and assumed that the gesture was a sign of encouragement. Here and there a dog ran freely. A spaniel was repeatedly chasing after and retrieving a stick being thrown by its master. A black Labrador standing at the edge of a rock-pool several yards forward of the throng was barking and wagging his tail as Captain Gilchrist approached through the air. Were these the final sights and sounds my grandfather saw and heard before the accident happened, before that morning's final misfortune, a calamity which resulted in his sustaining a fractured patella?

Chapter Ten

Proud Refusals

Grandfather's last memory prior to his falling to Earth prematurely, and with a force which caused him considerable pain and subsequently weeks of discomfort, was of a herring-gull gliding past on a course which was at a slight angle to his own, so that for a time man and bird were more or less heading in the same direction. The yellow-beaked gull was flying a yard above the Captain's head. For a second or so to the onlookers on the shore it seemed that the ponderous human being and the graceful creature with outstretched wings were competing in a race which could not have been more unevenly matched. There could be no doubt as to the eventual winner.

This became obviously apparent when the assemblage upholding the breeches buoy collapsed, the weakness and point of catastrophic failure being the spar to which Henley had secured the various lines and hawser. The result was that one minute Captain Gilchrist was sliding to safety and the next he was bemoaning the fact that, for a reason which would remain uncertain for some considerable time, the rescue apparatus had let the current incumbent down none too gently.

In one sense the Captain – my unlucky grandfather – was fortunate in that the height of his near vertical descent following the collapse was not great. Indeed, at the precise moment when the line carrying him slackened to become totally useless he can't have been more than twelve feet above the ground. It was not a height from which he would have expected, upon dropping feet first, to sustain serious injury.

On the other hand in the balance of fortune, it was unfortunate that the last man to leave the ship, the man who had witnessed his predecessors descend without a hitch, and who had, therefore, every reason to believe that the same equipment would work properly for him, had been distracted by the racing seagull to the extent that he was totally unprepared to effect a safe landing on the rock which seemingly rushed to meet him. In short Captain Gilchrist fell, and fell badly.

In the seconds before impact the configuration of the Captain's lower limbs was such that his left leg was relatively straight compared to the right leg. Not surprisingly, therefore, the former was the first to make contact with terra firma, and this was with the edge of the scaur. In keeping with the skipper's run of bad luck his left foot slipped off the edge to drop a further eighteen inches to land in one of Rankin Bay's famous rock pools. There was quite a splash, which caused several among the crowd of spectators to express their amusement in the belief that there was nothing seriously amiss. Those that had surmised thus could not have been more mistaken, for at the exact same instant that the 'Cap' Canaveral's unlucky Captain had made such a spatter with his straight leg, his right knee crashed down onto the shale. Notwithstanding the fact that shale is relatively soft when compared to the hardness of granite, in this instance the force which met the immovable object proved easy to resist, and fragile to boot.

My grandfather had no idea as to the extent of his injury or injuries in the moments that followed the impact, and initially, as if to follow the example set by the former humorists in the crowd, he too believed that there was nothing seriously wrong with him. His knee hurt like blazes of course, but that was to be expected, and the pain was not so sharp that he suspected a fracture. It was more a dull, persistent ache, and he hoped that it would eventually go away.

Gilchrist's first voluntary course of action after the involuntary one of clenching his knee and falling into the pool so that a large part of his body from the neck down was immersed, was to try to stand. Dripping with water and the odd slither of green, slimy seaweed, in this endeavour the Captain was obviously experiencing considerable difficulty, so much so in fact that in the company of one of the Board of Trade volunteers, the '*Cap*' *Canaveral*'s crew ran across the beach to come to their skipper's assistance. They gathered around the kneeling figure, the ill-fated ship's officer who was beginning to feel somewhat embarrassed at his being treated as a wounded hero.

"Easy there," the Captain ordered. "I only need two of you to help me out of this damned pool. If you, Walker, grab hold of this arm, and Cotton you take the other to help haul me up, I'll be on my feet in a trice."

"Are you sure you're okay skipper?" Walker enquired as he stepped towards the rocky edge of the pool where, stooping slightly, he placed a big hairy hand in the pit of the invalid's left arm at the shoulder while gripping the contiguous forearm with the other.

"My knee hurts like hell, but I don't think I've broken anything," informed the Captain as he peered up, over his left shoulder, at Walker's strangely benign looking beefy face.

Before another word was uttered, and to the Captain's surprise he felt himself being hauled to his feet in a lopsided manner, the impetus having come from his right where, upon turning his head in that direction, he had expected to see Cornelius Cotton's black smiling face, but where instead he glimpsed a stranger's stolid expression.

This individual was about twice his own age and an Englishman no doubt. His chin was clean-shaven, though his upper lip was adorned by a moustache which was grey and as thick as a decorator's paste brush.

"Come on lad… let's get you out of there and up on your feet," said the man with the unfamiliar accent, and in such a peremptory manner that the Captain had no choice but to obey.

In response to the Englishman having signalled with a nod of his head, Walker added his strength to the Captain's upward momentum, the result being that in the next moment my grandfather was standing on his own two feet. Now that the next step in mind was precisely that, to put one foot in front of the other and set off walking, though hardly surprising, it didn't help matters that the ground beneath his feet was so slippery and uneven, being comprised, along this part of the beach, of the layers of black shale which form the scars. People with no disability are wise to proceed with care on this surface. The treacherous nature of the ground did not, however, deter my grandfather from attempting a first tentative step on his own, though admittedly that step took a little more thinking about than usual. For prior to commencing the activity which most people take for granted most of the time, he first steadied himself on his uninjured leg in order to wrench himself free of the supporting arms: first from Walker; and then from the Englishman.

"Are you sure this is a wise move skipper?" enquired Walker with avuncular concern. "I mean wouldn't it be better to wait until we can carry you off the beach on a stretcher or something?" he continued, making, as he spoke, a quick survey of the ground that was likely to be their route.

Just yards ahead the shale became submerged beneath a band of pebbles. The band covered a stretch of beach about ten feet wide, though not uniformly. The pebbles ranged in size from small sea skimmers waiting to be picked up either by children or adults still young at heart, and rounded stones the size of ostrich eggs. This ground would also be difficult for Captain Gilchrist to negotiate, as would, albeit in a different way, the soft, golden sand which stretched from the sea-washed stones to the base of the cliff, and upon which the majority of onlookers were standing. Nobody was paying much attention to the wreckage of the breeches buoy, though, with typical canine curiosity, one of the free-range dogs was sniffing about its lamentable wreckage.

An appraisal of the ground which the skipper would have to cross just to reach the base of the cliff at Stoupe Beck prompted Walker to make a final plea to the Captain not to make the injury he had sustained worse than it already was.

"You don't have to do this skipper. I could give you a piggyback ride, or a fireman's lift," Walker suggested.

"We could take it in turns to carry you skipper," interjected Henley, who, though no one had blamed him to his face for the collapse of the breeches buoy, suspected strongly that the others thought him at least partly responsible.

The corollary in a psychological sense was that now, more than at any other time in the entire voyage, Henley wanted, indeed needed, to project himself in such a way that he would appear in a positive light.

The third comment in a similar vein was made by the Englishman.

"In my opinion Captain," he said, at last acknowledging the injured American officer's status for no reason other than that he was obviously held in some esteem by the men he commanded, "the comments and suggestions I've heard sound sensible enough, and if I were you…"

"Look here," said Captain Gilchrist, "I don't know who…"

"The name's Sanderson," the Englishman informed; "John Sanderson."

"Well Mr John Sanderson," the Captain continued vexedly, "judging from that white band you're wearing, my crew and I have you and the other guys in your team to thank for rigging up this thing and getting us safely ashore, so in all sincerity, on behalf of my men and I, that I do… but I tell you I'm quite capable of getting from here to wherever we're going on my own two feet, and that includes getting to the top of that darned cliff." By way of an afterthought, so as not to appear too gung-ho, he added, "That is if the path up is not too steep."

There was no need for him to repeat his statement of intent for Walker's sake. Careless of whether or not Captain Gilchrist noticed, the donkeyman gave Sanderson a knowing look, a look which the local man interpreted correctly as meaning that here they were dealing with a particularly bad case of stubbornness. Everyone that was interested in the little drama being enacted in their presence looked on with anticipation as the self-willed American took his first step. The limb thrust forward contained the injured knee. With considerable care the Captain gradually placed more of his body weight upon the cruciate ligaments, half expecting that – though he wasn't going to admit it to anyone – the suspect joint would buckle beneath him. To Gilchrist's delight he found that he was able to raise his left leg and take a step forward without experiencing excruciating pain. There was pain of a kind of course, but it was merely an accentuation of the dull ache which, though he believed that the more he manipulated the painful knee the quicker it would recover, was proving to be chronic.

Following the success of his first step, its execution being not unlike that demonstrated by a child when he or she is learning to walk, others followed, and although the determined pedestrian had declined all offers of help from his crew, he was prepared to accept the loan of a walking-stick from a gentleman who had approached with the sole purpose of offering the ornately carved length of wood. To judge by the donor's silver-grey hair and suited appearance, in combination with his general demeanour and peremptory manner of speech, it was obvious that the generous individual was a man of some refinement. He was of a type which was immediately conspicuous to American eyes for the reason that as the archetypal, upper-class Englishman no such creature existed back home. Whatever the Captain's feelings were towards such people, he was grateful to the retired Colonel – for that was the role ascribed to him by the sea-Captain – for the loan of the rather fine walking-stick.

"How will I return the stick to you?" enquired my grandfather of his benefactor as the latter was retracing his steps in order to rejoin his good lady wife.

"Give it to Charles when you reach the top of the cliff if you have no further use for it," said the walking-stick's owner, and in such a way that by some strange transmutation his words sounded more like affable advice than a command, which is what they were. "Failing that, just leave it behind the bar of the Rankin Bay Hotel and I'll collect it next time I call in for a swift half and a sandwich," the trusting gentleman added with a smile, as if he had, by his ostensibly altruistic act, provided an excuse for himself to make that visit sooner rather than later. "In any event, don't worry about it. There are several more where that came from."

"I shall probably leave it behind the bar," rejoined Captain Gilchrist as he returned his benefactor's smile while at the same time, a little alarmingly, raising the crook of the stick in salute.

Needless to say, prior to making the salutary gesture, my grandfather had ensured that both his legs were as steady as they could be under the circumstances. Then, having steeled himself for the hill he had yet to climb at a walk, the unlucky but noble Captain led his retinue of sailors across the soft sand. By this time the man with the moustache like a paste brush had begun to disentangle the breeches buoy from the lengths of line lying forlornly at his feet, and in this task he was soon helped by other members of the Board of Trade Rocket Apparatus crew who had, on this particular mission, achieved complete success, for not a single life was lost.

Chapter Eleven

A Letter Home

The following letter is one of several which came into my possession shortly after I began to research my grandfather's story, and I see no reason why it should not be published in its entirety.

c/o The Rankin Bay Hotel,
Rankin Bay,
Eskmouth,
Yorkshire,
England,

The best kept house in New Hampshire
1ˢᵗ November, 1919

Hi Mom, Dad,

I trust this letter finds you both well. The thought has just occurred to me that Penacook will probably be covered with snow by now, and I can imagine you both sitting in front of a log fire of an evening, you, mom, working at your sewing, and you dad, tying flies in preparation for your next fishing trip. I sure hope that this winter will not be as severe as the last, but if it is, I know you'll be able to keep warm burning the logs that dad and I chopped during the fall. Who would have thought that I would have gotten so many blisters?

Has grandpa Gilchrist found a replacement for old Rocky yet? I know how much he loved that dog, and how much he missed his company. It seems a particularly harsh twist of fate for him to have lost his 'best friend' so soon after losing grandma, so I reckon the sooner grandpa gets a new dog the better; and tell him from me that he ought to get one that's big enough to deal with the pair of coyote that did for Rocky. If this coming winter is in anyways as bad as the last, those critters will be coming down from the hills scavenging for food for sure; unless, that is, grandpa's already shot them. Tell him also that I don't expect him to be able to find a replacement for grandma so easily. At his age he's far too ornery for anyone to be able to put up with his moods.

If you're wondering about how I fared on my first voyage in command, and how I'm doing, I can report that I'm getting over the worst and making a good recovery. I tell you this at the outset to put your minds at rest, to reassure you that there is no reason at all for you to be worried. I am perfectly safe and making good progress towards being sound.

It's ten o' clock in the morning here, so you're probably both tucked up in bed as I pen this letter. I am seated at a polished wooden table in the lounge of the Rankin Bay Hotel. Despite the name, it's not the sort of place you would recognise as a hotel. It's just as you would imagine an English pub to be, you know, with log fires, brasses, warm beer. Apart from a wonderfully shaped barmaid called Rita (she has a great pair of fenders dad) and yours truly, the place is deserted. Rita, bless her, has just brought me a cup of coffee and a plate of cookies which she says are perfect for 'dunking'. They're called ginger-nuts and they're even harder than the hardest hard tack I've ever eaten. In fact, so hard are they, I reckon that if I didn't 'dunk' them they'd break my teeth.

Writing of breaks, my big problem at present is that I have to hobble around on crutches after sustaining a hairline fracture to my patella. The patella is what posh folks call the kneecap. The bone surgeon at the hospital I was taken to says that I can expect my leg to be in plaster for the next six weeks, so it would appear that I'm going to be stuck here for some time. I'm certainly not going to make it home for Thanksgiving, which is a disappointment because if things had gone according to plan I might just have made it. The good news is that there are worse places for a person to convalesce, but I'll come to that later. For the time being, let's stick with the news which is not so good, specifically how I came to crack my knee in the first place.

I'll give it to you straight: we ran into a storm which blew the ship aground. The Limeys launched a lifeboat from shore, and we thought it was headed in our direction until they rowed right on by. I later learned that the crew was making all possible haste towards another ship in trouble, the plight of which was thought to be worse than ours. In the event the ship they were looking for was nowhere to be found, at least not in the search area, which isn't surprising once you know that the engine failure which had instigated the call for assistance was soon repaired by the first engineer. I know that the English are a phlegmatic race, but I'd put money on there being some colourful language muttered in that lifeboat once the crew realised that they had put their lives at risk on what was little more than a wild goose chase. They must have rowed for miles.

We whose lives were considered to be less in peril were eventually rescued by breeches buoy, which is how I came to crack my kneecap. I was sliding towards what should have been a happy landing when the whole thing collapsed. I'd like to be able to blame *the Limeys for setting up defective equipment, but I can't. The blame has to rest on one of my own men, for his inability to secure a line. Rightly or wrongly, I'm not going to take the matter further. The man responsible feels pretty bad about what happened to my leg.*

Once I'd struggled up the path which leads from the beach to the nearest road at the top of the cliff, I was really tuckered. The guys that had rescued us by setting up the breeches buoy made room for me on their cart by carrying some of the equipment normally stowed on it. Then, pulled by an old horse called Dobbin would you believe, I was wheeled in relative comfort along some really pretty country lanes to the village of Rankin Bay. You'd like it here mom, the little, red-roofed cottages have been built in such a way that it seems that the building nearest the sea... on this side of the street that's the place where I'm staying, the Rankin Bay Hotel... is supporting a long line of cottages ascending the hill, and if you were to remove the hotel, then half the village would tumble down the slope into the bay.

I'm just putting my pen down for a few moments while I give the leg in plaster a good scratch. Rita reckons that a knitting-needle would be perfect for the job, but I'm happy to make use of the twelve inch rule loaned to me by one of the village boys. I know I only make matters worse by scratching, but sometimes the urge is irresistible.

At first I didn't think I had done any serious damage in banging my knee, but on the afternoon of the day of our rescue, the pain became almost unbearable, so much so that I was unable to finish the letter I was writing to the Company. Consequently I exchanged my hotel room for a bed in Eskmouth hospital, where I was laid up for almost a week. The x-rays taken within an hour of my arrival confirmed that I had indeed fractured my patella, and that I wasn't going to be climbing the rigging or playing baseball any time soon. Whilst we're on the subject of baseball, how did the Manchester

Fisher Cats end the season dad? Walker, my donkeyman, would no doubt like to know. Compared to your home-cooking mom, the food over here leaves a lot to be desired, but the nurses are pretty, and several have signed my plaster.

When I raise my head to peer through the window, the scene I gaze upon is one of sombre tranquillity. In shades of grey, sky and sea give the impression that they would merge as one, yet, like a pot of gold at the end of a rainbow, that dividing line we call the horizon persists. Adding to, rather than detracting from, this languid calm, the waves are unfurling gently along the beach where a small number of people are walking, either singly, or as couples arm in arm. Most are either headed for or returning from a gulley along the line of cliffs called Stoupe Beck, that being, because it's the closest, the best vantage point to see my ship. How forlorn she looks. Her graceful lines stuck fast on the rocks put me in mind of a once graceful lady, who, through no fault of her own, has come to grief, and as to how and when she'll be refloated... well... I have to say God only knows.

What I know is that if Henley is responsible for the relatively minor demonstration of incompetence which has resulted in my injury, I, as Captain of the Cape Canaveral, must take full responsibility for my ship's present ignominy, and for putting the company's finances in a weaker position than they would otherwise have been. I hope that the underwriters at Lloyds of London are feeling generous.

I'll close now, mom, dad, with a final word just to emphasise that you're not to worry. Things could have been so much worse. Happy Thanksgiving, and I hope to be home for Christmas,

Love,
Andrew

Chapter Twelve

The Endeavour Inn

After dropping the letter to America into the box embossed with GR to signify the reign, a red receptacle which, not being an example of the free-standing kind, is set into the wall of the building adjacent to the Rankin Bay Hotel, Captain Andrew Gilchrist set off up the hill that is King Street manipulating his wooden crutches with the consummate skill of a fit and expert user. It was my grandfather's intention to have lunch in the Endeavour Inn before going on to watch a football match in which his crew had been invited to play. These things he duly did, but not before first encountering aspects of British culture which were not only unfamiliar to him, but which, certainly in one instance, revealed the eccentricity of the English to an astonishing degree.

Beneath the sign – no longer a threat for being perfectly still – depicting Captain Cook's famous ship, and to the right of the inn's temptingly dark portal when viewed by the person about to enter, was an effigy of a man. The figure, which was approximately half the size of an adult male of average height, was, in the same vague sense, the same size as the girl, and bigger than the two boys, who were its acolytes.

The boys were dressed alike in grey, knee-length socks patterned at the top in a thick band comprised of three equally thin bands of red, white and black. Darker in tone than their hosiery, their short trousers also matched, as did their blue jerkins sporting winged collars and three buttons leading down a few inches from the neck. It was, however, by noting similarities in their respective colouring and style of hair, and by the close resemblance to the other of each impish face looking expectantly up at him, that my grandfather came to the conclusion that these lads were not just brothers, but were in fact twins.

The girl appeared to be a year or two older than her male companions, her accomplices, and the haughty, intelligent, yet nonetheless charming expression of this young teenager as she sought to look down her nose at the taller stranger, gave my grandfather the distinct impression that she was the leader of these youngsters, these juveniles whose intentions he had yet to fathom.

"Go on... ask," ordered the girl as the wounded sea-captain was about to pass, pushing the boy nearest to her rather forcefully in the back by way of encouragement.

Perhaps it was the combined look of disdain and perplexity on the Captain's face – disdain for the bandage-faced effigy dressed in rags and devoid of hands and feet, and perplexity derived from ignorance of what this business was about – that deterred the young scallywag from voicing the question as he had been bid.

"I asked last time... it's your turn," grumbled the boy who had received the jolt; and rather than risk rejection, the scamp whose courage had at that moment been found wanting, turned instead towards the straw-filled effigy seated with its back against the wall and its lifeless legs outstretched, and attempted to raise the brainless head from where it had flopped rather pathetically to one side.

In this endeavour he tried to no avail, and after the third attempt had proved to be no less successful than the first, he sat down on the cobbles by the side of the guy and proceeded to entertain himself by picking at the scab – the vestige of a wound which had almost healed – on his knee. He knew that he was the bravest of the brave when it came to clambering over rocks.

"Penny for the guy mister," demanded the scabby boy's brother at the same time as he took a step forward with palm outstretched.

Surprised by the effrontery, Captain Gilchrist looked first at the grimy little hand held out in expectation, and then at the girl, from whom, by means of a raised inquisitive eyebrow, he silently elicited a response if not exactly an explanation.

"A penny for the guy for Guy Fawkes night on November the fifth, on Wednesday," the haughty girl informed, though her voice and manner became increasingly flustered as the notion formed and grew in her mind that her words may be a foreign language to the stranger, and therefore sound like gobbledegook.

"And who was this Guy Fawkes?" enquired the stranger who, to the ears of his present audience, spoke with an unusual accent, though the words spoken seemed to be easy to understand nonetheless.

Captain Gilchrist, who, for the foreseeable future, had all the time in the world at his disposal, was content to rest the weight of his body on the soft padding at the top of each crutch presently tucked into his armpits; and though for the time being he was more than happy to converse with the children in order to learn as much as he could about local history and customs, the Captain was not of a mind to relent in one regard, that being his refusal to succumb to the pleas and outstretched palms of children begging. It was an attitude of mind which had evolved from his experience of walking through the ramshackle streets and waterfronts of some of the world's poorest cities, for in those situations he had discovered that

137

to give to a few was merely to encourage others to approach, to surround, to accost. Consequently Captain Gilchrist had decided a long time ago that although he would give to charitable causes whenever he felt inclined or was motivated by events so to do, he most definitely would not encourage children, and adults for that matter, to beg on the street.

"You mean to say that you really don't know who Guy Fawkes was," stated the girl in apparent disbelief.

"No; I don't," confirmed the Captain. "I'm an American, and as such I would ask you young lady whether you have heard of Paul Revere or Ulysses S. Grant?"

My grandfather was right in his supposition that the young lady hadn't.

"Are you a cowboy?" enquired the boy who had been picking at his scab.

"I'm a sailor," replied the Captain succinctly, before muttering quietly to himself, "though there may be a few that disagree."

"Do you know any cowboys?" enquired the boy who was interested in cowboys.

"As a matter of fact I do," replied the Captain with a smile. "In fact there's a member of my crew who used to be a cowboy… but he's not American… he's Canadian."

"Has he killed any baddies with his six-shooter?" asked the boy who up until this utterance had remained silent.

"I shouldn't think so," said the Captain with continued amusement at how simply defined, in the world beyond America's shores, were his country and countrymen in the minds of the young.

"Is that your ship that's wrecked on the beach?" enquired the girl who didn't share her companion's enthusiasm for the Wild West line of questioning.

"Yes; I'm afraid it is," replied the Captain ruefully.

"You can't be a very good sailor if you wrecked your ship," stabbed with words the boy who had been on his feet all the while, and who was rapidly gaining a reputation in Gilchrist's eyes for making comments that were dagger sharp.

By returning to the original topic of conversation, the Captain adroitly changed the subject, though not without first noting mentally that often in their innocent truthfulness children can be very cruel.

"So who was this Guy Fawkes guy?" the Captain enquired of the girl.

"He was a person in history who was captured before he could blow up the Government," the girl answered pensively, for the expression on her face clearly indicated that she was searching inwardly for as many facts as she could muster about the historical figure that was Guido Fawkes. "I think it happened during the reign of Queen Victoria," she added mistakenly. "There's a song we sing when we... I mean when one of the grown-ups lights the bonfire, and that's when we burn the guy."

The girl proceeded to give a melodious rendition of the rhyme she had learnt when she was ten:

"Remember, remember, the fifth of November,
The gunpowder, treason and plot:
I see no reason why the gunpowder treason
Should ever be forgot."

"I don't have much truck with people that try to blow up other people," said the Captain severely, "so why should I put my hand in my pocket for the sake of someone who tried, in my opinion, to do something wicked?"

"Our dad used to drive a truck in the war," said the boy who had been imitating the posture of a dummy, but who had since regained his feet, "but he was blown up by a German shell and sent to Heaven."

"I'm sorry to hear that," said the adult, who, despite his sympathy for the brothers, was becoming irked by the complexity of the conversation.

"What's wrong with going to Heaven when you die? That's where good people go isn't it?" the boy rejoined with yet more questions.

"If you believe that your father has gone to Heaven all well and good. No… What I meant to say is that I'm sorry that your father was killed in the war in the first place."

"Please give a penny for the guy mister," pleaded the boy whose previous comments had been so piercing.

"The only change I have on me is a few nickels and dimes, and you won't be able to spend them in any shop around here," the Captain informed, thinking, on the spur of the moment, that it would perhaps be a better course of action to decline the invitation to contribute to the children's coffers for a sound practical reason rather than keep his hands in his pockets, so to speak, on moral grounds.

"What are nickels and dimes?" enquired the boy whose knee was now trickling with blood.

"That's American money silly," answered the girl.

Sensitive to the accusation of being called 'silly', the young man with hurt feelings and a bloody knee turned, with a look on his face which spoke volumes about his sense of betrayal, towards the girl but said nothing to her.

"Well what are you going to use to pay for your beer when you go inside the pub?" the betrayed boy's brother enquired of the American.

"I have a pound note, and there's no way that I'm going to give you that," said the Captain emphatically.

"You'll have some proper change when you leave, and you could..."

"Come on... the tide is probably out by now... let's go and look at the wreck," said the girl, who by this juncture had become embarrassed at their persistent haranguing of the stranger, so much so in fact that intuitively she felt that the juvenile trio of which she was the unspoken leader had crossed the line between an enterprise which yielded a small financial reward, and begging for real. It was as if, having lost all sense of pride, they were intending to make a career of soliciting money from strangers. With the girl leading from behind, so to speak, she and the boys ran down King Street towards the slipway in The Dock, and beyond that the beach. The twins appeared to be exuberant, more than happy to have been relieved of their onerous and, in this most recent instance, unrewarding task. The same could be said of Captain Gilchrist as he set about the complicated business of entering the Endeavour Inn.

Designed to keep the warmth within and the cold without, the Endeavour Inn, like most buildings in Rankin Bay, be they public or private, has an inner and an outer door. For a person who has never tried, primarily because he or she has not needed to, to open doors whilst balancing on a pair of crutches, the procedure, like many activities performed for the first time, requires a certain amount of practice before the individual concerned can describe him or herself as being adept. Captain Gilchrist was undoubtedly becoming increasingly adept, but once he had managed with a

141

resounding clatter to negotiate the doors of the Inn, a narrow passage presented a further challenge, forcing the temporarily crippled sailor to adjust the style he exhibited going forward considerably. Needless to say, heard long before he was seen by the few people ensconced in the bar, his arrival was keenly anticipated by the four pairs of eyes turned towards the alcove – the alcove which at the end of the corridor formed the open entrance into the bar. Immediately upon entering Captain Gilchrist became conscious of the fact that his unusually noisy approach had excited the curiosity of the other patrons, and for a few moments he imagined himself to be not unlike the old sea dog who had stirred the imagination of the young lad in *Treasure Island*, the lad whose father had owned the Admiral Benbow Inn. Back in the Endeavour Inn, standing expectantly upon the threshold which separates the alcove from the barroom proper, Captain Gilchrist was tempted to recite the refrain which begins, 'Fifteen men on a dead man's chest... Yo-ho-ho and a bottle of rum!' From a sense of decorum, however, by checking the impulse which would have drawn more attention to himself than he already had, he refrained. The Captain was not, as you would expect of a person in his position, a diffident man, but neither was he overly extrovert. He considered his personality to be balanced nicely more or less midway between these two extremities.

"Good morning," bade the Captain as he quickly surveyed the occupants of the inn's unevenly lit interior.

The public area licensed for the drinking of strong liquor could be perceived as being two rooms in one, primarily because of the dividing partition which, from the wall opposite to the Captain's viewpoint, protruded about half way across the room in line with the end of the bar counter a pace to his right. Obviously, for the simple reason that it was the 'half' of the room that was farthest away from the two Georgian windows facing onto King Street, it was the area nearest to the newcomer which was most tenebrous, although such natural light as there was, was evidently sufficient to write by, for seated in the corner formed by the partition was a man who looked as if he would be more at home in a public library than a public house. His appearance was incongruous with the time and place, and not only in respect of his immediate surroundings, but in respect of the wider environment that was the entire village. To Captain Gilchrist's eyes nobody could look less like a man who earned his living from the sea, and equally from another perspective, nobody could look more like a man whose *métier* was to write, or perhaps lecture to the young at a top university, Harvard say, or Yale.

"I think good afternoon would be more appropriate," corrected the bespectacled figure following a quick glance at his watch, and peering over the top rim of his spectacles as he spoke.

Even in those few words Captain Gilchrist was able to detect an accent which he could not place exactly, but which he suspected was Irish in origin. The lilting intonation, though hardly strong enough to warrant being described as a brogue, was very different from the accent which he had grown accustomed to hearing in the precincts of Rankin Bay thus far. The Captain checked his watch and saw that the time was half an hour past midday. In a literal sense, therefore, the bespectacled man was right, but that didn't prevent the Captain from attempting, as it were, to defend his position.

"You're absolutely right to imply that we're well into the afternoon watch (and here he was referring to the pattern of ship's watches and not an actual timepiece), but I bid people good morning or good afternoon on the basis of whether or not I've had my lunch," informed the Captain cordially.

"And what happens if there's no lunch to be had?" replied the bespectacled individual.

The Captain was about to answer, but changed his mind upon observing that his interlocutor had lowered his head and eyes in order to return his attention to the business which had preoccupied him prior to the arrival of Johnny come lately, specifically the act of writing. The bespectacled man had clearly intended his question to be rhetorical. Looking on for a few moments after their initial and rather brief conversation had, for the time being, ended, Captain Gilchrist assumed, wrongly as it transpired, that the cursive script on the table directly in front of the penman constituted a letter.

It was during these moments of silent observation that Gilchrist was able to gain some measure of his former interlocutor by the latter's physical appearance, the most obvious feature being his glasses. The American had not seen spectacles like them, and in his view they were remarkable for the fact that the lenses were so large and perfectly round, as was, of course, that part of the frame which contained them. In the relatively poor light which prevailed in that part of the room, the Captain, when presented with the opportunity, had been unable to distinguish anything of the other man's eyes. What he had been able to note, however, was the bushiness of the eyebrows, the curves of which were almost as pronounced as the upper curvature of the spectacle eyepieces. The darkness of the eyebrow hair contrasted with that which grew in fair abundance on the scribbler's head. From their cranial origins two distinct wads of long, straight strands cascaded to left and right to form a parting above the right eye. The greater part of the forehead was hidden by these separate wads of hair like straw, but that didn't prevent Gilchrist from gaining the impression that the face and head were oval. The penman's ears were completely

144

hidden by the blond cascades, and his mouth, though small, looked accustomed to speaking words of greater grandiloquence than was usually heard in the shops, inns, and thoroughfares thereabouts. Taken overall, Captain Gilchrist sensed that the features he observed were indicative of high intelligence.

Unusually for this parochial and relatively insular corner of the planet, the man presently expressing his thoughts in ink was smartly dressed; he was wearing a tweed jacket and a matching shirt. To the surprise – and in some cases astonishment – of all that had beheld his demeanour, he was wearing a bow-tie.

Once the Captain had gleaned visually as much as he was capable of gleaning from the man whose hair resembled a collapsed haystack, he turned his attention to the Endeavour Inn's other patrons – the man with the pot-belly sitting on a high stool at the far end of the bar, and the couple who had been making an ocular study of the Captain for as long as he had been conducting the same with regard to the bespectacled correspondent.

Sitting with her back to the window, Jenny Fewster's older married sister, Sally Draycot, was impressed with what she saw, though she refrained from communicating as much to her husband sitting beside her – the fisherman known to this smallest of worlds as 'Cotty'. Sally, upon realising that she had become the object of the stranger's gaze, manipulated the shawl she was wearing around her head and shoulders with the sole purpose of letting her ringlets of auburn hair fall freely. These she shook prior to throwing back her head. At the same time she pushed back her tresses using both hands. The Captain could not fail to read the signal, as, in all probability, did Cotty.

Mrs Draycot's face was now fully revealed for the Captain's perusal, and the vision of loveliness that he saw in the moments following the instant when their eyes first met, and, as it were, held

145

each other in a limbo of inaction which seemed to last for an aeon, but which in reality amounted to no more than a few seconds, provided him with considerable food for thought. Projecting, he thought, sadness and longing in their moist limpidity, they were eyes which had the power to implore, and what they implored was to be provided with a little romance, to be released from a mundane life, from drudgery.

It has been said of people of a romantic disposition that they desire to eat bread that cannot be made from wheat, or words to that effect, but even if Sally had read or heard the statement – which she hadn't – she wouldn't have believed that the description could ever be applicable to her. Indeed, the most intriguing and tantalising aspect of Sally's romanticism was that she truly believed that the life she desired could be achieved, though she also accepted that such an eventuality would be extremely unlikely unless she were to make some drastic changes to her current circumstances. The ineluctable fact was that for a woman of her upbringing and limited experience of life outside the bay, the wrench which she occasionally dreamed of making was almost too great to contemplate with any degree of seriousness for long; and yet, if a suitable opportunity were to present itself, she could then allow herself the luxury of anticipation as she entertained the thought, the hope, of being able to make not infrequent first-class trips to London by train. At the most fanciful extreme of her imaginings she could visualise herself – in the company of a generous paramour – making a grand tour of European cities. In Paris she would have her photograph taken at the foot of the Eiffel Tower. She thought that a boat trip on the Blue Danube would be divine. In Venice she reclined, eyes closed, ears open, in the arms of her lover, and the sounds that she heard were Italian – the odourless waters of the Grand Canal lapping gently against the gondola's sides, the mellifluous voice of the gondolier serenading her with all the eye-moistening virtuosity of Caruso. She had read about such happenings and places in magazines published in the *belle époque,* in those halcyon years before the war, and the ambition to travel had haunted her ever since.

"Are you ready for another yet?" asked the familiar and far from romantic voice of her husband by her side.

The question, though considerate, was piercing for the fact that it epitomised the life she dreamed of escaping, and she could not help but scowl at the man whom she had married with her father's blessing. The ceremony had been held in Saint Stephen's Church five years ago last June, and though the years between then and now had not been hell insofar as they were an ordeal of physical and mental endurance, neither had they been the least bit fulfilling. In short, the years of her marriage had been a disappointment.

It goes without saying that she could not help being the person she was, just as she could not help wanting to share her life with a man the like of whom would be a fine catch for any woman. The scowl which she had instinctively and fleetingly revealed did not go unnoticed by the unassuming fisherman, and he was cut to the quick by the look's purport. He loved his wife dearly, and if he had been able to identify the canker which had been eating at her soul, and if, having identified the problem, it had been within his power to do anything about it, then he would have done all that was necessary. He maintained no illusions about his ability to move Heaven and Earth.

Noting the bemused and hurt look on her husband's sturdy visage, Sally's attitude towards him softened, and placing her hand on his muscular thigh, she said, "I don't mind if I do."

In addition to the words which she had uttered out of kindness, however, she also harboured the thought, "and I don't mind if I don't."

In the same instant that Cotty got up to go to the bar as yet devoid of a barman, the Captain sat down at a table where, as he rested his back against a wood-panelled wall, he was able to keep his rigid leg outstretched without hindrance to anyone. From this position he was the only customer to have an unrestricted view of everyone present. It wasn't a clear view in every case, for upon his having become seated the couple by the window had become shapes in silhouette. Whilst he had been upright, however, the Captain had been able to observe that the woman whose interest he had stirred was possessed of a face which, by virtue of the regularity of the bone structure and kissable softness of the skin, was more pleasantly handsome than strikingly beautiful. The appreciative American had entertained the thought that were he able to look upon such a face between waking and sleeping day by day, life would be sweet indeed, for it was a face which would gladden the heart of any man.

If there was a negative aspect to the woman's physicality as observed by Captain Gilchrist, then that undoubtedly was in the roughness of her hands, a roughness which betokened hard work in a predominantly cold, damp climate.

The demeanour of the man whose heart Mrs Draycot most gladdened was open, honest and cheerful, and in the few moments that Cotty's clean-shaven countenance remained imprinted upon the Captain's retinas, the observer beheld a face which revealed a preponderance of innate goodness, and perhaps not much cleverness. The overall impression that the Captain had gleaned from his observations was that for this couple's relationship to endure and flourish – and he had presumed that they were man and

148

wife – they would have to correct an imbalance which was obvious to behold at present, they would have to achieve equilibrium.

"He'll be back shortly… he's just gone to the heads," informed the pot-bellied man from his bar stool as Cotty approached.

The information imparted was not meant for local ears, ears that knew as much already, but for the benefit of the invalid who yet again was trying to find the perfect rest position for his injured leg.

"Thanks for that," responded the stranger to these parts who, somewhat naively, expected to be served, eventually, at the table nearest to him.

Looking about him, with an eye this time for those items in the room which were inanimate, namely the predominantly nautical articles and trinkets purloined or discarded from ships, all of which added to the decor, the Captain was amazed, and considerably perplexed, by an apparatus made of metal rods, each of which was approximately the circumference of a pencil. The strange assemblage was positioned high up on the wall which formed the partition.

After having given some thought as to what the contraption could be, and therefore what purpose it once served, Captain Gilchrist eventually gave up on his quiet speculations, and thinking that the only way to gain enlightenment on this occasion was to give voice to his ignorance by asking the direct question, that is precisely what he did.

"What on Earth is that?" enquired the Captain – but only after he had gained the writer's attention – subtly indicating the object of his curiosity by a nod of his head.

"That, my friend, is a dog carrier," the bespectacled man informed, as he too rested his eyes upon the focus of the Captain's interest.

His business in the heads concluded, the barman returned.

Chapter Thirteen

A Sporting Fixture

The invalid American was still smiling and chuckling to himself as he hurtled along Chapel Street with all the skill and determination one would nowadays expect of an athlete in the Paralympics. The cause of his mirth was the image of the dog-carrier, the object of his curiosity in the Endeavour Inn. Once the purpose of the contraption consisting of lengths of wire in the shape of a muzzle and a single length which was designed to penetrate the poor creature's rear had been explained, it was obvious that the artefact in question could not have been designed for any activity other than that which was indicated by its name. It goes without saying that the Captain did not take the instrument of canine torture seriously, and believed that it had only ever existed as a decorative joke. He was, after all, a guest in a land which was renowned for its regard for the welfare of animals.

On the level a person with two good legs would have had to walk exceptionally fast, or even break into a run, to keep up with the man levering himself forward on crutches. There were, of course, occasions when the disadvantage of his present method of making progress, in a physical sense that is, became noticeably apparent when compared with the gait of an able-bodied person. Indeed, a case in point had just occurred. He had met a middle-aged woman who had just emerged into the street a sidewalk's width from the doorway of Camberwell Cottage. Captain Gilchrist, smiling at the woman whilst manipulating his crutches so that they posed no danger either to himself or her, had stopped abruptly to let her pass. The slightly built woman looked – primarily because of the gaunt expression of her lived-in face – as tough as they come. Perhaps it was to keep faith with her recently acquired image in the beholder's eye that she failed to respond in kind, or in any way acknowledge the Captain's politeness.

"That's one person I'm probably wise to stay clear of," thought Captain Gilchrist as he watched the bird-like figure dressed most visibly in a floral-patterned pinafore disappear from view at the end of the street.

Undaunted, the Captain resumed his one-legged perambulation with renewed vigour, for this was a journey with a purpose. It was the Captain's intention to watch a soccer match scheduled to kick off at three o' clock, in just under an hour's time. The match was to be between two teams made up of the fitter members of the two Friendly Societies which were active in Rankin Bay, namely *The Lodge of Ancient Shepherds* and *The Oddfellows*. The field of play was to be the village sports ground, a venue which our prospective spectator had seen previously from his improvised seat aboard the cart belonging to the Board of Trade.

My grandfather was keen to be a spectator for two reasons. First, he hadn't had the pleasure of watching a soccer match before, and in view of the fact that the weather was behaving itself, he thought that the experience would be pleasant for being enlightening. Secondly, and this was the stronger of the two reasons, his crew were going to make up the numbers. Cotton and Henley were to play for the Oddfellows, whilst Crossman,

Landowska and Walker were to turn out for the Shepherds. It was with the afternoon's sporting contest in mind that the five potential soccer stars had journeyed by bus into Eskmouth that morning.

The main thrust of their mission was to purchase appropriate footwear. The next time that Captain Gilchrist expected to see his crew – newly shod no doubt – was when they emerged from the changing room in the sports field pavilion to take up their respective positions prior to kick off. The afternoon promised to be an entertaining spectacle, and to no small extent because of the lack of skill likely to be displayed by the Americans, soccer being a game about which they as a nation as yet knew little.

If my grandfather had been able to show admirable consideration and manual dexterity in avoiding a collision with the woman who was none other than Mrs Enid Fewster, he was not so fortunate when, upon turning the corner at the end of Chapel Street where the bakery then was, the crutch he thrust forward with his right arm clattered against one of two paraffin cans John Gretton was carrying, causing a slight spillage. The force of the collision caused the older man to spin on the spot until the uncontrolled momentum of his body – and the cans – was restrained by the gable end of Chapel Street that is farthest from the sea. The clatter of wood striking metal and metal striking brick could probably be heard from the other end of the street and from halfway up the bank, but fortunately for those people that had stopped in their tracks to wonder about the commotion, the noise was the worst of the incident. Naturally, after ascertaining that the old man was unhurt, my grandfather apologised. By so doing he effectively accepted full responsibility for the collision, although if an independent witness had been asked to arbitrate, the verdict would have been that neither party was to blame, that it was just one of those things.

John Gretton was one of the oldest men in the village, but that didn't make him slow on the uptake when it came to capitalising on a situation the ramifications of which, had, at first sight, appeared to be devoid of benefit. By John's quick reckoning, if the younger man had deemed it right and proper to have apologised – which indeed he had – then he must be to blame. He must be to blame for the pain – more imagined than real – which had suddenly developed in the octogenarian's right elbow. After he had removed himself from the yoke holding the cans which he gently lowered to rest on the pavement, the old timer attempted to rub away the pain. Or was he trying to coax it into being? Either way he grimaced appropriately.

"It's all very well you saying sorry and all that, but what about all the paraffin you've caused me to spill," fulminated the pensioner, in what some might say was typically miserly fashion. "Who's going to pay for that?"

The only real invalid present was a little taken aback by the sudden change of emphasis, the sudden focusing, and in a manner which was quite vehement, upon the commercial aspects of the incident. Captain Gilchrist looked incredulously from the cantankerous old man cosseting his funny bone to the dark patch on the pavement. He estimated that the surface area of spilt liquid was no bigger than a topgallant, and consequently he thought that his good nature was being taken advantage of, or at least such an attempt was being made.

"Why sir, in my opinion the amount of kerosene... that's what we call 'paraffin' in the States... you've lost isn't worth crying over," the Captain responded, trying by implication, by using words that cast doubt on his adversary's masculinity, to sting him into submission.

"That's easy for you to say," said Gretton as he stopped rubbing at the imaginary pain, "but there's been a war on you know, and every penny counts."

"We Yanks fought in the war too," asserted the American as he attempted to find some common ground, so to speak, in the hope of deflecting the pensioner's mind away from thoughts pertaining to financial reparation.

"That's not in dispute, but you didn't come in until the show was almost over," the Englishman rejoined, and thinking that there was nothing more to say on the subject worth saying, he once more turned the focus of his attention away from the sea captain's rather bemused countenance to the patch of spilt paraffin.

Captain Gilchrist's eyes followed the older man's gaze, and for a time the two men stood in silence as if transfixed, staring at the dark stain which to the American resembled a picture of a table as drawn by a child, and to John Gretton nothing in particular. The period of silence lengthened as each man waited for the other to concede. Eventually, after at least half a minute had elapsed, his patience tested to the limit over something which to his mind was so trivial as to be absurd, my grandfather put his hand in his pocket and took out a shiny new sixpence, which he duly offered to Gretton.

"There you are you old Scrooge," said the Captain, holding the coin between his thumb and forefinger for the shrewd businessman or money-grabbing capitalist – the relevant description being dependent upon one's point of view – to take.

"Make it a shilling and we'll say no more about it," said old John confidently. "I'll get back to delivering what's left of my paraffin, and you can get back to sailing your ship."

This time it was the Englishman's turn to use words sharply, and not only by the emphasis that he placed on the word 'paraffin'.

In seeking to double the sum he wanted to be paid in recompense, however, Mr Gretton discovered that his words served merely to provoke rather than persuade.

"You'll get no more money out of me than this coin I've got in my hand," said the Captain, conscious of the fact, as he held up the sixpence as if for inspection, that his face had flushed with the heat of defiance, with simmering anger.

He was less conscious of the fact that the volume of his voice had also increased.

Captain Gilchrist wasn't so exasperated, however, that he was unwilling at that juncture to step aside to let a familiar group of children – the same group that had earlier begged him to give a penny for the sake of Guy Fawkes – pass in single file. The Captain noted that the boy who had picked off his scab no longer had a bloody knee, though it was obvious that his shoes and socks, as well as the turn-ups of his short trousers, were soaked. It was this ragamuffin who brought up the rear of the trio presently being led by the girl. He laboured under the weight of the stuffed dummy hanging over his right shoulder, its legs dangling almost to the ground.

For their part, as they squeezed past the adults in heated discussion, the children sensed an atmosphere that was dangerously inflammable, and in twice as many ways as one. Indeed, so accurate was their intuitive appreciation of the situation they had come upon that they said not a word for fear of providing the spark that would set off an all-consuming explosion. For this reason the children seemed to be of one mind in voluntarily adhering to a maxim which they had no doubt heard many times, but with regard to the tenets of which they had hitherto refused to comply. Presently, however, given the volatile drama unfolding close by, they thought it for the best that 'children should be seen and not heard'.

In the event, engendered by the children's silent presence in passing, the short interruption to the international business being conducted in the street served to dissipate the heat from the men's discussion. Subsequently, realising that he was in danger of losing a tanner for the sake of wanting a shilling, John Gretton deftly took the coin from the proffered hand. After he had rather furtively placed the sixpence into his own jacket pocket, the old man placed the yoke – the yard length of wood from which the paraffin cans were suspended – behind his neck and across his shoulders. Expertly spreading the downward pressure throughout his body, he carefully raised the burden that ultimately provided for his creature comforts. Then, somewhat begrudgingly, he nodded to the seaman as he set off along Chapel Street in the direction of the sea, and, nearer to hand, his customers.

"Have a nice day," said Captain Gilchrist, little realising that one day his valedictory words would resound across the world like an anthem.

"Get away with yourself," replied the old timer, smiling wryly.

New to the nuances of the English language as spoken in England, Captain Gilchrist failed to grasp the meaning of this utterance, and would have shrugged his shoulders if he had been able to do so without their being a risk of his falling over. After adjusting his crutches so that once again they rested comfortably in the pit of each arm, he resumed his journey, a journey which had turned into a picaresque adventure.

In this regard, students that have dedicated their lives to studying the vicissitudes of fate, and who would therefore describe themselves as philosophers, will not be surprised to learn that the sequence of adventures in which Captain Gilchrist, and to no small extent his crew, had become embroiled over recent weeks, had not yet reached its culmination. How could it have? Like the rest of humanity, Captain Gilchrist and his men awoke each day to greet the sun, either as an apparition veiled by cloud, or as itself – the golden orb fully revealed. Then our group of shipwrecked sailors who had found safe haven would set about their daily routines, routines which, given the means, civilised people strive to perform and complete the world over. On occasion, driven by an impulse to give life greater meaning, to experience a little excitement, like canoeists in search of white water, these mariners would sally forth in the hope of making new discoveries. This latter quest was the reason why to a man the crew had accepted the offer to play in the soccer match, just as it was the reason for Captain Gilchrist's perfectly understandable lesser ambition. If he had been asked, the Captain probably would have stated that he could easily have foregone the confrontation with Mr Kerosene, but at a deeper level of consciousness he probably realised that the meeting with John Gretton – though as yet Captain Gilchrist had no idea of the old boy's name – had also added to the piquancy of his day; and only with the benefit of hindsight would he be able to describe the plethora of misadventures he had experienced of late as something completely different, as blessings no less. For these misadventures (or blessings) were to lead ineluctably to one more seemingly adverse happening, and an incontrovertible blessing, shortly after Captain Gilchrist had left the paraffin vendor's company.

The ascent up the bank, though the exertion demanded much of the invalid's strength and stamina, passed without further drama. The Captain chose to surmount the steep gradient by keeping to the centre of the cobbled road rather than by following the stepped footpath in the shadow of the humble dwellings. No doubt he considered the steps – all ninety-nine of them – would have proven to be more difficult to negotiate than the road's gradual incline, as steep as it was, and still is. In our modern era the metal road which replaced the cobbles is designated one-in-three.

On each of the three occasions that the Captain paused to rest, he turned one hundred and eighty degrees about to view the vista which he had seen only once previously. On the day of his arrival he had not taken in much of this particular view. This was primarily because the descent down the bank had been an exceptionally painful experience, his recently injured leg having been jarred repeatedly by the jolting of the cart as its seemingly square wheels trundled over the cobbles. On his subsequent journeys to and from hospital he had been unable to see a thing from the back of the ambulance. On the afternoon of the proposed football match the physical discomfort emanated less acutely from the knee enclosed in plaster, but, in making the climb, more grievously from the additional strain put upon his uninjured leg, as was the case with his upper limbs. The pain to which he had more or less grown accustomed – the dull, persistent throbbing in his knee – remained, and in fact at this juncture was felt a little more keenly than usual as a consequence of the increased blood flow commensurate with the greater effort. The corollary of all this exertion was that my grandfather's cardio vascular system needed to work extra hard, and at each of his static viewpoints, though he tried to take in as much of the panorama as possible, the main reason for his choosing to stop was to replenish the air in his lungs.

"There's never a van or a horse and cart going up the hill when you need one," said, jocularly, a man who surprised the Captain by his sudden presence.

The individual who had made this comment was making his way down the bank via the footpath. He must have appeared from one of the little bolt-holes or alleys between the cottages, for the Captain, who took the man to be a local fisherman, had not seen him approach. The tall, strongly built figure was carrying lobster pots, three of them – one in each hand, and one wedged between his right arm and that side of his body. The Captain had turned askance to see a smile beaming broadly back at him from a tough, but essentially kind, weather-beaten face. It was a countenance which seemed to epitomise the general character of these people amongst whom the sailor from Penacook, New Hampshire, had inadvertently found himself, and about whom he still had much to learn.

"If I had thought about it afore now, maybe I could have borrowed old Dobbin and ridden him bareback up the hill, tethered him at the top so that I could ride him back down again later," rejoined the Captain, assuming – probably correctly – that anybody from Rankin Bay would be aware that old Dobbin was a horse.

"Once a cowboy, always a cowboy," replied the Yorkshireman, who, as the gap between the two men widened, thought it necessary to look over his shoulder to speak.

The fisherman had realised from the other's intonation that the man with whom he was exchanging banter was one of Rankin Bay's American guests. Evidently their fame had spread. The gap between the pair continued to widen.

"It's usually injuns that ride horses bareback," hailed the Captain.

To this comment there was no reply, and Captain Gilchrist regretted that in this brief exchange it was he who had had the last word. It made him feel somewhat deflated, as if the wind had been taken out of his sails. Leaning upon his crutches, my grandfather watched the fisherman's uneven but nonetheless rhythmically bobbing gait as the latter descended the steps, eventually to disappear from view. Then, his breathing having almost returned to normal, his pulse no longer racing hell for leather, the Captain raised his head for the third and final time on this ascent, and surveyed a scene the beauty of which was perhaps marred, perhaps enhanced – he couldn't decide which – by a presence which was certainly piquant, probably more so to him than anyone. The view from here, this third and final resting place on the outward journey providing the highest vantage point, was naturally more spectacular than on the two previous occasions that he had turned to look, for then the vistas had respectively been less expansive for having been restricted by nearby buildings. In the distance, but dominating the scene beneath tranquil folds of cloud, in the Captain's perspective was the great sweep of land that curved up to, and stopped abruptly, at the land's ragged edge, the promontory that at the top is Point Pleasant. Appearing to be defiant in their very precariousness, perched thereupon were castellated walls, the function of which were as yet a mystery to the American officer. Their dominant position led the Captain to assume, mistakenly this time, that they had been built centuries ago, possibly not long after the Norman Conquest, to serve a military purpose. Almost as prominent in Captain Gilchrist's view were the five masts of his beloved ship tilting at the same angle to the perpendicular he had noted shortly after she had grounded. It was this aspect of the scene which was, understandably, the most piquant. The schooner's hull was hidden from view by the solid mass of a second chapel, the first being the building at the end of the street eponymously named. This second chapel, standing head and shoulders, as it were, above the surrounding cottages, provided for an obvious focal point in the middle distance, down from which the dwellings and commercial properties appeared as a ruddy mosaic of chimneys and roofs. To this American's eyes the scene that was a little strange for being foreign, possessed, nonetheless, a quality in keeping with his sense of universal harmony. The thought crossed his mind that as a boy he would have had great fun growing up here, provided, that is, his father hadn't drowned. He turned to gain the curvature of road that is the summit, whereupon he noted a likely place to tether a horse.

The journey between the top of the bank and the football pitch, though considerably longer than he remembered it to have been when he had passed that way by cart, was consequently more demanding physically than he had imagined it to be. This part of the journey, conducted mainly on the level, passed without incident; without incident that is until the moment when the Captain was walking along the lane which runs between the sports field and the embankment supporting the Eskmouth to Ravensborough railway line.

A rectangle of approximately six acres, the sports field presently a little way ahead and to his right, in summer served as a pitch for that other English game, the game which to American minds appeared more arcane than soccer. It was obvious from the occasional shouting that could be heard that a soccer match was already in progress, and that the source of encouragement was near. Already, despite his ignorance of the mores pertaining to the game, Captain Gilchrist was able to determine that the voices could be separated into two distinct groups; one group being those taking part and shouting for the ball, or, as was often the case, providing a warning of imminent encroachment from behind. In this context expressions which could be heard clearly and repeatedly were, 'yes, yes, to me', and, 'watch your back'. The latter phrase made Captain Gilchrist smile, primarily because the charming illogicality of the expression was new to him. By way of contrast to the sounds of active participation were the vocalisations made by the smattering of spectators. Their comments were usually of a more general nature and consisted of such partisan yells as, 'Come on shepherds, show them what you're made of', and, when support was directed towards The Oddfellows, 'Come on Oddfellows, pull your socks up, you're playing as if you've two left feet'. Above the clamour of voices with English accents, the Captain strained his ears to identify an American timbre using expressions which were of similar derivation, but so far he had heard nothing to this effect. What he heard periodically was the shrill blast of a whistle as the referee brought his influence and power to bear upon the game. Then could be heard cries of, 'that's rubbish ref', and, 'come on ref, you need your eyes testing. Anyone can see that that should have been given the other way'. The Captain pondered on what it was that should have been given the other way.

His ruminations on anything to do with the match were dismissed out of mind when he espied a woman emerge from around the bend in the lane and walk steadily towards him. The approaching figure caught sight of my grandfather more or less at the same instant that he caught sight of her. The distance between the couple upon their mutual realisation that directly ahead was a creature of the opposite sex was approximately sixty yards, though this gap was reducing by the second. When still too far apart to be able to discern in detail the other's facial features, both parties were instinctively aware that the person advancing, assuming that the grim reaper would take his toll naturally, was a long way from death's door. Their mutual recognition of each other's gradually discernible attractiveness instigated an event which was charming in its synchronicity. In the instant that my grandfather stopped in his tracks – balancing yet again on his crutches – with the sole purpose of attending to his hair, which, after recent exertions he felt to be in disarray, the young woman also halted. Her actions were no less indicative of incipient, and therefore tentative, sexual interest, and involved her removing the cap she was wearing and placing the item of millinery in the basket she had placed on the road. With both hands now free the young lady – who was none other than Henry Fewster's daughter Jenny – attended to her nut-brown hair. The fact that this was tied up tightly in a bun, which presently she had no intention of releasing, meant that this gesture served little practical purpose – in respect of her hair that is. Considered as an amatory sign performed with typical feminine subtlety, however, Jenny's hair-touching episode did not go unnoticed by the person for whom the gesture was made. The cheering that suddenly erupted from the football pitch indicated that one of the teams had scored a goal.

"Well done Shepherds, let's have another one," bellowed a touchline voice with gusto.

For Jenny to be making her way home from Millbeck Farm at quarter past three on a Saturday afternoon was an unusual occurrence. Mrs Higginbottom had been feeling 'under the weather' of late, and had asked Jenny if she would mind working a few hours extra to help with a few jobs around the farm, and in the house. Miss Fewster had agreed to the request, for she was not averse to earning a pound or two extra when the opportunity was offered. Moreover, she had been happy to help the Higginbottoms in their hour of need for more neighbourly reasons, though in this regard it is questionable that she would have worked the extra hours if they were to have been without pay. Feeling fatigued at the end of her long day – a day broken only by a trip home for a late breakfast, and to let her mother know that nothing was amiss –

Jenny had been in good spirits as she left the farm for the last time that Saturday, as she had set out along the lane heading for the shop which stocked the magazine she bought weekly without fail. In addition to the selfish altruism – or altruistic selfishness – already cited as reasons for her sense of well-being, there was now added a third, though the emotional effects of this latest encounter were initially to make her feel more flustered than delighted.

Like the paraffin vendor John Gretton, like the fisherman who had exchanged a few words with Captain Gilchrist near the top of The Bank, Jenny was aware that the clean-shaven, flaxen-haired individual approaching ever closer was the Master of the stranded ship in the bay, that he and his crew were Americans (she had no idea that one of their number was Canadian), and that they may be in Rankin Bay for some time. She was able to identify the person now only twenty yards away by the description provided by her father when she had, somewhat blatantly, asked him what the Americans in their midst were like. After making a few remarks which were disparaging of Yanks in general, Henry had described my grandfather to Jenny as being an ugly, puny-looking fellow with brittle bones, and that was why he was hobbling around the village with his leg in plaster. The appearance of the approaching figure, encumbered with a straight leg on crutches, brought a smile to Jenny's face, for she was able to see quite clearly that her father's description of the officer's more enduring attributes had been deeply ironic. The truth redeemed by seeing, her one wish at the moment – though if asked she wouldn't have admitted to it – was that she and the handsome stranger were not about to pass each other in the lane, like, dare I say, ships in the night.

Just as the hatless Miss was about to pick up her basket, she noticed a flash of blue sleeve appear from behind one of the many gorse bushes which adorned the roadside and the slope of the railway embankment with a rich mass of golden flowers in spring and early summer. Presently, at the onset of winter, the bushes in question were predominantly green, though where a few flowers persisted there remained splashes of yellow. Jenny glimpsed a boy's head. Moreover, there was no doubt in her mind that the blue sleeve which had first caught her eye was attached to a small hand, and the small hand was holding something it was eager to be rid of – a firework emitting smoke. The boy threw the firework and it landed only inches behind Captain Gilchrist's shoeless left foot, where it exploded with a terrific bang. It was as loud as a pistol shot.

In the moments following the sound likely to startle, Jenny, who was a witness to the scene in its entirety, became vaguely aware of a body scurrying away between the individual bushes in the roadside thicket which had provided his cover. Obviously Jenny watched this sequence of events with her eyes open, but nevertheless, she couldn't be absolutely certain that she had witnessed the young scamp who had perpetrated the minor act of terror scuttle away to rejoin his friends, or whether she had merely imagined his running in the direction of his confederates. If they existed and were in the vicinity, no doubt they would be lying in wait a safe distance from the action. Regardless of her uncertainty as to what had actually occurred in totality – a state of mind which she blamed largely on her fatigue – she had a good idea who the culprit was.

The fact that Jenny witnessed the action as it unfolded, and from a safe distance, meant that to the world at large the effect of the small explosion upon her nervous system had been barely noticeable. That said, however, she would be the first to admit that she definitely felt a shudder run through her body at the instant of the loud report, yet this was nothing compared to the effect –

dramatic in the extreme –which the firework going off had upon the unwitting Captain.

With both his eyes and all his attention focused on the comely creature drawing steadily nearer, he espied nothing of the action which preceded the big bang. Only when he realised that this particular bang wasn't a theory, but rather an actual event in which he was closely involved, was the schooner skipper able to react in a way that wasn't merely reflexive. Now it would be reasonable to assume that to a man of Captain Gilchrist's standing, a mini explosion – even one so close – would not make him jump out of his skin with fright. On the other hand, however, it doesn't take much imagination to appreciate that a surprise explosion occurring nearby is likely to have a greater effect upon an individual who is balanced precariously upon one leg and a pair of unwieldy crutches, than on a man or woman who has both feet planted firmly on the ground. This was the case with the Captain.

Upon turning to see what had happened only inches behind him, the Captain, perhaps because his movements were too hasty, or perhaps because what he was attempting to do on crutches required a greater level of skill and dexterity than he currently possessed, lost that precarious sense of balance and began a brief struggle with gravity which he quickly lost. Inevitably, the downward trajectory which he was unable to resist saw him plummet to the ground.

On his way down my grandfather caught sight of the look of horror on the young woman's face in response to his apparent misfortune. This look caused the seemingly hapless sea-captain to smile inwardly even as he sought to break his fall. The part of his body he used for this purpose was the fleshy part of his left upper arm. The crutches he had had to let go of, and these fell to the ground with a clatter. It was undoubtedly fortunate that he managed to avoid jarring his injured leg too severely, though the sudden movements insisted upon by the force of gravity did cause the Captain to grimace with pain nonetheless. Coincidental with the impact of soft flesh upon hard macadam, the anguished look on his face was accompanied by – certainly to Jenny's youthful ears – a clearly audible groan. The "Ugh!" he uttered had the desired effect, for it was the trigger that fired the starting pistol in Jenny's mind, and sent her running towards the victim of terror with all the urgency of a mother in fear for the safety of her child.

"I'll kill you if I ever get my hands on you Billy Cartwright," shouted the milkmaid at the top of her voice, directing her shrill threat towards the thicket wherein she had caught sight of the little terrorist.

In the apportioning of blame she realised that she could have been mistaken in having nominated the said Billy, when, for all she knew, the culprit could just as easily have been his twin brother.

"It wasn't me, it was him," came the plaintive cry from some way off, a cry which was quickly followed by a disingenuous echo.

For the duration of this verbal exchange, whilst Captain Gilchrist lay on his back awaiting the arrival of his angel of mercy, he gazed up at the blanket of cloud with a sense of contentment which was quite surreal in its other worldliness. The threat to murder the child – whichever of the twins was allegedly to blame – he did not take seriously, and he couldn't help but be amused, and more than a little impressed, by the distantly voiced defence proffered by the boys. He had seen neither hide nor hair of the miscreant who had thrown the banger, but the Captain was absolutely certain that it had to be one or other of the twins he had encountered initially outside the Endeavour Inn. He had already decided that there would be no reprisals when his eyes caused his mind to focus on a solitary crow flying – literally as the crow flies

– on a flight path which was ninety degrees to the direction of the road. The bird was flying inland, and though the recumbent observer was aware of people's tendency to ascribe human traits to different kinds of fauna, from his perspective it really did seem that the crow was flying with a strong sense of purpose, as if it knew precisely where it was headed, and whom it intended to visit. To the Captain's vivid imagination the crow's actions were reminiscent of a business-man – a banker say, or an insurance agent – about to make a call on a client.

"Are you all right?" Jenny enquired as she crouched to one side of the presently wistful officer

Her sudden appearance served to break the Captain's reverie, but he had no complaints when his view of the member of the Corvidae family was obliterated by an infinitely lovelier image. Jenny knew from the handsome face smiling up at her, and before the wounded victim was able to reply, that no serious harm had been done.

"Those Cartwright boys are out of control. They're running wild. Somebody should have a word with their mother about the things they get up to," fulminated the milkmaid, remarkably for the fact that she rarely expressed such ire. "Those two will end up in prison if they're not careful… you mark my words."

Jenny's agitation at this juncture was palpable, and prompted the man who had been gazing up at the sky so serenely to think that he ought to offer a few words of comfort."

"If it was one of the twins I met earlier who threw the firecracker, perhaps we shouldn't be too hard on them. One or other of them told me that their pa was killed during the war," said the Captain with avuncular concern for the tearaways. "I certainly wouldn't go so far as to risk being sent to the chair for them," he added, little realising that the significance of 'the chair' might be lost on Jenny.

A warning uttered only partly in jest, and revealed moreover in the sternness of his mien, soon gave way to a more pleasant demeanour as he beamed up at the prettiest face – once Jenny had moved out of silhouette – he had ever seen. It was a face made even prettier once all trace of aggression was expunged, so that in kneeling beside the ship's officer, the milkmaid's fine, slender neck, her unblemished, fresh complexion, her pert lips so promising of pleasure, her perfectly formed nose, her eyes which at one and the same time appeared lustrous and translucent and were hazel in colour, served to enchant the recumbent sailor who was all at sea though he was on dry land. Indeed, so taken was Captain Gilchrist with this vision of loveliness, that for longer than he would have thought seemly had he been conscious of the passage of time, he gawped like a love-struck youth who, night after night, yearns to be alone with the girl of his dreams, the girl who ever so cruelly robs him of sleep.

For Jenny the intensity of the Captain's gaze was not only disarming, but unsettling to the point that she felt her cheeks become suffused with a rush of blood as she became, temporarily, lost for words. In the moments of silence that followed she began to regret the vulgarity of her recent outburst and briefly wished that she hadn't given vent to her sense of indignation at what she had witnessed. Eventually, however, but in less time than it takes for a chameleon's tongue to catch an insect; she modified this thought so that latterly, and finally, she wished merely that she had expressed herself differently. Above all else she wanted to dispel any notion in the sailor's mind that she – Jenny the milkmaid from Chapel Street – could be capable of such a dastardly deed as murder. Perhaps it was because she knew that the man gawping up at her was American and likely to do things a little differently, that she considered the possibility that he had taken her threat to kill in a literal sense. It was, therefore, out of embarrassment at events just past and present that she averted her eyes from the Captain's persistent look, glancing down and noting the shapes of individual chippings held in place by the tar, and in so doing also observing a beetle crawl farther away from the danger of being crushed by a carelessly placed arm. Once the sensations in the young woman's cheeks had returned to normal and she had regained her composure, she dared once more raise her eyes to look at her beholder. This time she looked at him demurely, in a way which was reminiscent of the girl she once was, and in respect of whom many had been of the opinion that butter wouldn't have melted in her mouth. The fact that Jenny was a woman of twenty-two years of age, however, meant that her demure demeanour was not completely sincere and that hidden behind her expression of fawning innocence was inscribed an ulterior motive. In this regard our milkmaid was not unique, for the leitmotif inherent in that look has been expressed by countless women over aeons. With regard to the Captain's mien, she was pleased to note that he appeared to have emerged from his apparently witless state, though whether he had been left unscathed by the experience, or whether he had been deeply wounded in his soul, as yet remained to be seen.

"I know there isn't much traffic on this road," said the Captain as he raised his upper body so that his hands and forearms were resting parallel to each other on the ground, "but I'm sure that if we stay here long enough we'll be seen as an obstruction to somebody, and if not, then we may be run over."

Jenny smiled at the comment and then frowned at the thought, and although the Captain didn't say as much, the thought crossed his mind that if they were to be run over, the wheels responsible could be the Board of Trade Rocket Apparatus pulled by Dobbin. Now that, he concluded, would be a terrible irony. After retrieving her basket the milkmaid returned to assist the invalid get back on his feet. First she picked up the discarded crutches, and despite being thus encumbered, the arm she offered to assist the invalid proved invaluable to him. The fact that Captain Gilchrist wasn't a particularly big or heavy man didn't mean that he wasn't a strain on the young woman's physical strength, for she was hardly an Amazon, and consequently had to adjust her stance to prevent herself from being pulled down on top of the sailor and their both ending up in a heap. When three feet and the rubbery ends of one pair of crutches were once again firmly placed upon terra firma, a cheer erupted from the spectators watching the match. It was evident from the raucous comments that this time it was the Oddfellows that had scored. Jenny looked about her, and although she couldn't see what she was looking for because of the hawthorn hedge, which, apart from the white wooden gate close by, ran the entire length of the sports field, she remembered that located at the end farthest away from them, at the end she had already passed by, was a bench. This, she thought, would be a good place to lead the man in her charge, if he still wanted to watch what remained of the match that is. She estimated the distance involved to be just over a hundred yards. For his part, the Captain would have been happy to walk to the ends of the Earth in Jenny's company.

Chapter Fourteen

Getting Better Acquainted

There was no need for Jenny to accompany her new acquaintance to the one and only public bench on the sports field, but she had chosen to do so because of her continuing concern for the Captain's well-being, and because she was of the opinion that the stranger in their midst was someone whom she would like to get to know better. Not surprisingly the Captain had acquiesced without hesitation to the idea of watching the match in relative comfort, but had said to his carer – without much conviction – that he was quite capable of covering the distance involved unaided. Needless to say he was delighted to learn in this respect that his words had effectively fallen upon deaf ears.

In point of fact Captain Gilchrist's confidence in his own ability could easily have been subverted if, subsequent to the couple having set off together, the ball which had come flying through the air like a meteor in their direction, had not been effectively blocked and then diverted. The person who had done the blocking was of course the woman who had placed herself as a human shield between the invalid and the most likely source of danger, namely Jenny. The football – and it should be remembered that the ball used was bigger and heavier than the plastic-coated sphere so often 'skied' in the modern game – had been kicked with force by Cornelius Cotton, but unfortunately for him and his team not quite in the direction he had intended. After striking Jenny on her right buttock, causing her to evince with a yelp the momentary presence of pain, the brown sphere rolled harmlessly away. Before it had lost its momentum, however, it was retrieved by one of the local lads belonging to the team playing in red, predominantly. Grinning broadly, this individual thanked Jenny for saving his legs, as he put it.

"You're lucky your head didn't get in the way Jenny lass," the lad with the mordant wit added, "we might have ended up using *that* as a ball."

In respect of a comment which, in his opinion, was ungentlemanly in the extreme, my grandfather thought it for the best to keep his own counsel, certainly for the time being. The decision he made to keep quiet ran counter to his instinct and inclination, and there could be no doubt that had he been in a similar situation in Penacook, New Hampshire, he would have given the man who had uttered such words a piece of his mind, a verbal lashing for having shown a woman in his company so little respect. In marked contrast to the Captain's sense of effrontery, however, Jenny, once she had stopped rubbing her buttock and the pain had all but passed, felt not the slightest bit aggrieved at having been given the opportunity to protect the stranger, and as for her response to the notion that her head could have been used as a football, she merely turned haughtily, and totally dismissively, away.

"Is the young lady all right skipper?" enquired Cotton after he had run to the sideline where he had stopped dead in his tracks for the simple reason that he was uncertain as to whether the rules of the game permitted him to exit the playing area other than, as had been clearly evident, to retrieve the ball. He had, after all, heard mention of an off-side trap, and he thought that by stepping over the line he could possibly fall into it.

"I don't believe that my companion has suffered any serious injury," informed the Captain, pausing in his necessarily peculiar gait to examine Jenny as he spoke.

Once more the milkmaid felt herself blush under the skipper's questioning. Not thinking it necessary to speak further on the matter she merely nodded her affirmation that what the Captain had said was true.

"How's the game going?" the officer enquired, and though he was uncertain as to which side was winning, mainly his question was aimed at finding out how Cotton and the remainder of his crew were doing.

"Hey, black fellah, are you in this game or not?" shouted a voice with a Yorkshire accent, a sense of urgency and frustration clearly discernible in its stridency.

The reason for this encouragement, for urging the 'black fellah' to desist from holding an impromptu conversation with spectators, was that, with the ball at his feet, an opponent had just sauntered past the stationary figure. The person intent on setting up an attack on behalf of the Ancient Order of Shepherds was none other than Crossman. The Canadian appeared to be completely focused.

"The score is level at one a piece skipper," replied Cotton, seemingly careless for the present of everything else going on around him.

"I think you had better chase after Crossman," advised Captain Gilchrist finally, and after offering this advice, with Jenny by his side looking at the ground demurely, he resumed his quest to attain the bench.

Precisely two minutes later Jenny and he arrived at what for the invalid was to be the farthest point of that day's perambulation.

Wearily the invalid placed his crutches on the bench in such a way that the armrests pointed towards the top of the bench's backrest. After pivoting on one leg so that he was facing in the right direction, with a sigh he sat down, stretching out his unencumbered leg (the other made such decisions for him) at an angle which was more or less parallel with the crutches. Once she was satisfied that the man burdened by injury was comfortably seated, Jenny sat down by his side. Keeping her knees bent, the position she adopted was more upright, less slovenly.

"That's better," said Captain Gilchrist, glancing at his companion and smiling warmly to indicate that he was pleased to be in such attractive company. Then, in apparent contradiction of his stated reason for being where he presently was, instead of focusing his attention on the sporting contest taking place – now far enough away not to be in his face, so to speak – the Captain sought to fathom the meaning of beauty as represented by the landscape resting – seemingly at peace with itself and the world – beneath the soft yet leaden sky.

"It sure is pretty hereabouts," the officer observed, choosing on this occasion – without actually being aware that he had made a choice – not to look at the face of the woman for whom he had made the comment.

Seated as they were a few yards behind the goal-line, no less than two-thirds of the natural vista was unimpeded by the vigorous activity a football match creates.

"Yes ma'am, it sure is pretty round here," the American echoed.

From one extremity, from the scene he beheld over his left shoulder, the Captain slowly turned his head so as to absorb the full majesty of the promontory already familiar from other perspectives. Then, after following with his eyes the great sweep of land as far as to where the contours fall gently away, his gaze dwelt for a while on the open space, a cleft formed by the second hill which slopes directly in front of the couple's viewpoint at a distance of approximately a mile. To the Captain the outline of the hills brought to mind a bird's wings caught in a single moment of flight, or a flamboyant and shallow representation of the twentieth letter of the alphabet, namely the letter 'V'. The backdrop of sky he perceived to be between the two declivities was brighter than the remainder of the cloudy vastness, and presently evinced the sun's approximate position. Latterly the Captain's focus of attention flitted from one to another, and then to the third of a trio of cottages which faced south-east towards Point Pleasant. Their presence enhanced rather than detracted from the scenic beauty, and it was for this reason that Captain Gilchrist began to imagine what life must be like for the people living in the white-walled dwellings. He envied their occupants the views that would greet them of a morning, particularly as he had already heard comments in the bar of the Rankin Bay Hotel, comments which were not necessarily meant for his ears, that one of the great pleasures of living in the bay was being able to observe nature's more solidly imposing forms beneath an ever changing sky. The Captain believed it to be one of his more original thoughts that the scenes he carried in his mind – those which he had beheld recently and those which he was beholding at present – were representations of God's kinetic art. Indeed, the realisation was slowly beginning to dawn on my grandfather that from the day of his arrival the spirit of place, and not just any place, but this place – Rankin Bay – had been working with insidious intent upon his psyche.

That intent was, it now seemed, to enchant, and he was powerless to prevent it from happening.

"I'm sure there are places just as pretty as this where you come from," said Jenny blandly, for nothing more meaningful came to mind.

Her speech was hesitant, her manner diffident. The statement she intoned as a question was meant to stimulate conversation, to elicit as much personal information about the stranger and the place he hailed from as he was prepared to reveal. Just as the Captain was about to respond, the cheering voiced by the smattering of spectators that had not been otherwise distracted, and which also arose from at least half of the players, indicated that the Ancient Order of Shepherds had once again taken the lead. What's more, judging by the actions of his team-mates as they huddled around the ship's radio operator, either to pat him on the back or to tussle his hair, it was immediately apparent that it had been Landowska who had scored the goal. Captain Gilchrist waited for the hullaballoo to die down before he began to speak.

"It would seem that one of my men has been teaching you Brits how to score goals," he commented sharply, taking this opportunity to wave, as it were, the star spangled banner in respect of one individual's skill with a ball which was strange for being round. That said, he quickly sought to return his attention to the topic of conversation which Jenny had instigated, but that topic, perhaps because it hadn't really got under way, eluded him, so that finally he asked, "Now where were we?"

"You were going to tell me about where you come from in America," reminded Jenny, in a way which was helpful to the cause of both.

"Was I? Why, yes, I suppose I was," the Captain rejoined, clearly a little flummoxed. "Well parts of Penacook… that's the

178

town in New Hampshire where I was born and raised… are pretty enough, but in a different way to 'this sceptre isle', as your Mr Shakespeare put it. We have a great many elm and maple trees, and I haven't seen any here."

Already, from these few words, Jenny deduced that the American officer was better educated than she, but that didn't unsettle her in the slightest. On the contrary, it added to the speaker's charisma. For all practical purposes she could learn probably all there is to know about lobsters and fish from almost any of the fishermen living in Rankin Bay, but for all practical purposes there was only one person who could tell her about Penacook, USA, and he was sitting beside her; and how eloquently he spoke. She had not previously heard her village described as a paradise – either half or whole – but in her view that was all to the good in the sense that she was evidently in the presence of a man who could teach her so much about what she wanted to know.

"In fact, now that I've thought about it Jenny, I would say that Penacook and Rankin Bay are about as different as granite and glue," said Captain Gilchrist, without much thought as he brought to mind the frivolous comment made by the footballer who had retrieved the ball. "Oh! I'm sorry. You don't mind if I call you Jenny do you?" he asked politely, thinking that it would undoubtedly be a *faux-pas* if he were to overstep the mark by being overly familiar.

In reply to this question Jenny shook her head and said nothing. The glint in her eye indicated that inwardly she was delighted that her new acquaintance had called her by name.

"That's good," smiled the Captain as he held out his hand for the milkmaid to grasp, albeit lightly, briefly. "My name's Andrew… Andrew Gilchrist."

Jenny had wanted to use a French word to express her pleasure, a word she had learned from a wounded Belgian soldier who had stayed in Rankin Bay to convalesce during the war, but she didn't have the confidence to pronounce the word as she had heard it spoken, and so, without the slightest hint of nasal intonation, she merely said, 'enchanted'. Notwithstanding the flat vowel sounds typical of the county, for the fact that Jenny had not taken offence, that single word was music to the Captain's ears.

"To continue with your education on the history and geography of New Hampshire... you're not, by any chance, the same Jenny whose father is coxswain of the lifeboat, are you?" Andrew enquired as soon as the thought which demanded that his own education should take precedence popped into his head.

He had heard Henry Fewster refer to his wife and daughters by name, and now, somewhat late in the day, he thought it crucial to confirm that the person seated beside him, and the Jenny he had heard about, were one and the same.

Jenny provided an affirmative answer by stating enigmatically, "I've never had reason to doubt that I'm my father's daughter."

The effect of this confirmation of a kind upon Andrew's behaviour was to make him ponder whilst striving to look deeply into Jenny's soul – if, as people say, a person's eyes are the gateway to that ineffable idea. On this occasion Jenny withstood the scrutiny without blushing, and in a sense gave as good as she got when she delved just as deeply into Andrew's psyche. Indeed, so deeply did she delve, and so widely did her pupils open, that this time it was the tough sea-captain's turn to become flushed with colour. He sought to contain his embarrassment by returning to the lesson.

"To tell you that Penacook is a town of between three and four thousand souls, and that about seven miles from Concord... that's our state capital... it straddles the Boston to Maine railroad, means you know more about my home town than you did a little while ago, but I doubt you find this knowledge particularly exciting. Likewise, in telling you that our municipality has four churches, two chapels, three schoolhouses, one hospital, three hotels, twelve factories, and the largest flour and corn mills in the entire state," listed Andrew, pausing to catch his breath before continuing, "I doubt that your imagination is stirred to wonderful flights of fancy."

Jenny nodded her agreement, but no way did that mean that she wasn't enjoying the lesson. On the contrary, she presently believed that she could listen to Andrew recount facts which others may find tedious – such as which city is the capital of which state – all day long and not be bored.

"But when I tell you that Penacook is named after an Indian tribe which used to paddle their war canoes along the Contocook River, and that that tribe was one of the first in the land to come into contact with European settlers and – it almost goes without saying – regret it..."

"Why was that?" questioned Jenny, eager to learn more now that her imagination had been stirred. "I mean why did the Indians regret it?"

Jenny's interruption was hardly necessary, for what she had asked the Captain had been about to explain.

"They regretted it because the tribe was decimated by diseases the settlers brought with them, and against which the Indians had no immunity. Not only that, but many of those that didn't succumb to sickness were hunted down and killed by the English colonists... but don't feel too bad about it," the Captain advised, mainly because he had suddenly become sensitive to the possibility that he might have offended his student's sensibilities by implicating her – if only on the basis of shared birthright – in bygone massacres. "There were atrocities perpetrated by both sides," the Captain continued, "and the members of more than one colonial family... women and children included... lost their scalps."

"How terrible!" exclaimed Jenny with a shudder, although her sense of outrage would have been even greater were she not already to have an inkling of such dreadful deeds. Then she added, a little luridly perhaps, "But do go on."

"Well it wasn't only with the white settlers that the Penacook tribe managed to pick a fight. They constantly squabbled with other Alongquian-speaking tribes to the north, and with the Abenaki to the west."

"It sounds to me that they were a warlike bunch," Jenny commented, conscious of the fact that her most recent urging might have sounded just a little too enthusiastic, and that consequently Andrew might have interpreted her eager quest for knowledge as a kind of blood-lust.

"To a point," the Captain confirmed prior to elucidating further, "but in the White Mountains there's a peak named after the greatest of all the tribe's chiefs, and he, by all accounts, was a man of peace.

"I don't suppose he's anybody I'm likely to have heard of... like Geronimo or Sitting Bull," said Jenny.

"He was called Chief Passaconaway, which in English means "Child of the Bear'. Legend has it that he was a giant among men, and that he was able to perform magic."

"What sort of magic?" enquired Jenny, her enthusiasm to be given an insight into an esoteric world she could only vaguely imagine clearly visible in her facial expression.

Indeed, so enthusiastic was Jenny that she was literally sitting on the edge of her seat, and had turned her knees so that together they were pointing at Andrew's unencumbered thigh. Acting momentarily like a magnet to metal, her left knee came into contact with her companion's taut thigh muscle, but then, like two magnets with the same polarity, flesh and bone recoiled away from each other. The powers of attraction and repellence at work in their brief tactility didn't cause the slightest hiccough in the Captain's disquisition.

"You know... the usual things that people with magical powers tend to be good at... setting fire to water, making trees dance, making it rain cats and dogs, being invisible... basic stuff really, the sort of hocus-pocus you would learn in magician kindergarten." said Andrew rather flippantly. In a more serious tone he added, "I suppose what I'm really trying to get at by describing the Contocook and Merrimack country and the people that used to live there, and the folks that live there now, is that we Americans have a culture which is uniquely ours, and that we're not the rootless upstarts that many people on this side of the ocean take us for."

"I didn't..." Jenny tried to interrupt, but there was no stopping her impromptu teacher now that he was in full flow.

"In terms of what has been chronicled for the benefit of future generations, I know that our history doesn't have the same longevity as yours. I mean... I reckon that those walls up there were built by the Normans... and if my reckoning is not far out that would mean that they were built approximately five hundred years before Passaconaway became sachem of the Penacook Indians."

There was more than one word in Andrew's speech which Jenny could only guess the meaning of, but these shortcomings in her vocabulary didn't prevent her from grasping, as it were, the pedagogic baton which Andrew, because of his uncertainty as to when the imposing edifice atop Mount Pleasant had been built, had offered her. Evidently the Captain was now the student and she – the youthful and exceptionally pretty milkmaid – was his teacher. With absolute confidence in her superior local knowledge, Jenny's initial response to Andrew's supposition was to laugh. It was a joyful outburst which the Captain echoed.

"Why are you laughing at me like that?" Andrew was earnest to know, though he already had an inkling that something he had just said had been sufficiently wide of the mark as to appear ridiculous to his erstwhile student.

"I'm sorry for laughing, but I just found it rather funny to think that you should think that a hotel which was built in the eighteenth century could be over nine hundred years old."

Upon his becoming apprised of this knowledge the Captain felt a rush of blood to his face as he never had before, and this made him resent the fact that he had so little control over the outward signs of his emotional state. It seemed to him that everything he had said about his countrymen having a sense of history, and by implication, tradition, had been undermined by the mistake he had made. He was annoyed with himself for having been so naive as to think that the castellated walls he now scrutinised so intently could be as ancient as he had surmised. He wasn't in the least bit angry with Jenny.

"It's an easy mistake for a visitor to make," said Jenny, her intention being to dispel Andrew's embarrassment. "The person who built those walls… and even I don't know who the first owner was or when they were built exactly, and I've laid eyes on them almost every day of my life… must have had more money than sense."

She wouldn't have said as much, but Jenny's method of putting Andrew's mind at ease was to disparage the person who had designed the edifice in imitation of a Norman castle, imitation Norman at least in respect of its walls. The inner sanctum, of which only the roof and upper floor windows were visible, bore no resemblance to a Norman keep.

At that moment the sound of the referee's whistle being blown more shrilly than usual curtailed the couple's conversation. It became immediately apparent to the two pairs of eyes turned to see what the loud blast signified, that the first half of the match had come to an end, and the players began to huddle together in two distinct groups, presumably, Andrew thought, either to receive praise or be berated.

"You don't play football in America as the men here play it do you?" Jenny enquired, turning to look at Andrew as she posed the question.

"We play baseball and gridiron football," Andrew answered, "I suppose you could compare baseball with…"

"Good afternoon to you," hailed a voice with a distinctly Irish lilt from behind the backs of the seated couple.

The voice belonged to the writer who had amused the Captain in the Endeavour Inn. The former was standing in the lane looking over the hedge. He was smiling, and his radiant expression was particularly aimed at Jenny. It was as if he could do no other upon beholding such a captivatingly pretty female face. The Irishman's manner was relaxed, as might be expected of a writer recharging his batteries, as it were, between bouts of intense creativity.

"Do you mind if I come and join you?" the writer asked, directing his question towards the young lady, but then turning the focus of his gaze upon the Captain as he waited for an answer.

"Not at all," replied Captain Gilchrist, and before he was able to utter another word, Jenny beat him to it.

"You'll be able to keep our patient company," said Jenny, without the faintest idea as to the provenance of the animated portrait – for that's how the Irishman appeared – behind the hedge.

Following this comment Jenny turned to face the man whose company she was reluctant to share, and evincing some irritation said, "I really must be getting home. Mother will be getting herself in a tizzy about where I've got to."

No sooner were these words out of her mouth than Jenny began to regret having said them. Thinking that by her own voice she had gone a long way towards undermining her quest for independence, her sense of her own worth as a woman, she tried to make amends.

"But that doesn't mean to say that I can't come and go as I please," she said, somewhat disingenuously for the fact she had yet to put this statement to the test.

At that moment voices from the pitch once more erupted as the tightly-knit huddles began to disperse.

"Come on Oddfellows. Let's have a better second half," shouted the Captain of the team playing predominantly in red, adding to the verbal encouragement by loudly clapping his hands.

After changing ends, as they say, the footballers were taking up their positions in readiness for the second half to begin. Not surprisingly, not being familiar with the static formations adopted prior to the commencement of play, three of the strangers to the game needed to be told where to stand. Of the remaining pair one individual took up the correct position more by chance than design.

The encouragement rendered to the Oddfellows was reiterated with equal fervour by the Shepherds.

"Perhaps we can do this again sometime soon," said Captain Gilchrist as he struggled to his feet in defiance of instructions; for with the prospect of Jenny's departure being imminent, he was determined not to appear impolite in her eyes by being slovenly.

"Although next time I would appreciate my not having to fall flat on my back to gain your attention," he added bravely, a gleam of hope in his eyes.

"I shall be going to Chapel for the late-morning service tomorrow," responded Jenny with equal courage, equal optimism.

Then, rather incongruously given their location, and rather comically in the eyes of the approaching writer, the officer and a gentleman gave a slight bow, a gesture to which Jenny responded with a curtsy which was barely perceptible for being so fleeting. Finally, with a nod in passing to the Irishman, she departed the field of play.

Chapter Fifteen

Lightening the Load

"Here's one more for the pile Cull," warned a voice from the '*Cap*' *Canaveral*'s deck, and then, by saying to his youthful accomplice, "Let go," another plank of good North American timber plummeted the height of the schooner's hull to splash into the sea between the coble *Louise* and the larger vessel. "How many more can we carry?"

The person who had made this enquiry was now peering over the side watching proceedings. Being nearer to one than midnight, in nautical terms the hour had advanced well into the middle watch, and Cull the bellman was nervous. He was nervous because he knew that the business his cronies and he were about was highly dubious, despite what their leader Cotty had said to the contrary. Yes; the voice which had bellowed down into the inky blackness belonged to none other than Jenny's brother-in-law, and it was he who had persuaded the others to lend a hand in what the fisherman-cum-salvager had described as an undertaking deserving of, and indeed was likely to bring, high reward. The 'others' involved in this clandestine operation, were two lads named Dan and Izzy, both of whom, having already accumulated fourteen years' knowledge and experience, had left school and were looking for adventure. The fifth man in the conspiracy against the '*Cap*'

Canaveral's owners was Cull's chum, John Gretton. Despite the considerable difference in age between himself and the team's youngest members, he too was looking for a little excitement to help keep him sprightly, though obviously not so much as to cause him to keel over forever and a day. To this end Cotty had instructed the old-timer to keep watch ashore, to position himself approximately halfway between the slipway at Rankin Bay and the schooner. His job was to deter or delay nosey-parkers approaching from the direction of the village. He was to do this either by convincing the troublemakers – for that's how they would be perceived by the felons – that he had just returned from as near to the ship as he could possibly get, and that there was nothing of especial interest to be seen. If that rather weak stratagem was to fail, he was to trip on a rock and deliberately fall to the ground – albeit as gently as possible considering his age – and emit a scream the blood-curdling nature of which would be out of all proportion to the incident, to any injury – real or imagined – sustained. By that means it was likely that the pair bobbing about on the briny, and the pair aware of the more gentle swaying motion of the ship, would know that they were in imminent danger of discovery. The fact that it was his friend who had been posted as lookout was of little consolation to Cull, and did nothing to dispel his fear that they would all end up in gaol, regardless of their leader's positive slant on proceedings.

Other than fishing, the activity which the good and not so good people of Rankin Bay are renowned for was smuggling. It was as if the village had been purpose-built to receive and store contraband brought over from the continent to be hidden in many a cottage cubby-hole. Luxuries such as tobacco, tea, brandy and spices could be bought more cheaply in Holland than here. It is said that a network of tunnels used to link the cottages, their sole purpose being to enable the smugglers to escape capture – and subsequently the hangman's noose – when the excise men were hard on their heels. Often the beneficiaries of the illicit trade, the villagers knew on which side, so to speak, their bread was buttered, and did their utmost to assist the smugglers whose only crime was to deny the Government its tax revenue. In the eyes of these willing accessories, the amount being paltry, the offence was victimless.

The *Louise* was presently riding the swell with no more than a foot of water beneath her keel. Aboard her Cull was standing astride half a dozen planks stacked side by side in two sets of three. The lad helping him, Izzy, was trying to keep the load steady by sitting on the timbers the front ends of which were pointing down under the gunwales near the bows, whereas the rear ends protruded for at least a yard over the stern. For the fact that one or two details appertaining to the stowing of the cargo had not been considered beforehand, this arrangement had been decided upon by Cull, and so far he was feeling pleased that everything was going according to his plan.

"Once we get this one aboard that will be seven," informed Cull – his neck craned – as loudly as he dare.

The night being calm, above the slow, rhythmic swish of the waves unfurling gently along the strand, the sound of voices would travel far, certainly as far as to the shore. There was little likelihood of people being out and about at that time of morning, but if there did happen to be a lonely soul stumbling along the beach on a journey towards salvation, or a romantically inclined couple seeking closer physical union, there was no need, Cull had thought, for the 'salvage' men to draw attention to themselves by speaking more loudly and more often than was necessary.

By using one of the boat's oars just as often as a pole as for the purpose it was designed for, Izzy was able to guide the coble so that it drew alongside the plank now floating harmlessly on the current. This required considerable upper body strength on the part of the youth doing the work, but being a lad of stocky, thick-set build – a prop-forward in the making if ever there was one – he was evidently up to the job.

"We should be able to take another..." Izzy began, but the information which he was about to impart was to remain his secret, for Cull in his restlessness thought the time was rapidly approaching when he and his gang should leave.

"Another one is about all we'll be able to manage without getting ourselves in a pickle," overruled the veteran of many a dubious escapade, and in respect of what their final load should be his analysis had merit.

Sensibly, and without instruction, after carefully stowing his oar, Izzy moved from bows to midship, this being a better position from which to haul what was to be the penultimate plank aboard. The boat listed alarmingly as two surprisingly strong arms for one so young reached over the side to grasp and then raise the 'flotsam'. Unlike Izzy, whose ambition with regard to how much the *Louise* could carry was likely to have been considerably greater than Cull's, the older man had taken into account a number of factors which the eager youth hadn't. The first was that the higher the timbers were stacked aboard the coble, the more difficult she would be to manoeuvre back to the proposed landing-place, which, for security reasons, was to be between the slipway at Rankin Bay and Gunny Hole. From there it would be relatively easy to reconnoitre at least the lower part of the village to ensure that the coast was clear of prying eyes, and then unload the 'high-order salvage' prior to taking it to its ultimate destination in a matter of minutes. The destination was to be the ragged rows of huts where, in the main, the bay's fishermen stowed gear such as nets and lobster pots awaiting repair. The path leading up to the huts from the bridge at Bridge End was approximately one hundred and fifty yards from the slipway, and the slipway was in the region of a hundred yards from where they expected to land. Over this distance, Cull reckoned, it would just be possible for two pairs of hands to cover the ground carrying four planks apiece in a single journey. This line of reasoning – and it goes without saying that he counted himself as one of the self-employed stevedores – also influenced the bellman's reluctance for the *Louise* to carry a heavier load. At seventy-nine Cull considered himself to be quite youthful for his age, but even he was aware that there were probably parts of his body – parts he would have been hard put to name – which would probably rebel – and in this instance rebellion would equate to surrender – should the demands made upon them be too great. In this regard he believed that four planks were about as many as he would be able to carry when he was one of a team of two. The third and final consideration behind Cull's desire to stop at eight was the knowledge that the pair currently aboard the schooner would also be returning aboard the coble, and as things stacked up at present, that didn't seem too big a problem; but if the timbers were to be stacked to the height which Izzy had probably had in mind, the journey home, Cull thought, could prove problematic. There were times in Cull the bellman's life when he thought that he should have been an admiral, and this was one such occasion to be added to the list.

Cotty had been of the opinion that ten would have been the optimum number of timbers that the *Louise* would have been able to carry in safety, but that didn't deter him from going along with Cull's advice. He would have been loath to admit it, but he had grown weary of descending and ascending the ship's stairways in complete darkness. For the reason that his hands were free going up as well as down, at least he was able to fumble about without being encumbered by the load he was seeking to steal, which was hardly surprising given the length and the rigidly intractable nature of each item of booty.

The *modus operandi* adopted by the pair working aboard the schooner was, by force of circumstance, complicated, and as with every human endeavour, whether as simple as boiling an egg or walking the twenty or so miles from Rankin Bay to Ravensborough, or as complex as making a lobster-pot or building a boat, when that task is first performed there is bound to be room for improvement. It was only subsequently, once there had been an opportunity to huddle together and discuss the previous night's proceedings that Cotty and his crew were able to make some obvious improvements to the manual that in reality would never be written. For the present, however, they would have to fumble about in darkness. Nevertheless, for the fact that the strategy adopted was proving to be reasonably effective, the others had their leader to thank for having, three nights past, conducted a lone reconnaissance.

On that occasion the moon had appeared to shine as brightly as a searchlight, which was just as well, for Cotty had had no intention of drawing attention to his trespass by shining a torch. If he had have done so, for the game to have been up for sure, all it would have needed was for one of the Yanks to have taken a stroll after midnight, if only as far as to the end of the slipway. Any wistful musings bringing into soft focus the love of his life back home would have been dispelled in a trice upon the American observing a man-made light moving about aboard his ship. Subsequent thoughts would have been of a suspicious nature, or, alternatively, there might have been sudden alarm. No; the wily fisherman wasn't going to give himself away by showing a light, not even below deck, for Cotty was fully aware that the fastest form of energy in the universe is impossible to contain once a door or a hatch is inadvertently opened.

On the night of his lone foray aboard the schooner the task which Cotty had set himself was to navigate his way down into the hold and inspect the condition of the cargo with a view to 'salvaging' it. Even with the assistance of moonlight this was by no mean feat, but unfortunately the interloper if not for Captain Gilchrist and his fellow stakeholders, because of the ship's fundamentally simple design, and Cotty's night vision proving to be excellent in the near total darkness below decks, the mission was a complete success.

An integral element to Cotty's good fortune had been the discovery in the hold he was inspecting – the hold farthest aft – that quite possibly the chains holding one stack of timbers in place had snapped. Either that, or, as was just as likely, the load which they had been put in place to secure had slipped during the storm that had grounded the schooner. Whatever the cause, the result was that there were planks of wood strewn all around, and a number of these had come to rest as hazards. Indeed, pointing upwards at angles ranging between groin and head height, they appeared as traps put in place seemingly at random by the mysterious hand of fate. The pain which each of these impromptu pickets – pickets with sharp corners rather than whittled, flesh-piercing points – was capable of inflicting is not difficult to imagine. For Cotty such an infliction became a reality, albeit not severely, when, despite his having taken extraordinary care, and notwithstanding the lighter gloom consequent upon the hold being partially open directly above his head, the intruder received a glancing blow to his upper thigh. That's how the impact had seemed to Cotty, although by his stumbling against the inert object he had undoubtedly been the cause. The sharp pain in his leg had impelled the fisherman to curse beneath his breath. No doubt a more severe impact in a more sensitive place would have generated a louder expletive. Whilst rubbing the muscle to assuage the pain Cotty had been able to take stock of the situation and work out a plan which he believed would guarantee success. An image of a new hut to replace the dilapidated excuse for a building he was presently ashamed to own had come to mind. Then, an imaginary wad of pound notes providing the temptation, he had envisaged selling those timbers which were likely to be surplus to that requirement to other Rankin Bay folk, people that have no objection to bending the rules, or even, on occasion, to breaking them.

Craning his neck to look up through the gap between the sliding cover and the hold, and making mental adjustments in accordance with each new snippet of information he acquired, information derived from whatever source and by whatever sensory means, the prowler on a mission had set about honing his strategy. He gave no thought as to why the cargo in this particular hold should have been left partly exposed to the elements, but had focused instead upon the possibilities the gap presented, and in so doing he had estimated it to be a foot wide, wide enough to haul out, albeit rather painstakingly and over a considerable period of time, the entire load.

Standing amidst the displaced planks of wood, the inner walls of the schooner forming a huge cavern around him, a cavern in which timber which had not escaped the constraint set by chains had been stacked high, for a time the lone fisherman had felt a little daunted, and consequently, for a similar length of time – about thirty seconds – he had searched for a guiding star. Not one had appeared. In a sky of variable cloud, through the relatively small aperture available to him, the normally down-to-earth man from Rankin Bay had perceived only velvet darkness. The only sound had been the sea's reverberations.

The *Cape Canaveral* had added her usual groans to the night's sonority, but otherwise, as a complete entity, had barely moved. This was hardly surprising bearing in mind that she was then high and dry, the tide being out almost fully. The timing of the tide had certainly facilitated, and perhaps enabled, Cotty to make what was undoubtedly the most important discovery of his reconnaissance – his finding a rope ladder, the means by which he had clambered on to the schooner's deck. It was dangling over the port bow, presently the side facing the land. The lone adventurer could hardly believe his luck when he first set eyes upon this equipment, for without it neither his present purpose nor any subsequent related activity could have got off the ground.

Alone in the hold Cotty was able to visualise his plan coming to fruition in microcosmic detail. He was of the opinion, and had made decisions accordingly, that it would be more troublesome transporting the timbers over land than it would be to ferry them by boat. Once the marine option had become fundamental, he realised that he would have to put together a trustworthy team, and he knew just the men – and boys – for the job, scoundrels whom he would be able to persuade quite easily. He gave some thought as to whether he should leave the ladder where it was, or to alter its position so that he and a second member of his crew could ascend from the starboard side. He decided upon the latter course of action on the basis that he would be able to step onto one of the rungs directly from the boat, and this was preferable to stepping out of the *Louise* into thigh-deep water and wading around the *Cape Canaveral's* bows to the landward side, to the side where there would never be enough clear water for the *Louise* to manoeuvre. The fisherman was accustomed to working in cold, wet conditions, but he much preferred the comfort of keeping dry. The solution to the problem of how he was going to raise each timber the twenty to thirty feet up onto the deck had come to him just as a solitary star appeared in the aperture, the star's apparent isolation making it difficult, if not impossible, for an astronomer to identify never mind a common fisherman. The answer to Cotty's logistical problem had been staring him in the face. When the time came for him to effect his 'high-order' salvage, he would first lower a rope into the hold, and then, after descending by the stairs already known to him, he would tie the rope round each plank in turn in such a way that it would be an easy task for his accomplice to haul it up through the opening. He thought a bowline tied approximately a third of the way along would be perfect for the job. For a few seconds Cotty had entertained the idea that he could climb down the rope which, needless to say, he would have secured beforehand. For the simple reason that it would probably lead to disaster he dismissed the notion. The fact that this was to be a 'high-order salvage' operation didn't mean he had to take unnecessary risks.

Forward in time to the night of concerted action, Cotty made his way down into the hold for the final time, and there he found the rope dangling in readiness. Working as deftly as possible in the darkness to which his eyes had grown fully accustomed, expertly he tied the bowline around the last item of plunder, last as far as this particular expedition was concerned that is. In the main events so far had gone according to plan, the most significant exception being that Dan, after slipping on deck and falling rather awkwardly only seconds after he had clambered aboard, had sprained his wrist. Consequently, although he was able to lower and hold the rope in position without a weight on the end, it was impossible for him, using only one hand, to haul it up when there was a plank attached. The corollary of this was that rather than remaining in the hold after he had tied the bowline and given the order for each plank to be raised, Cotty had had to make seven ascents of the stairs to do the injured youth's job for him. This amount of exertion he hadn't anticipated, and he began to feel the effects of so much strenuous activity, for although Cotty was far from being a sluggish specimen of Yorkshire manhood, neither was he an athlete. Indeed, the heaviness of his breathing each time he had emerged on deck had revealed how much he was out of condition.

From his viewpoint on deck the only animate shape which Dan had been able to make out in the darkness below hitherto, followed the example of a rat which had long since scurried for cover and disappeared; but Cotty's absence was of short duration, for he soon reappeared, this time on deck, his obvious intention being to haul up the final plank of the night's tally. Wearily the unfit fisherman approached the opening over which Dan was crouched holding the rope.

"Shift yourself lad," ordered Cotty as he kneeled down beside the adolescent boy.

With his left hand – his good hand – Dan handed Cotty the rope, a considerable length of which lay coiled between them. The latter set to work hauling up the length of timber, but he was stopped almost as soon as he had begun by an insistent tapping on his right shoulder.

"There's a light on shore where there shouldn't be one," whispered Dan. "It looks to me like someone's smoking a cigarette. Can you see?"

Cotty's accomplice raised his left arm to point in a direction which was roughly at a right-angle to the side of the ship, and sure enough, when the fisherman raised his head and eyes to look beyond Dan's index finger, he too saw the unmistakable glow that could only have been a lit cigarette. No further confirmation was necessary, but as the two crouching figures continued to watch through the squares in the rigging supporting the jigger, they espied the sweep of an arm as the person smoking raised the cigarette from down by his (or could it be her?) side to his mouth. Like a fire's dying ember given, as it were, new life, the intensity of the glow increased as the consequence of an action which was completely the opposite to that which is required to rekindle a fire.

"It can't be old John can it?" enquired the youth in a volume which, at the moment of utterance, was easily drowned by the unfurling of a wave nearby.

"What's that you say?" questioned Cotty as soon as the most prominent background noise had diminished from one of its recurring crescendos.

"It can't be our trusty lookout can it?" said Dan, repeating the gist of what he had said if not the actual words, and knowing full well that the fifth member of the team should have been a couple of hundred yards nearer to the village than the position of the mysterious smoker. Moreover, it was also common knowledge that the old man didn't smoke.

If the truth be known, and in respect of this particular fact it generally wasn't, 'old John' hadn't smoked a cigarette since, in the biblical sense, he had last been with a woman; and that was all of two decades ago. No; although nothing of John Gretton could be seen from the deck of the schooner in the darkness, knowing him to be the occasionally cantankerous but nonetheless resolute man that he was, Cotty was certain that the man on watch would not have deserted his post to be in dereliction of his duty. The thought occurred to Cotty that perhaps the American Captain had designated a crew-member to act as night-watchman, to perform a role not dissimilar to 'old John's', albeit with contrary objectives. The man still breathing heavily from his recent exertions soon dismissed this idea on the grounds that the person smoking could easily have approached to within twenty yards of the schooner without getting wet feet, and that was considerably closer than he or she was at present. No; neither the man nor boy watching intently had any idea, at least one worth voicing, as to who the person ashore could be. The seconds passed into minutes, and gradually, as Cotty's breathing returned to normal, he became aware of how quickly his heart was beating. Alert to the possibility of imminent discovery, he realised, nonetheless, that he was relishing every second, every minute of this particularly tense period in the night's proceedings. The same could not be said of his accomplice, who was much more fearful of what might happen to him if he were caught, not so much from the machinations of the law, but from the verbal chastisement that he could expect to receive from his mother, and from the belt that would be wielded by his dad.

"Hello; is there anybody there?" enquired a familiar voice from behind the crouching shipboard figures.

Cull had intended his enquiry to be lower in volume than it was, but his judgement was awry. Perhaps this was because his hearing was not what it used to be, but whatever the reason, if this were a night of perfect stillness, his voice would have carried as far as to the shore, and perhaps even to the base of the cliffs. Fortunately for the 'salvagers', however, within earshot of the sea no such state exists, for even on the calmest of nights the wavelets continue to unfurl. Along North Sea shores the number of such nights may be counted upon one hand, but this night constituted neither thumb nor finger. The sea being only moderately calm, it was lucky for those concerned that the timing of Cull's enquiry perfectly matched a wave's crescendo, and words which were clearly, and somewhat alarmingly, audible to Dan and Cotty's ears were unlikely to have carried as far as to what was likely to be the nearest pair of ears on terra firma. In the excitement of the moment, however, Cotty was able to rationalise these events only vaguely, and the words which had originated and risen from the stern of the *Louise* were an unwelcome explosion in the team leader's ears. They provided Cotty with a dilemma which he knew he had to resolve quickly. The choices open to him were hardly legion. He could either remain where he was so as not to risk drawing attention to himself by his movement, in terms of mobility a course of inaction which would probably result in his having to call out as loudly as Cull had done simply to instruct the latter to be quiet, or, alternatively, he could make for the ship's side, and, leaning over as far as he dare so that his voice was directed downwards, in a loud whisper urge Cull to desist from making any further enquiries. He decided to make a move, and, after pressing down with his hand upon Dan's left shoulder – a gesture which effectively conveyed a non-verbal instruction for the youngster to stay put for the present – Cotty made his way as inconspicuously as possible – or so he hoped – to what he deemed to be quiet-conversation range of the boat crew. The sudden appearance of Cotty's head and shoulders at a point along the side of the ship directly above Cull and Izzy's upturned faces caused the bellman to pause for thought just as he was about to repeat – undoubtedly in a volume which in Cull's opinion wouldn't have been at all loud, but which, in Cotty's ears, would have boomed like thunder – the question he had asked earlier. Cotty beat the bellman to it.

"Will you keep your voice down?" aspirated the shadowy figure peering down at the pair in the boat.

The fisherman was able to distinguish between his confederates by their respective shapes rather than by any discernible features. It was to the thinner of the two that Cotty had addressed his command in the form of a question.

The terseness which Cull had discerned in Cotty's request made it perfectly clear to the bellman that he was being admonished. This left him feeling confused, so much so that he began to take umbrage, one consequence of which was that he was about to remonstrate with Cotty in his normal voice, just to let his leader know that he, Cull the bellman, knew what it meant to be discreet. Once again, and again fortunately for all concerned, Cotty took the initiative.

"There's somebody watching from the shore," informed the shipboard fisherman less sternly.

"What's that you say?" enquired Cull, unable, above the sea's relentless sonority, to catch the drift of Cotty's whispered words.

"For crying out loud: he said, 'there's somebody watching from the shore'," relayed Izzy, his nervous impatience, impatience born of fear and frustration, clearly evident. He virtually spat out the words.

In return Cull said nothing, and though he realised that nothing of his facial expression could be seen, he looked at Izzy scornfully.

Then, as if eager to receive further instructions, Cull raised his eyes in search of Cotty, and was surprised to find that his agitated leader had gone. The man at the helm of the *Louise* scanned along the '*Cap*' *Canaveral*'s rail fore and aft, but to all appearances it was as if the fisherman had been spirited away in the seconds it had taken for the bellman to scowl at Izzy. For his part Cotty had concluded that any further discourse with Cull at present was likely to be counter-productive, and certain that the need for hushed tones, if not total silence, had been imparted, he returned, keeping as low a profile as possible without actually resorting to crawling across the deck, to crouch down once more next to Dan.

"I hope that that chap yonder is as deaf as a post," the youth whispered as soon as Cotty had settled, the former having already ascribed male gender to the mysterious person on the beach.

"And as blind as a bat," added Cotty, aware that the expressions they had used, though commonplace, were nonetheless effective for that.

Indeed, on this occasion, and perhaps on no other, there seemed to be some greater significance revealed but vaguely by the inherent simplicity of their respective comparisons, and it goes without saying that neither Dan nor Cotty would have wished blindness and deafness to be inflicted – certainly as a permanent condition – on anyone.

"Where is he anyway? Where's he got to?" queried Cotty, his words barely audible to the youth by his side.

Gazing through first one, and then another, of the rectangular-shaped apertures formed by the portside rigging, Cotty was searching for the smoker's wafted signature, his cigarette's incandescent glow.

His search was in vain, as was Dan's, and man and boy spent the next five minutes straining to see like earnest lookouts or sentries whose senses, having originally been put on high alert, were gradually losing their acuity. The passage of time seemed much longer than the few minutes that had elapsed prior to Cotty becoming aware of a noise which at first he was unable to identify. It was the sound of Dan's teeth chattering, seemingly uncontrollably. The tough fisherman, no doubt from having been still for so long, was also beginning to feel the cold that numbs and stiffens. What's more, Dan, Cotty realised, had been motionless for at least twice as long as he had, and though he couldn't help but smile at the now constant chattering, he didn't want his youthful accomplice to suffer unnecessarily.

"Come on," he said quietly, "It's time we got off this hulk," and after giving Dan an invigorating slap on the back between the shoulder blades, Cotty turned to lead the way towards the starboard rail and the waiting *Louise*.

Chapter Sixteen

The Plan to Refloat

"She's a fine ship Gilchrist, a fine ship indeed, though you may wonder whether I am at all qualified to make such a statement, being a landlubber and all that. We'll certainly do our best to refloat her for you, won't we Sergeant?"

Standing six feet tall and ramrod straight, the Sergeant simply nodded his agreement to the words spoken by Captain Harnley, MC, of the Royal Engineers, words which were elsewhere received with smiles of faith and optimism by the other men standing on the scaur looking up at the graceful line of the '*Cap*' *Canaveral*'s hull, her five resolute masts, her taut rigging vibrating in the breeze. For a day in early December the weather, being bright and uncommonly warm in the sun's beneficent rays, was perfect for such a gathering. In addition to my grandfather and the two soldiers, the group consisted of Charlie Cook, Henry Fewster, and Walker, a small coterie which had come together to inspect the vessel and reconnoitre the ground on which the ship was stranded. The plan mooted was to refloat the schooner by drastic means.

The idea to place explosive charges against the rocks on which the ship had founded had been the brainchild of one Colonel Parker, that considerate individual who had offered the then recently injured sea-Captain, my grandfather, the loan of his walking-stick on that fateful day of his rescue by breeches buoy. It amused my grandfather when he learned that the gentleman on the beach that day was, in respect of his social status, exactly what my American antecedent had surmised – a retired Colonel. This sparse fact had been confirmed quite early on in my relative's enforced sojourn in Rankin Bay, and it was only recently that he had been able to form a fuller picture of the individual whose literally ground-breaking idea could see the five Americans and one Canadian enter their home port early in the New Year. The Colonel had, my grandfather learned, fought with distinction in the Boar War, but had missed the 'last show' for the simple reason that he had been too old to serve. He made no enquiry as to the reason why, but it came as a surprise to Captain Gilchrist, as it might have done to others in the assembled group, that the man who had effectively initiated this small but potentially explosive enterprise, was not among the throng. He was conspicuous by his absence.

"Well it would seem that there aren't any other options available to us, so naturally I wish your efforts every success," responded Captain Gilchrist, his attention distracted by the antics of a flock of birds running along the shore in water just deep enough to wet their feet. There were twenty to thirty birds in total. Heading towards the village, a few of their number made short flights seemingly to catch up with friends.

Captain Harnley, having with his own eyes followed the sea-Captain's gaze to its point of focus beyond the bowsprit, sought to improve upon his ornithological knowledge.

"Are those redshanks that I see scurrying along there?" enquired the Army officer, not expecting, as it transpired, that his question would be treated so ruefully by all within earshot, with the exception of the respectful Sergeant that is.

On reflection, however, the Engineer officer realised that his query must have appeared somewhat naive to those that make their living upon the sea.

"They're oyster-catchers wouldn't you say Henry?" answered Captain Gilchrist, seeking confirmation from the stalwart fishing-boat skipper and lifeboat coxswain. Even though he thought that Henry would be the person most likely to know for certain, the question was undoubtedly ingratiating for having an ulterior motive.

"They are that," replied Henry emphatically, and as he answered he took a step towards the stranded schooner skipper, though no practical purpose was served by this movement. "You'll often see them in the bay hereabouts... in greater numbers in winter than summer. My theory is," he continued, only too willing to reveal that his knowledge of local fauna was all-encompassing, "that the population that's here all year round is added to by migrant birds coming across from Norway. In that respect I suppose you could say that they're not unlike people, though you'll need to substitute a bunch of rebellious colonials for a band of marauding Vikings."

The American turned sharply to look over his shoulder at Henry just in time to catch sight of the twinkle in the bearded coxswain's eye, a twinkle which told him that Henry Fewster's comment, though barbed, was meant to be taken in jest. For his part, Captain Gilchrist wasn't so much irked – for momentarily irked he was – at being referred to as a colonial rebel as much as he was at him and his crew being described as a 'bunch' of anything. The word touched the raw nerve that was his self-esteem.

"It's not difficult to see how you were mistaken Captain Harnley," explained Henry, deferentially, "seeing as how both species have reddish-coloured legs."

"About eight sticks should do it I would say sir," interjected the Sergeant forcefully: he had no interest in birds and thought the present conversation irrelevant to the purpose of their visit.

It was a long drive back to their barracks in Ripon, and after the early start that Captain Harnley and he had made that morning, he didn't want to arrive back later than need be because of some esoteric self-indulgence on the part of his officer. The sticks the Sergeant had referred to were, of course, sticks of military dynamite.

The Engineer officer was more or less in agreement in respect of how much explosive would be required. In Captain Harnley's estimation ten sticks detonated in pairs would be sufficient to release the schooner from the clutches of the shale bedrock which forms the greater part of the bay. It was a relatively small amount of explosive given the length of the ship, but both experts were aware that they would not be trying to shift granite and that in comparison, in geological terms, shale is classed as a soft rock. Bearing in mind his experience of the breeches buoy, Captain Gilchrist, if asked to comment, might have disputed such a classification.

The sea-Captain and the soldiers leading, the inspecting group had already twice circumnavigated the schooner by the time the preponderance of their number had been distracted by the scurrying birds, though to every man present it had become immediately apparent on completion of the first 'grand tour' why it was that the *Cape Canaveral* had resisted all previous attempts to refloat her. The schooner had effectively become lodged between two shale strata, which, like a vice, held the hull in place, although pressure was applied only when the ship moved. These shale shelves had thus far proved too high to surmount even at the spring tide. At the last full moon high tide had been over six feet. The

Henrietta Maria and a tug from Hartlepool had been standing by with lines attached to their quarry ready to tow. Aboard the schooner sails had been made ready to be hoisted. Amongst the respective crews expectations were high, as they were amongst the sightseers that had gathered along the shore and cliff tops, that the *Cape Canaveral* would soon be free. For a time it had seemed that the ship had come to life as the hawsers were pulled taut and metal groaned, but the effort involved was to prove ineffectual, for the entrapping strata would not release their captive, and gradually, as the tide turned and the depth of water swirling around the now seemingly exhausted vessel had begun to diminish, in some quarters the high hopes previously entertained gave way to profound disappointment. Nowhere was this emotional plummeting felt more keenly than amongst the *Cape Canaveral's* crew, and for easily understandable reasons. Captain Gilchrist notwithstanding, to a man they had grown a little weary of Yorkshire wit and hospitality, finding the former rather caustic and the latter, by force of circumstance, austere.

Captain Gilchrist's attitude was more ambiguous, for he had become a man torn between two competing ambitions, ambitions which were diametrically opposed. Under normal circumstances he would have wished for nothing better than for the rocks which were restraining his ship to be wrenched asunder, thereby enabling his return to the States, admittedly with his pride hurt, but at least with his beloved ship intact. Part of him, however, half of that part of a man's being which urges him to take action, was in a state of rebellion against those wishes. The foremost reason for this anarchic state of mind was glaringly obvious, to himself certainly, but also, he suspected, to Henry Fewster. Other reasons, being more arcane, were more difficult for the ardent American to fathom, and whether in his introspection he was able to reach, as it were, the molten core that was his motivation for action is uncertain, but he certainly had a damned good try.

Not many people waking up each day on this planet will have experienced the vicissitudes that Captain Gilchrist did in the two months that had passed since he had lost control of his ship, and the intensity of the emotions he felt, and in one way or another, dealt with in that relatively short but eventful period, led him to believe that here in Rankin Bay was where life could be most fulfilling. Could the future here, he sometimes wondered, be his future?

With few exceptions his men and he had met with considerable goodwill and kindness in their coming and going, though it should not be overlooked that the presence of the *Cape Canaveral's* crew lodged within the community added to the local economy at a time of year when visitors were few. Demonstrating the enthusiasm of the perpetual scholar, that willingness to learn that is the predominant part of a man who believes that he has been put on this Earth to increase his personal compendium of knowledge, Captain Gilchrist had done his utmost since his arrival to learn as much as he could about local customs and traditions, hoping thereby, to gain a greater understanding of the general character of the people that for the foreseeable future he had no choice but to be among. In this regard he had taken every opportunity that had presented itself to enter into the cultural life of the community, and had attended such diverse happenings as the celebrations marking the failure of the gunpowder plot, followed, on the evening of the morrow, by his attending a lecture, the subject of which was the various kinds of apple grown in the British Isles. He considered himself to be reasonably knowledgeable about the rules and tactics appertaining to the game he now called 'football', and not 'soccer'. This quantum leap of sorts included his understanding the offside rule. Gradually his psyche was inculcated with our English ways, and the effects were incremental in the sense that the more he learned about this or that aspect of life in Rankin Bay past and present, the greater was his sense of belonging. There were times – few in number admittedly – when he almost felt apologetic for the fact that a couple of centuries ago his ancestors had left the fold to become, in Henry Fewster's words, 'colonial rebels'. Conclusively, to be specific about that which was implied earlier, it is safe to say that the strongest magnet working upon the Andrew Gilchrist's emotional mettle was the attraction he felt for Henry's daughter, Jenny.

Since that first tumultuous meeting in the lane when my grandfather had had the good sense to fall over in the hope of being attended to by a ministering angel, the milkmaid and the sea-Captain had been in each other's company on no less than seven occasions prior to the latter making his double perambulation to gauge the resilience of the '*Cap*' *Canaveral*'s geological prison. Like their first chance meeting, the next two encounters had been entirely fortuitous, but the subsequent five had been assignations. Neither party was in any doubt that their attraction was mutual, though it was as yet too early to say whether their feelings amounted to that mysterious state called love. For their relationship to be severed, however, and before the deepest bond it is possible for a man and woman to experience had had a chance to develop and flourish would have been dispiriting for man and woman alike, and it was for this reason that Miss Jenny Fewster and Captain Andrew Gilchrist occasionally expressed views in public which were contrary to their innermost desire. With regard to one physical manifestation of that desire, it was as recently as the evening prior to Captain Harnley's and Sergeant Harker's reconnaissance that the couple had enjoyed their first kisses. For both – to the sound of the sea's eternal rhythm they had embraced on the beach bathed in moonlight – the experience was blissful. It was little wonder that my grandfather was in two minds as to whether he wanted his ship to be released or continue to be imprisoned.

"How do you intend to detonate the dynamite?" enquired Charlie Cook, a man who was ever eager to get to grips with the details of any plan of action in which he was involved.

"I think at low tide we'll be able to detonate the charges electronically," answered Captain Harnley prior to picking up a piece of shale which had broken off from the main stratum located on the ship's starboard side.

He ran his fingers over the rock's smooth, flat surface, and then along its jagged edge. In his mind's eye he could see many such pieces flying through the air with terrific force, the force that would be released by the five explosions. The image raised questions about public safety. Subsequently, however, his imaginings became more personal, and eventually, having decided that there was little likelihood of embarrassing either himself or the others by doing what he now had in mind, by his performing an action which, in these circumstances, he had initially thought may appear too boyish, too playful, he launched the piece of shale as if it were a discus and he were the athlete he once was back at school in York, specifically the year in which he had won the *victor ludorum*. The upward trajectory of the improvised discus was true as it flew through the air at a perfect angle to the horizontal. There was no discernible wobble. The Army officer had not hurled his toy towards the flock of oyster-catchers – they were way off to the left of his projectile's line of flight – but alarmed as they were by the sudden demonstration of power, as one they took off to make for a calmer stretch of beach.

"Hard luck sir," said the Sergeant moments after the piece of shale landed with a barely audible thud a few yards short of the shallows. His presumption was that the Officer had intended his Herculean effort to produce a plop and a splash rather than the rather dull effect of the flat rock falling short.

"Thank you for that Sergeant Harker," responded the Captain, turning, as soon as he had observed the distance of his throw and regained his balance, to face the watching throng. "We won't have to go far to take shelter from the blasts," he added, returning the conversation to more serious matters as he massaged the bicep of his throwing arm. "The ship's hull would serve us perfectly in that regard, but from there, of course, you wouldn't be able to see anything. If you want to watch the action you'll have to stand back at least fifty yards, and as fifty yards in that direction," and as if to emphasise – though there was certainly no need – the direction he meant, with his back to the sea he pointed over his shoulder with his thumb, "will find you up to your waist in water, it will have to be to a point either up or down the beach that we retire a safe distance."

From where he had been standing beneath the bowsprit the Army officer took a few paces towards the cliff, his purpose being to survey the bay to the south towards Seal Point, to assess the lie of the land beyond the ship's stern.

"In my opinion, if you want to keep your feet dry whilst observing the earth-shattering effects of a few sticks of dynamite exploding in the shale bed, and, of course, stay perfectly safe, I suggest that, on the day, we retire to that flat-topped rock over there," and to give added direction to his words the young, fresh-faced officer raised his right arm and hand to point with his index finger at the large, prominent object, one of several such rocks along the coast that local legend states is a resting place for mermaids. The rock in question is (for it is there to this day) made of harder stuff than shale.

Taken aback a little by the implied delay of days, if not weeks, and seeking some light to guide him through the dark maze of his own uncertainty, rather suggestively Captain Gilchrist said, "It's a pity we can't get the job done right now… this very minute."

It was a bold suggestion to make, though nonetheless naive for that, because as yet the eager American was unaware that the team of two from the Royal Engineers hadn't brought any explosives with them. In their view this was simply a reconnaissance mission and nothing else. The Army officer looked first at Henry, and then at Charlie Cook. He was seeking moral support, and Charlie didn't fail to give it.

"Come, come, Andrew," said Charlie, managing to convey in those three words – for the purpose he intended – a potent combination of friendly familiarity and patronising condescension. "This is not the Wild West you know." At this announcement Henry Fewster and Sergeant Harker chuckled. "We can't behave like prospectors blasting their way through the Black Hills in search of gold. No sir; people take their morning or evening constitutionals along here, and children can turn up at any time to play on the beach making sandcastles, or to paddle and splash about in the shallows. My own favourite activity as a boy was to search for sea urchins in the rock-pools. Now I'm sure you wouldn't want anything so drastic as being blown sky-high to happen to your kids were they to pop up unexpectedly in circumstances similar to those that we're planning, and that could so easily happen to somebody's children, and simply because the adults involved… the people in charge… the authorities… us… failed to take proper precautions. No sir; that would never do. On the day when the charges are to be…"

214

Before the Board of Trade rocket crew leader had had a chance to complete his proclamation Captain Gilchrist interrupted. Serving, however, merely to defend his deflated ego, his interruption was to achieve little.

"I didn't say that we should proceed with blasting today," said the sea-Captain, "I stated only that it's a pity not to be able to do so, what... with conditions being... as near as damn it... perfect."

The emotion evident in the enunciation of 'as near as damn it', was assuaged considerably by an expression of support from a surprising quarter.

"That's perfectly true sir. That's exactly what I heard you say," said Sergeant Harker.

On this occasion, his exasperation assuaged before it had had a chance to develop into anything like full-blown anger, the sea-Captain expressed his gratitude for the soldier's support.

"Thank you Sergeant. I'm glad that there's at least one amongst us who is able to listen... and listen properly."

"Now if I may be allowed to continue," intervened Charlie ironically, and because it was obvious to everyone present that the overall mood had changed, that levity was no longer in vogue, nobody made any comment or quips, and the indomitable person that was Charlie Cook was indeed allowed to continue. "Up to a point I'm in agreement with Captain Gilchrist that there should be little or no delay in doing what we have deemed necessary, for I know that our guest... and dare I say friend... is eager to leave us, and who can blame him?"

Upon hearing this pronouncement the man of the sea doubted that the speaker and he were in agreement, but my grandfather realised that for the present he would do better to remain silent on the matter of his personal dilemma. Consequently the 'colonial rebel' nodded his head and smiled without showing his teeth at

Charlie's attempt at appeasement, and then he was all ears, so to speak, for the plan of action about to be proposed.

"That said, however," resumed Charlie confidently, like one who has assumed command, "we do need to allow ourselves sufficient time to inform various bodies. Our friends the boys in blue come readily to mind. I'll speak to the Chief Constable this afternoon... that is if I can get through to him at police HQ and he's not tinkering about with that new boat of his... about deploying some of his constables to keep any curious onlookers out of harm's way."

"The Army should be able to help in that regard," chipped in Captain Harnley. "I don't think that there will be a problem in bringing along a section... that's eight men usually... to assist with crowd safety. What do you say Sergeant?"

Happy to be used as a sounding-board, the Sergeant said, "Shouldn't be a problem at all sir."

"I think that we should also inform the Parish Council and Ravensborough District Council," Charlie Cook listed, "and I think it would be wise to have an ambulance standing by."

"What about providing cover in case of fire... aboard the ship I mean... just in case something should go badly wrong?" enquired Henry Fewster.

"I think that's highly unlikely," protested Captain Harnley, who, like the figure standing beside him biting his lip, and notwithstanding the sense he had that his professional competence was being called into question, began to think that the procedures being proposed would be more appropriate for dealing with the effects of a full-scale artillery barrage or a sequence of salvos fired from a flotilla of warships rather than, relatively speaking, the few small bangs he intended.

"Unlikely or not," responded Charlie, "there's no harm in our consulting with the fire brigade. Now all we need do is…"

"Is dynamite dangerous?" enquired the man who had been biting his lip, the man who had so patiently held his tongue whilst plans which in his view were ancillary to the operation to release his ship were being discussed. This question wasn't nearly as naive as it sounded, and it wasn't meant to be ironic, but lacking the qualification necessary for the query not to seem flippant, much to the questioner's indignation, it caused an outburst of raucous laughter. Curious as to what was going on, at that moment, having sneaked up apparently from nowhere, a group of children – five to be precise – ran out into the open from the cover provided by the '*Cap*' *Canaveral*'s stern. They seemed to be daring each other to approach the group of adults. Of the latter viewing the children unfavourably, Charlie Cook was first to comment.

"You see what I mean gentlemen. Where children are concerned you can't be too careful."

"That's a matter of opinion," muttered Sergeant Harker as the five men stepped off in the direction of the cleft in the line of cliffs known as Stoupe Beck.

To anyone observing from a distance – say from over a hundred yards away – the actions of the men appeared to be concerted, their limbs responding in unison to a silent command given to their collective subconscious, but from close-up, from a view point where it would have been possible to observe every detail, it would have been immediately apparent that a subtle game of follow-my-leader was in progress.

Charlie Cook led the way across the beach. When they were halfway across, from the back pocket of his trousers he pulled out a booklet smaller than his hand. He had only just remembered that he had brought the tidetables with him. After stopping in his tracks to read, a brief halt which caused the others to stop abruptly, he informed his audience that the tides on or about the twenty-first of the month would be perfect from the point of view that the tides would be at their lowest mid to late mornings, permitting the soldiers to set off from Ripon at a respectable hour whilst at the same time allowing sufficient daylight subsequent to their arrival for them to carry out the mission.

"What day is that?" enquired Captain Harnley.

"The twenty-first is a Tuesday," Charlie replied. "Is that all right with you... if we make the twenty-first our blasting day?" continued the rocket man as he returned the booklet to his pocket.

"That would be as good a day as any," replied Captain Harnley decisively.

Sergeant Harker was half-expecting to be asked to confirm that the date proposed would be suitable, but on this occasion his superior officer chose not to seek a second opinion. Captain Gilchrist, taking the opportunity provided by the pause in proceedings, had turned to observe the children that had been left to their own devices. He surmised that their ages ranged between nine and eleven. He could discern that they were four boys and one girl. Their voices shrill, they were trying to push one another – the girl included – into the sea as they walked along, increasing the distance between them and the ship with each youthful stride. They had evidently lost interest in the lifeless beast and were making their way towards the village. The *Cape Canaveral* had been there long enough for her to be no longer of interest to some.

"Is the twenty-first all right with you Andrew?"

"Henry?"

"I can't see my presence being of much use, but I'll be only too happy to come along and watch the fireworks... provided we don't have to launch the *Henrietta Maria* that is," replied the coxswain.

"That's settled then. I suggest we rendezvous at 10.00 hours at the lifeboat station on the twenty-first. In the meantime I'll liaise with the other agencies we've mentioned so that they will be able to deploy accordingly."

The arrangements finalised, Charlie again set off walking, and again the others followed. Walking in pairs save for the Royal Navy, the two Captains brought up the rear.

"When I asked if dynamite is dangerous," said the sea-Captain, addressing his remarks to the Army officer with whom he was more or less in step, but in a voice loud enough for the man in front to hear, "I meant is it dangerous to transport… to handle."

"That's a very good question," replied Captain Harnley prior to providing all that cared to listen with an insight into the depth of his knowledge apropos the chemistry of explosives.

Chapter Seventeen

Trouble at the Inn

On the night of 18th December – Saturday night – the lounge bar of the Rankin Bay Hotel was the busiest it had been since the last New Year's Eve celebrations. There was a festive mood in the air. With Christmas just around the corner, the convivial atmosphere was hardly surprising. The decor being seasonal, the walls were festooned in vibrantly coloured streamers. They had been pinned in such a way that, just below the ceiling, each streamer resembled a succession of waves running the wall's length.

The pictures that served as more or less permanent decoration on the interior wall were decorated with sprigs of holly. Each of the sprigs was resplendent with scarlet berries, and these, where they adorned photographs rather than prints of paintings, provided for a striking contrast with the monochrome images inviting perusal.

Three of the four photographs were scenes of Rankin Bay enduring winter weather, one, remarkably bearing in mind the salty air and how difficult it is for snow to settle on the coast, depicting Bridge End and the rooftops of the surrounding buildings under a covering of the white stuff. The other three showed the sea's fury, driven, no doubt, on each occasion by a howling gale, lashing against coastal defences.

The two prints were representations of paintings by Constable and Turner. They were 'The Haywain' and 'The Fighting Temeraire'.

On the side of the room which overlooked The Dock, three large Georgian windows had been artistically decorated on the lower panes with scenes involving snow and snowmen. These fenestrated decorations were only visible to those within when the curtains were open, whereas presently, because the hour was approaching half past eight in the evening, the drapes were drawn against the winter cold and darkness.

In the centre of the room, entwined around an otherwise unremarkable array of lights spreading their illumination as if from four corners or the cardinal points of the compass, sprigs of mistletoe offered the delight of a kiss to persons fully aware, and a surprise invitation to an unsuspecting few that had not raised their eyes and noticed.

The work put in by the hotel's husband and wife proprietors to bring a little festive cheer into their public rooms was greatly appreciated by villagers and visitors alike. Nothing I have yet described, however, created the desired effect as well as the item which was the focal point if not literally the centre-piece of the festive decor, and that was the Christmas tree. The tree in question was no bigger or impressive than the tree which had been installed the previous Christmas, or for that matter the Christmas before. It was the usual eight feet tall specimen of Douglas fir. What was special about the tree on display in the corner near the door of the Rankin Bay Hotel's now not so spacious lounge, what set it apart this year from every other Christmas tree in the village, was that it was festooned with electric lights. Compared with modern fairy lights the bulbs were large, of a size which nowadays would probably only be seen lighting up a tree as tall as a lamppost in a thoroughfare of brightly lit shops. The hotel's tree and lights were the talk of the village, and to the detriment of the Endeavour Inn's pre-Christmas trade, acted as a magnet to that establishment's regular patrons. Indeed, on the night in question, the only customers to enter through the portals of the inn renowned, particularly in Ireland, for the apparatus which appeared to be the epitome of canine cruelty, was Leonard Walmslow. He had deliberately chosen the peace and quiet of the near empty inn in preference to the fuss created by the latest attraction. The writer jotting down the impressions he had had of that day was joined later by a few villagers that, having grown impatient of the service – or lack of it as they perceived – in the busier establishment, had returned to where they didn't have to queue very long for a drink. Back in the Rankin Bay Hotel, at the end of the oblong shaped lounge opposite to where the bar is located, a log fire blazed.

Huddled together in an enclave around a rectangular table which had a polished wood surface and ornate wrought-iron legs, the latter making the thing heavy and therefore difficult to move even an inch, was the crew of the *Cape Canaveral* in its entirety. They were huddled together not for warmth, but simply because there wasn't enough space available for them to be anything other than matey. The man sitting closest to the fire – Henley – was complaining that the left side of his left leg was burning; not literally of course, but he certainly let it be known that the heat was causing him discomfort.

"Come on Sheldon… change places with me," he said, turning towards the Canadian sitting to his right at a right angle to him; and though in grammatical terms the words he expressed were undoubtedly imperative, they could hardly have sounded less imperious, sounding more like a plea.

"You've got no chance fellah," replied Crossman prior to raising his glass to drain it of the last dregs of beer.

Unfortunately, on this occasion Crossman's judgement was found wanting in two regards. First, there was a measure of liquid in the glass more than he had estimated, and secondly, and the two errors of judgement were not unrelated, he mistimed his actions to the extent that he attempted to imbibe before the last word was out of his mouth. The consequence for Crossman was an embarrassing but otherwise harmless dribble down his chin. This he duly wiped away with his sleeve.

"Now look what you've made me do," the Canadian added in a manner which was typically defensive; not necessarily of him specifically, but possibly anyone in his predicament.

It was perhaps significant that nobody laughed or thought the incident worthy of comment.

"Ask Cornelius to change places with you. He's been complaining about the cold ever since we grounded."

Cornelius acknowledged the truth of this statement with a nod of his head as he spoke: "What you say is right, but that doesn't mean I want to go to the other extreme."

It was at this point in the good-natured exchange of banter that Walker intervened.

"I think it for the best that we resolve this issue by implementing a rota. For example, if we all move round one in a clockwise direction... let's say every fifteen minutes... then we'll have each taken our share of the heat before the barmaid shouts last orders, that is unless she allows the fire to die down in the meantime. What say you skipper?"

"I think we should make the spell in the hot seat half an hour," said Captain Gilchrist in response to Walker's question, though he wouldn't have intervened if he had not been invited to comment.

"That way there'll be less chance of our being asked to leave because it's past our bedtime," the Captain added rather whimsically.

The sailors laughed at the significance of their skipper's words, as each man imagined how their proposed antics would appear to a casual observer should that person raise his or her eyes at regular intervals to see a seemingly strange ritual being performed. Notwithstanding Henley's physical discomfort, the mood of the group was convivial. It would have been the opposite if the bad news they had recently received had been the only news, but fortunately the tidings which had dampened their spirits initially had been counterbalanced by news of a more positive nature. Captain Gilchrist aside, the report which the '*Cap*' *Canaveral*'s crew considered to be unequivocally bad was that the day of blasting – the twenty-first of December – had been cancelled by the Army for urgent operational reasons. The skipper, being second from last in the chain when it came to this information being disseminated, had heard from Charlie Cook as recently as that morning that the plan to blow up the bed of shale had had to be postponed because Captain Harnley's skills, along with those of his men, were required in some far-flung corner of the British Empire named Iraq, where the restless natives were causing their imperial masters much trouble. Charlie, who had not been in direct contact with Captain Harnley, had received this intelligence from the Adjutant of the Royal Engineers Regiment based in Ripon late the previous afternoon. No doubt for security reasons there was little in the way of further detail. Known for certain, however, was that the plan to blow up the beach was postponed indefinitely.

When Captain Gilchrist first heard the news he didn't, as might have been expected of him, and as he might have expected of himself, experience that strange dichotomy of feeling which had previously pulled him in different directions. On the contrary, his emotional response with regard to his personal horizon was one of singular delight. The churning in his stomach told him everything he needed to know, apart from where on Earth Iraq is. Eventually enlightenment in the subject of geography was also provided by Charlie Cook.

The skipper of the stranded schooner may not have felt disappointment on his own behalf, but being a man of considerable empathy, he had been able to imagine how dumbfounded his men would have been upon learning of the postponement. He knew then that if he had imparted this news in, as it were, an undiluted form, his crew's sense of disappointment would have been all the greater for their having had such high expectations of the explosive action plan, for they had believed that this next attempt to refloat the *Cape Canaveral* would not fail. After all, no lesser an organisation than the British Army would be involved. How could they not succeed, particularly after all the work which they – the *Canaveral's* crew – had put in unloading the remaining timber? This had been done following the last vain attempt to refloat the ship, when it had not gone unnoticed that their cargo had been seriously depleted.

In his role as messenger to his men, fortunately for my grandfather barely an hour after he had heard the news he had been loath to pass on, he received a telegram from Company headquarters stating that if there was no likelihood of the *Cape Canaveral* being refloated before Christmas, then the members of his crew were to travel to Liverpool by train in time to board the *Cap St. Vincent*, a schooner of the same line bound for New York on January 6th. When it came to addressing his men Captain Gilchrist had opted to use a turn of phrase that he had picked up from Walker, an idiom which had become common speech on and off the ship, common to the point of tedium.

"Which do you want to hear first," the Captain had enquired, "the good news or the bad news?"

Frequently, when the individual or group of people respond by saying that they want to hear the good news first, they may well be treated to the bathetic and therefore rather disappointing reply, 'There is no good news'; but such flippancy wasn't going to be indulged by Captain Gilchrist, certainly not out of his own mouth. In reply Cotton had spoken up on behalf of his shipmates, and nobody had seen fit to contradict him when he had requested to hear the bad before the good.

We know that in the eyes of his crew the Captain was not thought to be a cruel leader; far from it; and therefore, if the judgement of that same crew wasn't wide of the mark, it was unlikely that he would want to assume the role of torturer and deliberately make his men suffer. In any real sense he certainly wouldn't, but it has to be said that on the occasion in question the man in charge had taken some small satisfaction in noting – after he had responded to Cotton's prompt – the transformation which had taken place on each of the faces arrayed before him. The misery which had shrouded each visage turned ugly, as effectively as a cumulus-nimbus cloud may darken the light from the sun, had amused, and therefore pleased, the Captain simply because he had it in his power to enlighten souls that were previously heavy, previously dark.

Nevertheless, he had let his men suffer for several moments longer than need be, giving Henley sufficient time to express vocally what most of the others had also been thinking.

"Trust the limeys to screw things up for us."

He had gone on to express the opinion that when push came to shove limeys weren't to be trusted. It was little wonder that Henley had had to change his accommodation more than once during his two-month sojourn in England.

When the torturer about to turn healer had thought the time had come to alleviate the pain, he had been taken aback by the reaction of his men. Just as when the sun appears from behind a cloud, each man's face had lit up upon his learning that the good news was not an invitation to a dance at the village hall, which, though not unwelcome, would have been poor compensation for the depth to which their spirits had plummeted, but a trip home, and soon, in two and a half weeks time. Crossman and Henley had emitted whoops of jubilation as they made their way to the Rankin Bay Hotel to celebrate. Walking side by side down King Street, it had been left to Walker to commiserate with his Captain for the fact that he wouldn't be going with them. He was to stay with his ship – or close by – for the time being in the hope that a sensible plan to refloat her could be devised, a plan which in all probability would involve his taking on a replacement crew. Following hard upon his commiserations Walker had seen something in the sudden and rather exaggerated dolefulness of his skipper's demeanour that had told him that all may not be as the Captain wanted certain things to seem, and that consequently any expression of sympathy might have been misplaced.

Walker had had more than an inkling of the Captain's attachment to a young lady by the name of Jenny, but up until this moment he would have thought it incredible that the relationship was serious enough for the skipper not to mind not going home with his crew.

"What's the name of the place dynamite man has been sent to?" enquired Walker of his Captain, after the six sailors, in accordance with the planned rotation which closely resembled a game of musical chairs, had changed seats for the first time, so that, to Henley's relief, it was Crossman's turn to be in the hot seat. Fortunately for the Canadian, and much to Henley's chagrin, the fire was less intense than it had been.

"It was previously called Mesopotamia... which means the land between two rivers. It used to be ruled by the Turks, but the League of Nations has just ceded it to the British, and that's prompted a revolt. It would seem that the Arabs in that part of the world don't want to be ruled by anyone... not the British... and certainly not the Turks. I learned all this from our friend Charles this morning. It's amazing what that guy knows. He's a walking encyclopaedia. He also told me that Iraq is the cradle of civilisation... the place where people first began living..." (At this point the Captain paused in his discourse as he struggled to find the appropriate word.) "...civilised lives around five thousand years ago..."

Walker was about to say something of consequence but was beaten to voicing his thoughts by Cornelius Cotton, who, having listened intently to the history lesson, had taken umbrage at the idea of any country having control, or even suzerainty, over another. Being mindful of the fact that his forebears were slaves, this attitude comes as no surprise. Cotton knew that in this regard his honest opinion would be heard sympathetically by people whose antecedents had rebelled against the dictates of the British.

"Up the revolt!" exclaimed Cotton, raising his glass for whoever felt inclined to chink against his.

Cotton's words and action were echoed and imitated in fashion by three of his confederates. Crossman, whose family was loyalist and royalist to the bone, and Captain Gilchrist, who was sensitive to the possible negative ramifications such a toast presented, declined to participate. In the latter's opinion the sudden outburst at best seemed thoughtless, and at worst it seemed despicably duplicitous to be toasting the enemies of their friends. With considerable concern as to what effect the sound of American voices raised in support of an Iraqi revolt was having upon their generous hosts, the Captain looked about him for signs of disapproval on faces that were familiar, and on others that he hadn't seen before. It was with some relief that he noted that his doings, and more importantly those of some of his men, continued to be largely ignored. That is not to say that the declamations made by the descendents of slaves and colonial rebels had not caused an eyebrow to be raised in a corner of the room overlooked by the Captain, for there had been more than one such silent expression of incredulity.

Cotton completely ignored the fact that Crossman had refused to participate in promoting the cause of insurgency. He did this because he couldn't expect anything other than fealty to the crown of England from a Canadian whose ancestry wasn't French. He wasn't going to let his skipper off the hook so easily.

"How come you don't care to drink to the success of freedom skipper?" the sailor enquired.

"I'm all for people being free to choose their own destiny Cornelius," replied the Captain, addressing the crewman by his first name – which was something he rarely did – in an attempt to gain unquestioning acceptance for what he believed was the sophistry inherent in what he was about to say, "but often the situation in a country rived with unrest is more complex than outsiders – people like us – looking in are able to fathom." Then, before Cornelius was able to respond to this statement, Captain Gilchrist showed him his empty glass and said, "It's your round matey."

The notion of taking it in turns to go to the bar to buy drinks was still a little strange to the Americans, but Captain Gilchrist had assimilated certain local mores rather well. Indeed, so well had he assimilated this particular aspect of British culture that if it had not been for his New England accent he could easily have been taken for a native. Not so Cornelius Cotton, for the appearance at their table of the most obviously buxom of the barmaids led him to believe that he could remain seated and still procure their respective 'poison'. He asked the young woman, who in his estimation was about twenty years of age, and who had arrived in their midst to collect empty glasses, if she wouldn't mind taking their order for drinks and bringing them to the table. She turned down his request, but as if to compensate the sailor for his disappointment, by leaning forward from the waist – ostensibly to wipe the table – she provided Cotton with an awe-inspiring view of her ample bosom. His sense of propriety told him that he should avert his eyes, whilst at the same time the artist within him told him that he shouldn't. There can be no doubt as to which factor took precedence, for in short he ogled. It was left to Henley to spoil Cotton's pleasure and at the same time save him from further embarrassment.

"I don't suppose you can put another log on the fire can you? It's getting a little chilly in this corner," he lied, his intention being to turn up the heat for the man in the hot seat, to make him sweat.

"I'll be back in a jiffy to warm things up for you," the barmaid said as she gained her full height, which was all of five feet two inches above the ground, a fact which seemed to emphasise and enhance the rounded pulchritude revealed by her décolletage. Her name was Rita. Burdened by a tray stacked mainly with empty glasses, with a backward glance Rita smiled lasciviously over her shoulder as she parted the sailors' company. Her smile was generous, for it was directed at no one in particular.

"Hey! You can't make that ten minutes can you?" called out Crossman, aware that after that passage of time he would have vacated the chair which was closest to the fire. To all intents and purposes his words fell on deaf ears, for there was no reply.

There being no other recourse open to him, reluctantly Cotton rose to his formidable height, and, following in the barmaid's footsteps, threaded his way through the throng to do what was necessary for his team's morale. Maybe it was because of the difference in height between them, but whereas Rita the barmaid had had to repeatedly signal her presence and her wish to be let through with, "Excuse me", after, "Excuse me", Cotton was able to part the waves, as it were, without uttering a word. It was as if the people impeding his progress became instinctively aware – for the backs of many were turned towards him – of the tall, dark stranger's presence behind them. It was as if the American were able to communicate his apologies telepathically directly into the skull – be it hirsute or bald – confronting him. At the bar he had to stand in the second row of the phalanx waiting to be served. This gave him the opportunity to look over the heads and shoulders of people – men mostly – leaning forward half-crowns in hand, to leer at Rita's voluptuous curves from a greater, therefore less provocative, distance than he had done previously. Presently the main focus of his attention was standing at the sink washing the glasses she had just collected.

Perhaps it was to rest his eyes that after a few moments the sailor broke his reverie and looked about him for no other reason than to gain an impression of the faces at either side. His ears were receptive to their chatter, for the local accent, whether it was asking for a whisky chaser or a packet of crisps, never failed to amuse him. Upon looking to his left Cotton's eyes lighted upon the face of a beautiful woman whom he surmised was approximately thirty years of age. Standing by the curtained window, this manifestation of female beauty was completely different from that displayed by the busty barmaid, for the serenity revealed in this woman's face was totally enchanting. She certainly cast a spell on Cotton, and its power transfixed his eyes.

There can be no doubt that the attraction was mutual, for the woman found herself gazing at Cornelius as intensely as he was gawping at her. It could be argued that in some respects this was hardly surprising, and for the most obvious of reasons. At the end of the second decade of the twentieth century people with black skin were rarely, if ever, seen in Rankin Bay. It was this rarity value, and his tall stature, which enabled Cornelius to present a striking figure wherever he went in the village. In this regard the black American had grown used to being gawped at, and was not offended in the slightest when passers-by considered him to be an object of curiosity. After all, had he not witnessed a similar phenomenon when the ship he was on had put into Conakry, and he and the white man he had befriended had gone ashore together to savour the delights of the town. There it had been the person with white skin who had been in the minority, and who had, therefore, come under scrutiny, notwithstanding that a white face in Conakry was undoubtedly less of a rarity than was a black face in the Yorkshire fishing village. Obvious factors aside, however, there was in the look shared by the serenely sad woman and the black American sailor a recognition of each other's attractiveness, an appreciation which given the right circumstances could have developed into a meaningful relationship. On this occasion, however, such a flourishing was out of the question, and it wasn't going to happen because the sad-eyed woman was none other than

Sally Draycot, and the man standing beside her, the vague figure that had remained peripheral in Cotton's line of sight, was her husband Cotty.

Mr Draycot had been under some duress of late, and for good reason, for old John had gone missing; and because of his own negligence, this was an eventuality for which Cotty felt personally responsible. In the early hours of that fateful morning when he and his fellow amateurs had first purloined part of the ship's cargo, the team of 'high-order salvagers' had forgotten all about the old man who had been posted as lookout on the beach, at least until well after daylight had dawned, by which time he was nowhere to be found. After a couple of days had passed to give the missing person a chance to turn up of his own accord, searches involving friends, neighbours and the police had been organised, but with no result. Whether he was alive or dead, there was no trace of the man, so it seemed as if he had been spirited from the face of the Earth. One wit said that perhaps he had assumed the behaviour of a cat and gone off to a secluded place to die. Others said that he had perhaps gone to visit relatives, or even 'a fancy woman' in Ravensborough, and that sooner or later, like a rather aged prodigal son, he would turn up and laugh at those same friends, neighbours and police that had gone to so much trouble to look for him. A totally serious suggestion was that he had fallen – possibly following a heart attack – and been washed out to sea. This was the hypothesis which Cotty subscribed to, although he did wonder whether there was any connection between the mysterious smoker they had espied from the *Cape Canaveral's* deck and John's disappearance. What Cotty knew for certain was that not he, Cull, nor the two lads were directly responsible for old John having gone missing, yet still the feeling of guilt persisted. This feeling was accentuated by the fact that Cotty couldn't tell those involved in the search exactly what he knew without incriminating himself and his chums. Moreover in this regard, he couldn't be absolutely certain, despite their having discussed the matter amongst themselves and having agreed not to divulge what they knew of John Gretton's last known whereabouts, that their secret would not eventually be revealed by one of their number, inadvertently or otherwise. Already, on two occasions he had had to provide reassurance to Cull and Dan that no good would come of their spilling the beans, so to speak, as to the business in which they and John Gretton had been involved. Without doubt, unless he was out on the briny plying his trade, it was this last consideration which most often kept the normally redoubtable fisherman awake at night, and several times over recent weeks he had lain in bed staring up at the dark, featureless ceiling, his mind going over the mystery as to his friend's possible whereabouts; but more often than not it was the consequences of their secret being revealed which preoccupied him; and all the while, in blissful ignorance of her husband's sleeplessness, Sally lay sleeping beside him.

Unused to such psychological pressure, it didn't take long for Cotty's forebodings to become apparent in his waking hours, and eventually in public; not demonstrably at first, but the signs were there to see for those that knew the fisherman well, and no one knew Cotty as well as his wife did. She had noted, and indeed had commented upon, the fact that her husband was less inclined to put out to sea of late, and that he often cited the weather, or the tide, or the swell, as reasons for not launching his boat. He wasn't able to give up on fishing completely of course, for he wouldn't have been able to make a living of any sort without putting in some effort, but the days when he could have earned a herring and didn't had definitely increased. One practical excuse he gave was that he needed to do some work on his hut, to get the building shipshape, as it were.

A more disturbing consequence of Cotty's present sensibility, a change which Sally had observed over recent weeks and was at a loss to understand why, was her husband's propensity to drink more than he had done previously. This increase in her spouse's consumption of alcohol hadn't occurred suddenly, but had been more insidious for being gradual. There were, of course, financial implications. It doesn't take a genius in economic theory to realise that when there is less money coming in, the more of that lesser amount spent on drink the bleaker will be the outlook. With the percipience of a woman of sense Sally could see the proverbial storm clouds gathering over their personal horizon, and was determined to take action to prevent their darkly nebulous forces from being precipitated. To this end she had already determined to let her husband do as he wished – within certain parameters – up until Christmas, but once the holiday was over, she would put her foot down to quote a phrase which the women of Rankin Bay, to the consternation of their men folk, used to say frequently. Given the way events were about to unfold in the hotel lounge on that Saturday evening before Christmas, Mrs Draycot probably came to wish that she had put her foot down a lot sooner than was her intention, for not far off being half-seas-over, Cotty left his wife's side to approach Cornelius Cotton. The fishermen's attitude was far from friendly.

"What's yours love?" enquired Rita of Cornelius, casting her eyes down to her most alluring assets, surely her intention being that the sailor's gaze would follow.

Unfortunately for the couple involved in this mainly non-verbal courtship, their interaction – from one side proactive, from the other less so – was rudely interrupted.

"Who do you think you're looking at paleface?" said Cotty into Cotton's left ear, so loudly and aggressively that the sailor instinctively raised his left hand as if to cover his eardrum whilst at the same time leaning with his head and torso as far from the source of the sound as was physically possible.

"I assure you sir, I was just minding my own business," responded Cotton, hoping, by the politeness of his reply, a politeness which he suspected the locals considered quaint, to diffuse the situation. "If I have offended you in any way I'm at a loss to know how," the sailor added with a quizzical look.

The general hum of conversation around the bar ceased suddenly as the people that were gathered there focused their attention on this latest, rather interesting, development, one which was potentially explosive.

"You were ogling my wife" accused Cotty, careless in his half inebriated state about making a scene.

"Come on Cotty man," hailed, from across the bar, a voice which was familiar to the fisherman's ears, "get back in your corner. Haven't you heard, this is the season of peace on Earth and goodwill to all men?"

The voice belonged to Cull, his diminutive figure being almost hidden from view by the burly frames of two Eskmouth fishermen.

"Just you keep out of this Cull. It wasn't your wife he was eyeing up," slurred Cotty, his emotional state – his rising anger – clearly evinced by the raised finger he pointed at his friend.

"Chance would be a fine thing, wouldn't it Cull?" called out one of the local wits anonymously.

For his part Cotton, although he considered 'ogling' to be an inappropriate word for the look which Sally Draycot and he had shared, if he hadn't been previously, the Texan sailor was now fully aware of what had riled his accuser. He didn't consider that his response to the Englishman's harsh introduction had been in any way disingenuous.

Meanwhile, in the corner farthest away from the little drama being enacted, Cotton's fellow mariners, their attention having been gained by the background hush that had gradually permeated throughout the room, had become vaguely aware that something out of the ordinary was going on at the bar. Even when they eventually realised that an altercation was taking place, and that their own man was in the thick of it, at their skipper's recommendation they as yet made no move to intervene.

To say that Mrs Draycot was embarrassed by the events unfolding before her eyes would be an understatement. She was shocked by her husband's behaviour to the extent that she appeared to be petrified. Mortified she certainly was, and though she might have wished for the ground to have opened up beneath her feet, she knew that the only sure way of escaping her continuing humiliation was to leave, and this she dared not do for fear of exacerbating the situation, for the only practical means of attaining the exit was to pass within an arm's length of her husband and the stranger. What she specifically feared was that Cotty would grab her by the arm to detain her, and that she wouldn't be able break free of his grip. Up until recently she knew her husband not to be a violent man, but she also knew that over recent weeks his character had undergone a change, a change evinced by more erratic behaviour, and this gave her cause for concern. Cotty had never laid a hand upon her – in anger that is – but in his present mood there was no telling what he might do. Consequently, like everyone else in the room she watched and waited, but unlike several of those watching and waiting, she hoped for the best but feared the worst. The worst, as conceived by her imagination, was that her unpredictable spouse would pick up a glass and use it as a weapon.

Ostensibly the motivation for Cotty's aggressive posturing was provided by the green-eyed monster, but it should also be borne in mind that the jealous fisherman was one of those patrons whose ire had been fomented by Cotton's tactless praise for the revolt in Iraq. The irate Englishman was well aware that a plan to free the trapped schooner using dynamite put in place by sappers based in Ripon had had to be shelved because the soldiers that would have been involved had been sent at short notice to the Middle East. Upon hearing Cotton's toast of 'Up the revolt', he had said to his wife that if the soldiers were to return home safely they should come to Rankin Bay and blow the ship to smithereens. He had also added that at least then there would be 'brass' to be made from the sale of scrap metal. There might also have been a deeper cause behind Cotty's resentment, but he was sober enough not to let himself be viewed as a racist bully. For several moments the fisherman who had hitherto acted so spontaneously was at a loss as to what to do next, so he simply stood there, like an actor in a melodrama awaiting his cue, glaring at the person who was the target of his enmity. The thought crossed Cotty's mind that he was in danger, as the Chinese would express it, of losing face, that as a consequence of his dynamism – as he perceived the action he had taken in respect of his and his wife's honour – fizzling out pathetically, he would become the laughing stock of the entire village, and henceforth appear a consummate fool in the eyes of Mrs Draycot.

Cotton, having concluded that the irksome individual he was having to contend with was behaving the way he was because of how much he had had to drink, adhered to one of several maxims which had been taught to him by his mother, and that was to ignore

– if at all possible – bad behaviour and praise that which is good. To this end he calmly ordered his pints of warm beer, watched as Rita placed each amber-filled glass with its white, frothy head on a round tray, handed over a ten-shilling note, duly received his change, and carefully, ever so carefully, stretched out his arms to pick up the tray now heavily laden. Notwithstanding the fact that he was aware of his would-be aggressor's continuing glowering presence beside him, Cotton believed that he had dealt with the situation satisfactorily. Indeed, the thought occurred to him that not only would he emerge from this encounter completely unscathed, but rather his reputation would be enhanced considerably, particularly in the eyes of the ladies, which should serve him well in future liaisons. Unfortunately this thought, occurring just as Cotton was about to turn his back on his assailant, generated a smile on the mariner's face which anyone – not just Cotty – would have perceived as an expression of self-satisfaction amounting to smugness. Cotty saw it, and that wry smile – toothless for being close-lipped – goaded him into action more acutely, and therefore more effectively, than ever a red rag did to a bull. Some devil in Cotty awoke him from his torpor, from his stupefaction, and without giving the thought which flashed before him the slightest consideration, deftly he stuck out his foot to catch the heel of the American just as the latter was about to step forward. This was undoubtedly a cunning move on the part of the fisherman, and for no other reason than that not a single soul saw him do it. The effect was devastating, certainly for the person whom Cotty perceived to be an enemy of the Crown, and for his shipmates. The falling body that was Cornelius Cotton quickly followed the upturned glasses spilling their content. If there appeared to be little room for manoeuvre prior to the incident, the impression had been beguiling for the fact that almost in an instant a cavernous space had opened up for the sailor to fall into as the throng of people in his immediate vicinity, not wishing to be soaked in beer, compressed themselves into any vacant space in an attempt to get out of the way. Whereas a few were successful, others were not so lucky, but at least no one was injured by the glasses flying through the air, none of which broke as it landed. Unfortunately, however, a glass was broken clumsily underfoot, and it was Cotton who suffered the greatest misfortune because of this occurrence, for having already let go of the now useless tray, he had positioned his hands palm down to break his fall. The result was that he cut his left hand on one of the largest shards. After first inspecting this hand to gauge the severity of the cut, and finding, despite the presence of a significant amount of blood, that his injury was superficial enough to be ignored for the present, he turned on his side to glare up at the aggressor.

"Did you enjoy your trip mate?" Cotty questioned sarcastically, the grin of the victor who has gained his triumph by dastardly means besmirching his face.

Coming on top of his ignominious fall, this verbal thrust was too much for Cotton to take lying down, and like a black panther roused and let loose from the cage of civility, he rose to his feet with an agility rarely seen in a man of his height and build, and launched himself at Cotty with a blood-curdling cry. It was as if at that moment all the injustice, all the iniquities, which had been meted out to him and his forebears by the likes of the obnoxious individual presently staring down at him was being channelled through his veins, compelling him to become a terrible avenger. With his left hand – the bloody hand – he grabbed a handful of the fisherman's clothing just below the throat. This was to pull the head of the man whom Cotton knew to have been the person who had tripped him within range of his right hook, and this he delivered with telling effect. Dazed by the speed and ferocity of the retaliation, the fisherman was unable to put up any defence and felt the full impact of Cotton's fist on an area of his face which included the bridge of his nose, the upper part of his left cheek, and his entire left eye. The first blow delivered, Cotton had drawn back his right arm to deliver a second, but was prevented from doing so by Walker, who had been the first of the *Cape Canaveral* cavalry to arrive. Almost upsetting their table, they had made their move when the realisation eventually dawned that their man really was in trouble, and that Cotton quite possibly hadn't simply tripped and fallen by accident – like a buffoon – which is what they had at first assumed. Captain Gilchrist, having, by some deft manoeuvring managed to place himself between the two antagonists, instructed Cotton to let go of his victim. Cotty, when free, was quick to realise that the time of fisticuffs had ended, and that the likely best course of action open to him was to assume the role of the injured party. Rita evidently thought it now safe enough to arrive with a dustpan and brush to sweep up the broken glass.

"What's going on here?" enquired Captain Gilchrist, turning the focus of his attention from one to the other of the pugnacious pair.

"That… that man attacked me for no reason," responded Cotty as he straightened his shirt and pullover.

"That's right… he did that," resounded a voice from the throng. "We all saw him do it."

It soon became apparent to Cotton that he was in a difficult situation for the fact that the violence which had been perpetrated on him had not been witnessed, whereas his own aggression had been plain for all to see. He realised that people would think he had responded the way he had simply because Cotty had poked fun at him. He glanced down at Rita kneeling at her work, and although in Cotton's view her voluptuous charms were more obvious to behold than ever, on this occasion the industrious barmaid did not return his searching look, and he divined that there was little comfort to be obtained in that direction.

Turning to look his Captain directly in the eye, unapologetically Cotton said calmly, "He tripped me. He did it deliberately."

"I did no such thing," Cotty retorted, and then added, "If this is the way members of your crew behave when…"

The fisherman wasn't allowed to finish the speech he intended, but was cut short by Captain Gilchrist. The latter wasn't going to be lectured on how he should maintain discipline amongst his crew. Not wishing to let the Englishman gain the moral high ground, and noting that the man he was addressing was wearing a gansey, by intonation he asked, "You're a fisherman I believe?"

Despite being perplexed as to why his occupation should be relevant to the present conversation Cotty answered proudly, "I am that," he said, and thinking it necessary to supplement this succinct answer with information about his lineage in this line of work he added, "…as was my father and my grandfather."

"Well Mr." began the Captain, only to pause in order to elicit the fisherman's name. The fisherman, either, in Captain Gilchrist's opinion, because he was too dull to take the hint, or because he was reluctant to give his name, needed further prompting. "I'm sorry, I didn't quite catch your name," the Captain said expectantly.

Immediately the thought occurred to Cotty that what he might be expected to say at this juncture, and therefore what he perhaps should say, was, "That's because I didn't give it;" but for reasons which he conceived to be diplomatic, he decided not to risk irking the American by completing the cliché. Instead he responded unequivocally. "The name's Draycot, but people round here know me as Cotty."

Perceiving there to be some advantage to be gained by continuing with diplomacy, the fisherman held out his hand for the Captain to grasp and shake. Reaching out to his erstwhile adversary in such a manner was as yet out of the question. It almost goes without saying that under normal circumstances Captain Gilchrist would have gladly grasped the proffered hand, but on this occasion, believing the gesture to be premature and somewhat disingenuous for being ingratiating, he declined the offer, and left Mr Draycot to withdraw his hand – a hand which the passing seconds revealed had evidently been thrust forward to no purpose – as soon as he felt inclined so to do. All around them the social life of the hotel was returning to normal, and realising that they had witnessed the best (or the worst, depending on one's point of view) of the action, the people enjoying themselves generated a welcome for being familiar hubbub. For the present Cotton wisely left it to his boss to speak on his behalf. He was glad that the skipper hadn't shaken his opponent's hand.

"Well there are signs of a struggle on you both, so I suggest that we part company and let time heal your wounds, and perhaps whatever ill-feeling there is between you," advised the Captain.

Embarrassed by rejection Cotty responded sharply. "You must be joking if you think I'm going to let this lie. I'm the innocent party in all this, and I have witnesses to prove it. This doesn't end here you know," warned Cotty, pointing his finger at Walker's back.

At the sound of Cotty's raised voice once again the hubbub died down, and to the sound of the fisherman's wounded pride, threatening, by implication, further action, in single file the Americans left the room. In the doorway the Irish writer, sensing the less than happy mood among those leaving, stood aside to let them pass. Upon gaining the street, without saying a word Cotton led the way to the Endeavour Inn. He was hoping for a quiet drink.

Chapter Eighteen

A Parting of the Ways

"It's not the Ritz, but at least the temperature is a few degrees warmer in here than it is outside," said Walker as he stepped through the waiting-room doorway.

The waiting-room Walker surveyed upon entering formed part of Rankin Bay station, a building which, because of its quaint architectural style, would have beguiled the Americans as to its purpose had they beheld it upon their arrival in the village. The complicated arrangement of walls and roofs juxtaposed at different heights and angles more closely resembled an English country cottage – one that in this instance was situated adjacent to the track – than any railway station they had set eyes on previously. After the several weeks that they had been stranded however, weeks that were on the cusp of turning into months as the more appropriate reckoning of time, such quaintness no longer surprised them. Indeed, on more than one occasion the topic under discussion amongst themselves had focused upon how, generally speaking, buildings reflected the national character. Then it had been expostulated that the 'Brits' gave as much, perhaps more, consideration to the aesthetic appearance of their permanent structures as they did to functionality, whereas back home it was felt that the converse was more often the case.

By stopping suddenly to conduct his cursory inspection the *Cape Canaveral's* donkeyman caused a chain reaction not dissimilar to the effect, on the trucks or carriages being pulled, produced by an engine-driver when he pulls into a station or depot and applies the brakes. The sudden and unexpected blockage was felt most emphatically at the back by Landowska and Captain Gilchrist, but in different ways for the reason that the Captain, distracted by the conversation he was holding with the woman by his side, walked into the New Yorker's back. A chain reaction going in the opposite direction to that which had begun the sequence was only prevented by Landowska arresting his forward momentum so as not to bump into the man in front, namely Cotton.

"I'm sorry," said Captain Gilchrist, "I should have been watching where I was going."

Landowska, still with his back to the Captain, turned his head to glance over his shoulder and give a barely perceptible nod to acknowledge the apology. More noticeable was the smile he evinced in the direction of the woman who had laughed out loud at the incident. This was none other than Jenny Fewster, and it was now common knowledge, certainly amongst the *Cape Canaveral's* crew if not the entire village, that she and the skipper were, to use the modern vernacular, an item. In the eyes of the couple in question they thought of themselves as 'going out together'.

"Come on. What's the hold up?" hailed Landowska, fully aware – skipper apart – that it was the most senior member of the crew he was addressing. "It's freezing out here," he added; and as if to emphasise his comment about how cold it was, he changed hands in the sense that the hand which had been holding the suitcase he was carrying he now placed in his pocket for warmth, and the hand which he had kept enclosed in cloth for a similar reason he now used to grasp the case. The one thing that he didn't need pointing out to him was that his present situation would be improved considerably were he to wear gloves. He regretted having lost the pair that had been in his possession.

The still air chilled, and people in the open exhaled carbon dioxide like engines emitting steam. In the stillness these exhalations, like the smoke curling from two of the station's chimneys, were slow to dissipate. Nobody on the platform about to enter the waiting-room knew for certain what the temperature was, but they could tell by the vaporous clouds constantly being created by their breathing, and by the way frost persisted in the shadows as yet untouched by the sun, and by the sensation akin to pain emanating from the body's exposed extremities – and some that were not exposed – that this was the coldest day of the year so far, though the fact that the date was only two days after Epiphany meant that there would be many an opportunity for the temperature to fall further. An appealing aspect of this winter weather when high pressure was dominant was the brilliant sunshine radiating from a cloudless sky. Presently, to look in the direction of Point Pleasant was to be dazzled by sun-reflecting glass. The bright light glinted on the wings of gulls wheeling and diving out to sea. All in all, for the time of year it was a good day to begin a journey.

After being made aware of the hold-up he had caused, and conscious of the fact that he was letting cold air into the room and relatively warm air out, Walker heeded the prompt from Landowska and stepped forward in order to take a place on one of the plain wooden benches which made for more or less permanent fixtures on three of the four walls. The most prominent features on the wall devoid of seating, the wall opposite the gable end, was a coal fire and, on the chimney breast, a framed picture of George Stephenson's Rocket. The fire, as evidenced by a single tongue of flame, was burning rather pathetically.

In front of the fire was a hearth in which there was a copper scuttle half-filled with coal. Adjacent to the scuttle was a trio of utensils – a brush, a shovel, and a pair of tongs – normally referred to as a companion set. Walker took only a cursory interest in all these items, these features, and after throwing his holdall down on to the paved floor close to where he intended to place his feet, he sat down within range of the heat which would soon be radiating from the fire, or so he anticipated. One by one the others squeezed through the open doorway into the room, Captain Gilchrist bringing up the rear one step behind Jenny. Once inside the Captain firmly closed the door behind him.

For the reason that Jenny and the mariners were not waiting to meet a passenger travelling on the train from Eskmouth – the train bound for Ravensborough due to arrive in twenty minutes – it would be safe to assume that the sailors were waiting for the train in order to begin a journey. This wasn't going to be a day-return excursion to the resort farther along the coast, but rather the beginning of a journey which would take weeks and cover thousands of miles. The majority of the party in the waiting-room of Rankin Bay Station were going back home to the States.

A casual observer wouldn't have needed the deductive powers of Mr Sherlock Holmes to be able to discern who was going to be travelling and who wasn't. The absence of material possessions in the form of luggage revealed that Jenny, Captain Gilchrist, and, unfortunately, Cornelius Cotton, were, for the foreseeable future, not going far.

In keeping with company instructions Captain Gilchrist was to stay behind as planned, and it was now plain for anyone with eyes to see that this prospect was far from being anathema to him. He had, in his official role, but without wearing any insignia denoting officialdom, come to the station this bright, cold morning to say goodbye to the men who, without exception, had become his friends during the weeks that had passed since he last had a ship to command, at least one which was able to float. Upon looking back over the preceding weeks Gilchrist realised that the increased familiarity which had developed between the crew and himself had been the inevitable consequence of their changed circumstance. Surrounded, as Henley would say, by limeys on their own soil, the Yanks and their adopted Canadian had closed ranks, so to speak, and as there was no longer any need to summon the crew on deck to hoist or lower the sails, there seemed no need to maintain shipboard discipline. Cotton had managed to land himself in trouble regardless.

The unfortunate aspect of Cotton having to keep the skipper company through no choice of his own was that following the fracas in the hotel lounge a week before Christmas, Mr Draycot, perceiving and promulgating himself to have been the victim of a violent assault by the Texan, had walked to Eskmouth to make an official complaint. Given the serious nature of Cotty's allegation, the authorities in the shape of Constable Birtram arrived at a certain Rankin Bay address two days before Christmas to arrest Cotton and take him into custody. First on the doorstep to the Constable, and subsequently to the desk Sergeant and then the duty solicitor, Cotton had tried to explain that he was the innocent party in this unpleasant business, and that if there was any justice in the world, it was his accuser who ought to have been arrested. Cotton's words hadn't fallen upon deaf ears, but they might as well have done for all the good that they served that day. The problem for Cornelius was that the police, in making their enquiries, had found several witnesses prepared to make statements recounting exactly what they had seen. Not a single person had come forward to say that he or she had seen the accused being tripped prior to his fall. This made Cotty's act of sticking out his foot surreptitious indeed. The upshot of Cotton's time in police custody was that he was charged, and then, thanks to the timely arrival of Captain Gilchrist, duly released on bail. For the defendant the cheery prospect of being able to spend the Christmas holiday with his shipmates was counter-balanced less positively by a requirement for him to submit his passport. Crude by today's standards, this simple document with its mug shot stapled into place, had been the only means of identification that Cotton had had in his possession, and without it he knew that there was no guarantee of his being readmitted into the United States. It had been, therefore, with considerable reluctance that the defendant had handed this document over in exchange for a handwritten receipt which, for safe keeping, he had passed to Captain Gilchrist. From the moment that he had been informed that it would be weeks before he could expect to appear in court, Cotton sensed instinctively that he would not be returning home with the rest of the crew.

It would not have been in the least bit surprising for him to have felt despondent as he sat with his friends in the waiting-room awaiting the arrival of the train which would take the others on the first, and probably the shortest, leg of their journey, but on waking up that morning he had decided not to let his disappointment mar what overall was likely to be an optimistic mood. Despite there being moments when he couldn't help but look upon the world rather wistfully, on the whole, and to his credit, he was succeeding in maintaining a cheerful countenance. For their part, though not a word in this regard had been spoken amongst themselves Walker, Landowska, Henley and Crossman tried not to let their undoubted delight to be leaving appear too euphoric, but it was hard work. Indeed there were times when they were forgetful, and then they appeared to be unconcerned about their friend Cotton's situation. If asked the skipper would have described his own emotional state as being on even keel, but in reality he was on another plain altogether.

"Do you think that somebody will come to arrest us if we put some coal on the fire?" enquired Henley of anyone who had a mind to answer.

By this time everybody apart from Jenny was seated. Rather than follow Walker's and the others' example upon entering, she had made a beeline for the chimney-breast to study the artwork on display. The painting, which she knew to be an original watercolour, was hardly the work of a professional artist, and although it was probably of little monetary value, Jenny considered the depiction to be of historical interest. She was eager for one of the Americans, or the sole Canadian, to enquire about the significance of the 'funny' little engine which was the forerunner, not only of the train which her acquaintances from across the Atlantic would soon be boarding, but every train in the world. Perhaps it was because they already knew everything there was to know about Stephenson's Rocket that nobody showed any interest, but no comments or questions were forthcoming. Realising that artistic appreciation and the dissemination of local knowledge was at this juncture superfluous, with the intention of feeding the fire Jenny stooped to unhook the shovel from the companion-set. This action she did not complete, for the waiting-room door opened to reveal the stationmaster's smiling face. The face she recognised belonged to Tom Beresford, a trusted friend of the family's, which, in this case, meant primarily of her father. Jenny liked Tom because his face reflected his manner. In combination they revealed not only considerable experience and strength of character, but also an avuncular kindness. She always felt safe and at ease in his presence. Topped by a navy-blue cap, the stationmaster's head – neck craning around the door – had appeared first, and nonchalantly, like a seasoned campaigner who is rarely surprised by the world and its workings, he took from his mouth the pipe he was accustomed to smoking and began to speak.

"Is everything all right for you in here?" he enquired prior to catching sight of Jenny. When he did espy the lovely lass smiling back at him he said, "Hello Jenny love. I didn't expect to see you here. How are your mum and dad keeping... well I hope?"

Tom was also about to enquire about Jenny's sister and her husband, but upon noting the presence of the man whom Jenny's brother-in-law had accused of actual bodily harm, the stationmaster thought it wiser to hold his tongue, at least for the time being, on that particular matter. While waiting for an answer to any of the questions he had posed, Jenny's friend stepped into the waiting-room and closed the door behind him.

"Dad's gone and caught a cold, and that makes him grumpy," answered Jenny, "but mum's well... bearing in mind that she has to put up with Mr Grumpy. As you can see, I'm in the best of health... and spirits," she added, putting great emphasis on the last two words as she glanced at Captain Gilchrist.

Jenny proceeded to introduce the family friend to each member of the 'Cap' Canaveral's crew, leaving her special friend till last. In the event she had surprised herself for having taken such a lead, and this new-found confidence she attributed to the spiritual illumination she gained from being in Andrew's company.

"I was just about to put a little more coal on the fire," the milkmaid added once the introductions were completed.

"You'll do no such thing," responded Mr Beresford sternly, but so as not to allow the young lady's expression to be despondent for long, he made amends by saying, "I'll do that for you."

251

One or more of the sailors chuckled as the stationmaster advanced across the room. Tom gave a knowing wink to Captain Gilchrist as he passed. After picking up and then tipping forward the scuttle, thereby allowing what Beresford hoped would be a sufficient amount of coal to tumble on to the fire to keep it going rather than suffocating what little combustion there was, he straightened his back and said, "My apologies gentlemen. I seem to have been negligent in my duty this morning. I doubt you'll feel the benefit of this lot before your train arrives."

Tom was looking somewhat ruefully at the black heap where seconds before a flame had been; and as for the waiting-room's other occupants, they didn't feel that the temperature was now lower than a few moments ago, but to their eyes it certainly looked as if it was.

"Never mind… perhaps the train will be late and you will feel the benefit," said Tom with his customary smile.

He turned his back to the fireplace, and with Jenny – who had turned to face in the same direction – standing by his side, the stationmaster studied the faces and postures of the sailors seated facing inwards. Most obvious was the considerable space between each figure, and as the stationmaster was something of an amateur anthropologist – in the same way that he was an accomplished amateur in almost every field of study – he concluded that though the crew seated before him was ostensibly a fraternity, each male individual had sought to dominate his own sizeable space, his own immediate environment.

"I hear that you're leaving us this morning," said Tom, beaming down at the man sitting nearest to him, namely Walker.

"Not all of us unfortunately," Walker responded. The skipper over there and Cornelius here are staying behind… though for very different reasons."

"Ah yes," muttered Tom rather pensively, and as if to give emphasis to his thoughtfulness, he sucked on his pipe whilst at the same time gazing at some far horizon perceived only inwardly. After this pause for thought he continued, "I heard there was some trouble at the bottom house before Christmas. Don't tell me it involved one of you, did it?" the stationmaster questioned, though he knew perfectly well not only that it did, but also who the belligerents were.

The stationmaster's manner of speaking caused Walker some confusion, and consequently he transferred the focus of his attention from Mr Beresford to Jenny, encouraging her by this silent communion to translate that which was unintelligible to him.

"The Rankin Bay Hotel is known by Tom and his friends as the 'bottom house'. The Endeavour Inn is the 'middle house', and..."

Interrupted by the person she was informing, Jenny had to curtail her translation of the local vernacular as it pertained to Rankin Bay's licensed premises.

"...And the pub on the right as you go up the hill – The Jack and Jill is it? – is known as the 'top house'," said Walker, eager to let it be known that he had grasped the logic of the positional naming.

Perched nearest the door, Captain Gilchrist, thinking that the time had come for him to put the stationmaster in the picture as he perceived it, opened his mouth as if to speak, only to close it again out of deference to Jenny.

"It's not necessarily 'unfortunate' that you're not all leaving us," she said as she searched for, and found, the Captain's admiring eyes.

She was aware that she no longer blushed to behold them. Indeed, rather than embarrassment, her countenance beamed great affection.

"I'm sure that's true of the skipper," interjected Cotton, "but I know what I'd rather be doing in half an hour's time, and that's sitting in a railroad car with my buddies here rather than going back to the village with you and the Captain, and you know I don't mean any offence by that. After all, it's true what they say Miss: two's company and three's a crowd."

"I take it that you're the man the police arrested?" enquired the stationmaster, again, and without doubt because of a glaringly obvious physical characteristic, knowing full well that it was.

"That I am," admitted Cotton without hesitation, "but I assure you sir... though I regret losing my temper that Saturday night... I assure you that I am not to blame for starting the violence.

The look he gave the stationmaster, whose appearance, if it were not for the pipe he now held, resembled that of a defence lawyer standing before him, was the epitome of sincerity, and therefore, in this instance, innocence.

Tom made no further comment on this specific matter, but chose instead to approach the same general topic from a different tangent.

"I also hear that your ship was plundered of some of its precious cargo," he said knowingly, yet inviting confirmation that he had not been misinformed.

"It might not have been so precious... but it was certainly worth making the trip around the coast from Bristol," Captain Gilchrist said at last, "and certainly, if you can throw any light upon the theft I would be much obliged," he added.

Before responding Tom withdrew the pipe from his mouth and proceeded to search his trouser pockets for a box of matches, an item which he found at the second attempt. It was as if he was deliberately keeping his audience in suspense as he first took the time to reignite the tobacco. Consequently, after two or three strong inhalations on the pipe now returned to the orifice for which it was designed, his head became partially hidden in a cloud of smoke. This noxious effusion was disdainful to Jenny, prompting her to leave Tom's side and walk across the room to sit down next to Andrew. The Captain reached out to hold her hand prior to leaning forward to look across her. He was all ears, so to speak, for what the stationmaster had to say.

"Well," began Mr Beresford once the smoke had cleared, "let's just say that a little bird told me that a certain individual from these parts… the man you hit," he informed as he narrowed his eyes to focus once again upon Cotton, "has built himself a new shed up by Fisherhead.

"That's an area by the side of the track leading up from Bridge End," informed Jenny. "That's where most of the fishermen's huts are… quite ramshackle some of them."

"Well Jenny my dear," Tom responded, "one or two of them are not as ramshackle as they once were. I would go so far as to say that Cotty's… that's the nickname," he interposed whilst making a gesture towards the Texan, "of the man you thumped… I would go so far as to say that Cotty's shed is quite palatial, relatively speaking that is. Now it seems to me Jenny my dear… and you know that I'm not the kind of man who goes looking for trouble… quite the opposite in fact… and nor do I want to create trouble for anyone else either… least of all your sister's husband… though I do think that Henry should take him aside for a quiet word… but it seems to me that if Cotty's insistent on pressing these charges, you Captain may want to go up to Fisherhead and have a look around... you know... make a few enquiries as to where they got the wood to build those new sheds of theirs."

In the belief that he had spoken in accordance with his own concept of natural justice, and with sufficient understanding and diplomacy for him to be optimistic that there would be a satisfactory conclusion to this business. Tom beamed across at Jenny's astonished face and said, "I believe that Cotty has painted his shed Bay brown."

This rather unnatural colour had become prevalent throughout the village ever since a ship carrying a consignment of paint had run aground the previous winter. It was the colour of the saddle on the rocking-horse which Jenny had been given as a child, and which was still in her possession at home. It was, therefore, Dudley's image which flashed into mind whenever she heard 'Bay brown' mentioned.

"I thank you for providing me with this intelligence sir, and I promise you that Mr Cotton and I will be paying this man... Cotty you say his name is... a visit at Fisherhead. I'm sure Jenny will be more than happy to show us exactly where we'll find our quarry."

Made suddenly aware that she was being asked implicitly to act as a guide on a path which could conceivably land her brother-in-law in prison, Jenny was far from sure that she was happy to do Andrew's bidding, but, somewhat meekly, she nodded her willingness to comply.

For his part Cotton was delighted to have been given the opportunity to be proactive in respect of his future, rather than having to be more or less passive until the time came for him to appear in court. Moreover, the course of action which he envisaged the skipper and he would take necessarily meant that they were still in this together. This sense of camaraderie was of great comfort to the Texan, for hitherto he had imagined having to spend the foreseeable future in limbo, a state – one perhaps not unfamiliar to an American citizen – of 'splendid isolation'. Now he would no longer have to kick his heels, so to speak, whilst the skipper enjoyed intimate hours – intimate in an emotional sense – in Jenny's company. Nobody present was insensitive to the fact that the ambiance in the room had lightened considerably.

"Well… unless my practised ears are mistaken gentlemen… and that would be a first I assure you… that's your train I hear approaching," informed the stationmaster.

For a few moments, like members of an orchestra responding to the conductor's baton when he or she calls for hush at the beginning of a performance, the prospective passengers, and those bidding them adieu, stopped all movement. Unlike musicians, however, who then wait upon a silent signal to sound the right notes, the people in question listened intently for the train's mechanical rhythm. Once heard there soon followed a general kerfuffle as the sailors picked up their belongings and filed through the door on to the platform. Mr Beresford brought up the rear. No sooner was the waiting-room completely vacated when, accompanied by a hissing of steam, the engine in the green and gold livery of the Eskmouth and Ravensborough Railway Company, with four carriages in tow, drew alongside the platform. For many, particularly those waiting to board, it was a magnificent sight.

Chapter Nineteen

A Meeting of Minds

The confrontation – anticipated on one side, unexpected on the other – between Cotty and Rankin Bay's two remaining American guests took place two days after the parting of the ways signalled by steamy effusions and many jocular valedictions shouted back and forth between the train slowly picking up speed and the station platform. Prior to their setting out for the as yet – to American eyes – the undiscovered part of the village known as Fisherhead, Jenny had pleaded with Andrew to let her accompany him and Cotton on what ostensibly was a fact-finding mission. She was of the opinion that if her brother-in-law was where they hoped to find him, and indeed where he might be expected to be at that time of day – mid-afternoon – then her presence could be of use: of use to which side she didn't say. It was a working day, and as well as having been up well before dawn that morning to go to the farm, she had gone to bed much later than usual the night before. The effects – undoubtedly detrimental – of having had less sleep than she deserved showed on her face. She looked tired. Her manner was fraught.

Ensconced once again in the hotel lounge deserted but for the three people in discussion, an old man at the bar whiling away his time, and the buxom Rita, if Jenny was aware of the irritability her demeanour projected, she chose not to let it detract from her purpose, and argued that because neither of the visitors knew her brother-in-law's mind as well as she did, it would be unwise not to take her with them. She also expressed her belief that, generally speaking, women bring a pacifying influence to bear on situations involving men that, at the mercy often of a volatile combination of testosterone and overweening pride, are likely to be at loggerheads.

In respect of the points put forward by Jenny, on this occasion Captain Gilchrist could not have disagreed more, and unequivocally expressed the opinion that Jenny's presence at the meeting – were it to take place as anticipated – would likely do more harm than good. The Captain didn't actually say that this was man's business, but that's what he thought, and he thought it Company business to boot. Taking into consideration the fact that the young woman with whom he was besotted to the point of being in love was looking far from radiant, and appeared disturbingly fractious, added to his conviction that the decision he had made not to let her come along was right. His final word on the subject was a resounding, "No".

The single word, declaimed so emphatically, aroused Jenny's anger. Her initial reaction was to call Andrew's bluff by stating that this is a free country and that she would go wherever she chose whenever she chose provided she didn't trespass, and that no chauvinistic bully – a foreigner at that – was going to stop her. Subsequently, however, and without explanation, she changed her mind, and exhibiting a sequence of gestures which clearly evinced her resentment, with an unnecessarily loud clatter which caused the formerly unconcerned to look her way, she vacated her chair. Before departing the company of the two men staring sheepishly, though nonetheless resolutely, up at her, she turned to Cornelius and said that she hoped he would get what was coming to him.

This parting comment left Cotton somewhat confused, and for several moments he pondered the logic of what had been said to him. He decided against trying to regain Jenny's attention as she stormed towards the door, and thought it safe to speak freely only when the firebrand filly was out of earshot.

Captain Gilchrist had just seen a side of Jenny which he had not encountered previously, and though some of the things she had said whilst in high dudgeon had cut him to the quick, prompting him to think that there would be difficulties to overcome if their relationship was going to be permanent for being happy, the cause of Jenny's outburst he ascribed to a combination of fatigue and worry. Nonetheless, he realised that there was a demon in her soul which liked to have its own way; and because he also realised that the same demon exists to a greater or lesser extent in everyone who is not a saint, the difference of opinion which ostensibly had been their first quarrel didn't affect his love for Jenny in the slightest.

In weather similar to that which had prevailed at the leave-taking two days earlier, though at this time of day the sun was hidden from view to every denizen of Rankin Bay save for those individuals that chanced to peer through the topmost windows of the tallest buildings, the Americans set out on their quest, their aim being to walk along New Road towards Bridge End and then on to Fisherhead.

Before they had gone a few yards Captain Gilchrist left Cotton's side and ambled over to the receptacle for charitable donations resembling a cod. At the top of the slipway, whilst searching in his trouser pocket for a suitable coin, he couldn't help but observe the sea creeping up towards him and then receding. This calm refrain was strangely reassuring in the sense that it seemed to echo the rhythmic pattern of aeons, and therein was a message which informed the onlooker that whatever task he was about this day; it would matter little, for small and inconsequential is the individual human being compared to the boundless seas and oceans. The remarkable consequence of this wordless communication was that the Captain became suffused in a spirit which in its quiet calm was dauntless, and although only a few moments ago this aspect of personality had not been totally lacking, it wasn't as much in evidence then as now. It was as if the sea's ceaseless motion had transferred some of its formidable strength, its power. From amid a handful of coins the Captain selected a shilling, and this he placed in the fish's mouth.

Upon returning to his subordinate's side, he slapped Cotton on the back and said, "Come on bud… let's go and find out what the rats have been doing while we've been getting some shut-eye."

From that moment Cotton, who had stopped in his tracks when the Captain, without saying a word, had suddenly wandered off in the wrong direction, knew that they would win the day, even if the forthcoming confrontation were to become an Anglo version of the gunfight at the OK Corral, that is to say a fight without six shooters.

The two men on a mission gained the rough track leading up and inland from Bridge End in a matter of minutes. Parked, as it were, on the left-hand side of this track were three boats, one of which – the largest – was the cobble *Louise*. The keels of two boats – Cotty's cobble included – rested on wheeled bogeys, whereas the third boat in line, the boat farthest up the slope and away from the bridge – the smallest of the three – had been left high and dry, and looked as if it hadn't been near water for some considerable time. The hull of this boat, and therefore its superstructure – it was the only vessel in sight to possess a wheelhouse – tilted to starboard at an angle of approximately thirty degrees from the perpendicular. On the grassy bank to the right of the path more or less opposite the line of boats, Dobbin appeared to be enjoying his semi-retirement. Grazing without a care in the world, he could hardly be bothered to raise his head in acknowledgement of the human presence.

The cabins the two men were looking for, that miniscule part of the world known as Fisherhead, occupied directly ahead an area of level ground to the left of the track, whilst to the right an old but still serviceable tractor was parked in front of a stack of lobster-pots. These were supported by an otherwise seemingly purposeless dry stone wall. The wall had given way in places, and a number of discarded stones were lying on the ground. There was nobody in sight as first Cotton, and then the Captain, turned from conducting a visual survey of the village from what to them was a different viewpoint. The perspective may have been new, but the columns struggling to rise from the cottage chimneys in the still air were only too familiar, as was the not unpleasant odour of wood smoke. Intelligence that Fisherhead was not completely deserted was provided at this point by the unmistakeable sound of a person sawing wood. The sawing stopped, and there followed the equally unmistakeable sound of someone using a hammer. The Americans, putting their backs into the hill in their determination to attain their goal, looked at each other questioningly, and the question silently asked was, "Is this the moment of truth?"

The first sign of life to appear in the vicinity of the sheds stepped into view just as the Americans drew level with the tractor and the first dilapidated excuse for a cabin, one which obviously wasn't of recent construction, and, what's more, wasn't painted the right colour. The figure who had stepped into view and then, upon noting the approach of the two men, had disappeared from view just as quickly, was a boy. He was wearing a navy-blue duffle coat with the hood up, a covering which made it nigh on impossible for anyone, at the distance the Captain and Cotton were, to identify the youngster, except perhaps for the mother who had dressed him that morning for school. After a few moments had passed, during which time the Captain and Cotton were able to dismiss the first half-dozen or so sheds from their enquiry, and at the same time identify a couple of pristine, and therefore likely, culprits ahead, the boy reappeared from the gap – no more than a foot wide – separating the penultimate and the last fisherman's cabin that formed the community at Fisherhead. This time the boy's hood was down, enabling Captain Gilchrist to identify him as being one of the same urchins who had solicited him for money for the benefit of Guy Fawkes all those weeks past. In the belief that it was the twin who had scuffed his knee, Captain Gilchrist said, "Hello young man. How's your leg?"

For all the effect this question had upon the lad's demeanour, the Captain might just as well have been speaking Greek. The boy's blank expression prompted the speaker to elucidate.

"The last time we were in conversation your knee was bleeding... unless, that is, I've mistaken you for your brother."

The boy didn't have a chance to reply before, emerging from the same gap as the whippersnapper had done, Cotty appeared. The fact that his fist was clenched around the end of a weighty claw-hammer gave a persuasive quality to his already stern countenance.

"Oh! It's you," the fisherman said dismissively.

"I'm afraid so," responded Captain Gilchrist rather disingenuously for the fact that he wasn't in the least bit afraid.

Cotty couldn't help but notice that the Texan was keeping a wary eye on the hammer, the tool which just happened to be in his hand, and which, for the present, he was holding innocently. When, however, the fisherman recognised that the implement was perhaps being perceived as a dangerous weapon, the malicious demon in him proceeded to contract and extend certain muscles alternately, the result being that the palm of his left hand was hit repeatedly with the head of the hammer, specifically the face normally used for driving nails into wood. There could be no doubt that the gesture was meant to instil fear – if there was none there already – into the hearts of the men confronting him. Even so, the fisherman had no intention of wielding the hammer as a weapon, and eventually, having hit his left palm six or seven times, he spoke to allay any fears his gestures might have created.

"You needn't worry about this," he said, directing his words primarily at Cotton after first glancing down at the gently repetitive impact of metal upon the flesh said by some – in respect of the lines therein – to indicate the future, "the next time we do battle it'll be in court."

Assuming that he had met the Americans by chance, and convinced that for the present he had nothing more to say on the matter, Cotty was about to turn away to return to the task he had been about at the back of the shed, but was detained from so doing by Captain Gilchrist's arresting words.

"It's about that that we've come to talk to you," said the Captain, raising his voice slightly, not in anger, but to emphasise the fact that Cotton and he had come to Fisherhead for a reason, and that they were not going to be fobbed off that easily.

There followed at this time a contribution to the conversation which, though unexpected, was of greater significance than anything which had been said thus far, to the extent that it determined the future of everyone present. Spoken by the boy, the gist of his words brought a smile to American faces, and caused the Englishman to blush, first with embarrassment, and then with anger.

"You're the Captain of the ship that was going to be blown up by the soldiers aren't you…" enquired the boy, more out of a desire not to be left out of the proceedings than to be informed about that which he already knew, "…where Cotty got the wood to build his new shed?"

If Cotty had been a vampire the boy's revelation, uttered as if it was of no consequence whatsoever, would have been the stake that the vampire-slayer had driven into his heart.

"That's another thing we've come to talk to you about," said Captain Gilchrist authoritatively, and then to the boy he said, "I am indeed, and I thank you young man."

The delight beaming up from the boy's upturned face, delight at his contribution – in certain quarters – having been appreciated, was soon dispelled, however, when Mr Draycot spoke.

"If you don't sod off home, I'll hit you over the head with this," he said, raising the hammer above his head as if he was about to commit the horrendous crime.

The fisherman's actions and demeanour were too theatrical for the threat to be taken seriously, so neither sailor stepped forward to intervene as the boy's protector. For the time being the vampire-slayer stood his ground; but as brave as he was, the lad who now realised that he had well and truly put his foot in it – as is frequently said in this part of the world – instinctively raised his arm to protect his head, just in case. Not wishing to take his threatening gesture to any regrettable extreme, Cotty gently lowered the hammer so that the wooden shaft came to rest once more against his thigh, the steel head against the side of his knee.

"I'm sorry Cotty," the boy whimpered apologetically, "I know Cull said that I shouldn't say anything to anyone about you collecting the wood, but the words just came out of my mouth… I didn't think about what I was saying. I hope I haven't got you into trouble. I haven't have I… got you into trouble I mean?" the youngster questioned meekly.

For several moments Cotty was in a quandary as to what to say or do, and for their part the Yanks simply stood by watching and waiting for the next development in a sequence unfolding to their advantage without any input from them. Indeed, independently of each other they perceived that for either to intervene presently could just as easily be detrimental to their cause as beneficial.

Not yet having fully come to terms with the situation in which he now found himself, there was as yet considerable consternation in Cotty's voice when he said to the boy, "Listen son, you couldn't have dropped me deeper in it if you had tried. I have a good mind to…" At this point the tough fisherman noted that the lad whom he knew had lost his father in the war was on the verge of tears, and consequently the adult softened his tone. "Go home son. Go home before that empty head of yours gets me into more trouble."

In search of moral support the boy looked first at Cotton and then at Captain Gilchrist. The latter nodded to indicate that he should do what Cotton had said. Fed up with adults and their scheming, the lad responded by pulling up his duffle-coat hood prior to setting off to steer a path between the sailors as he headed towards Bridge End. Sulking in the way that only small boys can, he kept his eyes lowered to the ground. Meanwhile the Americans, having stepped aside on either side to let the boy through, showed their appreciation and respect by standing to attention and giving a formal salute.

"And when you see that brother of yours, tell him that if I catch him trying to break into my shed again I'll…" said Cotty, struggling to bring to mind a suitably terrible punishment: he succeeded only after stammering hesitantly. "… I'll… I'll have his guts for fishing line."

"That was me," the identical twin responded, his admission of guilt resounding with defiance as he turned to face the three men for the last time before breaking into a run. His former sulky expression had given way to a mischievous grin.

"What that lad needs is some discipline," said Cotty, "because the way he's heading he'll come to no good."

"And who is going to provide it Mr Draycot?" enquired Captain Gilchrist, astonished that the fisherman should be lacking in self-awareness to the extent that he failed to see the hypocrisy inherent in the comment he (Cotty) had made.

The fisherman was not so witless, however, that he was blind to the significance of Captain Gilchrist's question, and consequently, projecting a snide, irritating grin, he said, "I suppose you think that I'm the last person in the world to be making such a comment, seeing as how my friends and I salvaged a small amount of wood from your ship."

"Not salvaged… stole," corrected Cornelius emphatically.

In response to the fisherman's searching look Captain Gilchrist simply nodded to confirm that he agreed unreservedly with his friend's choice of word.

"And as for the amount you took being small, well it was certainly enough for you to be able to build a new shed… and not just yours by the looks of it," Cornelius added.

Once again Cotty smirked as he turned to inspect his pride and joy, running his fingers lightly over the paintwork prior to blurting, "It's a fair cop gentlemen… the question is, what do you propose to do about it. You don't expect me to take this thing down do you?"

"That's exactly what we expect you to do," replied the Captain, seizing the moment to assert his authority. "And what's more," he continued, "first thing in the morning we intend to report this matter to the police. After all, why shouldn't we now that we have a reliable witness?"

The Captain turned to look for the boy, but he was nowhere in sight. Nonetheless, the action of seeking left Cotty in no doubt as to the solidity of the case against him. Following his most recent pronouncement the speaker paused to let the full force of his words hit home. Then, softening the tone of his voice in an attempt to gain the desired response, the Captain offered the fisherman the chance to get off the hook on which he had been well and truly caught.

"Unless, that is, you drop the charges you brought against Mr Cotton here."

This time it was the fisherman's turn to be surprised, for he had not anticipated that such an offer would be on the table, so to speak.

"Charges which shouldn't have been brought in the first place," interjected Cotton forcefully, "seeing as how you deliberately tripped me."

On the basis that negotiations were at a sensitive stage, and that the outcome, therefore, was in the balance, the Captain signalled to Cotton to be quiet before he continued. "Well Mr Draycot, what do you say?" Are we going to have a *quid pro quo* in respect of the charges, and I mean those that have been made as well as those we shall make if we fail to reach an agreement. Is commonsense going to prevail so that they're dropped all round?"

Neither Mr Cotton nor Mr Draycot was familiar with the Latin phrase used by Captain Gilchrist, but they had a good idea as to its gist, and there seemed to be no good reason on either side not to abide by what had sounded like its ineluctable logic.

"And I can keep the shed?" questioned Cotty of the Captain.

"It's a fine shed," replied the American. "It would be a pity to have to knock it down; and besides, the timber would no longer be of any use as a marketable commodity now that it's painted in such an unattractive colour.

"People round these parts are not going to turn their noses up at what the tide washes ashore if it can be of use to them," Cotty responded, "whether it's tins of paint or wood."

"The wood from our ship wasn't exactly jetsam," remarked Cotton.

"You went out in a boat at night and…"

Cotty didn't allow the Texan to finish, but overruled him by saying, "Your entire ship was washed ashore… a careless thing to let happen if you ask me."

"No one is asking you," interjected Captain Gilchrist, sharply for the fact that he sensed that his authority was possibly on the point of waning, and he would rather it didn't. "Well Mr Draycot, do we have an agreement that you will drop all charges against Mr Cotton here, and in return we'll say no more about the wood?"

"We do indeed," replied the fisherman, and much relieved he held out his hand for the Captain to grasp.

Chapter Twenty

A Tragedy Occurs

It had been with some reluctance that Captain Gilchrist had shaken Mr Draycot's hand that day, but he had thought it the right thing to do to cement the deal he had just arranged between the former antagonists. The thought had flashed through the Captain's mind that it would have been improper to have done otherwise, and being perfunctory, there had certainly been no warmth in the tactility.

Cotton was of a different opinion, for he had not felt it incumbent upon him to follow his Captain's lead, and his response upon seeing Draycot's hand subsequently extended in his direction, had been to keep his own hand down by his side. Evidently Mr Cotton had not been prepared to be reconciled with Mr Draycot so easily, and indeed, had been irked when the fisherman, for whatever motive, had treated him – as Cotton perceived it – contemptuously when he had said, in the same instant that he had thrust out his hand, "No hard feelings Cornelius."

Three days after the agreement solemnized by his handshake with Captain Gilchrist, Cotty had travelled into Eskmouth to do as he had promised, a task which he had undertaken with some trepidation, and rightly so, for he had to demonstrate considerable resilience in explaining his reasons for not proceeding with the case against Cotton. If he hadn't realised it beforehand, Cotty was left in no doubt that policemen take strong exception to timewasters, and was even threatened with being brought to account for that reason. In his bid to escape the police station it had been made absolutely clear to him that he would be charged if he ever 'tried it on with them again'.

In the days and weeks that followed Cotty's return from Eskmouth the relationship between the American sailors and the man who had been their bane mellowed considerably. From its frosty inception at Fisherhead – when all hostilities ceased – to the beginning of the year's shortest month when Cotty made the invitation he would live to regret, the process of reconciliation progressed through several phases, almost, therefore not quite, imperceptibly. In this regard what can be stated unequivocally is that from one extreme of the pendulum's swing to the other mutual mistrust and disdain gradually transmogrified into their opposites, and ultimately the ties of friendship which developed appeared to be stronger than one would normally expect over such a short period of time, and perhaps for the very reason that turbulence and enmity had been transformed. In practise an interested party, or the Irish writer say, could have most easily observed the outward manifestations of this bond developing more often in the lounge of the Rankin Bay Hotel, but not exclusively so, for our protagonists also visited the bar of the Endeavour Inn. Initially, whenever the two men chanced to meet in these public places – and I refer specifically to Mr Cotton and Mr Draycot – they said not a word, but rather greeted each other with a tentative nod of the head, this accompanied on each side by a stony face. It was at the third meeting in such circumstances that the ridiculousness of their silent rituals caused the stony expressions to crack, and naturally what ensued were grins, first on one face – the darker of the two – and then on the other. Subsequently, perhaps mindful of his recent transgression in this regard, Cotty asked the Texan if he would object to his calling him by his Christian name. Cornelius replied that he had no objection whatsoever, provided that he – Cotty – didn't mind being called by his sobriquet. Following this early blossoming, on a different evening Cotty offered to buy his new friends a drink. This offer was accepted and then reciprocated. A pattern of sociability was established and there followed, often with the three men seated at a table, but occasionally also in the company of others, Cull included, the telling of yarns about the sea and voyages to distant lands, or alternatively, stories of the giant cod – or was it a shark that got away? These tales were invariably accompanied by loud guffaws, and there was much backslapping. More often than not the rivalry between the Brits and Yanks was forgotten altogether, though there was the odd occasion when it manifested itself, albeit now never so caustically as to upset either set of sensibilities. After heeding advice which the skipper had given Cotton in private, the crewman never again mentioned his support for the rebel cause in Iraq. He wondered why he had ever done so in the first place.

Eager to foster and then, as it were, cement friendly international relations, Captain Gilchrist was not averse to whiling away an hour or two in Cotty's and Cotton's company, though not surprisingly he chose to spend the preponderance of his free time – time which he was able to determine – with Jenny. On occasion Jenny and her sister Sally joined the boisterous boys gathered around the seafarers' table, but their presence – either singly or as a family pair – was the exception rather than the rule. This was because the women in question – being the imaginative creatures they undoubtedly were – were in no doubt that their conspicuousness had a marked effect upon the men's behaviour and conversation. They sensed that the ambiance they helped to create was more genteel than it otherwise would have been. Consequently, like ladies that leave the gentlemen to their port and cigars after dinner, the Draycot sisters knew when to make an exit, leaving the fishermen and sailors to continue with their masculine banter over warm beer in an unhealthy fug. It was just possible that the two people most relieved in learning that the Yanks and Brits had become good friends were Jenny and Sally, and for obvious reasons. The last thing they wanted was for there to be a family feud.

Once the sword of Damocles in the form of a prospective court appearance had been removed, and there was no longer any chance that either party would be sent to prison for his alleged act of criminality, there was no practical reason why Cotton should stay in England other than to keep his skipper company. Both men knew that sooner or later one of them – Cotton – would have to go, but neither pressed the issue to make the departure happen; not the crewman *vis-a-vis* the skipper; and not the skipper *vis-a-vis* the ship's co-owners. If the truth be known Cornelius and the buxom barmaid were 'seeing' each other, but as yet rather secretly, so that not even Captain Gilchrist was aware of the real reason why the man who until recently would have jumped at the chance of a passage home was now inclined to tarry. The instructions were for both men to stand by, for the present and foreseeable future. It was apparent to Captain Gilchrist that his colleagues back home were in a quandary as to what to do with the *Cape Canaveral.* Meanwhile, bearing in mind that over three months had passed since the ship had grounded, the schooner remained stuck fast to be pounded intermittently by high seas and wintry weather.

More than once the thought had crossed the Captain's mind that Cotton and he were in danger of losing their sea legs and becoming soft by being so long ashore with so little to do, and because he couldn't be with Jenny morning, noon and night, he didn't need to be asked twice when the invitation was put to him. If only that invitation had been to take a trip on a charabanc to the races at Beverley, or, if an excursion of greater cultural depth was preferred, a visit to the Minster in York, a city in which it would be possible, if a little light relief were required for balance, to do a little shopping in shops the like of which were not to be found in either Eskmouth or Ravensborough. Equally, a day return on the train to Ravensboroough would certainly have provided for a relatively safe break in the sailors' daily routine, safe that is compared to the offer which Cotty made and the Captain and Cotton – the latter of his own free will – duly accepted. The proposal, made after two or three pints of beer had been quaffed, was for the Americans to accompany Cotty on one of his fishing expeditions in the *Louise*, a dangerous business for the uninitiated to become involved in at any time, but particularly so in winter. No doubt the Yanks wouldn't have hesitated regardless, but seeing as how the fisherman had couched the invitation in such a way as to invoke feelings of national pride, they couldn't possibly refuse. The owner of the *Louise* also chided the Americans by saying that they only dare put to sea in vessels half the length of a football pitch, this notwithstanding the fact that he had no idea as to the sailors' experience of small boats. They could, like Captain Bligh and his loyal crew cast adrift in the Pacific Ocean by *HMS Bounty's* mutineers, have been in similarly dire straits for weeks on end for all he knew. No such exploit had cropped up in conversation. When all was said and done on the matter, the upshot was that the Anglo-American trio would rendezvous at Fisherhead as soon as the morrow. They were to meet at six am. By being one of the crowd when the invitation was made and accepted, Cull the bellman would also be one of the crew, as would one of the lads, namely Dan.

This early in February the weather on the Yorkshire coast was never going to be warm and balmy, but unfortunately for accomplished fishermen and novices alike, the climatic conditions which greeted Cotty and the others as they left their respective dwellings were particularly daunting. Under normal circumstances even a fisherman of Cotty's experience would have questioned the wisdom of putting out to sea in such weather, but the problem, and sometimes danger, of playing the card imprinted with a symbol denoting the vice or virtue that is national pride is that its effects are likely to be reciprocal. For the sake of the card he had played, as it were, this was certainly one occasion when the Briton wasn't going to be deterred.

The makeshift crew which the *Louise's* skipper had put together was only too willing to spring into action when Cotty manoeuvred the tractor, onto which the bogey supporting the boat was to be hooked, into position. Despite the debilitating effects of the cold, the first coordinated action of the day was successful at the first attempt without mishap. Subsequently, at the behest of the lad who had recently grown accustomed to being called Dan the Man, Cull and the Americans clambered aboard.

Dan the Man wasn't in the best of moods, and for good reason. He too was old enough and wise enough to realise that it was verging on foolishness to put to sea in such hazardous conditions, particularly with an inexperienced crew. His own powers of persuasion as yet not fully developed, he also regretted having succumbed to Cotty's emotional blackmail, for his boss had told him that because their nocturnal escapades aboard the *Cape Canaveral* were no longer a secret known only to the four people directly involved, if it wasn't for him (Cotty), he (Dan) would have been arrested by now and so could have been looking forward to appearing in court, where, in all probability, he would have been found guilty and given a hefty sentence. Consequently, therefore, he (Dan) owed him (Cotty) a favour. Dan resented the fact that he had allowed himself to be duped.

Nonetheless, having informed his parents the night before that he was getting up early to look for crabs among the rocks, Dan the Man clambered aboard the tractor to seat himself on the wheel arch. He felt the cold through the seat of his yellow oilskin trousers, and because at that moment his mother's words of warning about how sitting on cold surfaces would lead to piles – an ailment he knew nothing about from personal experience, a status quo he was happy with – he raised his body a couple of inches to place one gloved hand under his bottom. Mindful of the giant wheel directly beneath him, with the other he held on to the back of the tractor seat for all he was worth.

Holding on was what Cull should have done more firmly, for the forward momentum of the tractor when Cotty first pressed down with his foot on the accelerator pedal was transferred to trailer and boat with a jolt, the sudden lurch forward being instrumental in the three passengers losing their balance, none so dramatically as Cull, for he fell to the deck with a thud. The younger, stronger men, having stayed on their feet, were soon on hand to help the old timer to his. The experience left Cull dazed for a while, but as soon as his head was clear of fuzziness – as clear as it was ever going to be – the thoughts which came into being therein caused him to question his participation in the morning's work, so much so in fact that as the tractor, trailer, and crew trundled down the track from Fisherhead, he considered the pros and cons of handing in his notice, notice which in this instance would be a matter of minutes, half an hour at most. The thoughts which occupied Cull's mind as Cotty weaved round the largest pot-holes were that the others – and it didn't really matter who the others were – only let him come along to make up the numbers, and that they probably considered his presence to be more of a hindrance than a help. Not for the first time in his long career Cull saw himself through the eyes of others. Generally speaking this is an accomplishment rarely aspired to therefore rarely achieved; but Cull never failed in this exigency, whenever it suited him that is.

By turning right at the seaward side of the bridge, the tractor and its short-haul travellers met the wind head-on, and though the power of nature's invisible force was enhanced for being funnelled by the rows of cottages built into the gorge which dictated the layout of the village, it didn't augur well for the immediate future. Not only was the wind strong, it was cold, and the wind-chill effectively reduced the temperature by five degrees, if not on thermometers, then certainly upon the flesh it gnawed.

By the time the fishermen had travelled halfway along New Road, Cull had convinced himself that he would only get in the way of things in the limited space the *Louise* provided, and that he would inform Cotty of his decision at the earliest opportunity. After all, at his venerable age he didn't need to be macho, and the drumbeat of national pride was not the stirring factor it once had been. Indeed, he had decided long ago that it would be preferable to die at home in bed than be washed out to sea perhaps never to be seen again, a fate which he was sure had befallen old John. The excuse he would give was that he was still dazed after banging his head. Moreover, he had paraffin to deliver, and he thought he would begin his round earlier than usual.

For their part the Americans were not immune from harbouring feelings of reticence generated by concerns about safety. Between them their knowledge and experience of the sea was considerable, but as their current mentor and leader had correctly surmised and intimated, their affinity with small boats was negligible. More than once the deep-sea sailors sought the gateway to each other's soul in the darkness that soon would begin to lighten, and what each man searched for was his comrade's reassurance that all would be well. In these moments of uncertainty, as they inwardly questioned their sanity, the man from New Hampshire and the man from Texas hadn't previously felt the bond between them to be as strong as it now was, so that differences in rank and status seemed of little consequence; yet at the same time both were intuitively aware that once they were back aboard a vessel not in the control of a 'crazy' Englishman, a vessel many times bigger than the boat the size of a bath-tub they were about to launch, then the old distinctions would return, and it could not be otherwise.

For the present, however, and within sight of the sea's white horses emerging from the inky darkness, the Captain, holding on to the hood of his rainproof jacket, turned to the Texan and shouted, "This is another fine mess you've got me into Cornelius."

It's stating the obvious to point out that the seemingly enhanced whiteness of a black person's smile is engendered by the contrast between teeth and facial skin tone, but on this occasion in particular, hard upon following his comment, Captain Gilchrist was sure that Cotton's smile was whiter and broader than he had ever seen previously.

Perhaps, the Captain considered, the surrounding darkness also provided for a greater contrast.

"What's that you say?" shouted Cotty from the tractor's seat, looking over his shoulder as he steered into The Dock.

Thinking that the task of trying to speak above the noise of the wind and sea combined was not worth the effort, Captain Gilchrist signalled with his hand that he had said nothing of importance. Cotty, attending once more to the task in hand, turned the tractor, in as wide an arc as possible in the relatively small space available, round to the left. For a few moments the vehicle appeared to be heading up the hill that is King Street, away from the sea. Nobody, however, was under any illusion that Cotty had given up on the idea of going fishing this morning, and likewise everybody concerned knew that he was simply manoeuvring in order to be able to reverse down the slipway into the sea. Here, in what is the largest public space in the village, light was provided by a solitary gas lamp situated at the foot of a flight of steps which lead up to a promenade known locally as the "quarterdeck". There was no activity in or around the three boats laid up in front of the hotel, and that was significant.

Slowly, carefully, Cotty reversed the tractor towards the slipway, and needless to say it was now pushing rather than pulling the *Louise*. At the first attempt the driver, who was fully alert and in control of his faculties, failed for the fact that the trailer, boat and crew slewed sharply to the right: the whole caboodle jackknifed. The bows of the *Louise* almost came into contact with a fish sooner than expected, a fish made of metal. Indeed, only inches separated the boat and the cod whose mouth is permanently open for charitable donations when Cotty applied the brakes.

At this point, and without a thought for the people sleeping in the nearby cottages, at the top of his voice Cull said, "Stop!" The command was given not to prevent Cotty from causing the destruction of a Rankin Bay landmark, but rather to deter him from moving off again before Cull had done what he was intending to do. His intention was to get out of the boat, and seeing that Cotty was now watching his every move, this he did with consummate effort if not skill, as, with less obvious difficulty, did the

Americans. Dan took this opportunity to jump down from his perch and proceeded to join the others now waiting at the top of the slipway.

Upon joining the little coterie initially he made no comment, but merely leaned on the fence that exists to prevent people from falling no small height into the stream-channelling, concrete gully below. He looked out to sea and noted that above the eastern horizon the sky had lightened considerably, and the pattern revealed, though predominantly shades of grey, included red and pink striations. He also noted that the waves emerging from the gloom and rushing towards the shore in quick succession were not as high, and therefore not as intimidating, as he had anticipated, and what's more, they were petering out before they reached the slipway. To the uninitiated observer this could just as easily have indicated that the tide was on the ebb as flowing in, but Dan knew for certain that it would be high tide within the hour.

The young man turned to the others and said, "It looks a little scary here, but we should be all right once we've cleared the scaurs. The conditions are ideal for cod. What do you think Cull?"

"What I think is that when you bring to mind the sea conditions in which your man over there could have put out in and didn't, that he's off his rocker to put out today."

Cull directed his words towards the questioner, but he spoke them loudly enough for the Americans to hear.

"Anyway," Cull added, "what you get up to today is no longer any concern of mine, for I'll not be going with you."

"Does Cotty know?" enquired Dan, and though the answer to his question would have been simple enough either way, he failed to hear, or see in the shape formed by the bellman's lips, Cull's reply.

For whatever reason – perhaps it was to encourage his crew not to stand idly by, but rather make their way down to the sea in readiness to launch the boat – Cotty had chosen that moment to rev the engine, just as Cull had been about to speak. Subsequently, by applying less pressure on the pedal, less noisily Cotty inched his way down the slipway, preceded, of course, by the *Louise*. Led by Dan, the others followed behind the reversing tractor, and it wasn't long before the water was lapping over their wellington boots. After he had driven into the sea as far as it was practically safe to go, his mind now set on freeing his boat, without cutting the engine Cotty clambered down into the surf. He was momentarily detained from completing the task he had in mind by the weight of a hand on his shoulder. The hand belonged to Dan.

Dan, placing his mouth barely six inches from Cotty's left ear, shouted, "Cull says he's not coming with us."

Cotty, though surprised, wasn't unduly alarmed by this news and simply said in reply, "Why not?"

Despite not having been informed precisely by Cull as to why he was staying ashore, but having sensed that there was an element of fear behind the decision, Dan replied, "He's not feeling too well."

Cotty gesticulated to the Americans to get into the boat and prepare to row. Even though they were standing close by in water shin-deep, they had not been privy to what had been said between Cotty and his protégée. Turning in the opposite direction, the *Louise's* skipper espied Cull's wiry frame standing half-way up the slipway. The latter seemed determined to keep his feet dry. The fisherman signalled for the old man to wait where he was, and then, with only Dan to assist him, he attended to releasing the *Louise*. Once she was afloat and steadied only by Dan's capable hands and the initially less than expert ministrations provided by the Americans working the oars, he clambered back into the tractor's driver's seat prior to pulling the trailer clear of the boat's stern. Then he drove up the slipway, but only as far as where Cull was waiting. Once alongside he vacated the driver's seat for the second time, and without enquiring as to the reason behind the old man's change of heart, he invited his crony to take his place behind the wheel. The invitation was couched in such a way that, even if he had wanted to, the recipient wouldn't have dared to decline it. The order Cotty gave was for Cull to take the whole kit and caboodle back to Fisherhead, where he was to park up – without unhitching the trailer – and place the ignition key in the inner rim of the tractor's right rear wheel. Was that something which Cull was able to do? Yes it was, and he would do it willingly. Cotty assisted the bellman to climb aboard.

Now that there was an amateur behind the wheel, it didn't come as a surprise to Cotty that when Cull did manage to put the vehicle into gear, it was reverse that he found initially; and although he quickly realised his mistake, it wasn't soon enough to prevent the assemblage of wheels rolling down the slipway towards the *Louise's* stern. The sight, and the ensuing thought that Dan could soon be crushed between boat and trailer, caused Cotty's heart to miss a beat, but fortunately for all concerned the fisherman needn't have worried, for Cull was not so incompetent that he was unable to rectify the mistake. Indeed, once he had applied the break and subsequently selected first gear, the assemblage began to move, slowly at first, in the right direction. Only once Cull had observed that the trailer had cleared the slipway did he apply more pressure to the accelerator. Sensing that Cotty would continue to watch until he, Cull, had driven round the corner near to where the village sweet shop is situated, as a valedictory gesture the old man raised his hand.

In the sombre grey light now pervading the village, Cotty was well able to see the backhanded salute: it caused him to mutter aloud, "Don't you dare drop a clanger and crash Cull. Why don't you keep both hands on the wheel for God's sake?"

For the watching fisherman the situation was that once the assemblage of vehicles under Cull's control was out of sight, it was then out of mind, and so, without another moment's delay, and much to Dan's relief, Cotty rejoined his crew. It was immediately apparent to the new arrival that the lad was having an almighty struggle trying to keep the *Louise* under control, even with the assistance of the Americans manipulating the oars. Upon grasping hold of the cobble's starboard quarter, and signalling with a nod for Dan to imitate him and give one final push, the thought flashed through the fisherman's mind that he ought to apologise to the Americans for the absence of power from the outboard motor protruding – rather conspicuously in its idleness – over the boat's stern. The two-stroke engine was presently inoperable, the reason being that a certain individual – none other than he who was presently exerting himself in tandem with Cotty – had, some weeks previously, failed to tilt the engine upon entering shallow water, and consequently had wrecked the propeller. The busting of the boat's only item of machinery had happened prior to the bust-up in the hotel, but 'being strapped for cash' as Cotty put it, as yet he hadn't been able to replace the damaged component. The fisherman determined that he would only refer to the idle piece of equipment if asked about it. This was because he didn't want to embarrass Dan by bringing the subject to the fore, particularly as he was of the opinion that he had perhaps already lambasted the lad for his oversight more than he should have, and on the last occasion had told him that he would say no more about the matter. No; today, and on days to come for the foreseeable future, the

Louise would be powered by muscle rather than horsepower. With this thought in mind, Cotty determined not to go far; no farther than a mile off-shore.

Wading out up to their waists in togs designed for that purpose, eventually Cotty signalled to Dan, whose centre of gravity was several inches lower than the fisherman's, to clamber aboard. Exhibiting the agility of youth Dan did just that, and once seated immediately picked up the two remaining oars and secured them in the rowlocks. Seconds later, demonstrating less agility overall, but much more strength in his upper body, Cotty hauled himself out of the water and, stumbling over the nets which with a bit of luck would soon be lowered over the side, he sat down next to Dan. He was about to relieve the young man of the starboard oar, but instead got up again to check that the engine was securely tilted so that the skeg stayed out of the water. The corollary of this action, performed to prevent further damage to the engine's lower parts, was that the *Louise* was effectively now rudderless. The check completed to his satisfaction, Cotty reclaimed his seat next to Dan and took possession of the oar he had been about to grasp a few minutes earlier. Then, twisting his torso through almost ninety degrees, he looked over his right shoulder at the po-faced Americans, and grinning widely, above the noise of the water being churned into foam around them, he said commandingly, "Come on… put your backs into it, or we'll be here all day."

Making the kind of effort which would not have shamed Hercules, Cotty and his crew worked the oars more or less in unison, the result being that to the fisherman's surprise the cobble made good progress. Soon they were approaching the buoys marking the entrance to the channel which ran between the scaurs. The fisherman had no idea how many times he had strained his neck to orientate himself – and by extension the boat – in relation to the black port-side marker buoy bobbing up and down at a distance ahead that was diminishing far from steadily, but he knew that it had been many, and each time he had glanced over his shoulder he couldn't help but focus first on the black American's face, and on every occasion save the last, the expression he beheld was one of questioning incredulity. Beyond the entrance to the channel the sea's swell became noticeably heavier, and though the waves rushing towards the shore were no longer breaking over the *Louise's* bows to give the crew – the Yanks in particular – a soaking, making headway now seemed doubly difficult. To the men more used to being on ships the experience was proving to be disconcerting to say the least, and even the local lads sensed that they were flirting with danger. Nevertheless, onward they rowed.

No sooner were the marker buoys two to three boat lengths behind when Captain Gilchrist felt a sharp nudge on the right hand side of his ribcage. The demand for the skipper's attention was administered by Cotton's elbow. At first the Captain thought that his friend was experiencing some difficulty, but he was soon made aware as to why he had been nudged so forcefully when Cotton enquired as to the identity of a man watching the *Louise's* progress from the top of the cliff.

At first the Captain, who had been experiencing difficulties of his own in respect of working the oar in the rowlock, searched along the top of the wrong cliff for the person Cotton had described, but eventually his eyes did come to rest upon the silhouette of a man, and the shape he saw he recognised in an instance.

"That's the Irish writer I told you about a while back… you know… that guy I first met in the Endeavour Inn… I wonder how he's getting on with his novel," the Captain said, as volubly as possible into Cotton's ear without actually shouting.

"I just hope that it is a novel he's writing," Cotton responded, "and not our obituaries."

Catching the drift of the words spoken primarily for Cotton's benefit, and not wishing by exclusion to remain in ignorance of what was going on in the village, Cotty enquired further.

"What's his name?" asked the fisherman succinctly, calling out his request for information whilst, for obvious reasons, keeping his back turned to the person he was addressing.

"Leonard Walmslow," replied the Captain, inadvertently pausing in his oar-stroke as he tilted his head back into his hood in order to be heard more clearly.

The break in the Captain's rhythm caused his and Cotty's respective oars to crash. Fortunately there were no grievous consequences, and once the Captain had regained the stroke, a rhythm largely determined by the man in front, the necessarily brief and staccato exchange was resumed.

"I've never heard of him," said Cotty.

"That's because he writes books," the Captain responded with sarcasm.

The Americans grinned at each other in a way which suggested that they had just scored an important point against the Brits in unsporting competition. The fisherman glanced at Dan and tut-tutted.

At this juncture Cotty, having decided that they were far enough from shore, called a halt to rowing and stowed his oar. He instructed the others to use their respective oars to keep the boat steady – though he realised even as he spoke that that was something of a forlorn hope – whilst he attended to the net. Unable to stand unaided for long, by placing in turn one hand over the other along the gunwale, he proceeded towards the stern to where the net was. His hope was that it wouldn't be tangled. It was then, at the precise moment that he let go of the gunwale to take hold of the brightly coloured net – it was orange – that the fateful and calamitous event occurred.

In a materialistic, secular age, in an age which often seeks to denigrate the notion that there is such a phenomenon as spirit, it may seem facile to speak or write about the 'hand of fate', but from the description of events narrated to me by my grandfather, and from the pieces which I read in the Ravensborough Courier and the Eskmouth Gazette – and not forgetting the fictional account in Leonard Walmslow's great prizewinning novel, 'The Wreck' – there is no doubt in my mind that such a notion has efficacy.

I have seen manifestations which are difficult to rationalise. On an otherwise relatively calm day climatically, I have been amazed to see the wind rise suddenly and ruffle my son's hair, and it seemed to me that the force measured by anemometers and seen only by its effects on things – smoke, leaves, hair – was making a singular statement, and that statement without words indicated the presence of the Holy Ghost. That manifestation happened a long time ago, but more recently, within the last month in fact, I was equally amazed to see, upon gazing through the book-room window, a serpentine shape in motion. This kinetic art delineated by the action of the wind upon leaves and grass only an inch above the ground resembled a fast-moving mamba approaching the window. In a similar vein I have taken delight in the actions of the windhover, and am convinced that on a number of occasions my exultation has been reciprocated. There is more in heaven and earth…

I have digressed, and so as the author of this narrative and the protagonist's grandson, I beg the reader's pardon for taking a liberty, for intruding into a tale which is surely remarkable enough without my having to invoke powers which may be construed as being supernatural. The fact remains, however, that the invisible force did play a major role in what became for two of the men on board the *Louise* that day, a life and death struggle, a role which was exceptional notwithstanding the prevailing conditions.

Up until the moment when Cotty had removed his hands from the gunwale to attend to the net, the wind had been blowing directly onshore, making it just about possible for a man with knowledge of the bay to predict how the boat would handle. There was only one such man aboard and Dan had great faith in him, for he believed that Cotty knew what he was doing. The fisherman did indeed know what he was doing, but even he wasn't able to foresee such a sudden increase in the strength of the wind as it gusted from an unlikely quarter, from the South.

Indeed, if, in terms of direction, the forces of nature had continued to behave in accordance with expectation, then much of the power manifest in the sudden and exceptional gust would have been deflected by the Louise's bows, and that which remained would have hit its target squarely in the back, knocking him forward. Then all Cotty would have needed to do to steady himself was to stretch out his arms and grasp the *Louise's* stern either side of the redundant outboard motor.

What actually happened, however, was that the fateful gust caught the *Louise* side-on just as the cobble was lifted atop one of many crests: that the boat didn't capsize and tip her entire crew into the maelstrom was nothing short of a miracle, and certainly for the down-to-earth Englishman there was no such divine intervention. Caught in the most vulnerable of positions, the poor fellow was blown over the side, the side which had tilted from the horizontal to such a degree that the gunwale was where one would normally expect to find the keel. For my grandfather the sight of the fisherman's arms flailing as he sought to grasp something solid to save him was a sight which haunted him far into the future, as did the plaintive groan which Cotton emitted when he realised that nothing was going to prevent him from ending up in the briny. The inevitable splash occurred. If, at that moment, either Dan or the Captain had been able to react speedily, one or other could have thrust out his oar for Cotty to take hold of so as to be hauled back aboard. Alarmingly the opportunity for impulsive action was gone in the time it takes for a sailor on watch to shout, 'Man overboard', and though at one point there was a real danger that the *Louise's* keel would come crashing down upon Cotty's head (an eventuality which may incite cynics to wonder which would come off worse), the opposite occurred, and despite the best efforts of two of the crew, the gap between the *Louise* and the grim-faced fisherman grew from feet to yards.

If, as he maintained, the actions of my grandfather were the nautical equivalent of being too pedestrian, the same cannot be said of Cornelius Cotton's reaction to the crisis unfolding in the water. Even though he wasn't a strong swimmer, no sooner had he removed his boots than he dived overboard, seemingly to save his former enemy.

By the time Cotton had made a splash – literally – the man who hadn't entered the water of his own freewill was approximately twenty yards from the coble. This gap between him and the boat was increasing ever wider, and though this was remarkable for one reason, it wasn't for another because the fisherman seemed to be making every effort to put as much distance as possible between him and the *Louise*. Those who remained afloat by virtue of wood sealed with pitch were experiencing considerable difficulty making headway in any direction. Such a pretty kettle of fish, bearing in mind that the number which had previously been considered to be the minima in respect of handling the boat in such conditions had been depleted by half, was to be expected. To add to their problems – though unlike the men in the water, they weren't as yet in immediate danger of drowning – the present seating arrangements made the task of manipulating the oars with any degree of coordination considerably more difficult than it would have been had they been adjacent to each other.

"We have to turn the boat around and make for the slipway," shouted Captain Gilchrist, realising, perhaps rather belatedly, that the time had come for him to take command of the situation.

Even above the cacophony created by the wind and sea, the authority and determination in the Captain's tone was clearly audible to the other member of the *Louise's* crew.

"But what about Cotty," Dan protested loudly. "We have to save him."

"Our best chance of saving Mr Draycot is to launch the lifeboat," replied the Captain, and assuming that Dan would make no further effort to countermand his decision, his next instruction was wholly practical.

"Use your right oar (each had grasped an oar which had been discarded) to back-paddle and help me turn *Louise* around," he ordered.

Watching the fisherman's head and shoulders disappear and reappear intermittently as they were carried – and perhaps were propelling themselves – in a direction which was at variance with that which the *Louise* would be taking, pained Dan considerably, but realising that the sea-captain's decision was eminently sensible, he complied with the order given. Captain Gilchrist pulled on his oar for all he was worth whilst at the same time allowing his eyes to skim, as it were, over the heaving water in the hope of catching sight of Cornelius. Not surprisingly the man from

New Hampshire was anxious that the Texan had failed to surface, or if he had, had become submerged again without either oarsman having caught sight of him. The Captain spent a few moments pondering over what could have happened. At this time the mental processes involved in contracting and extending muscles were subsumed to the extent that his body as an entity resembled a machine which has been programmed to perform repetitive tasks. Of course, there was the remote possibility that each time he turned his head askance to look, the relentless undulations of the sea served to hide the would-be lifesaver from view; and then, returning to the negative tack, surely, he thought, Dan would draw his attention to where Cotton was located if the latter were to emerge. Unable for the present to fathom what had become of his crewmate, the Captain glanced up at the cliff to see if the novelist was still watching. Mr Walmslow was also nowhere in sight, but at least in his regard the Captain was able to formulate a plausible hypothesis as to what the Irishman had been up to since he had first been observed. His supposition was that Walmslow, having noted the perilous predicament of those at sea, had made his way post-haste to raise the alarm, and thereby initiated the launching of the lifeboat. Whilst these thoughts were at the forefront of Gilchrist's mind, however, no such preparations were apparent, and the foreshore was as deserted now as when they had left it less than an hour ago.

Once – by the depleted crew's sterling efforts – the *Louise* had turned more or less through one hundred and eighty degrees, with their backs to the shore, the Captain called out the time. "In… In… In…" he instructed intermittently, repeating the monosyllabic command until he was certain that the rhythm was established. The *Louise* fought her way towards the buoys marking the channel. Finding, upon entering the navigable gap between the scaurs, that they were equidistant between each buoy, inwardly, silently, the rowers congratulated themselves for the fact that the boat in their charge was positioned perfectly. Their despondency at the plight, quite possibly loss, of their respective friends didn't preclude their feeling a profound sense of relief at the prospect – in all probability soon to be achieved – of grounding the boat. At this point in time they were fifty to seventy-five yards from the slipway. With thoughts running through his head as to his course of action once he was back on dry land, the Captain was startled to hear Dan's youthful voice calling for him to look in the direction indicated by his pointing finger.

"There he is," the lad shouted, "it's the black bloke I'm sure… your friend Cotton."

It goes without saying that in order to point Dan had to let go one of the oars, and it was perfectly natural, and with regard to navigation, advisable to do as he did and stop rowing altogether. In the next instant the coble lost power completely when the Captain also paused, in his case to look along the line indicated by Dan's finger. He peered into the steely grey sea heaving in the middle distance, but couldn't see any sign of life in the direction indicated. To ensure that he hadn't overlooked anything, the Captain searched to right and left of the imagined compass bearing, and from the marker buoys all the way to the horizon. The entire procedure took only seconds. Nothing out of the ordinary could he see, but whilst searching he heard a boom, a thunderous noise the significance of which didn't at first make an impression, a fact which he later attributed to his eagerness to confirm Dan's discovery.

"Are you sure your eyes weren't playing tricks on you?" the Captain enquired disappointingly.

"I'm certain that it was him skipper, though I only caught a glimpse," Dan replied, without his even being aware of how loaded with meaning was the epithet he had used.

The import of the single word 'skipper' was not lost on the Captain as two sets of eyes peered over the *Louise's* portside bow, and because it wasn't noon on a Sunday – the time and day when the cannon located at the top of the hill was test-fired – it eventually dawned on the 'fisherman' who had yet to catch a fish in these waters that the *Henrietta Maria's* crew had been summoned for real.

"There... over there... I'm sure that's somebody in the water," Dan shouted at the top of his voice, once again raising his arm to point, this time a few points north of the direction he had earlier indicated.

On this occasion Captain Gilchrist saw the entity too, and although he was unable to focus for long enough to be able to discern without a shadow of doubt that the floating body was even a human being, never mind his friend, he eventually came to the sickening conclusion that it was unlikely to be a piece of flotsam or the trunk or branch of a tree, but in all probability was indeed Cornelius. Of course what dismayed the Captain more than anything was that whereas he had hoped to see the tall Texan swimming with gusto as he battled against the swell in his gallant attempt to save the Englishman, he had perceived instead what had appeared to be a lifeless body. The entity which he presumed was Cornelius again disappeared from view. In a similar vein, last seen swimming in the direction of Gunny Point, Cotty was also nowhere to be seen. The unspoken difference of opinion on this matter was that the Captain presumed him to have drowned, whereas Dan, being a local lad and possessed of least some knowledge in respect of currents, presumed that the fisherman had made it to the shore.

Concerned primarily for the fate of the Texan, Dan turned to face the man whom he had designated to be in charge and shouted, "We have to run the boat around. We have to try to save him."

Whilst weighing up the pros and cons of the voluble suggestion a wave washed over the coble filling the bottom of the boat to a depth of several inches. In the same instant Captain Gilchrist heard voices calling to each other from the top of the slipway behind him. The sounds denoting activity of some urgency caused the Captain to turn his head to look, and what he saw was heartening, for the *Henrietta Maria* was being hauled towards the slipway by its crew. They were pulling on lines attached either side. The Captain thought it safe to assume that she would be launched and underway in a matter of minutes.

"Come on mate, let's go… let's turn this thing around," Dan sought to encourage, his nominal familiarity sounding disrespectful in his eagerness to bring his influence to bear.

Aware, that if he didn't propel and steer the *Louise* in one direction or another, that there was a risk that the coble would come to grief on the northerly most scaur, the Captain resumed rowing with the sole purpose of regaining the centre of the channel. Aware also that to make for the open sea with a seriously depleted crew that was feeling the effects of fatigue, and in a boat that had no effective rudder, was simply asking for trouble, the Captain made a decision which was contrary to that which Dan had tried to persuade. The course of action which the Captain communicated was that they would let the lifeboat come to Cotton's rescue; either that or recover his body.

Chapter Twenty-one

Captain Gilchrist is Reunited with his Crew

A large volume of water had passed under the keel of many a ship since Jenny Fewster had sighted the *Canaveral* battling against the storm on that dark and windy October morning nearly six months earlier, but not, as was obvious on this pleasant April fool's day, in a volume that was deep enough to enable the schooner in question to be refloated. There the ship lay, in exactly the same position in which the milkmaid with the creamy complexion had seen the bare masts secured by rigging rising from the sleek lined hull each time she journeyed to and from work via the cliff top path. In the darkness of her pre-dawn perambulations Jenny had still been able make out the schooner's dark shape against the lighter surroundings. In her opinion, which, though hardly professional, was better informed than some, the vessel which had become almost synonymous with Rankin Bay wouldn't leave in a month of Sundays, and my grandmother said as much to her fiancé, Captain Andrew Gilchrist, as the couple walked hand in hand down King Street. Their destination, as on many recent occasions, was the lounge of the Rankin Bay Hotel.

My grandmother had accepted my grandfather's proposal of marriage only three days previously. It was a proposal which she had been astonished as well as delighted to receive. Consequently, one might have expected the couple's respective demeanours to reflect an inwardly blissful state. Contrary to this expectation, however, presently the couple's expressions were, as they climbed the steps to enter the hotel, as sombre as dusk in early November, and with good cause, for this was no mere social outing.

The couple had arranged to meet one of the co-owners of the *Cape Canaveral*, an individual with a much greater stake in the ship, and, unlike Captain Gilchrist, in her sister ships bearing the names of global locations akin to promontories gleaned from the pages of an atlas, than the Captain's meagre percentage. The name of the august gentleman Gilchrist was about to meet for the first time on British soil, and to whom he was about to introduce his future wife, was Mr Robert Fox of the New Hampshire Foxes. The gentleman in question, in partnership with the cousin who had remained behind to look after the day-to-day running of the business, was effectively grandfather's boss, though for how much longer that relationship was likely to continue was a debatable point, and for a number of reasons.

There was a stoical element to the Captain's introspective dolefulness, for although he was fully aware that this was no formal meeting, he foresaw that he would have some explaining to do, and no doubt a host of questions to answer to boot. Moreover, he knew also that the ensuing exchange of information would be a complex business for the fact that Mr Fox had not arrived alone. After having docked in Liverpool the previous morning, the co-owner of the shipping-line, accompanied by the '*Cap*' *Canaveral*'s former crew, had disembarked from the Cap St. Vincent to board a train at Lime Street station. It was the first of three they were going to catch that day, the third disgorging the party at the tiny station from which the majority had left for home several weeks previously, the station serving Rankin Bay.

The return of Crossman, Henley, Landowska and Walker was intended to serve a double purpose in that not only would they be able to attend a memorial service in honour of their lost shipmate, but also they would be on hand if, metaphorically, the last Sunday in Jenny's month of Sundays was in the offing. Such an occasion, quite literally, was a distinct possibility, for in anticipation of his boss's arrival Captain Gilchrist had solicited the good offices of Charlie Cook to ascertain whether or not the Army – the Royal Engineers in particular – were yet in a position to provide assistance by using explosives. To Charlie's and the sea-captain's great surprise, they learned from the Adjutant that Major Harnley had recently returned from Iraq, and subsequently, following two telephone conversations with the officer in question, arrangements were made for a team from Ripon to travel to Rankin Bay on the first of April, its mission to get the job done once and for all.

Conscious that he could be perceived in some quarters as being the cause of this furore, it was with a certain amount of trepidation that the Captain opened the hotel's outer door for his bride-to-be. In the sense that the truly brave man or woman is he or she who overcomes his or her fear in order to succeed, he recognised that he would need to summon up a considerable amount of moral courage merely to enter what he conceived at that moment to be the lion's den. Of greatest concern to the Captain was that he had no idea how well, or indeed how poorly, he would perform with Jenny by his side. Naturally, in the long term, and most definitely imminently, he hoped that the presence of his beloved would encourage him to achieve more than it would have been possible for him to do were he alone; but such thoughts didn't preclude his having doubts, and the idea that he may – in the next few minutes – be made to look a fool in front of Jenny filled him with dread.

Jenny, aware that this was a momentous occasion in the life of her affianced, and demonstrating, in respect of another's feelings, that kind of sensibility for which her gender is renowned, albeit often mistakenly, smiled at Andrew as he let her pass, and once over the threshold she held out her hand for him to hold. If it was up to her – and it wasn't – they would enter the lion's den conjoined. Andrew willingly grasped hold of the offered hand, but did so merely to give it a tender squeeze before letting go in order to open the inner door. In the necessity of having to conduct what then was a wholly masculine business, he was perfectly at ease with the idea of introducing his fiancée (how could he be otherwise when he had proposed it?), but unwilling to enter the room holding hands. Once again Andrew held the door open for Jenny to enter before him.

The arrival of the couple caused those ensconced within to turn their heads. Finding safety in the familiar, Jenny beamed as her eyes rested upon the welcoming transatlantic faces turned towards her, the faces of people who months earlier had departed Rankin Bay Station as acquaintances, but who, she now believed, had returned to the village as friends.

The patrons espied by the couple were divided into two distinct groups, the nearest of which – from Captain Gilchrist's and Jenny's perspective – comprised a trio standing and drinking coffee next to the bar. Members of the other group were seated around a table in the far corner. This group was comprised entirely of the '*Cap*' *Canaveral*'s crew. Despite the earliness of the hour to a man they were drinking beer.

Upon entering Captain Gilchrist's natural inclination was to approach the far table and shake each man's hand, but he overruled this impulsive desire and instead merely greeted his crew with a perfunctory gesture. His considered course was to steer Jenny and himself in the direction of what appeared to be, and undoubtedly was, the more authoritative group sipping from miniature cups.

"We had better have two more cups please Rita," requested the only local member of the trio, namely Charlie Cook. "And I think that we had better have a fresh pot if you would be so kind," Charlie added, noting not for the first time that morning the heavy bags, so to speak, under the barmaid's eyes.

Then, by way of a compliment, a voice with a strong New England accent, asserted, "That sure was a great cup of coffee Miss, and I for one would love to imbibe more."

The word 'imbibe' was new to Rita, but from the context she had a good idea as to what it meant, and she took pleasure in the compliment as she repaired to the kitchen to do as she had been bid. The two strangers present were Major Harnley, Royal Engineers, and the co-owner of the shipping line, Mr Robert Fox, otherwise known to his employees as wily Bob. The physiognomy of Mr Fox, though familiar and therefore presenting no surprise to Captain Gilchrist, created a strong impression on Jenny for the fact that he appeared to be a giant when compared to the others present, and in physical stature they weren't particularly short. The story of Gulliver and his travels – a book which Jenny had read and enjoyed – enabled the young lady to see herself as a denizen of Lilliput in the presence of this American Gulliver who stood at least six feet six inches tall; and with reference to a different tale (though she had yet to discern any lupine traits in the character of Mr Fox), she could imagine herself wearing a red cape with a red hood and saying, "My, what big hands you've got," or with equal candour, "My, what a big head you've got."

Compared to his peers Mr Fox really did have a big head, and for the fact that it was covered in thick, grey hair which grew down at the back over his collar, it gave the newcomer the appearance of an aging lion. This leonine bonce was possessed of a face which was craggy and tanned. The limpid blue eyes set above a fleshy nose denoted perspicacity, and, rather incongruously, also revealed a capacity for cruelty as well as kindness. The eyes smiled at Jenny as she approached, so too the mouth as wily Bob spoke.

"And who is this treasure you've brought along to delight us all Andrew?" he enquired with all the suavity of a New England politician playing host at a large reception, and then, allowing no time for the Captain to answer, he added, "So this is the young woman you intend to marry. I can see why you were so reluctant to leave my boy."

Words which to the Captain sounded pointedly ambiguous poured like balsam into Jenny's ears. She blushed with embarrassment – something which she hadn't done in a long time – as wily Bob bowed to take hold and kiss the feminine hand he raised. The former milkmaid was hardly accustomed to such genteel behaviour. My grandfather's reaction, as he described it, was blatantly neutral. At this juncture Charlie Cook assumed the role of Master of Ceremonies and commenced the round of introductions, some of which were superfluous. Once these had been made Captain Gilchrist complimented the Major on his recent promotion and enquired as to the state of play in Iraq. Feeling a little overawed to be present at a conversation about such weighty matters, a conversation to which as yet she had neither the knowledge nor the confidence to contribute, Jenny took the bold step of excusing herself so as to join the '*Cap*' *Canaveral*'s crew at their table. First she took the cup and saucer which Major Harnley offered her, and greeted Rita as if they were old friends, which was hardly the case. Andrew encouraged his fiancée's departure with a nod.

"If my age were half what it is you wouldn't have a chance of winning that girl's hand Gilchrist," were the words which resounded in Jenny's ears as she left one group to join the other. "You lucky devil," wily Bob added.

The response of her husband-to-be she failed to hear as Crossman, leading by example, stood to greet Jenny as she drew near.

"Good to see you again Miss Fewster," said the Canadian, "though you probably think that we're like bad pennies."

"What do you mean?" Jenny asked naively as she placed the coffee-filled crockery she was carrying upon the table. Then she sat down on the chair which Henley had brought from another table. This time the men followed her example.

"You know," replied Crossman, "like bad pennies you try to get rid of but seem to keep turning up in your pocket."

"Not at all," Jenny responded, "and I'll be annoyed if you persist in calling me Miss Fewster. The name's Jenny to my friends, and I like to think of you all as my friends."

It was Walker who changed the tone of the conversation by asking, "But you do know why we're here, I take it Miss…" At this point the donkeyman paused as he pondered how best to correct his near *faux pas*, and then, with more than a hint of reluctance in his voice, he said simply, "…Jenny."

"You're here to attend the memorial service for Cornelius aren't you?" Jenny thought it polite to ask. "According to Andrew you may be about to return to your ship. The presence of Major Harnley tells me that an attempt to refloat her is being planned."

Walker smiled when he heard these words, not so much for what they conveyed, but rather for the manner of their delivery. It seemed to the donkeyman that Miss Fewster was striving to adopt a manner of speech appropriate to her new and elevated station in life.

"There's more chance of flying to the moon than getting the *Canaveral* off the rocks," interjected Henley.

"That remains to be seen," responded Jenny.

"What exactly did happen to Cotton Miss," enquired Landowska solicitously. "Do you have any idea?"

There was a pregnant pause as Jenny raised her cup to her mouth and sipped. For a future wife of a sea-Captain this was not the simple procedure it would appear, for Jenny had got it into her head – perhaps she had read as much in a magazine, or in the pages of a guide to etiquette – that the correct way for a lady to hold a teacup was to keep the little finger raised. About cups containing coffee she really had no idea, and was, therefore, confused. Consequently, unlike a fiddler crab's giant claw, her little finger went up and down for no apparent reason. Once again Walker smiled.

"From what Andrew... from what your Captain has told me... and I'm not sure whether I should be the one telling you this... our friend Cornelius made a bold bid to save another man's life. It had been Mr Draycot's idea to invite your Captain and Cornelius for a morning's fishing aboard the *Louise.* That's one of the cobles you see lined up at Fisherhead..."

"Draycot... Cotty... is that the same louse who caused Cornelius so much trouble in this very place, right where the skipper and the others are standing?" enquired Crossman vehemently.

For having been Cotton's closest shipmate, of the 'Cap' *Canaveral*'s crew it was Sheldon who felt their loss most keenly.

"I know he can be awkward at times, but I don't think I would ever describe him as such," responded Jenny in a tone which, if her sense of indignation hadn't been sincere, would have sounded affected: evidently she was rising to the challenge of her new role.

"So the crew consisted of three in total?" asked Walker, attempting to ensure that nothing that was worth knowing about this dreadful business was left to supposition.

"There were four," replied Jenny concisely, but then, after a moment's deliberation, she elaborated, "They took a lad named Dan with them. Heaven knows what Cotty was thinking of taking out one so young in such a heavy sea."

The gravity of Jenny's pronouncement, together with the seriousness of her expression, was infectious, and for this particular group a prolonged silence ensued. Eventually, after a lapse of approximately twenty seconds, Miss Fewster resumed her narrative.

"It was Cotty of all people who was tipped out of the boat. The *Louise* was hit by a freak gust of wind just as he had got to his feet to see to the nets."

"Serves the idiot right," remarked Crossman.

Jenny ignored the comment and continued.

"In next to no time Cornelius dived in after him. Andrew said it was the most selfless and courageous act he has ever witnessed. The problem was… and is… that Cornelius failed to surface, at least not for an age, and when they did catch sight of him… if it was him… the body looked to be lifeless."

Walker opened his mouth as if to speak, but then, without having uttered a word, closed it again, for the speaker holding court, as it were, seemed to have read his thoughts.

"Andrew thinks," said Jenny, "that Cornelius must have been knocked unconscious… or even killed… by the coble's keel soon after he had entered the water. An alternative possibility is that he hit his head on a submerged rock. Cotty thinks the former theory the most likely. He says that the entrance to the channel and the channel itself are usually clear, though he did point out to Andrew... and anyone else who cared to listen... that even he couldn't be certain, letting it be known... as if people from these parts didn't know already... that the power of the sea can be formidable."

"You mean to say that the..." (The speaker stuttered as he struggled to find a suitable epithet.) "...the man Cornelius tried to save survived, and the hero who went to his rescue... Cornelius... has, in all probability, drowned," said Crossman summarily, astonished by what he had just been told.

Jenny nodded guiltily.

"What puzzles me," said Walker questioningly, "is why the two in the boat weren't able to recover the body."

That was one of the questions I put to Andrew. What Cotty had told him was that after wading ashore at Gunny Point, he worked his way round the base of the cliff until he reached the cleft he had climbed once before as a boy. After reaching the top the first thing he did was to make his way to my house to raise the alarm. You do know that my dad... that my father is the coxswain of the lifeboat don't you?"

To a man the *Canaveral's* crew nodded.

"What Cotty hadn't realised was that the alarm had already been raised... probably by somebody watching from the shore... I've no idea how he failed to hear the cannon."

"His ears would have been filled with sea-water," commented Walker, "and that..."

"That could have affected his hearing," completed Henley.

They were of course referring to Mr Draycot.

"Anyhow," resumed Jenny after she had paused to take – for that morning – her last sip of coffee, "the long and short of it is that

Andrew made the decision not to risk the lad's... Dan's... life by venturing into open sea for a second time."

At this point in the exchange Jenny couldn't help but notice the changed expression on Walker's face, a look which seemed to indicate that he couldn't quite believe his ears.

"Captain Gilchrist's first concern was for the safety of his crew," said Jenny emphatically, "and what's more, he knew that the Henrietta Maria was about to be launched."

"I thought I could feel my ears burning," sounded a familiar voice from behind Jenny's back. The hand she felt and espied resting on her shoulder she also recognised. Andrew's tone of voice gave a clear indication that the initial meeting with wily Bob had not gone as badly as he had thought it might.

"I was just explaining to Mr Walker and the others why it is that Mr Cotton's not with us," said Jenny.

She had been about to conclude her statement with her usual term of endearment when addressing Andrew, but given the circumstances she decided against it.

"There's just one more thing I'd like to know skipper," said Walker, ponderously raising his heavy head as he turned the focus of his attention from Jenny to the Captain.

"What's that?" enquired the Captain peremptorily, sensitive to the possibility that the question about to be posed could place him in a difficult position.

"Why wasn't the body recovered by the lifeboat?"

"We had to get clear of the channel before the Henrietta Maria could be launched. You've seen it... you know how narrow it is," the Captain added, a little defensively. He was, of course, referring to the channel. "And you don't need me to tell you that a man standing six feet tall takes up a lot of space in a room such as this, but put him in the immensity of the sea or ocean and you can imagine how difficult it could be to find him."

"That's if you're not looking in the right place," interjected Henley.

Captain Gilchrist ignored the interruption.

"That's all I can tell you for the present. Who knows? Perhaps Cotton will be washed up on some lonely stretch of beach eventually."

"Perhaps he already has, and nobody has been able to identify him," commented Walker coolly. "Where is the coxswain anyway... I thought he would be part of your little gathering at the bar?"

What the Captain considered to be the latent aggression in Walker's tone caused him to deliberate for a moment as to whether now would be the time and place to reassert a modicum of his sea Captain's authority, but thinking that his own sensitivity might be the problem, he decided not to be a disciplinarian just yet. In consequence of the donkeyman's offhand manner, however, he concluded that the cosy familiarity which had developed between him and his crew would have to be dispensed with soon.

"My father went to Eskmouth first thing for a meeting with the Chief Constable," informed Jenny.

"He's arranging... hopefully... a police presence for this afternoon," the Captain added, sensing by reading the faces of his men that they believed the meeting to be connected with Cotton's disappearance, which it wasn't. "We're going to set off the charges at fourteen hundred hours... that's two o'clock for your benefit Henley... precisely."

"Today you mean?" Crossman enquired, astonished, and impressed, that a day of anticipated lassitude was about to turn dynamic.

"I mean today," averred the skipper. "It's up to you whether you come along to watch the fireworks, but we need to be aboard and ready to sail by six. Walker, I'm leaving it to you to ensure that this rabble of a crew is where it should be at the appointed hour."

There were mock remonstrations at the Captain's provocative, yet far from serious, ascription of the '*Cap*' *Canaveral*'s crew as a rabble. With the good humour of a sportsman who knows that the game is afoot, Captain Gilchrist smiled at Jenny, and she at once rose in response to the silent communication that it was time to depart the sailors' company.

The Final Chapter
Iconoclasm

Even today, when we are blessed with the greater mobility provided by highly efficient vehicles, the number of times in a year that it is possible to see a policeman in the precincts of Rankin Bay can be counted on the digits of two hands. Many that are law-abiding citizens will no doubt consider such blue-serge minimalism to be laudable on the basis that the upholders of the law evidently have little cause to visit a village in which the presence of a patrolling police car could cause mayhem; not, you understand, because the hordes of drug pushers would likely do themselves an injury as they scurry for cover; and not because the ladies of the night would begin weeping and wailing for no longer being able to offer their services; but because one car too many in the narrow street thronged with tourists and free-range children can easily lead to a jam the like of which requires a diplomat's patience and a chess player's perception to clear.

At the onset of the third decade of the twentieth century the environment in the village was different for being less orderly and less congested, but the number of routine police patrols was not greater – and nor was it less – than in modern times.

It isn't difficult to imagine, therefore, the level of interest that was generated late that morning when a dozen constables debussed at the top of the bank, and then, in a column of twos, marched smartly down the hill behind their Sergeant. There having been little time for the news to spread regarding the exceptional event which had been planned for that afternoon, rumours were rife as to the reason for the presence of so many boys in blue. A clever observer, one capable of deductive reasoning, might have put two and two together had he or she also espied four individuals in Army uniform going about their business. For the fact that they were so few, and had been ordered to keep a low profile, the soldiers were generally less conspicuous than the marching column. Among those villagers not gifted with foresight or deductive powers, rumours abounded as to why it was that the police had arrived in force.

Tongues wagged. One individual was heard to say that the coppers had come to arrest the American sailors for smuggling timber, and that it had come to light that the ship's Captain and his crew had grounded the schooner deliberately for that purpose. A continuation of this fabrication was that the owner of the *Cape Canaveral,* being an upright, Christian gentleman, had tricked his crew into returning to Britain to face the music, so to speak. This story was considered plausible, and consequently it spread around the village like a virulent strain of influenza.

A rumour which was thought less convincing was that the '*Cap*' *Canaveral*'s crew had been involved in a sinister conspiracy to murder that poor 'darkie'. Astonishingly, however, this mischievous tale was thought credible in some quarters, and those that did give it credence went on to speculate that the same vagabonds and murderers were probably responsible for doing away with old John, of whom neither hide nor hair had been sighted since his disappearance. The suggestion that the old timer had been killed by the sailors because they wanted to benefit from the sale of his internal organs was met with universal incredulity and spasmodic laughter.

Fortunately for Captain Gilchrist and the others they remained in ignorance of this outbreak of bad-mouthing, and were saved the ordeal of having to confront and deny any accusations of murder that might have been forthcoming. The truth-teller who saved them was no less a rascal than Cull the bellman.

Minutes after the police had arrived in The Dock to be given final instructions before dispersing to go about their duties, at two minutes past twelve Cull rang his bell, the sound of which invariably preceded a pronouncement. Delivered in a voice which had never been stentorian, Cull manfully informed the villagers that explosive charges would be detonated close to the ship named the *Cape Canaveral* at two o' clock precisely, and that the police were advising people to keep away. He also informed that on no account was anyone to venture along the beach beyond Stoupe from now until the all-clear had been given. The path along the top of the cliff would remain open.

Now that the denizens of Rankin Bay were fully apprised as to what was about to happen, those that had given credence to the malicious gossip either grimaced or chuckled as they ruminated upon either the wickedness or fancifulness of their respective imaginations. Of course, it was impossible for the man who was soon to marry Henry Fewster's youngest daughter to be involved in anything as underhand as smuggling, or as nefarious as murder. Needless to say, having been advised to stay away, the majority of the villagers that were currently idle, or that were employed in work which could be put aside for an hour or two, made their way towards the ship in order to witness the spectacle. This was in keeping with police expectation. On the slipway there was considerable activity as one after the other of the boat owners launched his boat with the intention of watching 'the party' from a safe distance out to sea. First away was Jack the lad in the *Red Lobster*.

Before long there was a line of people strung out along the tops of the cliffs. They led and followed others that were making their way down and up the steep paths where the two natural clefts separate the high plateaus. They followed one another mainly in single file. This was because the path was fenced on the landward side. Here and there, however, where the trail was wide enough to allow it, two people could be seen walking and talking together, side by side. Conjoined pairs were formed by parents holding the hands of children. The kids usually trailed behind slightly. The progenitors sensibly kept their progeny in tow and away from the cliff edge where a wrong step combined with the potentially harmful effects of gravity could have serious consequences. On this pleasant spring day the villagers on the move were in a holiday mood, but that didn't preclude their being prepared for a change in the weather. The forecast in the local newspaper was for sunshine and showers. In anticipation of there being more of the former than the latter, some carried easily portable chairs; and in anticipation of there being more of the latter than the former, others carried umbrellas. Thermos flask in hand, Captain Gilchrist escorted Jenny along the beach as far as the police cordon, whereat he gave his beloved a peck on the cheek in recognition of the fact that they were about to part company, Jenny to ascend by the steep path to join her mother and sister at the top of the cliff, the Captain to pass – with permission – through the line of police constables. At one thirty-five the Captain handed the thermos flask to Jenny and set off to join Mr Fox, Charlie Cook, Henry Fewster, the Chief Constable, Major Harnley, and the three other soldiers from the Royal Engineers, all of whom were doing things in the vicinity of the ship on the seaward side. Captain Gilchrist recognised the figure of the person whom he believed to be Sergeant Harker. He was incorrect in one respect only, and that was that the former Sergeant had been promoted to Staff Sergeant in the interval since they had last met. If everything was to go according to the plan in respect of which the Staff Sergeant had, and would, play a significant role, then in a short while the *Canaveral* would be free of the scaur forever.

Initially standing eight to ten yards apart, six police officers – one of whom was a female officer on secondment from the Metropolitan Police – held a line across the beach a little north of Stoupe Beck, from the base of the cliff to a point a few yards from where the sea gently unfurled over wet sand. Since their arrival the ground they had to cover had been gradually extending. Not even a Londoner could fail to notice the phenomenon, at least this once. This wasn't really surprising considering that she, being the officer posted farthest from the cliff, would be the first to get her feet wet were she to be in the same position when the tide turned. The thought perturbed her as to when that might be.

At the southern extremity of what was considered to be a safe distance from the schooner's stern, only two policemen were standing sentinel. The opinion was that members of the public were much less likely to approach the danger area from that direction. That opinion was validated, and so with little to do, and to lessen the strain on their vocal cords, the two constables gradually drew closer together so as to pass the time discussing such important matters as Eskmouth's chances of beating South Bank in the Amateur Cup Saturday week. Without doubt the boys in blue that needed to be most responsive, and for whom as a consequence the time passed relatively quickly, were the four constables and the Sergeant in position along the cliff top path.

Ten minutes or so after Captain Gilchrist had been allowed through the police cordon the remainder of the '*Cap*' *Canaveral*'s crew approached laden with diverse items of luggage. They had been interrogated *en route* by the Irish writer, who had even gone to the trouble of taking notes whilst walking. The crew members thought they would be rid of Mr Walmslow's company sooner than in fact they were, for their intention had been to follow their Captain and make a tidy pile of their luggage on the beach on the port side – the relatively safe side – of the ship, and then retire a safe distance if necessary, which could be in the opposite direction, towards Seal Point. Henley had argued with the policeman in front of them that with the schooner's hull between them and the explosions, there would be the safest place of all. Walker knew that Henley's reasoning wasn't going to make headway, but even he was surprised, when informed by a callow police officer who was probably half his age, that the mariners in waiting wouldn't be allowed to proceed further until after the explosives had been detonated. The three Americans and one Canadian, along with the note-taking Mr Walmslow, had no choice but to do as they were bid and wait. Meanwhile, the cordialities having been dispensed with, the staff-sergeant showed the sea-captain the positioning of the charges. They consisted of four lots of four cylindrical sticks of dynamite wedged into the rock necessarily close to the '*Cap*' *Canaveral*'s hull. The Captain wondered whether the explosives were too close to the ship, but said nothing about his concerns. Five minutes before the scheduled big bangs, the group led by Charlie Cook and the Chief Constable retired the requisite distance. Only a few of this coterie were able to make effective use of the large rock which, on the occasion of Major Harnley's previous visit, had been considered suitable protection.

Consequently Charlie Cook and the senior police officer, Henry Fewster and two soldiers, retired a further ten yards as far as the extended line of police constables. Behind the rock Major Harnley connected the plunger, and then, to Captain Gilchrist's surprise, the Army officer invited him to do, as it were, the honours. My grandfather's first instinct was to accept, but upon catching sight of what he perceived to be an envious glint in wily Bob's eye, he offered the instrument of destruction to the *Cape Canaveral's* majority stakeholder. Wily Bob beamed as he took the offering. Mr Fox placed the plunger between his knees on a plateau of rock. He then told the others to keep their heads down: this instruction found no detractors. Finally, after first looking about him to check that nothing was obviously amiss, with a determined thrust he exerted the necessary downward pressure. By this action he created the current which in the next instant exploded the detonators, and they in turn detonated the dynamite. In that there were four almost instantaneous explosions everything seemed to have gone according to plan, and once the fallout of rock fragments and sand had landed and settled, there were cheers all round. On the cliff top path Colonel Parker, the man whose idea it was, raised his hat and cheered. Others followed his example, and soon loud hurrahs resounded. Mr Fox took a bow. Upon espying Jenny standing between Sally and their mother the Captain waved. With a wave of his hand Mr Fox acknowledged the cheers of the people watching in boats.

"Well… well… well!" expressed the *Canaveral's* owner with a broad grin. "That's the first time I've blown up anything. Let's go and have a look-see."

Leading a retinue which at the rear consisted of the schooner's crew, wily Bob led the way back to the ship. Stepping with caution over the altered scaur, eventually, like an eager novice filled with high expectation, he was able to scrutinise his handiwork, able, as ill luck would have it, to gaze at the gaping hole below the waterline. For at least a minute the owner stood in silence, aghast at what he had done. The retinue also looked upon the scene just as gravely. For a time the owner was able to remain phlegmatic, but his equanimity came to a sudden end when he heard his Captain, who was actually addressing his comment to Major Harnley, say, "You were only supposed to blow up the scaur, damn it."